LOVE BITES

Timber Creek
Book 2

B. PERKINS

AIMEE VANCE

Revel Books

Revel Books
Paperback ISBN: 978-1-963848-04-5

Cover Design and Illustrations
Copyright © 2026 Aimee Vance

Character Art
Copyright © 2025 Mellendraws

www.aimeevancebooks.com

To the ADHDers:
Your passion is a super power.
Never be afraid to use it.

Chapter One

MAX

Two in the morning wasn't exactly prime time in Midwestern hillbilly towns. The cracked parking lot next to the local park was empty, the only streetlight flickering in and out several hundred yards away. Crickets chirped in the faint moonlight, answered by an owl hooting in the trees above me, unaware I lurked in the shadows beneath it. Just like the oblivious fucker who climbed out of the van advertising for a local electric company while a nondescript black sedan pulled up next to him, headlights off.

"Have you ever been on time even once, Joe?" He bent down, arms on the roof of the car as he peered inside, staring into the backseat. "Where'd you find this one?"

"Foster care." The door chimed as Joe exited the car, the first man stepping back to make room. They spoke in hushed voices, but between my supernatural hearing and the quiet of night, their voices carried like a cocking gun. "Her case worker filed a complaint she was acting odd during a full moon and asked for her to be rehomed. Like shooting fish in a barrel, Frank. This is getting too fucking easy."

Joe yanked open the back door and reached inside, dragging a small figure out of the car towards the van. They moved awkwardly, shoulders jerking to the side telling me their hands were bound behind their back.

Shadows curled around me, blending in with the night sky

as I leaned against an old oak tree on the opposite side of the parking lot, listening as these lowlifes buried themselves with every word they spoke. On and on they went, talking about their latest kidnappings, confirming tonight was merely one in a long string of cases I'd been hunting down for the last several months.

Since shifters were outed to the human world several years ago, supernatural society had been plagued with a kidnapping problem. My job working for the Paranormal Relations and Interspecies Council — sometimes not-so-affectionately called the PRICs — encompassed a wide range of not-quite-above-board responsibilities, but this was the best part. Even if I hadn't been assigned to help bring kidnappers to justice, I would have found a way here tonight. Not because I had some hero complex to protect the innocent, but because I loved the taste of evil.

"Think she's a wolf?" Joe said, a cigarette dangling from his lips as he flipped on his lighter, casting a glow over his face. "Delta wasn't happy when the last girl turned out to be just a crazy ass human."

My mouth tingled, my fangs begging to be released as if sensing my prey with the mention of *Delta*. I'd heard that code-name from more than one kidnapper lately, and hopefully this was enough to prove to the PRICs that this was a much bigger issue than they wanted to recognize.

I'd been tracking these two deadbeats through podunk towns for weeks after intercepting a police beat 200 miles away, but catching them in the act made this an open and closed case. As much as the chase was half the fun, I was ready to move on. Too long in one place made me edgy, and edginess only led two things — fucking, or feeding.

Considering how slim the pickings were in rural Kansas, fucking was off the table. But with any luck, feeding was very much *on* the table.

Frank jabbed a thumb at the full moon hanging in the sky as he opened the back door to his van. "We'll find out soon enough."

I rolled my eyes at their ignorance, picking a piece of lint off my black shirt. Humans now knew about the existence of wolf shifters, but propaganda was everywhere. Despite West Larkin assuring the world that wolf shifters had little in common with werewolf lore, many of the violent and terrifying myths persisted. Including that wolves could only, and always did, shift on the full moon.

Joe almost dropped his lighter, taking a step away from the girl he pushed towards the van. "Shit. Is it even safe to —"

She lunged at him, snapping her jaws. He let out a high-pitched yelp and I suppressed a chuckle.

"Don't you know anything?" Frank said, yanking her back against him. "You can't be turned into a werewolf. That's just superstition."

"I'm not a *werewolf*," the girl snarled, probably upset at what was, to shifters, something of a slur. She curled her lips, teeth glinting in the moonlight. "But I can still bite —"

Joe slapped her hard across the face, and she went down, crashing onto her knees with a gasp.

Rage flashed through me as a crackle of lightning shot across the dark night, drawing the attention of all three of them to the cloudless night sky.

I'd seen enough.

"You really should do your homework before class, kids," I drawled, appearing a few feet away from them and dissolving my shadows.

Joe yelped again at my jump-scare, the whites of his eyes showing all the way around his irises. "What the *fuck* —"

With a flick of my hand, shadows erupted, dragged him to the ground and sealed around his mouth, silencing him. Black bands of my magic held him as tight as the ropes tying his victim's arms, and I closed my fists, squeezing them tighter until his eyes bulged with a muffled scream.

"Much better." I quickly scanned the girl for any more serious injuries before meeting her gaze. "You good, short stack?"

She pushed to her feet, and her nose gave the barest twitch, the only sign she was trying to figure out who, or what, I was.

Frank was too busy gaping at the shadows smothering his buddy to notice when my attention switched to him.

"Pretty nifty, right?" I tilted my head to one side, lifting a brow in question.

The acrid scent of his fear filled the air as he turned wide eyes on me, quaking in his boots. "W-what are you?"

Leaning in, I whispered, "The monster in the shadows. The one you feel in the prickle at the back of your neck when you're alone in the dark. Everything you've ever feared, come to life."

His eyes flicked between me and the van, as if wondering if he could move fast enough to get in and drive away, which only made me smirk.

"You can try. In fact, go ahead." I waved a hand at the van. "Make this fun for me."

He didn't move, so I stepped towards him, my hands flexing at my sides.

"Take her," he blurted, pushing the teenage girl towards me. I reached a hand out to steady her, then stepped forward, blocking her from his sight. "Just let us go."

"Oh, I'm definitely taking her with me." I held my hand up, inspecting my fingers as the inky magic in my veins painted my usually olive skin the same color as the night sky, feigning boredom. "But what's that human saying about having your cake and eating it too?"

I flashed a grin a second before he broke into a run. Letting out a sigh of relief, I rolled my shoulders and finally let my fangs descend. It had been far too long since my last hunt.

Somewhere in my mind, my father's voice rang through, giving me specific orders *not* to bite anyone, but it was so hard to remember all those little details, especially when his list of rules had been growing nonstop since before the first World War.

Keeping my back to the girl so she didn't see my canines, I said, "Wait here, and I'll get you somewhere safe. Hope you're not afraid of some blood."

In a heartbeat, I vanished and reappeared beside Frank, halfway across the parking lot. He ripped at the van door handle, but I slammed it shut again, his panting breaths turning to whimpers as my shadows surrounded us, blocking out what I was about to do from any street cameras, as well as the girl.

Technically my job description was to *find* the kidnappers, subdue them, and turn them over to the PRICs, but accidents happen all the time, right? Not my fault he tripped and fell into my mouth.

"Please!" Frank screamed until my shadows dipped into his mouth, choking him. My fangs sank into his neck, his body going rigid under my hold as he flailed uselessly.

The tangy, copper taste washed over my tongue, like the first drink of water after the hottest day, quenching a thirst I usually denied myself. Human blood was so much more satisfying than animal for a vampire like me, and when that human deserved to die for trafficking kids?

Like the finest Italian vintage.

It only took a few moments to drain him of enough blood to kill him. I let out a sigh as I licked my fangs clean, wiping my mouth as they receded back into my gums. I didn't need to give the poor girl a heart attack when I was supposed to be rescuing her.

Soon enough, his lifeless body slumped to the asphalt. I pulled him up by the armpits, heaving him unceremoniously into the back of the van, then poured the spare tank of gasoline I found over his body, around the inside of both the van and Joe's sedan, and in a ring around them.

My phone buzzed in my pocket as I tossed the empty can back into the van. I answered it as I headed back to the girl and Joe, still restrained by my shadows on the ground.

"Wow, an actual phone call? Am I in trouble, Premier, or did you just miss my dulcet tones?"

"Not now, Massimo," came my father's voice, sharper than usual. As the head of the PRICs, he wasn't used to anyone sassing him, but it was my favorite hobby. "Come to Headquarters immediately."

I glanced down at the blood spattering my jeans and leather jacket, licking my tongue over my teeth. Not exactly Headquarters apparel. Not to mention it would be a *dead* — pun intended — giveaway I hadn't followed orders. Again.

"Kind of in the middle of something, actually."

"*Now*, Massimo." He hung up.

What a guy, my father.

Letting out a breath, I strolled back over to the girl now sitting on the concrete, staring at me with a mixture of confusion and wariness.

A look I was very familiar with.

Squatting down in front of her, I asked, "Do you know who I am?"

For good measure, I revealed my wings — the unusual black feathers catching her eye immediately. Most of the supernatural community had heard of the Dark Angel — I was the only one of my kind with wings as inky black as mine — but she shook her head.

"You're — an angel?"

"Debatable," I muttered, but my feathered wings, despite

being opposite the typical angel white, led most to believe that was what I was.

The human world might have just learned about wolf shifters, but the supernatural world had recently had its own shock — vampires. The species had successfully hidden in the shadows — literally — for centuries. Even five years after they were revealed to the general supernatural society, there was still a lot of secrecy. My ancestry was one of the Premier's best kept secrets.

"I promise I won't hurt you. We need you to make a statement for the Council. I'm going to bring you into Headquarters, and then we'll get you home."

"I don't—" She swallowed, her gold-rimmed eyes staring up at me. "I don't have a home."

My jaw worked, a deep sigh escaping. "Have you heard of Timber Creek? West Larkin?"

She sat up straighter as a little of her fear dissipated. "Yeah. I've heard of him."

Not surprising. Timber Creek's Alpha had made quite a name for himself. Now there was a guy with a hero complex. But even I could admit he was one of the good ones.

"He's made a sanctuary of sorts, takes in shifters like you. You'll love it there."

Her eyes darted to Joe. "What about him?"

I stood, adjusting my jacket as I looked at the human scum still staring wide-eyed at me behind his shadowy restraints. Sweat beaded on his brow.

"He's coming with us, too." With his mention of Delta, hopefully there was a lot more than blood to get out of him. Apparently, interrogating him would be someone else's pleasure for the night since my father needed me so urgently.

I turned back to the girl. "Do you trust me?"

Biting her lip, she gave a shaky, not at all convincing nod.

Good enough. With a shrug, I grabbed Joe's lighter, flicked

it open, and tossed it. A *whoosh* sounded as the gasoline caught fire, circling the vehicles.

I yanked Joe up to his feet by his elbow, then took the girl's arm — much more gently — and we vanished into the night as an explosion boomed behind us.

Chapter Two

MAX

I loved strolling through PRIC Headquarters. The gleaming white floors and walls. The utter lack of character or personality anywhere with its austere modern architecture. The constant sneers of disdain from every uptight angel in the place as they caught sight of me and hurried away, all too aware of my less-than-savory reputation.

My all-black attire, hair, and wings had always set me apart from other angels, but the muddy boot prints and flecks of dried blood I left behind me with every step? Those were special to tonight, and I loved leaving my mark.

"Ah, Gabriella, pleasure as always." I smirked at the angel sitting behind a white marble desk beneath an aptly labeled but unironic sign reading LOBBY. She stood and circled the desk, her white wings gleaming as she frowned at the three of us. Like most angels, Gabriella's silver hair and eyes matched that of her formal business attire, a boring grey wrap dress and matching heels that added to Headquarters' clinical feel. Her gaze flicked to the girl at my side, then to the man bound by shadows at my feet, before looking down at the tablet in her hand.

"Massimo," she said, nails tapping on the screen as her frown deepened. "There are no pending assignments here for you showing acquisitions. Have you followed the protocol?"

"Ah." I reached forward, swiping aggressively across her tablet as electricity buzzed along my hand, zapping the device until the screen went black. "So weird how that always seems to happen for me, isn't it? Must be a glitch in your *protocol*."

She sighed, bringing the now useless tablet to her chest.

"And these are —?" She raised a silvery brow at the girl, then the fucker at my feet, seeming to spot the dirt I tracked in and wrinkling her nose.

"Human garbage for interrogation." I kicked Joe with the steel toe of my boots, having replaced my dark shadow magic with my angel powers to hold his arms behind his back. He groaned at the kick, the sound muffled by his gagged mouth. "And —" I quirked a brow at the girl, realizing I hadn't stopped to ask her name.

"Hailey," she offered quietly. "I'm a wolf shifter."

I nodded in thanks. "— here to make a statement against her kidnapper here."

Gabriella pursed her lips, then walked back to her desk and typed in a code on a keypad there. A moment later, another angel in a full grey suit emerged and dragged Joe away unceremoniously.

I turned to go when I felt a tug on the sleeve of my jacket.

"You're leaving me?"

My brows furrowed as I glanced down to Hailey's small hand on me, then back up at her. Her wide eyes met mine, and unless I was mistaken, she seemed to be pleading with me to stay.

As gently as I could, I plucked her hand off my arm. Wolves were so damn touchy.

"You're safe now, Hailey. Gabriella will take good care of you, and we'll get you to Timber Creek shortly." I shot the angel a warning look, but like the professional she was, Gabriella merely gave a curt nod in return.

But Hailey was still biting her lip. And it made me feel... something.

I grimaced.

"I can… check on you later?" I offered, at a loss for what to do.

Gabriella barely stifled a snort.

Taking a steadying breath, Hailey gave a brave-faced nod. My hand moved on its own, patting her awkwardly on the head.

What the fuck?

Clearing my throat, I gave Gabriella one last nod, then got the hell out of there.

Unlike most angels, I hadn't grown up in Headquarters — a combined residence and office space for angels in a realm all its own. White hallways as empty and boring as the Lobby circled an atrium, revealing what I liked to think of as a fancy birdcage in the center. The only difference between areas were the labeled floors and hallways, but even those were white on white, embedded in the walls in a maze of *bland*. This wasn't home, but I knew my way around well enough to find my father's office.

Wings flapped in the distance as angels flew from floor to floor, going about business as usual as I approached the atrium. I stopped on the edge of a platform jutting out into thin air, a hundred-foot drop below me, letting my black wings spread wide. With a deep breath, I launched into the air, only needing a few beats of my wings to lift the few stories to the top floor, entirely dedicated to the Premier, the leader of our supernatural society and my father. Dark wings fully extended, I felt the weight of every pair of eyes here, the same way I always did. The Dark Angel, both literally and figuratively.

I relished in every wince at the sight of me.

My secret heritage wasn't widely known, but with vampires joining the fold of supernatural society, more and more questioning gazes lingered on my dark features, so different from my father.

So different from *every* full-blooded angel. Because I wasn't one.

Daddy's dirty secret.

Malachi Russo, Premier, the shining silver plaque next to his door read as I reached his office, and I rolled my eyes. All it needed was a magical ticker of the number of days since he'd last set a drink down without a coaster to display how practically perfect he was.

Striding into his office without knocking — he'd demanded me here immediately, after all — I smirked when his gaze hardened at my attire, polar opposite to his crisp charcoal pinstripe suit and white button-down.

I held my arms out wide. "Present, as ordered, Father dearest."

He sighed, closing a manila folder on his desk. "Close the door."

It slammed with an effortless twist of my magic, and I threw myself into one of the armchairs — white, now to be stained with human blood — across from his desk.

To my dismay, he hardly seemed to notice. His grey hair seemed whiter, his olive skin paler, the faint wrinkles bracketing his mouth deeper. Angels didn't age the way humans did, a fact my several hundred-year-old father could attest to, but today he looked… older.

"We have a situation."

I didn't bother righting myself in the chair, not feeling the need to pay attention yet. With my father, a "situation" could have been anything from another species was outed to the human world, to his pristine white rug had a stain he couldn't get out.

Suddenly, he frowned, sniffing the air, and gave me a once-over before glaring at me. "You killed them? Again?"

I put my hands up. "Oops."

"We need them *alive* to get more information."

"I kept one alive this time. He's on his way to Interrogation now, and he even mentioned Delta. Aren't you so proud?"

With a deep sigh, he spun in his chair as a screen built into the wall behind his desk turned on, playing a news clip from earlier today.

"Police are still searching the Boston area for the attacker. Residents have been advised to walk in pairs at night and be on the lookout for a man described as at least six feet tall, last seen wearing a dark hoodie. The autopsy revealed puncture marks in the neck which the Medical Examiner believes to have been caused by — and this is not fantasy — fangs. Whether this was a cosplayer gone overboard, the work of a werewolf, or something else, only time will tell. For Nightly News, this is —"

Malachi muted the video. I raised my eyebrows.

"Next snack? I mean" — I held up my hands — "my apologies, is that victim's attacker my next *mission?*"

He shook his head. "The victim was drained of blood."

Hm. A rogue wolf shifter *could*, theoretically, do that. It would make a hell of a mess, and there would be far more damage to the body than neat fang pricks like the newscaster described, but it wasn't impossible. Not likely, but neither was the idea that —

"This was a vampire, Massimo," he interrupted my thoughts. His steely grey eyes met mine pointedly. "And it was no accident that they got carried away, or left the body. They're sending a message."

I righted my legs, resting my elbows on my knees as I leaned forward, not quite believing the most secretive species of supernaturals would be so blatant. "What message is that?"

Malachi pulled a photograph from the manila folder on his desk, tossing it over to me. It showed a female body face down on a dark street — presumably the one from the news report — sickly white from blood loss, with the words *back off* written in blood across her bare shoulders uncovered by her halter top.

I held the photo closer, examining it for any minute detail.

A dark figure stood with their back to the camera, but in view, nonetheless. If it was a vampire, they made no efforts to use shadows to hide themselves from the street cameras that had captured the news footage, nor any attempt to cover their kill. Both were unusual for a vampire used to hiding and operating in the shadows, gifted with the ability to hide themselves and erase memories of their presence with magic.

They were gloating.

"My best guess? The Conclave heard about us trying to track them down as part of the census, and they want us to stand down or else —" He gestured to the photo. "They're saying they can make this sort of thing start happening all the time if we don't do as they demand."

I scratched along my jaw, still not seeing how this related to me.

For the past few months, I'd been helping my father track down supernaturals living on the fringes of society. All too often, I ended up discovering they were missing, which led me to their kidnappers. Our main goal was to prevent situations like Hailey found herself in tonight, especially for these at-risk kids with no one to notice they were gone. Malachi had a hunch it was all connected somehow, but until we had a complete census of who and where supernaturals resided, it was hard to see the full picture.

Shockingly, not all supes were on board with the idea of a census. The main holdouts being the vampires, via the Conclave — the organization that lorded over all vampires, headed by the oldest, most lethal of the species.

"That's where you come in," Malachi continued, seeming to read my mind.

But mind-reading wasn't a skill *angels* had, and dear old Dad was as Angel as they came.

I snapped my fingers. "Let me guess. You want me out there spreading the good word to the community about the joys of togetherness. All for one and one for all, right? Should I coordinate some photo-ops kissing babies and visiting donut shops —"

"Community outreach, Massimo? Honestly." He shook his head.

We shared a glance that was almost conspiratorial. For all my father's good intentions, interacting with the public was probably the last thing he ever wanted to do. Wasn't high on my list either. "Do tell, then."

"I know you don't know much about vampire society but—"

"Whose fault is that again?"

"—the Conclave is only a small minority of their people, and even less of a representation than our angel Council used to be. The Conclave members might not want this, but individual dens might be willing to cooperate. With one of their own." He leveled a meaningful look at me.

I glanced around the room behind me, then pointed at my chest in question. His jaw twitched.

"Look." He sighed, and suddenly, there was something unfamiliar in my father's eyes. Something like… concern? "I've kept you away from as many of your kind as I could for a reason, only asking you to step into the role of Dante when absolutely necessary."

I frowned at the use of my alternate identity I used when interacting with vampire society, at my father's insistence I keep my heritage and ties to him hidden. "And let me guess. This is now absolutely necessary."

"You've gotten the smallest taste of how dangerous vampire dens can be," he said, reminding me of the one and only assignment he'd given me to meet with some vampires on the East Coast. I'd almost died, and we'd never spoken of it again. "They're not an accepting species. They like to act first and ask questions never. Their rules are archaic and barbaric, making the Mafia look tame. But we can't just let them attack humans, or other supernaturals, like this without consequences."

I sat back in my chair with a dark laugh, because wasn't this an ironic twist? Malachi had kept my heritage as the darkest secret, explaining my unusual features as the angel's version of a genetic mutation — appalling enough to the perfectionist angel society to make them all react like I was a leper. He'd held whatever knowledge he had about vampires so close to his chest, even *I* knew next to nothing about my mother's people.

Obviously he knew enough about vampires to sire a half vamp son, and yet, in the last minute, had shared more insider information into vampire society than he had in my whole life. I knew better than to ask questions about his past, but this all felt a bit too convenient.

"They've *been* attacking humans and supes and whoever the fuck they want for centuries, unbeknownst to almost everyone. Why ride their asses about this now? We can deal with getting the other supes in order first. Find this damn *Delta* and bury the whole organization six feet under."

"*Now* they're making the news," Malachi said, handing over the rest of the folder. Half a dozen other reports already filled it from around the world. "Boston. New York. Paris. London. Rome. Tokyo. They're hitting major cities around the world and shoving it in our faces. Testing us, to see what we'll do. There's already too much attention on the shifters the public *does* know about now, and discussions have begun on how we protect the other supernatural species — whether we reveal them on our own terms, or continue to hide them as we've tried to do for centuries. There was a Council meeting last month to discuss our plan moving forward—"

I hummed, resting my elbow on the chair's arm, and

pressing a finger into my temple. "Let me guess, the vamps didn't agree with your ideas."

"The only way we control the narrative is if we are the ones to tell the world about ourselves." He held up the folder of evidence the vampires were leaving around the world. "This isn't it."

"So, what did the Council decide?"

Malachi sat back in his chair, steepling his fingers. "Nothing, as of yet. My idea to slowly introduce the world to the idea of more supernaturals wasn't one the Council was fond of."

"What did the vamps want?"

His stare turned deadpan. "To disappear and let the Conclave self-govern once more, but we can't let that happen again. We all need to band together."

"What do you mean, *again*?" I leaned forward. "You know how vampires have gone under the radar all these centuries, don't you?"

"A thousand years ago, vampires were exterminated. Or so it was thought," Malachi began, and I nearly held my breath in disbelief that he was finally revealing this to me. "As I've said, vampires are dangerous, their powers equal to, and in some cases greater than, even angels'. They are supernaturals' greatest predators, almost impossible to kill, and the greatest threat to our secret existence as they prey on humans. The other species came together, and hunted them to extinction, letting their lore pass into myth and legend and stories. Clearly, they weren't *all* killed."

"And clearly, not all supernaturals believed they were gone," I added pointedly.

"Everyone was told they were gone completely," Malachi continued. "To the best of our knowledge, they had been eradicated. Only a few angels remained vigilant, and passed down to their successors the truth — that vampires were very real once, and that if there had been any left, they might return."

"Conspiracy theorists will love this one," I muttered under my breath, and Malachi cut me a glare. "So, what, you went looking for them one day? Tripped and your dick slid home?"

The lamp crackled on his desk. "That is a story for another time."

I rolled my eyes. "As always."

"Massimo."

"So, you go looking for them a little over a hundred years ago, you obviously find them" — I gesture to myself — "then what? Did you single handedly decide not to tell anyone else they were still around?"

"The Council met to decide what to do. But the fact was, vampires had been quiet. They weren't causing problems, they didn't interfere with the other species. Their terms were simple: live and let live. We don't bother them, they don't bother us." Letting out a sigh, Malachi rubbed a hand down his face. "At the time, our options were limited. We couldn't be sure of their numbers compared to ours, and we had other preoccupations."

"And you agreed. With vampires. To just leave them alone, unchecked, and trust they would keep their word."

"If your tone is suggesting that was a foolish decision, I'll remind you hindsight is 20-20."

"So this is retaliation?" I raised an eyebrow, looking down at the folder. "For going back on your word to let them live separately?"

"Yes. But we can't let this stand, not when the Conclave is letting vampires be so blatant."

"So your proposal is…"

"The Conclave is corrupt. That much was evident even a century ago. I refuse to believe they represent the will of their people. Despite vampires' violent nature, I have reason to believe most of them don't *want* to be secluded anymore. Wouldn't want to essentially declare war on the rest of the supernatural world like this."

I narrowed my eyes. "Reason?"

"The first step," he continued, ignoring me, "is talking to them — to the *people*, not the Conclave. We need to know what the general vampire population actually thinks. If we can get them to work *with* us, instead of against us, we could save a lot of lives."

I shuffled through the reports in the folder. Bloodless bodies and bite marks left in places meant for humans to find. They knew the media would pin this on the shifters, not having a better explanation, and it would ruin any efforts the Council made to present the rest of the supe world as non-violent.

"*If.*"

Malachi nodded as I set the folder on his desk. "Yes. If."

"And if *not?*"

I met his gaze, but he didn't answer. We both knew the answer anyway. Like he said, vampires were violent. Snack first, questions never.

When he spoke next, his voice had dropped from his Premier tone to the one I almost never heard anymore. The fatherly one. The one that, every once in a while, revealed he did in fact have emotions somewhere deep, *deep* down.

"If there were anyone else I could send in, Max."

I blinked. He almost never called me that, despite it being my preferred name.

This was getting ridiculous.

"Why send anyone else when I'm clearly the best for the job?" I rapped my knuckles on the chair, looking around vaguely for a drink, but of course angels were too uptight to keep alcohol at work. Freaking PRICs. "Where do I start?"

Malachi grimaced. "Well, that's the other thing. Your last meeting was arranged ahead of time, but that won't work if we're trying to avoid the Conclave. Dens are almost impossible to find."

My eye twitched. "Great. I'm so glad we had this whole

conversation then. I love giving up my hard-earned interrogation to some junior angel enforcer for nothing."

His tone went right back to Premier mode as he continued, "Are there any wolves you trust?"

I frowned, wondering where he was going with this. "Why?"

"You need one." I zoned out as he explained everything he knew about locating dens and how a wolf's keen senses might be the key, but I was stuck on the whole *someone you trust* thing. "But when I say dens are dangerous, I mean it. Find someone you can take with you, someone who will protect your back."

And there was the crux of the matter.

I trusted no one.

I stood to go, more than ready to go find myself a whiskey, a hot shower, and possibly an outlet for all of this pent-up frustration. Not necessarily in that order.

"Before you go." Malachi stood also, the two of us almost the same height, and hesitated a moment before opening his desk drawer and pulling out an envelope. His fingers tightened around it. "I — I debated whether or not to give this to you."

Always the dramatics. "Hand it over or not, then."

"It's from your mother."

My heart stopped.

There had been a time in my youth when I'd been *desperate* to know my mother. To know anything about her, or her people. I'd grown up without a single other vampire in my life, and the one time I'd gone looking had not gone well.

"I don't want it," I snapped, years of anger, of resentment, heating my blood.

"It was left behind in the Council chambers after the Conclave was here last week, but it's addressed to you—"

"Oh, *now* she wants to reach out?"

"— And it might help with what comes next."

I stared at him. "Hunting vampires, you mean." Tilting my head, I studied his face. "Have you read it?"

He shook his head. "Of course not."

I hummed. As if such a breach of privacy were beyond him. Hilarious.

"Just take it, Massimo. Read it or not. It's yours, and it was my duty to deliver it."

"Such a diligent messenger pigeon."

The lamp on the desk flickered, then sparked as Malachi's irritation got the better of him. My job here was done.

"Fine." I snatched it out of his hand, crumpling it as I stuffed it into my pocket, striding for the door.

"Be careful out there, son. Don't get into any fights you can't win. We still have a lot of things to get done together to make this world safe for our kind, and I'll need you back in one piece to do them."

Of course, his main concern was my skill set, the greatest tool in his arsenal. The worst part was I could hardly fault him — his motives were pure, making the world safe for all supernaturals. So what if the casualty was our relationship? Sometimes I wondered if that was why he'd fathered me at all, assuming it was intentional. To create his ultimate hybrid weapon.

But this wasn't the Oprah Winfrey show. Our feelings didn't matter.

I flexed my wings, shooting him a look over my shoulder as I readied my shadows to get the fuck out of here.

"Don't you know, Pops? There *is* no fight I can't win."

Chapter Three

SUMMER

"Trust me on this one, babe. You do *not* want to ride a camel. They spit."

I looked up from where I sat on the floor of my bedroom just in time to see my best friend Indi pluck the camel ride photo off my bucket list bulletin board. With a flick of her fingers, she set it on fire, her bracelets jangling on her pale, freckled wrists. The scent of charred paper mixed with the ink, changing it in the most subtle way.

I wrinkled my nose at the smell. "Hey! When I said you could help, I didn't mean you could light my dreams on fire."

"Just one gal trying to save another gal's pelvic floor." Indi held her hands up, stepping away from the bulletin board hanging on my coral bedroom wall, her floral skirt swishing across my wood floors. She squinted at the wide array of pictures and doodles I'd been saving for the last several years, currently spread across every available space in my room.

"You know shifters heal fast," I said as I got up, scraps of paper drifting to the floor around me. Since the camel ride was now off the table, I pinned a picture of an elephant to the board instead. "And besides, my pelvic floor has seen little to no action in quite some time."

Indi shook her head, but couldn't hide the smile my sad love life caused. "Trust me, a camel ride is not the action you're looking for. But no more fires, I promise."

She plopped onto my fluffy white duvet, the gold bedframe

creaking as she reached for the stack of pictures and little labels I'd doodled. With a yellow pillow in the shape of a daisy tucked under her head, she started reading through them. "Ride on a plane. Eat gelato in Italy. Put a lock on the Pont des Arts. Kiss the Blarney Stone," she read, her black eyes flicking up to mine. "Have you done any of the things on your bucket list yet?"

I hesitated to answer, knowing how she'd react, but she knew me well enough to see the truth written on my face.

"All right. New plan. We're going to mark at least one of these off before your birthday next month. You've been saying you're going to start living the life of adventure you've always wanted for years now, and you're stalled here in Timber Creek."

"I'm not *stalled*," I huffed, looking down at the sandy beaches of Bali in my hand. "I'm just busy. I have my family, my bakery-slash-bookstore, and my apartment. That's a lot of dreams already come true for this almost-30-year-old."

"Okay, well I dare you to pick one to do tomorrow, and I'll even do it with you."

I knew what she was doing, pushing me like this. She thought I'd chicken out, or back down. Instead, I shot her a sugary grin, holding up another magazine cutting. She cringed.

"Anything but that. You're on your own there."

"Oh, come on." I laughed, turning the paper to look at the whitewater rafting advertisement for a trip down the Colorado River. "You hardly get wet at all."

Indi leveled a stare at me. "That is patently false. And what if I went overboard?"

I shrugged. "Hold your breath?"

Indi rolled her eyes. As a demon with literal fire in her veins, she, like most of her species, *hated* water. It wouldn't kill her Wicked Witch of the West-style, but most demons avoided it whenever they could, especially the frigid snowmelt that made up our Colorado streams. As a wolf shifter, I didn't have the same problem.

"Okay, okay, what about…" I shuffled the scraps of paper heaped around me, looking for something a little more demon-friendly. "Aha! Ziplining! You can't have any objections to that. No water at all, unless it rains."

Indi grinned. "That's more like it. Book it."

I reached for my phone to look up the website, but halted before my hand even touched it when my brother called into my mind.

"Summer? Are you home?"

Indi shot me an inquiring look, and when I gestured to my head to indicate someone was mind-speaking with me through our wolf pack bonds, she set her mouth in a line.

"What's up, Terran?"

Instead of responding, my ears pricked as the downstairs exterior door that led up to my apartment opened, followed by Terran's footsteps — and another, lighter set of steps. I smiled, recognizing River's gait.

"One sec." I nodded to the apartment door, but Indi had already heard them too. We headed out to the living room, and I pulled the door open right as my older brother Terran reached the landing, his five-year-old daughter River right behind him. He wore a black shirt with a pair of faded jeans, a trucker hat thrown backwards on his head to keep his shaggy brown hair out of his face. His eyes were the same hazel as mine and our brother West's, nothing like his little blonde-haired, blue-eyed daughter.

"I know it's your day off with the bakery closed and I tried, I really did, to find someone else to watch River for me tonight, but Cruz got stuck in Nevada after a drift race and Dad's having some situation with a Willie gone rogue, and I'm out of options," my brother said in one long breath, his eyes quickly darting around the room as he gripped his daughter's hand. I didn't love that I was his *last* option, but at least he knew he could count on me. "Oh, hey Indi."

My best friend offered a curt nod, then squatted down in front of River. "Did your dad forget he can call me and we can be buds too?"

River smiled, her two front teeth missing as she looked up at her dad. "I do like Indi. Her red hair is really pretty."

When River and Terran chorused, "Like Merida," — River in glee and Terran with enough resignation to betray he'd heard this comparison many times before — something I could have sworn looked like a blush crept over Indi's freckled cheeks.

River let herself in, zooming over to my couch, skidding across my rug, and diving head first into my collection of novelty pillows that she loved — sherbert rainbows, succulents, cupcakes. Any pillow I found in a cute shape and my coral-yellow-sage green color scheme was a necessary purchase.

Terran's eyes slid back to me. "West has a bunch of Alphas coming in tonight. I hate asking you to step in on your night off —"

"River!" I cut my brother off, skipping over to grab her hand and pull her down the hall. I could read between the lines — Terran didn't want River anywhere near those other Alpha shifters, and I was right there with him. Most of them were decent people, but there were one or two who did *not* need to know about River, my brother's half-human daughter. "I was just thinking about calling and asking if you wanted to have a sleepover tonight. We can bake, and have a dance party, and read a book. Just us girls. Sound fun?"

"You're a lifesaver," my brother's voice rang in my mind, and I waved over my shoulder. *"I don't know what I'd do without you."* He muttered a stiff goodbye to Indi, then made his way quickly back down the stairs.

"I love sleepovers at your house," River said as I opened

the door to my bedroom, looking at the mess I'd made with my bulletin board. She paused in the doorway, then tilted her head to look up at me. "Did you have a tantrum, Aunt Summer? Sometimes my room looks like this after I have big feelings too."

Indi chuckled, leaning against the doorframe with us. "She's not wrong there. This is a lot of chaos, even for a demon."

"It's organized chaos," I defended myself, hands on my hips as I looked down at the scattered stacks of colored pictures and slips of paper.

"Hmm."

"*Semi*-organized. I know where everything is. Well, I know roughly what pile everything is in." I ducked to the floor and started putting things back in the bin my other brother's mate Jade and I had labeled several months ago, piling all of the art supplies back into the corner of my closet. A closet that had, for a few magical days, been beautifully organized by Jade with labeled aesthetic bins and all, but was now back to its usual haphazard mess. What Jade didn't know couldn't hurt her.

"Did you just mess it all back up again?" River asked.

"No," I lied, shoving the last of the papers out of sight. Being called out for my mess by a five-year-old was a new low. "Who wants cookies?"

River jumped up and down, racing towards the stairs that lead to my bakery, *Love Bites*, beneath my apartment.

"So about tomorrow," Indi said as we followed the energetic little girl down the stairs.

I shrugged. "I don't know yet. It depends on how long Terran needs me to watch her."

"I can watch River and you can go by yourself."

An involuntary shudder ran through my body, and I stuck my tongue out. "Times are not that desperate yet."

Indi laughed, pulling out her phone as it buzzed. "I have to go sign for this shipment and finish inventory at the store." She started towards the shop's front doors, calling behind her, "Adventure awaits you, Summer. You're the only one in your way."

I sighed as she left, headed towards her general store down the street. Streetlights turned on all along Main Street as the dark clouds warned of a spring storm, overshadowing the valley. This high in the mountains, the scent of petrichor lingered in the air, bathing everything in my favorite smell. Soon, everything would bloom and the scents would be almost overwhelming in their intensity, but I savored the crisp air, breathing deep as I flicked the lock on the doors once more. Hopefully the rain wouldn't delay the Alpha's meeting tonight, but it was anyone's guess how long these things went.

Ever since my oldest brother West took over as de facto leader of the shifters in North America, more and more responsibility had fallen on his shoulders. Five years ago shifters had been outed to humans, the first of the six species of supernaturals to be shoved into the spotlight. There was no way to undo what the humans already knew but the Council was working overtime to keep the rest of the species hidden for as long as possible.

Since then, West had been battling shifter-human relations as well as a growing population of shifters needing to relocate to pack grounds for safety. Not all Alphas were as accepting as him, and it was something he was trying to fix.

Luckily, he'd been learning to set some boundaries and delegate now that his mate Jade was living with him. If I ever wanted to see any of those items on my bucket list ticked off, maybe I needed to start doing the same.

"What kind of cookies are we making?" River asked as I joined her in the kitchen, a genuine smile on my face as I took over helping her tie on her mini *Love Bites* polka-dot apron. Pulling a hair tie off my wrist, I wrangled her pale blonde curls into a high ponytail, keeping it out of her face, then planted a kiss on the top of her head. I loved my niece more than anyone on this earth, and taking care of her — no matter that it derailed my plans — was never a burden.

"Let's look and see what I have." I pulled down glass jars from the shelves over my workstation, each neatly labeled after Jade went wild back here one day, showcasing chocolate chips, caramel pieces, crushed candies, and any variety of toppings a little girl could dream of. I was proud I'd managed to at least keep *this* area organized and tidy. "What are you thinking?"

"What about those s'mores ones Cruz loves with the mini marshmallows?"

I grabbed a box of graham crackers, the jar of mini marshmallows, and a container of chocolate chips as I headed towards my industrial mixer. "That is the best idea I've heard all day. Should we save him some?"

She tilted her head in thought. "Depends how many we make. I think I want to eat at least six."

"At *least.*" I nodded in agreement, positive we were both about to have a stomach ache by the end of this. "Did you wash your hands?"

With a mid-air karate kick, River leapt off her stool and scampered over to the sink, shouting over her shoulder, "Music, Auntie!"

I smiled. "On it! Which album?" I knew better than to ask if she wanted to listen to Taylor Swift—the answer was always yes.

"1989!"

"Solid choice."

Welcome to New York blared over the speakers as I measured the dry ingredients, pouring them into a mixing bowl one at a time. River hopped back on her stool, shaking her butt to the music as she sang the wrong lyrics and followed my instructions.

I hugged her from behind, planting kisses along her neck to make her giggle. "I love you, sweet pea."

"I know," she said confidently, her eyes glued to the oven as we watched the cookies bake. "I'm your favorite."

"You sure are."

"Do you have a husband?"

"Nope." I glanced down at my phone, replying back to my dad's third text that yes, River and I were good, and no he did not need to leave and come get her. Despite years of helping out with River, everyone always seemed braced for disaster when it came to me.

"Why not? You make *really* good cookies," River asked while she licked marshmallow off her fingers, rapid-fire interrogating me. A dozen cookies cooled on a rack behind us, even though we'd both inhaled three a piece right out of the oven. The warm chocolate scent wrapped around me like a blanket, the ultimate comfort.

"I *do* make good cookies," I agreed, putting my phone back in my pocket so I could dry the mixing bowl before putting it away. If only dating were as straightforward as following a recipe. "Ready for your bath?"

She nodded, taking off towards the apartment. I wasn't sure I'd ever seen the girl walk — everything was a race.

Up in my bathroom, I turned on the water in the standing tub before grabbing a black-and-yellow striped bumblebee towel, complete with a little face and antenna on the hood, for River.

"Do you *want* a husband?"

I laughed, staring up at the ceiling as the water filled the tub. "It's on the bucket list."

"What's a bucket list?"

"A list of all the things I want to do, the places I want to see, and adventures I want to go on someday."

"Oh, like how I want to go to the moon."

"That's a great bucket list item, sure."

"Is a baby on your bucket list?"

A snort escaped me at her blunt questions no adult would dare ask so freely. "Someday, maybe. I don't know. Can't you stay little and be my baby forever?"

"No," she deadpanned. "I'm not a baby anymore. I'm almost *six*."

"But you were such a cute baby, with that pretty blonde hair and those big blue eyes."

"Do I look like my mom?" she asked, and my hand stilled in midair, accidentally pouring too much lavender bubble bath into the water. River's mom had left her on Terran's doorstep as an infant, throwing him for a wild loop. She'd never met her mom, and it was a sore subject for everyone, no matter how much we all loved this sweet little girl.

"You do." I grinned, squatting down next to the tub as she got in the water, splashing it around her legs. "But you also look like *my* mom. She had pretty curls like you do, and bright blue eyes."

Twirling my fingers in her hair, my heart lurched at the reminder of my own mother sitting beside the tub while Aspen and I played in the water a lifetime ago. It had been 15 years since she passed, but not a day went by that I didn't think of her.

"Tell me about Grandma Cora."

"Well." I ran my fingers through the bubbles, lost in my memories. "Her hair was golden-brown like mine, but curled just like yours. Half me, half you!" I splashed some water up on her belly and she giggled. "And if you think my cookies are good, then you would have loved hers. She was the best cook I've ever known."

"That's what Daddy says too." She nodded, laying back in the water with only her little face sticking out of the bubbles. "That's why he works at the restaurant, even though sometimes it isn't very fun. He says he can feel her there."

Tears pricked my eyes, but I nodded. "She's everywhere here in Timber Creek. Did you know that's why Papa loves his buffaloes so much? They were Grandma's favorite."

River sat up covered in bubbles. "Yes! He talks about her all the time while we check on the Willies. But he said she liked to eat them." She scrunched her nose, and I laughed.

"Sometimes, yes. I think she saw everything as food though."

Her little eyes squinted as she stared up at me. "We don't eat Willie. They're our friends."

I nodded, wiping the smile off my face. "You are most certainly right. No more buffalo burgers."

That agreed to, River quizzed me on everything from why the trees stop growing high up on the mountains to when my dad's peach crops would be ready so I could make peach cobbler while I rinsed her hair and pulled the drain.

Teeth brushed and in pajamas, I glanced at my phone to check my messages for any word on how the Alpha meeting had gone, but saw nothing. More than likely any plans I had for tomorrow were squashed, knowing River would be spending the day with me. "Ready for bed?"

"Can I sleep with you?" River asked, holding a Highland cow stuffed animal that had the same haircut as her father.

"Of course you can." Her little hand slipped into mine and we made our way to my bed, pulling back the duvet and climbing under the covers.

"I had fun tonight," she said with a yawn, snuggling into my side. "You're my favorite too, Auntie Summer."

I flicked off the lights, then curled on my side to throw my arm over her. "Good."

"You'll never leave me like my mom did, will you?" she asked, and my heart lodged itself in my throat. "Papa says Timber Creek is too small for you. He's afraid you'll leave next. Like Aunt Aspen."

I leaned down, brushing her hair off her forehead as I kissed it. Moonlight caught on the bulletin board across the room, shining a spotlight on all the places I wanted to go and the things I wanted to do, but this…

This was on my bucket list too.

Everything else felt selfish in a way I couldn't let myself voice, a choice I'd have to make to leave my family behind. Sometimes dreams were just that, right? Only dreams.

Who needed to see the world and fall in love when I had so much already to be thankful for?

If losing my mom so young had taught me anything, it was that no moment could be taken for granted, and you never knew how long you might have with the ones you loved. Being able to help my family, to make cookies and have dance parties with River — that was what really mattered.

"I won't leave you, River," I whispered as she let out a long sigh and closed her eyes. "You're my world."

Chapter Four

MAX

I landed on the back deck of West Larkin's house with a thud, pulling back my shadows at the last second. Mountains framed the picturesque mountain lodge the Timber Creek wolf pack called home, a chill spring breeze blowing through the surrounding pines, filling the air with their resinous scent.

Jade, West's mate, looked up and waved from where she sat in an Adirondack chair on the large back porch, sipping iced tea and utterly unfazed by my sudden appearance.

A startled gasp sounded from beside her, and I belatedly realized Hailey sat with her, staring wide-eyed at me. Freckles dotted her pale skin, her long brown hair tied up in a bun as she sat curled up in an oversized green pack hoodie. I hadn't realized how young she was when I picked her up, but now that I could really take her in, there was no way this girl was more than 16.

"Shit, sorry." I vanished my wings as I moved towards where they sat. "I didn't mean to scare *you*, but this one is fair game." I jerked my head at Jade, who threw a cashew at me.

"Overgrown crows don't scare me."

Hailey offered a shaky smile as she caught her breath, and I pulled up a chair to join them. Unable to stop myself, I scanned Jade quickly, a force of habit every time I saw her since I got her out of a bad spot a few years ago.

But she looked good. Great, even. Relaxed in a way I'd never seen her before, her tan skin bright and healthy with all the sun she got here, her signature green hair falling in waves around her shoulders. No longer the scrawny, scared girl from all those years ago — no, now she looked strong, confident. At peace.

"To what do we owe this visit, Dark Knight of mine?" Jade tilted her head, swiveling to Hailey. "Ours, I guess."

"Searching for your worse half." Jade chuckled, and the sound was so hard-earned from her, I couldn't help but smirk in return. "Hailey, are you settling in okay?"

It had been a few days since I'd brought her into Headquarters, then made sure she was placed here, with West and Jade.

Jade made significant eye contact with Hailey. "I told you he only looks scary. Max is a big ol' softie deep down."

I scowled. "Careful, pup."

"Oh, right." Jade mimed zipping her lips shut, then whispered, "Our little secret."

I rolled my eyes. "I see everything's fine here." Still, my gaze slid to Hailey, seeking confirmation.

She nodded, a slight blush creeping across her cheeks at my attention. Not an unusual reaction for me. "Jade has been helping me set up my dorm room and introduce me to the pack."

"The dorms are open now? How old are you?"

"Sixteen," she confirmed my earlier guess, her eyes narrowing slightly in a show of teenage rebellion I loved to see on her, because it looked so *normal*. "I'm fine on my own. I was going to file for emancipation before—" she stopped, swallowing. "Before."

Jade patted her knee. "Hailey's going to fit in just fine here. The pack opened the dorms a few weeks ago, and Atlas moved in to keep an eye on the younger ones. They have their own rooms, but he's there to watch out for everyone and in case they need anything."

"I didn't even know bear shifters existed," Hailey said, referring to Atlas, and pulled her hands up into the sleeves of her hoodie. "He's nice though. Big."

I held back the chuckle at her description. Atlas was former Special Ops and one of the most formidable fighters I'd ever met, and yet he truly was a teddy bear at heart. He was the perfect fit to look after young shifters ready for a taste of independence.

The screen door slid open, and West came out to join us. I stood to shake his hand, the geometric pack tattoos on his arms standing out as usual on his suntanned skin.

"Hey, man. Did we know you were visiting?" he asked, resting a hand on the back of Jade's chair.

"Surprise visit."

His eyes met mine, realizing I must have something to discuss for me to show up unannounced. Leaning down, he pressed a kiss to Jade's forehead before whispering something in her ear that had her flushing from her cheeks to her chest. Then he straightened up and gestured back to the house.

"Let's talk in my office."

I bade Hailey goodbye and good luck settling in, gave Jade a teasing salute, then followed West inside.

A tingle, like electricity, skittered over my skin as I stepped over the threshold. I shook it off, then stopped when I noticed West studying me, head tilted in thought.

"So you don't need an invitation? That one's a myth?"

"For me, it is," I answered his vague question, both of us leaving my vampire heritage unsaid. He was one of about a handful of people who knew what I truly was, not the Dark Angel story most believed.

I flexed my fingers, the last of the sting dissipating. He didn't need to know that I did experience *some* discomfort without a direct invitation into someone's home. At the end of the day, not receiving an invitation couldn't keep me out.

West nodded slowly. "And, for the others?"

The full-blooded vampires, he meant. And I got where he was coming from — with vampires now exposed to our society and almost an unknown entity, an Alpha like West would want to know everything about them. To assess how much of a threat they might be.

If only I had more to tell him.

With a shrug, I said, "Guess you'd have to ask one of them."

His brows rose. "You don't know?"

"Shit, am I gonna fail the class, teach?"

West grunted, then continued through the living room, heading towards his office.

I nearly tripped over a remote control car as I followed after him, swearing softly, and West's chuckle said he heard me.

West's house was nothing like the sterile, minimalistic one I'd grown up in. For one, it actually looked like a child lived here. There were toys, children's art on the fridge, a well-loved rainbow blanket on the couch, all evidence of his little niece that lived upstairs with West's brother, Terran.

But even beyond those things, it was just... warm. Comfortable. The sofa was huge and the cushions full to bursting, there were family photos on the walls — signs of *life* everywhere. A stray hat left on the counter, a plate of cookies wrapped by the fridge, a pitcher of iced tea steeping in the sun on the windowsill.

In his office, West shut the door behind us and took one of the leather seats in front of his desk, gesturing me to the second one. With the dark, raw edge wood furniture and even more family photos, it, too, was in stark contrast to my father's cold, clinical office.

"So, what really brings you here? Do you have news?"

I nodded. "The night I found Hailey, I took in one of the guys that grabbed her."

West went stock-still, that way only shifters could, his usually hazel eyes flashing gold with his wolf for a moment. "Bennett?"

"Not him." I shook my head at the mention of his mate's kidnapper. "But, this guy is in the same ring. We'll have Bennett soon."

"How soon?"

"Give us a week or two." I eyed West. "You want him, he's yours."

West flexed his fingers — a common tic among shifters working to keep their claws retracted. "Just put him away. It's what Jade wants."

I raised a brow, not hiding my surprise that West wouldn't want to rip out the throat of the guy who abducted and drugged his mate not too long ago.

Then again, judging by the muscle twitching in his jaw — fighting his fangs — and the flicker of his eyes between his human ones and his wolf, that likely *was* what he wanted to do.

"You were so much more fun before you were domesticated." West leveled a flat glare at me, and I held up my hands. "But as you wish. The offer stands. People go missing in the system all the time."

He gave a grim nod, but I knew he wouldn't take me up on it, now he was house broken.

My second order of business was a bit less straightforward. I twisted in my seat, not even sure how to bring it up. Not sure *why* I was bringing it up.

"Is there something else?" West asked, astute as always.

I grimaced. "Yes, sort of."

I told him about my new orders from Malachi to track down the vampire dens. West's brow furrowed further with each sentence, until he was all but glaring at me.

"So, that's it? I understand what a problem this is, and you know I don't want people getting murdered, but what the fuck,

Max? You're just abandoning our whole attempt to get supes organized and find all of these kidnappers?"

"I'm not abandoning anything," I told him. "But Malachi believes the vampires will only keep escalating things, keep pushing the boundaries, and we can't have that, so it's taking priority. Do *you* want random innocent people showing up drained of blood left and right and blamed on your puppies? Because that's what's happening."

West sat forward. "What about all the *other* supes? Who still need help? Kids like Hailey?"

His eyes flicked to the door a second before his brother, Terran, slipped in, shutting it quietly behind him. He'd no doubt been drawn to the room by West's agitation. Wolves were connected like that through their pack bonds, sharing emotions as well as some telepathic messages; West had probably been filling him in mind to mind as we spoke.

I tightened my jaw. "Does this reaction mean you won't help?"

West sighed. "I'll try to come up with a list of wolves who might be up for something like this — no, *not* you," he shot at Terran, who'd just begun to open his mouth. "I need you here, and so does your daughter."

"This will be dangerous, Terran," I added in support of West's command. No way in hell would I drag that little girl's father away from her when I couldn't guarantee he'd come back in one piece. Still, I couldn't resist throwing in, "And you're not exactly the wolf you used to be."

His jaw clenched, and I smirked. But he knew I was right.

He crossed his arms, leaning back against the office door. "It has to be a wolf? I can't send Atlas or Cooper with you?"

"My father seems to think so, but we're working with a lot of unknowns here. All I know is they need to be a Tracker, with the keenest sense of smell."

The brothers' gazes met again as they held another silent conversation. Wolves were so annoying with that shit.

"Secrets, secrets are no fun," I cut in, waggling a finger at them. "But this brings me to the other reason I'm here." I looked to Terran. "Does Quentin still work for you?"

Terran pushed through the swinging saloon-style doors to his restaurant, Buffalo Willie's, as the scent of salty fries and burgers hit us in a wave. With the log wood siding and whiskey barrels doubling as tables, the place looked right out of an old Western, albeit with modern lighting. One wall was even covered in old sepia-toned Wanted posters, some of which held some familiar names and seemingly displayed with pride.

"Quentin, you here?" he called out, heading for the kitchen at the back and gesturing for me to pick a booth. "Take a seat, I'll send him out. You want something to eat?"

I smirked. "Don't think you have what I want on your menu, man."

Terran grunted in response before disappearing into the kitchen.

"Hey, Max!"

Leif, West's adopted son, was setting out rolls of silverware and gave a wave. I tilted my chin up in acknowledgment and slipped into a booth, drumming my fingers on the table. He looked like he wanted to chat more, but my mind was elsewhere, small talk not on my agenda.

A moment later, Quentin emerged from the kitchen, untying his waist apron as he approached.

The young-twenties vampire looked about the same as the last I'd seen him — black hair, unnaturally pale skin with colorful tattoos covering scrawny arms. But unlike a few years ago, he'd lost that haunted, gaunt look — maybe not quite *healthy*, but certainly better than he'd been when I'd found him.

"Quentin." I waved at the seat across from me. "Please, have a seat."

He slid onto the bench, eyeing me warily. "Something wrong?"

A fair question. I'd never sought him out before, and we only had one thing connecting us — something I doubted he ever wanted to rehash.

"No — well, yes, but nothing that's your fault. I need your help."

He furrowed his brows.

"Your den — your *old* den — I need to know how you found them, and where it is."

Quentin straightened, then his eyes darted around the mostly empty dining room. Leaning forward, he lowered his voice as he said, "I wouldn't say I found *them*. It was more of a *right place, right time* thing. Or wrong place, wrong time, I guess. As for *where*, I can't —" He shook his head. "I can't tell you."

"You're not in trouble, Quentin. *They're* not in trouble, as of now. I just need to find them."

"No, that's not what — I mean I *can't* tell you. It has to do with my bond to — to *him*."

I narrowed my eyes. "Grigor?"

Quentin winced, all the confirmation I needed. Grigor, the vampire who had taken a vulnerable human and turned him, then kept him as his personal snack for years. Not the greatest guy.

I lifted a hand halfway to Quentin's forehead, ready to use my combination of angel and vampire powers to see into his memories. He might not be able to *say*, but I should have still been able to see it. "May I?"

"It won't work, but you can try."

He tilted his head towards me, and I touched my fingertips

to his temple. As an angel, I could extract memories, but as a vampire, my powers were even more than that. Darker. Deadlier.

I could change them, erase them, replace them with something else entirely, leaving no trace of my presence.

Quentin grimaced as my magic invaded his mind, searching for the location, but where it should be was only a dark fog. I dropped my hand, sitting back, and Quentin shrugged.

"Well," I mused aloud, drumming my fingers again. "They must have been close to where I found you. I can't imagine he'd let you out of his sight for long."

I raised an eyebrow for confirmation, and Quentin nodded.

"So the den is somewhere in Boston." Quentin had been blood-drunk in a club in Southie when I'd found him, about to feed in the middle of a crowded dance floor before I dragged him out of there.

What a coincidence this latest attack on the news was right in Grigor's backyard.

But this *bond* Quentin spoke of made me realize… "What else can you tell me about Turned vampires like yourself?"

"What do you mean?"

"I understand your blood requirements are greater than for a Natural vampire, and you have some bond to your Maker." Another wince. "What else?"

The truth was, the vampire Conclave usually had Turned vampires put down — their need for blood made them a liability — so Quentin was the only one I knew.

"The main thing — besides the blood — is I can't manipulate minds and memories the way Naturals can."

An even greater problem for feeding then, since vampires typically erased their victim's memories to hide their tracks. The photos of the vampire leaving their kills behind resurfaced in my mind, making me wonder if that was what was happening around the world. Was the Conclave now letting Turned vampires loose on society, letting them feed freely without erasing the victim's memory after?

"As for the bond." Quentin swallowed. "It's hard to explain. Makers are supposed to be responsible for any vamps they turn, since we can't alter memories. It's not quite a parent-child relationship, or at least not a *healthy* one, but a guardian of sorts. In return, I'm… drawn to him. I wanted to help him."

"Are you still?"

"It's less now. It was hard at first, being here and so far away from him. With time, I've learned to ignore the pull. But I think, if I saw him again…" Quentin trailed off with a shrug.

"All right." I set my hands flat on the table, leaning back in the booth. "What do you know about wolves being able to scent dens? Any truth to it?"

Quentin jerked back, a confused expression clouding his face. "I'm not sure about that, but most vampires *hate* wolves. It's part of the reason I've stayed in Timber Creek so long — no one would think to look for me here among so many wolves."

My tongue ran across the tips of my canines, deep in thought as the bells over the door jingled, followed by a wave of sweet lemon verbena I knew immediately.

I turned to see Summer Larkin enter, her long honey-brown hair tied up in a ponytail with a pink bow. She wore a rainbow tie-dye t-shirt with a *Love Bites Bakery and Bookstore* logo, a pair of ripped jeans, and platform pink sneakers.

I could get a sunburn just looking at her, she was so sunshiney.

"Daddy!" Terran's daughter River called as she dropped Summer's hand and sprinted across the restaurant through the kitchen saloon doors. Summer smiled, offering a wave to her brother through the kitchen window, then turned to chat with the people seated at the nearest table.

She flitted around the dining room with ease, smiling and laughing with everyone she greeted, which was just about everyone in here.

"— next?" Quentin finished a sentence I hadn't heard any of.

"Next —" I started, but then Summer spotted us, and a smile broke over her face as she came over.

"Well look at this small world," she said, looking between the two of us. "I didn't know you two knew each other! Then again, I guess you *are* both vampires, maybe you go way back?" I fought not to jolt at her nonchalant statement — like it was common knowledge I was a vampire — but she barreled right on. "Hm, or maybe not, since Q is Turned and you're" — her hazel eyes met mine, tracing over my face slowly as she sniffed the air, before she finished — "half, I'd say. Natural. Actually, how old *are* both of you? Quentin, I assumed you were young, but I guess looks probably don't mean much for vampires, if *Twilight* is anything to go by." She chuckled at her own joke, propping her hip against the booth. "Then again, you don't sparkle, so maybe *Twilight* isn't the most reliable source." Her gaze slid to me, and she jabbed a thumb in my direction. "Now, this guy I'm pretty sure is ancient, if the socks he wears are any indication."

I discreetly shifted my ankles under the table. "What's wrong with my socks?"

Summer merely made knowing eye contact with Quentin, the two of them clearly trying not to laugh.

"Summer, stop harassing my patrons!" Terran shouted from the kitchen, and Summer shot us both a *Yikes* face.

"My bad! Enjoy your" — she glanced at our empty table, biting back a smile — "uh, wood varnish lickings, apparently. I'll have to message Stephanie Meyer — that certainly wasn't in the books."

Another beat later, she breezed back out the front doors, and I snapped my gaping jaw shut as my gaze cut to Quentin.

The real question was, how did she know I was half? And Natural? "Did *you* tell her —?"

Quentin shook his head vehemently. "I did not."

I tapped my fingers on the table and got out of the booth, clapping him on the shoulder.

"Thanks for everything, Quentin. But I've got a wolf to follow."

Chapter Five

SUMMER

"You know, stalking is only cute in dark romance and, personally, I'm more of a rom-com girl."

I turned on my heel, and Max froze in his tracks, guilt written all over his face. "I wasn't *stalking* you. Someone sure thinks a lot of herself."

"Hm." Hands on my hips, I faced him as we stood in front of my bakery.

Dressed in black to match his dark hair and making his deep blue eyes pop, Max stood out like a sore thumb against the bright yellow siding and floral multicolored paint on my shop windows. There was something in his expression — besides the guilt — that said he was assessing me for some reason.

Interesting.

I assessed him right back.

He was the definition of tall, dark, and handsome. Olive skin that wasn't just suntanned but spoke of some sort of Mediterranean heritage and the darkest brown hair that was messy in a way that said he spent some time in front of the mirror, making it just-so. And that smirk he always wore — it was as deadly as his hidden fangs.

"Hankering for another spinach and feta croissant then? I think I have some I could heat up."

No one in their right mind would turn down one of my

spinach feta croissants, so I knew I'd have him hooked. More time for me to figure out what his deal was.

I pulled open the door and walked towards the kitchen, Max's footsteps stalling behind me somewhere in the middle of the café section that took up one side of the shop's space, filled with multicolored metal tables and chairs, interspersed with plants and cute lamps and a few comfy armchairs.

"How did you know what I ate for breakfast?"

I slipped into the kitchen, grabbing a pink apron and sliding it over my head, taking over for Olive behind the counter so she could ring up a bookstore customer. I opened the glass display case full of muffins, scones, cookies, bagels, and, of course, croissants. "Wolf, Maxy. I have exceptionally strong senses, even if you did brush your teeth after. Now, cinnamon toothpaste — that's a bold choice."

Grabbing a pair of tongs, I pulled out a croissant and slid it into the toaster oven behind me.

"I didn't say I actually wanted one, sunshine," Max said, slowly approaching the counter.

"But they're delicious, and now I know you like them." I grinned as the timer beeped, pulling it from the oven and plating it for him. "My treat."

He glanced between the croissant and my face, an expression I couldn't quite read flashing across his face before he reached a tanned finger across the counter and pulled the plate towards him.

My smile wavered under his attention, a rush of heat washing through me the longer his gaze lingered, seeming to take me in for the first time. Suddenly I pictured him in a white frilly tunic and fitted trousers, myself in a corseted gown spread beneath him on a bed covered in red rose petals, feeling the heat of that attention everywhere in my body like the heroine of the bodice ripper book I fell asleep reading the night before.

"Anything else?" I asked, willing my heartbeat to chill out.

I did not need to romanticize every single person who came into my life, imagining every possible scenario and if I'd become the future Mrs. Massimo Russo. Not in a million years.

Even if I had any actual interest in Max, our lives did *not* fit together, and never would. I was a small town girl, and he — well, it was safe to say this little town wasn't big enough for the likes of him.

"How did you know?" Max asked, then took a bite of the croissant, buttery flakes flying everywhere with the crunch in a way that I did *not* find endearingly adorable. A flake caught on the edge of his lip before his tongue darted out to get it.

"Know — know what?"

He brushed crumbs from his black jacket. "Back there. How did you know those things about Quentin — and me?"

Oh, that. "How could I not? I mean, sure, you both smell like vampires, but also different. Can't you scent the difference?"

His sharp blue eyes narrowed on me, which I took as a *no*. "I'm an angel, Summer."

I pursed my lips, staring at his dark hair and deep blue eyes, then glancing down to his shoulders where I knew, if he hadn't glamoured them, deep black opalescent wings would hang. Max might parade around and advertise himself as a full-blooded angel, but ever since Quentin arrived and I'd met my first vampire, there was no hiding the distinct metal-and-smoke scent that I assumed all vampires had. Max's was different, that same scent mixed with a bourbon and sandalwood smell that was distinctly *him.* "Okay."

Max looked around the mostly empty bakery to the bookshelves lining the left side of the café, filled with a colorful assortment of romance novels, finishing his croissant in silence.

I chatted with Olive and sent her for her break, taking over the register and preparing for the lunch crowd soon. Max lingered, rapid texting on his phone, observing the café and me in turn.

Why was he still here?

The weight of his attention sat on my shoulders like a bag of sand, making my whole body aware of his focus every time it landed on me. I could feel it zapping across my skin like a livewire.

"Maybe it's time to stop reading romantic suspense," I muttered to myself as I reorganized the books on the shelves, placing them back in alphabetical order.

"Why do you only sell romance novels?" Max's deep voice said from right behind me, and I jumped, clutching my heart.

"How did you do that?" I looked over my shoulder, realizing our faces were mere inches apart. He placed a hand on the bookshelf above my head, his sandalwood scent invading my senses. "Sneak up on me like that?"

"Maybe your senses aren't always as sharp as you think."

I narrowed my eyes. "Is there a reason you're loitering around here?"

"I'm not *loitering*. I'm a customer, and I'm lingering. This is a bookstore; lingering is usually encouraged. How long have you been running this place again? You should know that by now."

"You're not going to buy anything, so you're not a customer. Ergo, *loitering*."

I turned back to the books, staring down at the one in my hand.

Max's hand reached around me, a finger tapping on the cover. "*Married to the Monarch.*" His breath slid across the sensitive skin of my neck, like a sensual caress. "What's this one about? A woman dreaming of a pampered life? Maybe I'll buy it."

A high-pitched chuckle escaped me as I clutched it to my chest. "No. It's a marriage of convenience, where the son and daughter of two feuding monarchs are forced to wed in an agreement for peace between their kingdoms."

"So, *Romeo and Juliet* style, forbidden romance. How astoundingly original."

I spun, leaning my back against the shelves as I tilted my chin up to look at Max. This close, I couldn't help but notice the hint of amusement in those deep blue eyes, but I wasn't about to let him stand with the dismissive comment. "Not at all. *Romeo and Juliet* is a tragedy. This is a *romance*. There are only happily-ever-afters on these shelves. I like to imagine there's a happy ending for everyone out there, somewhere, just waiting for them to find it. That's why I only sell romance novels — I am an eternal optimist."

He trailed a finger down the spine of a book thoughtfully. "In my experience, not everyone deserves a happy ending. Isn't it naive to think otherwise?"

I leveled a look at him; this was an argument I'd heard before. "Naive, or hopeful? Forgiving? Isn't it overly dogmatic to assume people can't change, or aren't worth a good redemption arc?"

His dark brows rose, a glint of something dangerous in his eyes. "Even killers? Vampires?"

"I thought you said you were an angel?" I lifted my brows to match his expression and he smirked, the hint of a dimple on his tan face entirely too seductive. Heat pooled in my belly, and suddenly, I wondered if angels or vampires or both could scent arousal the same way shifters could.

"Anyway." I pushed off the shelves and ducked under his arm, heading towards the correct section of shelves to put the book away. And to put some much needed space between us. "Was there something else you needed? Tea? Coffee? Mafia romance?"

"Now you're just making things up." Max followed me towards the two black shelves in the back corner of the store, full of dark covers and darker deeds, even if they *also* had happy endings. "Who the hell would want to read about the Mafia?"

"Oh, my sweet summer child," I said and his chuckle rumbled from behind me. "Mafia is but the tip of the dark romance iceberg. And I've got news for you — *all* of these books are made up."

"Yes, I am aware of the meaning of fiction."

He pulled a book off the shelf, flipping through it, and I eased over to pluck it from his hands. The last thing we needed to add to this conversation were the logistics of using a gun in certain places.

"Oooh, maybe we don't start with that one. I'm not sure you're ready for reverse harem if you've never even heard of Mafia romance."

His head tilted to the side. "Reverse harem?"

I patted his chest, and instantly regretted it as tingles spread from my hand all the way up my arms. "One woman. A whole bunch of men. Good times all around."

"A *whole bunch*?"

"Usually four, but it varies." I shrugged. "If that sounds interesting, I've got something a little — ah, *tamer* than that one to get you started. I'm sure you could learn a thing or two —"

"Not interested."

"You sure?" I pulled out the book I had in mind, waving it in a rainbow motion. "The more you know."

His eyes widened at the four bare-chested men on the cover, taking the book from my hands gingerly, like it was a bomb set to detonate. "This is what you're into, Little Larkin?"

A common misconception. "I didn't say I'm *into* it, just like I'm not actually into sentient doors or dragons and bloody battles. But hey, a little fun reading never hurt anyone. Here." I pressed it into his chest when he tried to pass it back. "Enjoy."

Walking back towards the counter, I peered over my

shoulder as Max studied the shelves, pulling each dark book down one at a time, muttering under his breath at the absurdity of the titles and covers.

"So, you've stalked me, had a croissant, *lingered* — care to share the real reason you followed me here?"

He put the last book in his hand away, straightening the uneven spines before walking towards me.

"And here I thought we were enjoying a little bonding, but whatever. Before we get into it, I need you to shut down any mental connection you've got going on with West. Because I'm pretty sure the favor I'm about to ask you for might make him want to murder me."

Well that had my attention. "Color me intrigued." I glanced around the shop, only a few patrons hanging around in the café. "Give me fifteen, and I'll meet you up on the roof."

Chapter Six

MAX

It was impossible. It *should* have been impossible.

Summer could *scent* me? No other wolf, or any supe, had ever been able to scent that I was half-vampire in all my years. Sure, my father had mentioned looking for a wolf with keen senses, but I'd never imagined this.

There was a chance that West had told her what I was after he'd found out during our hunt for Jade, but he seemed like the kind of male who could keep a secret.

As instructed, I'd taken the stairwell up to Summer's roof, where I now paced aimlessly through neatly arranged rows of raised garden beds. Flowers of every color bloomed in between vining plants beginning to grow over trellises, framed by the scenic Rocky Mountains circling the little town. Everything was alive and fresh, just like the woman who lived here. It was easy to imagine how gorgeous this would all be later in the summer. If I hadn't been so distracted by Summer doing the impossible, it would have been... nice.

Bit overboard, in my opinion, but to each their own.

Then there was the *other* distraction — I glanced down at the "reverse harem" book I was still, inexplicably, holding. What the fuck was that woman reading?

I flipped it open, scanning through some pages until the word *cock* caught my eye. Glancing around the roof to check I was alone, I held the book a little closer.

I gasp as Knox pulls me astride him, lining us up and slamming his cock in me in one thrust. As he sets our rhythm from below, Ajax's hand reaches around my jaw from behind, tilting my head to his and capturing my lips in a devouring kiss. His other hand grips my hips, then my ass, his fingers slippery with lube as he breaches my

—

"All right, I brought the tea anyway, since I want some and what better way to use the last of my peach syrup. The bourbon is optional depending on the turn of this conversation — oh, you must be at a good part for that blush."

I slammed the book shut, but quickly switched my slack jaw for a smirk as I wiggled the book at her. "Is your family aware of your salacious reading material? This is downright scandalous."

"Next thing you know, I'll be flashing my ankles. The horror!" Summer gasped as she hiked her jeans leg up, showing off her crew socks. With a chuckle, she set the basket containing a pitcher of iced tea, a bottle of bourbon, and two cups down on a turquoise metal garden table, then sat on the chair beside it.

"I'll have you know I've given out many a book recommendation over the years, and some people have even told me I saved their relationships. But if you want to be the one to tell my brothers about that book, be my guest. Just make sure you tell me in advance so I can be there with popcorn as their minds explode." She waggled her eyebrows, pouring us each a glass of tea.

With a shake of my head, I took the seat across from her. "Let's get back on topic."

"Yes, this mysterious favor."

"You can scent me." I met her eyes, hesitating, as she took a long drink of tea.

"Is that the favor? What is this, a smell kink? You want me to huff you and puff you and blow —"

"*No*, what does that even —" I broke off as Summer

started laughing at me again. "Okay, you have your mental links shut down?"

Summer tapped her temple. "Fort Knox up here."

I glared at her, remembering the name from the book, but tried to move past it. "You know something about my work for the PRICs, for Malachi?" She nodded in a *sort of* way, so I continued. "He wants me to track down some vampire dens, but they're notoriously hard to find. Almost impossible. Except, my father found mention of a legend that some wolves have senses acute enough to find them. Since you appear to be unnaturally good at scenting us —"

"*'US'?*" Summer's air-quotes and dramatic questioning tone should have been on Broadway.

"Yes, you were right, I'm half-vampire," I said, and she gasped, hand to chest and all. I rolled my eyes. "I want you to help me test my father's theory about the best way to find dens."

"Sure." She shrugged, taking another long sip, and I fought not to let my jaw drop.

"Well, I wasn't finished explaining what exactly I'm asking of you."

"You want to see if I can smell a whole pack of vampires, right?"

"A den, but yes. It's not that simple though."

"Sounds pretty simple to me. You point me in the right direction, and I find the nearest charred blood bank, right?"

I frowned. "Charred blood bank?"

"Not charred, per se. More smoky copper. You really can't smell yourself? Do you have allergies? Can you *get* allergies? Maybe you should go see an otorhinolaryngologist."

Brushing a hand across my face, I leaned back in my chair, staring at her. Why was she agreeing so easily? There was no way this sunshine-emitting, tie-dye wearing woman was fully comprehending the severity and complexity of the situation.

"This is dangerous. Vampires do not play nice. Your brother will kill me if we do this and you get hurt."

"I'm confused. Do you *not* want me to agree to help you?"

"I want to make sure you understand the situation. This isn't one of your books, sunshine. This is *actual* danger."

She grinned. "Good thing for you, I've been needing some adventure in my life lately. This wasn't technically on my bucket list, but I can add it in, no problem. Besides"— she stood up and went to a control panel on the wall, triggering the sprinklers to water the plants around her— "I have three brothers. I'm not exactly helpless. And for all your tough guy act, I hardly think you'd ever let anything terrible happen to us."

"Bucket list?"

She clapped her hands, turning back to me but ignoring my question. There was something slightly manic in her eyes that set off an alarm bell in my mind, and when she spoke again, her words started coming out faster and faster. "Now, I assume we'll be traveling, because obviously I'd already know, with my super keen nose, if there were any dens nearby. So that means I need to pack, and let Olive know what's up and get some shifts moved around, but I can probably be ready to go in a few hours."

"Summer —"

"Okay! Two hours, tops. I'll make it work, Tim Gunn style. We got this. Oh my gosh, how fun, I can't remember the last time I took a vacation! Where to first, partner? Nope!" She held up her hands. "Surprise me. I'll pack for everything. We'll be able to sneak in some sightseeing, right? It sounds like we'll have to wander around, so yes, sightseeing. Great idea. Oh, I can use my new suitcase! This will be great."

I waited to see if that was the end of it, or if she had more she needed to get out. When her eyes only widened expectantly, I sighed. "Summer, no. I want to test Malachi's theory with you on this *one* den that I suspect is somewhere in Boston. But if it works, then I'll find someone else — you have the store, and your family, and probably no actual combat experience, sibling squabbles notwithstanding."

She deflated a little more with every word, then crossed her arms. "Some other wolf with super senses, you mean."

"Yes, exactly."

"When you've never — and I mean *ever*, and Goddess knows how old you are, we already covered the socks — been sniffed out before and I'm right here in front of you, ready and willing to help?"

I faltered, then went for it. "We think you'll have to taste my blood to surpass their cloaking spells vampires use to hide their dens." Her brows shot up at the advice my father had given me. "There are more vampires near a den to increase the scent, but all the more reason for them to cloak that scent. Part of our magic enables that. But Malachi's belief is that, if a wolf *tastes* vampire blood, it can negate some or all of that cloaking magic."

Wrinkling her nose a little, Summer hummed. "Well, blood's not exactly my kink, but that's not the grossest thing in the world."

My jaw did drop this time. "What? You're actually willing to do that."

"Couple drops of blood?" She shrugged. "You know I'm a wolf, right? I take my steak rare, buddy. Practically mooing. Does it have any fun side effects? Now *that* would make it more interesting for the bucket list."

"That's not —" I sputtered, my brain stalling for a minute, then tried again. "Do you know what blood sharing means for vamps?"

"That we're really, really good friends? Or enemies, I guess, depending on if the blood was a *willing* thing or not. I could just bite you. Frenemies. Best of both worlds."

I shifted in my seat to hide the effect the image of her biting me had on my body, then reached for the bottle of bourbon, unscrewed the lid and took a long pull straight from the bottle. "It means you're a Source, a whore, or a spouse."

"To other vamps, maybe."

"Which is who we'll be meeting with."

"Whom we'll never see again."

"You don't — you wouldn't care?"

She lifted her arms. "What strangers think of me? Not particularly."

Why was I more upset about this than she seemed to be? Why was she not *getting* this?

Summer tilted her head, honey-brown hair cascading over her shoulder. "Maybe *you're* the one who cares, tough guy. But do you care if they think that about me, or think that *you* would have a Source/whore, or that yours would be me?" Her eyes widened comically again, only I was almost sure she was dead serious. "*Or* are you worried that they'd know that *I'd* know that *they'd* know I'm only *pretending* to be —"

"What are you rambling about?" She was losing me. Possibly herself as well.

"The way I see it, we have an easy out here, partner of mine." She leaned back in her chair, a mischievous glint in her eye I had a feeling I'd come to know well.

"Enlighten me."

"Massimo Salvatore Russo, will you fake-date me?"

Chapter Seven

SUMMER

Max frowned at me. "That's not my middle name."

"Dang. What a missed opportunity. You're straight out of a Mafia romance, so it seemed fitting. Like an Italian Don, laundering money in the back of a mediocre restaurant. Makes me want a meatball."

He pinched the bridge of his nose, letting out a long sigh before he looked up at me again. "This isn't one of your books, Summer. We won't be fake dating because there is no *we* here, and it's not dating vampires care about but marriage — no rings means you're still on the literal table. We're not even going to approach the den — just see if we can find it and then I'll go back alone after I bring you back here. I will not be responsible for mixing West Larkin's little sister in vampire business."

Simmering started somewhere in my gut, because fuck that. *West Larkin's little sister?* Like I hadn't heard that my whole life. My eyes flashed to my wolf's, and Max startled at the sight. My wolf paced in my mind, ready to bare her teeth, but unlike Alpha wolves, there was no fight for dominance between her and I — I was in control of my own mind. We were two souls living peacefully together, equally pissed off by his comment.

"You know, I'm actually a full-grown adult," I said coolly, trying my best not to let the rejection get to me. "And I'm more than aware of the differences between fiction and reality, and capable of making my own decisions. So, how about you *never* say anything like that again, I'll go pack for Boston, and when we regroup in two hours we can pretend this part never happened. *Capisci?*"

Okay, maybe I was a tiny bit hurt he was so appalled by the idea of dating me — or marrying if that's what it took — even if it was for show. But I was sick of everyone in my life viewing me as the sweet little Larkin sister, of everyone being afraid to come anywhere near me for fear of my brothers, of this whole town continually underestimating me. I was a low-ranking wolf in the pack dynamic, a little sister, and a woman — a hell of a combination in shifter society that lead to way too much babying — but I was not about to be dismissed because of those things I had no control over.

Indi was right — there was no time like the present to start setting boundaries and living for me, instead of everyone else. I *did* have control over that.

I wanted to do this.

I wanted to go to wherever it was we were going and do whatever it was we were doing, even if I knew almost none of the plan. It sounded dangerous. It sounded different. It sounded *fun.*

To his credit, Max looked a little chagrined about his outburst. "You know Italian?"

"I know a lot of things about a lot of things. I took classes for a year but then I got bored and switched to French, which wasn't nearly as romantic as everyone says. All that throat clearing. It's got nothing on Italian."

A slow smirk crept over Max's face. "*Sono d'accordo, fiore.*"

I hustled right the hell out of there before my panties could set themselves on fire, but those words in his sultry voice seared themselves into my brain, replaying all the way down the stairs to my apartment.

An hour and a half later, I lay on my lavender suitcase with white daisies, squishing the two sides of the case together as much as I could to get the zipper to close.

Sure, Max said he'd bring me back after this one little test, but who was he kidding? After 24 hours, he'd be putty in my hands, and forget all about that little *send me home* part of his plan. We'd be gallivanting across the globe, finding vampire dens at every turn, in no time flat.

And, boy was I prepared. I packed for everything — sundresses, sandals, a parka, my favorite poncho, overalls, wool socks, hiking boots, swimsuit, little black dress, shorts, pants, tees, 16 pairs of underwear — I stopped mid-zip.

Did I need my ren-faire dress?

No. I kept zipping.

Unless —

I shook my head. No, if I *needed* a ren-faire dress at short notice, I could run to a thrift store and improvise.

Thus assured, I finished zipping my suitcase closed with some effort and wheeled it out to my living room. Then I squinted down at my current outfit and went to change.

Twenty minutes later, I burst out of the stairwell door back onto the roof where we'd agreed to meet, lugging my suitcase behind me.

Max's eyes darted to it immediately — couldn't blame him, Betsy was *beautiful* — then back to me, tracing over my appearance. His lip twitched.

"First of all, *no*" — he pointed to the suitcase — "and second of all, what are you wearing?"

I gestured between us. "What, I thought this was the uniform? It screams *undercover,* which is kind of against the point but who am I to argue with a professional such as yourself."

In a last-ditch effort to match Max's aesthetic, I'd raided my sister Aspen's clothes she left behind in my guest room for black jeans, black Vans, and a black hoodie. Aspen was almost color averse.

He gave me a flat stare. "And what did you tell West, exactly?"

"Just that Max Russo, infamous Dark Angel bad boy and ex-con, is whisking me off to corrupt my innocence and feed me mercilessly to a den of hedonistic blood-suckers. Why?"

His face paled before he caught on and cursed under his breath.

"You're not actually scared of my brother, are you?"

"Scared? No," he scoffed. "But I don't need the headache of dealing with an Alpha tantrum right now."

The truth was, I hadn't known what to tell West, since I wasn't sure when we'd be back and Max seemed to want to keep this under wraps. For now, I told him I was headed east — not a lie — to source apple orchards for some bakery items. That wasn't entirely implausible as I did occasionally travel to source the good stuff myself, just never as far as the East Coast. He probably assumed I meant Denver, but that was on him for assuming.

He only had to buy it long enough for me to convince Max that this partnership of ours did not need to be a dirty little secret.

Max leaned forward to take my suitcase from my hands, peering down at me. "Have you traveled by flicker before?"

I nodded. Flickering was how demons essentially tele-ported, and Indi had taken me with her a few times. It was horrible.

"Well, this is worse." Max slipped an arm around my waist, my stomach fluttering at his nearness. I had to tilt my head back to meet his gaze, my chin all but resting on his chest, his sandalwood scent and warmth intoxicating. "Buckle up, buttercup."

I wrapped my arms around his waist a heartbeat before

darkness enveloped us, swirling like an arctic breeze as the ground fell away. Vertigo scrambled my brain, and I slammed my eyes shut. Cold sank into my bones until my teeth chattered, and I pressed my face into his chest just for the warmth as my veins turned to ice. Air and static rushed through my ears, silent and deafening, but my grip on Max's shirt never wavered, nor did the feel of his hand on the small of my back.

Slowly, the cold receded, and my feet met solid ground again, my breaths sawing out of me like I'd just run a marathon.

As I fought to catch my breath, I pried one eye open, but darkness still surrounded us.

My fingers still dug into Max's shirt, holding on for dear life, and our entire fronts were pressed together.

"Max?" I breathed, not quite sure why I was whispering.

"Yeah?"

"Is it supposed to still be dark?"

He leaned down, lips trailing over my ear sending a shiver down my spine for an entirely different reason than a moment before. "Have you heard of *shadows*?"

I smacked his chest, and the low chuckle that responded nearly made my knees buckle.

I stepped back, straightening up and getting my hormones under control. Hopefully.

With a deep breath that didn't help clear his scent from my nose at all, I took in our surroundings as my eyes adjusted to the dim light, then shot Max a look.

"Are we trolls?" We'd landed under a bridge, large enough that where we stood it was almost dark as night and littered with all manner of trash.

"Would you rather land in the middle of Copley Square? Might defeat the whole *staying hidden* thing we've been going for, but I'm always up for making a scene if you are." He jerked his head towards the far end of the bridge as he took off. "This will be a pretty brief partnership if a little city grime offends you, *principessa*."

I elbowed him in the kidney, eliciting a satisfying *umph*, and reached for my suitcase. He jerked it out of reach.

"I can carry my own."

"Really? This thing weighs as much as you do."

I tilted up my chin. "I'm going to take that as a compliment to my legendary packing abilities."

"What the hell is even in here?"

"Don't worry your pretty little head about it. Now." I skipped a little as we emerged from under the bridge, and the city appeared in front of us, the lit-up Boston skyline rising above the river. "Where to?"

"What do you mean, there's only one bed?" Max all but snarled at the receptionist when we arrived at a hotel several blocks away. "I specifically requested two when I booked this room just a few hours ago."

"I'm sorry, sir, there must have been a mix up," the flustered man responded, clicking around his screen. "Our only remaining room is a single King." He glanced between the two of us, then added, "Big concert at Fenway this weekend."

My eyes widened. "Really? Who? Please say Taylor Swift."

Before the receptionist could respond, Max cut in, "Let's just find another hotel. There's a thousand in this city."

The man cleared his throat. "I think you'll find much the same situation anywhere else, sir. The whole city is booked up."

I put a reassuring hand on Max's arm, though it seemed to have the opposite effect as his jaw tightened. "It's fine, we'll take the room. My fiancé here is just old fashioned, you understand." I shot the guy a wink, and Max went red under his tanned skin.

We finished checking in, and made our way all the way up to our room before Max held out a hand to stop me.

"Fiancé? And what exactly do you want to do about this one bed situation? Just so you know, unlike what the lore says, I don't actually sleep in a coffin."

The door beeped as I held out the key and pushed it open, walking inside the small room.

"One, yes, fiancé. If the only thing keeping you from bringing me along on this quest is a marriage of convenience, then we might as well start practicing, hm? Engaged can be our trial run. And two, we'll do what one always does in a one bed situation —"

"I'll sleep on the floor."

I held up my hands, shaking my head. "The readers will riot."

"Readers?" Max muttered as he shut the door behind us, one hand still on the handle as that muscle in his jaw flexed.

I plopped down on the white duvet, running my hands over the smooth fabric as I tried not to focus on how chiseled his jawline was, and how badly I suddenly wanted to lick it. "Sleeping on the floor is the absolute worst outcome in a one bed trope, which you'll know soon enough now that you're becoming a book boyfriend. We'll share."

"Book boyfriend? If you expect me to ravish you with three other dudes, think again, wolf."

I cocked my head, ignoring his comments. "You don't turn into a bat or anything, right? I'm not going to wake up with you suspended from the ceiling above me?"

The scowl. I bit my lip.

"If it'll make you feel more comfortable, we can pillow-barrier it up. But that guy was right — we'd probably find the same situation in every hotel in this city, so we might as well save our time and our feet and just suck it up." I chuckled, then winced. "Bad choice of words."

Max sighed, flipped the lock on the door, and in two long strides he stood between my knees, deep blue eyes locked on mine. A strand of his black hair fell across his face, and my hand twitched with the need to brush it away.

"This *never* gets back to your brothers. *Capisci?*"

If I wasn't mistaken, maybe Max *was* a little scared of West. I patted his chest reassuringly.

"Maxy, believe it or not, I rarely talk about my sleepovers with my bros. Now, are you a left side of the bed or a right side guy?"

Chapter Eight

MAX

Everything was loud.

I stared at the ceiling, the blackout curtains doing nothing to block out the sounds of the T, bell dinging and wheels screeching as the subway car turned. Car horns alternated in a chaotic rhythm with sirens and drunken passersby on the street below. Boston was alive even in the early hours of the morning, hours after Summer put her ear plugs in and fell asleep.

I'd never been much of a sleeper — blame the vampire genes, probably — but in the same room, same *bed* as Summer Larkin?

My head turned against my will, staring at her sleeping peacefully, hands under her face as she laid on her side facing me with a smile on her face, because of course she smiled even while unconscious. Her hair was tied up in a knot on the top of her head, but several tendrils had come loose, draping over the side of her face, only adding to the angelic look she had going on. The sheets draped over her body, but I saw the skimpy yellow pajama set she wore before she snuck under the covers, and the sight was seared into my mind.

And this pillow barrier was a joke. It did nothing to stop her intoxicating scent from reaching me, nothing to dull the beat of her heart, or the memory of how she'd refused to take no for an answer the day before.

She was a puzzle, one my mind refused to let go of until I could figure her out. I couldn't decide if she was incredibly short-sighted and impulsive or the bravest woman I'd ever met, but the moment she'd met my glare with one of her own, I'd barely held myself back from pinning her against the wall and silencing her with a searing kiss.

Just the memory of it had my fangs descending, ready for a taste of her. I ran my tongue over them, willing them to recede. I'd just fed a few days ago, even if I hadn't had time to fight or fuck the adrenaline out of me — I should have been fine.

But I wasn't fine.

I was *ravenous.*

My fangs pricked my lower lip as I looked back up at the ceiling, the taste of my own blood doing nothing for me.

With a long sigh, I gave up on sleep even though it was only four in the morning. Slipping silently from the bed, careful not to wake Summer, I made my way to the shower. I just needed a few minutes respite from her sweet scent invading my nose, and I'd be able to think again.

Not waiting for the water to heat up, I stripped and stepped under the frigid water. Goosebumps raised on my skin as I tilted my head back, drawing shadows around me to clear my thoughts.

I still couldn't wrap my brain around how exactly Summer had convinced me to bring her along and give this a try. One minute I just wanted to run the idea of testing her powers by her so I knew if there was any truth to the whole wolves-scenting-vampires thing, the next her arms were wrapped around my waist as I vanished us across the country.

The memory of our bodies pressed close together had my cock twitching as I washed up, and I gritted my teeth. I could *not* have an interest like that in Summer.

Summer was… good.

I had enough scars lacing my skin to tell the tale of the many dark deeds I'd done, both at my father's will and on my own. There was no saving me, and I'd only poison someone like Summer, leeching her of any light she had inside her just like my shadows leeched the world of color.

Reminding her she was West's little sister had pissed her off, and rightfully so, but the facts were the same — she was as off limits as they came for me romantically.

And my original plan was still in place. As business partners, we'd try to find this one den as a trial, and if it worked, I could find another wolf to find the rest of them. Summer would go back to her life, and we'd go back to passing acquaintances.

Simple.

After dressing, I ran a towel over my hair as I left the bathroom, doing my best to stay quiet. Steam billowed out of the doorway as I opened it, and I was nearly bowled over by a yellow blur on her way into the bathroom.

"Give me five minutes and we're making this town our oyster!"

The door slammed, followed by the shower running again.

"I don't think that's the saying," I muttered, but I doubted she heard me. She was already belting out song lyrics.

Fucking hell, she was naked in there now. I took a long, measured breath, which only served to fill my lungs with her lemony scent from the still-warm bed.

I gripped the dresser, letting my head fall between my arms as the wood creaked under my fingertips, and worked to keep my fangs from descending. Maybe I needed to feed again. Just to take the edge off.

"Almost done!" she called as the water turned off.

I sat on the edge of the bed to put my shoes on as I calculated the plan for the day. It was still early, but she was a baker, probably used to early mornings. We could scope out the city to get our bearings before the hunt began tonight when vampires were most likely to be active.

I was still trying to get my reaction to her under control when Summer emerged from the bathroom.

"What are you thinking for breakfast? Because, damn, could I eat after all that travel. Is it also called flickering, or do you have your own name for it? Should traveling like that be tiring? Well, it was, or maybe I forgot to eat last night, or maybe it's jetlag? I've never had jetlag before." Summer paused, clipping on her crossbody bag, and tilted her head at me. "Do you eat breakfast? Beyond croissants, I mean. Oh, crap — do you need blood? I have no idea —"

I stood, trying not to grin at what was clearly her sight-seeing ensemble. White sneakers, those figure-hugging jeans again, and a breezy pink Hawaiian shirt.

"Breathe. It's called vanishing for vampires. And no, I don't need blood." *Yes, I do. Yours.* "But breakfast sounds good."

"Awesome!" Summer grinned. "Okay, so while I was waiting for you to finish up your beauty routine, I found these two restaurants that look amazing and are already open. One is just down the street, and the other one is downtown but it's right next to the Public Gardens, which I *really* want to check out while we're here, and then maybe we can do part of the Freedom Trail — not *all* of it, maybe just over to Faneuil Hall, unless you want to keep going — so if you don't mind —"

When the hell had she researched all this? "Gardens it is."

Summer fist-pumped the air. "Ducklings, here we come!"

I furrowed my brow as I followed her out of the room, closing the door behind us and heading for the elevator. "Ducklings?"

Summer's eyes met mine in the elevator's reflective doors. "*Make Way For Ducklings?*" She raised her eyebrows significantly, then frowned. "Did you not read that one as a kid?"

"Apparently not."

"Probably wasn't written yet, right?" She smirked.

"Oh, she's got jokes today."

Her fist half-heartedly met my shoulder, but the little touch was enough to remind me how badly I wanted to taste her.

We stepped onto the elevator and I hit the button for the ground floor. "Have you really not been to Boston before?"

"Nope. But I can Google like the best of them."

The elevator dinged, and Summer waltzed out, pulling oversized heart-shaped sunglasses from her bag and sliding them on.

"Keep up, Maximus. I'm on a mission."

"So you don't need blood everyday like food."

"Nope."

"And your fangs obviously retract."

I sipped my black coffee while Summer lobbed question after question at me between bites of her fresh berry French toast, topped with a mountain of whipped cream. We sat at a café on the edge of the Public Gardens, tourists and traffic bustling all around us.

"Obviously."

"And you don't turn into a bat or sleep in a coffin. Garlic?" she asked while wiping a stray bit of whipped cream from her chin with her thumb, then licked it off. My fangs tingled, but I didn't look away, enraptured by her unintentional erotic display.

"Great with butter."

"I saw your reflection in the elevator."

"Very astute."

"What about the whole blood lust thing?"

"Some vampires do experience something like the blood madness you're probably picturing, but it's more common in Turned than Natural vampires."

"So you've never experienced it?"

"Blood madness?" I scoffed. "No."

"Because you're half?"

"Because" — I furrowed my brow — "because I'm half, and I manage my blood requirements well, and I'm not an irresponsible, impulsive delinquent."

Summer hummed, taking a sip of her orange juice. "What about the other blood lust?"

"What do you mean?"

Her brows shot up as she leaned closer, lowering her voice. "You know. Like, feeding during sex?"

I blinked.

"It's always this life-changing orgasmic experience in the books."

The damn books again. Fuck, was it getting hot here? I rubbed the back of my neck.

"Aw, you're uncomfortable. That's adorable. Okay, moving on. What about wolf bites?"

I breathed a sigh of relief. Talking about feeding during sex was the last thing I wanted to be doing when I needed to keep Summer firmly in the friend zone. No, not even the friend zone. The business-partnership-acquaintance zone.

"I imagine a good bite would be painful, no matter the species."

"But you don't know if it kills or poisons a vampire?"

I shook my head.

She narrowed her eyes, swirling the last of her French toast in the whipped cream. "Maxwell, I'm beginning to think you don't know much more about vampires than I do."

I chose not to respond to that, her observation hitting a little too close to the truth for my liking.

Sightseeing with Summer was like getting a history lecture from a golden retriever puppy hopped up on cocaine. She walked backwards, arms wide as she gushed out endless facts I still couldn't figure out when she'd had time to research, much less memorize, the brightest smile on her face.

I followed her through the Boston Public Gardens, listening as she told me about every fresh bloom that lined the walkways, then posed for a picture next to the George Washington statue. Giving him the finger.

"Did you know this was the first public botanical garden in the United States?"

I opened my mouth to answer, but she gasped so loud I turned around. Summer was pointing excitedly towards a row of duck statues.

"Get my picture like I'm one of the ducklings!" She threw her phone at me then crept up behind the ducks, squatting down and wiggling her butt. My thumb hesitated on the camera button, my heart doing a weird fluttering thing. I didn't know if I'd ever seen anyone as vibrant and full of life as Summer, and it was hard to look away.

I cleared my throat, took the picture, and held the phone back out to her. She took it, stared at the picture with a bright smile, and laughed. "This is perfect. Remind me to send this to my dad later, I'll definitely forget."

I nodded, shoving my hands deep in my pockets as I followed her.

"So" — she spun around, walking backwards again — "what's up with the shadows thing? Is it like a glamour? That's the only thing I can think of to relate it to. You don't *actually* disappear, just hiding in plain sight. So you're just manipulating the light around you, right?"

"Close enough."

"Ohmygosh the swan boats! C'mon, we're riding one —"

And that was how I found myself amongst a sea of tourists

on a *swan boat*, of all things, while my lemon Italian Ice — the correct flavor, both for authenticity and also because I had lemon on the mind — melted in my hand.

"Smile!"

Summer snapped the photo before I could even register what she was doing.

I glared at her. "Absolutely not. Delete that."

"Hm." She pursed her lips. "No way, I look fantastic. Also, you *do* show up in photos."

"Clearly." With a snap of my magic, her phone was in my hand.

Her eyes widened, looking pointedly at the humans around us on the clear spring day. But they were too busy sightseeing to have noticed anything, and besides, we were relatively hidden in our seats.

"Do not delete that photo."

I rolled my eyes, but settled for cropping myself out of it, then passed her phone back. "Try that again and I'm keeping your phone until we're back in Colorado."

Summer snorted, grabbed my Italian Ice, and took a large spoonful for herself. "Sure. See where ultimatums get you, tough guy. Need I remind you — *three* older brothers? You will rue the day you put your foot down."

The rest of the day was a whirlwind of Boston facts, snacks, and alternating sun and drizzle as we explored the city, fruitlessly searching for any hint of vampires. Even Summer's usually smooth, shiny hair was adorably fluffed up and frizzy by the time we made it back to the hotel after dinner.

Scratch that. Not adorably. Just, frizzy.

While Summer took a power nap before our evening plans, I slipped out onto the balcony. Cars zipped by as the sun lowered behind the buildings around us, casting the world in a pink hazy glow. At least outside, the distinctly urban scent washed away all hints of Summer from my nose, replaced by exhaust fumes, stale beer, and trash, a far cry from the clean mountain air of Timber Creek.

Switching my focus, I pulled out my phone to read through missed messages from the day, scowling at the last email from the Council.

Krista, a witch I'd had an unfortunate, on-again, off-again situationship with and who'd been involved in the Black Rose Coven takedown a few months ago, had finally been sentenced.

Two years in the Iron Keep for her part in the kidnapping and imprisonment of shifter kids just like Hailey. I gritted my teeth. It wasn't nearly enough for what she'd been involved with, but I wasn't the most impartial when it came to my cheating ex-girlfriend.

When the sliding balcony door cracked open, all thoughts of Krista vanished as I looked up from my phone.

"Okay, admittedly — and this isn't a flex, just a fact — my boobs are bigger than Aspen's, but honestly the fact she even owns anything like this is mind-boggling." Summer stepped out onto the balcony, wrestling with the top of the sleek, skin-tight black mini dress she wore.

I nearly choked on my tongue as I stared at the dark fabric highlighting every single one of her curves, and that stopped *far* too high up her toned thighs.

Thighs I suddenly pictured wrapped around my waist. Or my head. Both, in turns, if possible.

"What is it?" Summer glanced from me, ogling her, to her dress, and smoothed it down. "Is there a stain or something I missed?"

"No." My voice was pure gravel, but I was too busy fighting my adrenaline and my fangs to care. I met her eyes, my hand raising of its own accord, reaching out to her. Drawn to her, unable to resist the pull between us. She took it, her palm so much smaller, warmer than my own, and I raised both our arms.

On instinct, she twirled with the motion, giving me a 360 view.

Perfection.

Her self-conscious giggle snapped me out of it, and I dropped her hand unceremoniously, stepping back. *Away*.

"Okay," she said, laughing again. "Are you changing? I just have to put my shoes on."

She lifted the sexy black heels she'd been holding in her other hand.

Fuck me. We needed to get out of this room. Needed… other people. Buffers.

"If you're finally done powdering your nose, let's get out of here." I gestured back into the room, closing the sliding door behind us.

This might have been a huge mistake.

"I love this song! And the lights!" Summer grinned in the middle of the dance floor, bouncing and swaying to the music. "A+ to my first club!"

I couldn't stop the corner of my mouth twitching as I put a hand between her shoulders, gently guiding her over to the bar. I needed a drink.

"How is this possibly your first club? You're — what, twenty-eight?"

"Twenty-nine, for another month at least. My parents were kinda literal with the *Summer* thing. And what part of Timber Creek screams *club scene* to you?"

I chuckled. She had me there.

"How old are you, by the way?"

I tried to flag down the bartender, but they didn't even glance our way. "Older than you."

"Aw, c'mon. Angels are like, ageless, right? So what, are you forty? Two hundred? Give me something. And don't worry, I won't make fun of you. My best friend Indi is ancient."

She waved at the bartender, golden-brown loose curls sliding over her shoulder as she leaned over the counter. Of course, he saw her immediately and hustled right over. Figured.

"I'll have a mojito, and he'll have an old fashioned."

I raised a brow, but said nothing, remembering the drink I'd had on the balcony earlier and her ability to scent out what I'd last eaten in Timber Creek. No matter how much my attraction to her made this complicated, I'd chosen one hell of a wolf to accompany me.

Summer waved a hand to encompass my entire being. "Am I wrong? But c'mon — age, now. Or I'm drinking yours too and I won't even like it."

Sighing, I leaned an elbow on the counter, turning towards her. She mirrored my pose, and the rest of the bar seemed to fade away, the two of us in our own little world as our gazes met.

"A hundred and twenty-five."

Hazel eyes searched mine for a minute, then Summer patted my arm. "Aw, you're a century baby. Were your parents all, *new century, new life?*"

Our drinks arrived, saving me from delving into that, and I took a long sip.

"Back to work, wolf. You dilly-dallied all day. Any senses going off detecting vampires nearby?"

Summer hummed, leaning back against the bar to survey the room full of writhing bodies and flashing lights. How she could smell anything aside from sweaty bodies and alcohol in here was beyond me. "So far, the only vamp I sense is you, buddy."

I nodded, not having expected anything else. "Are you still willing to try it — with my blood?"

Tapping and swaying to the beat without seeming to realize it, Summer held out her glass. "Spike me up."

Scowling at the mere suggestion of doing such a thing as sharing blood in public, I grabbed her wrist, tugging her out of the main room.

The hallway to the bathrooms was already occupied; the couple grinding up on each other didn't even look over as we passed through.

At the end of the hallway, we found a storage room, and I closed the door behind us as Summer flicked on the lights.

"How do we do this? Couple drops in my drink, or do I just give you a good chomp?"

I eyed her. "You're so nonchalant about this, I don't think you fully understand the implications of blood sharing with a vampire."

Summer threw her hands up. "Look, we came all this way. You need to find dens. I'm willing to try this. Now I think you're just procrastinating."

She was right, I was. Everyone I'd ever bitten had no memory of it, essential to keep my persona as the Dark Angel intact. It's not like I could just bite a girlfriend without explaining my fangs.

And the truth was, I'd never allowed anyone to taste my blood. Yes, I'd fed from others, so maybe that was hypocritical of me. But allowing someone else to taste me like that required an amount of trust, of vulnerability, that I'd never had.

I was aware that this was just a few drops of blood. Summer was hardly going to drain me dry. But if a few drops might allow her to find a whole den, what would it mean for us?

At the very least, any vampire we encountered in the next few days before the effects wore off would know she'd had my blood, and there was no ring on her finger to brand her as mine.

Would her family be able to sense it?

Would it give her an increased ability to sense *me*?

I realized I was tapping my fingers against my leg and made a conscious effort to still them. Why had I spent so long running from my vampire heritage, instead of trying to learn everything about it that I could? Why hadn't I paid more attention to the few vampire interactions I'd had to know more about all of this?

But she was right. We were here, and we had to try it.

One thing I did know was that blood sharing could get — well, *heated*.

"Okay," I said, trying to psych myself into it, then internally rolled my eyes at myself. I was acting like some virgin bride on her wedding night. "Couple drops. But don't say I didn't warn you."

Summer waited expectantly, clueless to my inner turmoil.

Keeping my eyes on her, I let my fangs drop, and bit into my thumb.

I held out my hand to drop it into her cup, but she must have misinterpreted my motion. The next thing I knew, Summer's soft lips had closed around my thumb and I had to fight my knees from buckling.

"Oh, fuck —"

She *sucked*.

Chapter Nine

SUMMER

He was midnight rain.

Refreshingly cool, like a mountain stream, quenching a thirst I'd never known I had. This was nothing like the animal blood I'd tasted in my wolf form — elk or deer we hunted in the mountains, their blood warm and rich and coppery.

If I'd ever had any doubts about Max being anything but *other*, this shut it down. Max tasted like the finest ice wine, cool and just sweet enough to keep me coming back for more.

I'd had enough; I only needed a few drops. But I couldn't stop.

From the shocked expression on his face, I belatedly realized he'd meant to drop his blood into my drink, but the second my wolf had scented his blood, she'd taken over.

"Summer."

A finger landed on my chin, but I batted it away.

"*Summer.*"

In a flash, the finger turned into a full hand around my neck, pressing me gently, but firmly, into the wall behind me, and finally his thumb left my mouth with a *pop*.

I drew my gaze up to his, and his deep blue eyes swirled.

Swirled?

No, wait, that was *my* eyes doing that.

I glanced around the room — the whole place shimmered.

Max swore under his breath, his hand around my neck loosening ever so slightly. "I was afraid of this."

"This?" I echoed, drawing out the *s* like a snake, then breaking into a fit of giggles. "That's not even a word, Maxy."

"You're a little blood-drunk. It'll fade in a bit."

"I hope not." I grinned at his narrowed eyes, then gasped. "Max! It's working! I found a vampire!"

Instantly, he went on alert. "Where? In the club?"

I shook my head. "Closer." I booped him on the nose and burst out laughing again.

He rolled those pretty blue eyes and I reached up, squeezing his cheeks together as I drew his face down to mine.

"Don't be mad at me," I said in a mocking tone, my heart racing as I held him close, sharing breath. Whatever I meant to say next fled my brain faster than a herd of wild Willies as I stared at his lips, the peek of his canines sticking out over his plump bottom lip.

Maybe it was the blood, or the close proximity, or maybe just the pheromones in the air around us from the club, but suddenly I wanted to kiss him more than anything I'd ever wanted in my entire life. I lifted up on my toes, needing to see if his kiss tasted like his blood, that same sweet intoxicating delicacy I needed another hit of.

"Summer." His voice was lower, holding a warning tone that did nothing to break the spell I was under.

"Hmm," I mumbled, leaning in, lips tingling, eyes closing as I prepared myself for that euphoric feeling again.

His hands landed on top of mine, gently lifting them off his face as he stepped back, eyes as dark as the shirt he wore. "Easy there. Let's get some air."

Without waiting for my response, he grabbed the door handle and ripped it open, the handle coming off the door completely as it rested in his palm. Another bubble of laughter erupted from me as he stared at it, then dropped it on the floor and stepped out.

"Nice," a sleazy guy nearby said, giving me a leering once-over as I straightened my dress and followed Max out of the closet. "She's hot."

I flew into Max's back as he stopped abruptly, spinning on the guy who'd said it. Magic hummed in the air as his focus honed, and I glanced down at his hands. What looked like black ink spread up his arms from his fingertips, painting his arms in shadows as he reached forward and slammed the guy against the wall.

"Hey man!" he spluttered, his beer dropping to the floor and splashing all over my shoes. "What the hell!"

"I'll have you wishing for hell."

Max's canines — no, fangs — punched out again. I pictured him sinking his teeth into this guy, into anyone but *me*, and my gut churned, rioted.

No.

I jumped into action, grabbing Max by the arm, my skin almost ghostly against that black inky magic.

"Out. *Now.*"

Max's gaze flicked to me, and I crossed my arms under my boobs, pushing them up. Both he and the scumbag he held pinned against the wall looked down, just like I knew they would. "You done here, Maxwell House?"

Max turned back to the guy pinned in front of him, his lips pulling back in a snarl, but my focus drifted. Something niggled at my senses, like an itch on a phantom limb, and I turned towards the club, my nose in the air as my eyes closed, focusing on the wide array of scents and sounds.

Something was different.

Chalk it up to Max's blood, but my nose worked like a metal detector, sorting through the rabble until it settled on three bodies moving through the crowd on the far side of the bar. All three carried that same smoky metallic scent Max did, but different.

My eyes flew open, and I stood on my tiptoes, trying to see over the crowd.

"My spidey senses are tingling!" I tried to whisper-shout over the music to Max. The lurker chuckled.

"If that ain't innuendo, I don't know what —"

In a flash of darkness, the guy crumpled to the ground.

My jaw dropped. "Max!"

Max waved a hand at the pile on the ground. "He's alive. Let's go. Lead the way, sunshine."

I was still staring at the guy, trying to reassure myself he was, indeed, still breathing, as Max's large hand grasped mine and tugged.

Back on the dance floor, the gyrating mass of bodies was still in full swing to the pounding music, but the vampires had disappeared into the crowd. I tried to ignore everything but the pull on my magic. Easier said than done with the way Max's blood still turned every flash of the strobe lights into a glitter bomb.

"Close your eyes." Max's lips were at my ear to be heard over the music, and then his arms wrapped around my waist from behind.

Right. We were on a dance floor. Needed to blend in and all.

Go big or go home.

I closed my eyes, and let my hips sway, brushing my ass against him. A low growl let me know my retaliation had succeeded, his hand settling on my hip and squeezing.

Don't write checks you can't cash, Maxy.

Then — there.

Opening my eyes, I tapped Max's hand resting on my hip before I darted through the crowd, slipping and dancing effortlessly through the bodies in pursuit of my prey. I didn't turn to see if Max was keeping up — I knew he would.

Reaching the far side of the dance floor, I scented the

vampires again, but they were gone now. I followed the trail to the club's side door, and pushed it open into the cool night air.

A moment later, Max burst out as well, and I chuckled. "Took your sweet time."

He scowled. "Don't go where I can't see you."

I lifted a shoulder. "Keep up, then." I took off down the street, my wolf pushing forward in my mind now that we were on the hunt. Briefly checking my surroundings, I let her in, bracing as my body shifted into a tawny wolf.

My clothes dropped in a puddle on the ground, and Max swore as he bent down to grab them, hugging them to his chest. "Are you fucking kidding me?"

I yipped, then darted across the street *Frogger*-style dodging cars, and turned when I realized Max had gotten stuck waiting for a truck to pass. My tongue lolled out as I watched, but I kept moving, following the magic, when a cloud of shadow materialized in front of me. I skidded to a halt with a yelp, and Max emerged from the darkness.

"Do I need to get a leash for you, wolf?"

My wolf growled, her teeth bared and hackles rising before darting around him. The night grew darker around me, Max covering me in his shadows as I ran down the crowded streets undetected, letting my nose guide me.

A few times I paused, afraid I might have lost the trail, but then I'd feel it again, and keep moving. The air turned salty as we wound our way closer to the ocean, and I slowed my steps as the magical signature grew stronger, the metallic smoky scent thickening unmistakably.

Only a single flickering streetlight and the moon lit the dark street as I stopped to looked up and down it. On one side of the street, a junkyard; on the other, a boarded-up warehouse behind a cheap wire fence. Standing this close, the scent was almost choking in its intensity.

In a blink, a wash of magic shook my body as I transformed back to my human form. I gestured at the warehouse, dark and foreboding as Max approached from behind me. "A little cliché, don't you think? Practically screams, *there's a dead body in here.*"

A choked sound escaped him and I turned to look as my clothes slapped against my chest.

"Get dressed," he mumbled, his back turned to me as he stared up at the night sky. I grinned, slipping back into my dress and heels.

Darkness swept around us, and I realized Max was cloaking us in his magic even more than before. The chill followed, and I wrapped my arms around myself as Max's sharp eyes darted around the area.

"All good. And this is the place."

"You're sure?"

I snorted. The appropriate response to dumb questions. "The fact you *can't* sense them is what's more surprising here. It reeks."

Max stiffened at my comment, but didn't respond, instead pulling out his phone and tapping away at it with his back still turned. Then he tucked it back in his pocket, and turned to me with a decisive nod. "All right. Let's head back."

I jolted. "What? No way. We have to go in there and check it out! This is not the part of the story where they go home."

He frowned, but I wasn't leaving, at least not yet. My head tipped back as I inhaled deeply, then tip-toed around the side of the building, following the trail of the vampires who'd been here last. I could have scaled the fence easy enough, but my wardrobe choice wouldn't make it graceful and I'd already shown the world my bare ass once tonight. Shifters were used to nudity, but Max's rejection when I'd tried to kiss him earlier stung just as much as everything else, and I wasn't about to give him a free show.

"Summer," he whispered from right behind me as I kicked

at the part of the fence where the scent was strongest, my foot going right through the magical barrier. "Leave it."

I opened my mouth to offer him a sassy response as I stepped through, but jerked in surprise as a man appeared in front of me.

"Who knew they delivered food to this part of town?"

Chapter Ten

MAX

"I'd probably be gamey, not gonna lie."

Summer's nose wrinkled as she stared down the vampire in front of us, the male casually leaning against the crumbling brick wall. Like the stories told, his skin was moon-white, dark hair slicked back from his face and dark eyes to match, and a lithe body made for deadly speed. But nothing was as ominous as the fangs protruding over his lower lip while he offered her a grin that was far from friendly.

He chuckled, his eyes scanning her body in that damn dress, highlighting her luscious curves. "And a mouth on you too. This must be my lucky night."

I tensed, my fangs descending as I assessed him, ready to step in front of Summer. Before I could move, her hazel eyes blazed her wolf's gold as she lifted her nose and snapped her jaw. "Seems like I might be the one with the luck tonight."

Something flashed across the vampire's face and his head tilted in interest, as if he'd just now noticed she wasn't some damsel he could chomp down on, but a full-blooded wolf shifter, a predator in her own right.

"I'm here to see Grigor," I said, breaking their stare-off before he had another moment to notice just how tempting Summer was. "Is he still here?"

For the first time, he looked at me, recognition showing as his eyes narrowed. "What's your name? You look familiar, and I thought I knew all of us on the East Coast."

"Dante," I said, and luckily Summer didn't react to my alternate identity.

The vampire subtly straightened, apparently having heard the rumors of the rogue vampire who sold himself as a supernatural hitman. My reputation obviously preceded me, despite the fact I'd never met this vampire before.

For the last few years I'd led a double life, existing on the outskirts of vampire society as Dante — my *actual* middle name — and in the rest of the supernatural world as Massimo Russo, Premier angel Malachi Russo's son. The worlds could not collide or any chance I had an in with the vampires would be shot, so I kept my dark angel wings retracted and hidden from view.

The door behind him cracked open, and a second vampire appeared in head-to-toe black leather, contrasting her white hair and whiter skin. The only splash of color on her was the dark red tint of her lips as she eyed me with interest. "I thought that was you at the club, Dante." Her tongue darted out between her lips, running across the tip of her right fang. "It's been a long time."

Not nearly long enough, I thought, but kept it to myself. I lifted my chin, stepping one foot in front of Summer. All vampires were dangerous, the combination of mind control, shadow walking, and strength making them one of the most powerful supernatural creatures, second only to angels with their lightning abilities. Nicolette was old and exceptionally powerful, Grigor's second in command for the last century, and I hated her. "Nicolette. Never a pleasure."

She tossed her head back and laughed, the moonlight glinting off her teeth. "As I remember, there was quite a lot of *pleasure* last time, Dante. Maybe you need a demonstration to remember just what pleasure feels like."

Summer cleared her throat loudly, her fingers lacing

between mine. The warmth of her grip was a shock to my system, and Nicolette glanced at her, dark eyes squinting.

"As fun as this little walk down memory lane is, we're here to see Grigor."

Nicolette pursed her lips, then nodded and the first vampire stepped aside to let us pass. My heartbeat drummed in my ears to the same rhythm as the music, a trancelike vibe that warned of the deadly creatures within. It took all my control not to grasp Summer to my side as we stepped into the warehouse, but my scent all over her and my violent reputation were hopefully enough of a statement. Forcing my fingers loose, I dropped her hand, placing my palm on her low back as we followed Nicolette. Our footsteps echoed down a dingy hall before we pushed through a set of dark curtains, and Summer staggered to a stop in front of me.

Like the club we'd left, people writhed on a dance floor, sweaty bodies grinding against each other to the beat of the music. Unlike the club, dim lighting glinted off gold-edged furnishings set into nooks in the wall, upon which lay scantily clad men and women, their heads thrown back in seeming bliss, all while vampires feasted on them. Some couches had more than one vamp per plaything, and another had multiple humans to one vampire, her fangs deep into one's neck while her hand slipped down into another's pants.

"Are they—" Summer started, and I pushed her forward away from the orgy breaking out. "Yep. Nevermind."

"Don't stare. They'll take it as interest."

"Got it. Eyes only on you then."

I missed a step, and Summer winked.

Nicolette wove through the dance floor, a path clearing as we moved towards the front of the large warehouse turned den. From what I could tell, most of the victims here were human, and likely had no idea what was happening to them as tongues licked over bite wounds and sank into flesh. At the very least, they would have their memories wiped before they were set loose again.

The steady beat of the music, the flashing lights, and the strong scent of blood and arousal in the air was a heady mix.

And I'd brought Summer Larkin straight into this den of debauchery.

West was going to murder me.

In front of us was a raised platform, girls dancing in cages on either side of a golden throne. Grigor sprawled across the throne, shirtless and bored with one leg over the armrest, appraising the room. His long blond hair hung past his shoulders, a hint of shadow in the veins across his bare chest. He snapped his fingers and a man — no, more of a *teen* — stepped forward, knelt, and offered his neck.

Shadows shot through my veins in my anger as Grigor bit into his neck, blood spilling carelessly down the teen's neck as he drank. His victim's face was a mixture of pain and lust, hands moving over Grigor's skin as he moaned.

A giggle bubbled out of Summer beside me, and Grigor's blood red eyes jerked our way, teeth still in the boy in front of him.

I clenched my jaw as his gaze raked over her, tossing the boy aside as he stood to his full height. In an instant, the red in his eyes faded to an icy blue. His long strides made him look like he was gliding as he approached us, eyes narrowed at Summer before flicking to Nicolette and, finally, me.

His smirk was pure ice as he stepped forward, not bothering to wipe the blood from his chin. "Dante. You brought a pet." Shadows danced under his fingertips as he brought his hand up to trace the edge of Summer's jaw, but she recoiled at the near touch, making Grigor's smirk grow. "How cute. Is she in exchange for the one you stole from me?"

I kept my face blank. Technically, he had no proof Quentin's escape was my doing, merely that I'd been in the area around the same time. "Quentin wanted to leave, so he did. Last I heard, the Conclave frowned upon keeping Sources against their will. You can take it up with them if you have an issue."

"Then I'll just have to convince her to stay, hm?" Grigor circled behind Summer as his fingers traced just above her skin, never touching but a clear threat. "I promise to make it good for you, pet. You'll forget all about Dante in an instant."

Summer chuckled. "Oh, you don't want me as a pet. Trust me, Grogu. I shed."

Grigor's pale eyes hardened. "It's Grigor. And I didn't say you could address me."

Summer ignored him as she waved a hand at his throne, amusement lighting up her face. "I'm sorry, are you serious? You have an honest to gods throne? What is this, *Game of Thrones* night at the vamp club? At least add some pyro so you get the full dragon feel, if that's what you're going for, Gringotts."

I fought back a grimace, my hand shooting out to grab Summer's again, but it didn't seem to derail her. The more she continued to speak out of turn, she unknowingly told him she was unclaimed, the defiance something that would be near impossible if she'd been a normal human or other supernatural claimed by me. I wanted to slap a hand over her mouth, but it was already too late.

"Can we speak to you privately?" I cut in, dropping her hand and taking a step forward to draw his attention back to me and begging Summer to get the hint to quiet down.

"Do you have my pet?"

I didn't answer, and Grigor shrugged like it was out of his hands.

"Then we have nothing to speak about. Return the boy to me and then we can discuss whatever you like. Nicolette will see you out, unless you're here to dine, in which case" — he licked his lips — "I'll insist we all watch." Reaching out a hand, he trailed a pale finger down Summer's jaw, down her neck, despite her low growl. "Such a pretty thing."

My hands clenched into fists. But he turned, heading back to his throne, when Summer spoke up again.

"Aren't you curious how we found you?"

I whirled on her. "*Summer.*"

Slowly, Grigor faced us again, tongue dragging across his fang as he considered her, then me, and I could have slapped myself. If her question hadn't intrigued him, my reaction just had.

In a heartbeat of supernatural speed, he appeared directly in front of us, one hand around Summer's throat, and the other tangled in her hair, tilting her head back to meet his eyes. To delve into her mind. Milliseconds passed in slow motion as shadows enveloped them, Summer's mouth hanging open as her wolf's golden gaze met Grigor's. My fangs snapped out.

A snarl left me as I dove between them, shoving her back and him off her. He flew back against his throne, but in an instant was back in front of me, black veins angry under his skin. I ducked the swing he threw, and then we were a tangle of limbs and snapping jaws and teeth.

I could feel the attention of the club turning to us, but thankfully most of them were too high on the feast or drunk on actual substances to care to step in.

If only I could say the same for Summer, but no. A swirl of honey-brown hair swept in front of my vision as she leveled a solid kick at Grigor, sending him doubling over to his knees.

His roar finally had the other vampires pulling to their feet, forming a semi-circle around us. Nicolette stood directly behind Summer and me, blocking any retreat.

"You steal from me" — Grigor spat a glob of blood onto the floor — "you trespass, *and* you attack me? The Conclave will be hearing about this, *Dante.* They've left you alone too long, unchecked. Your days are numbered."

Inky darkness rose like a fog around him, the shadow of his leathery wings emerging as black bled into his veins. As though they were entranced, the vampires of his den mimicked his actions, closing in around us.

"I'm going to take your pet," he snarled, taking a step closer, "and drain her dry while you watch."

My eyes flicked around the room, assessing the situation, but I couldn't fight off this many vampires at once, especially if I had to keep an eye on Summer too. As half-angel, I had the ability to dip into my father's lightning powers as well as my mother's shadows and strength, but not without revealing myself for what and who I truly was. Magic hummed under my skin, feeling the spells put in place around the den. Vanishing wouldn't work within the den itself, but the spell's barrier ended just outside the warehouse. We needed to get out. *Now.*

I'd been an idiot to try this with Summer. I had only one avenue left to try to get out of here without a fight.

"I always knew you'd be back," Nicolette said against my ear, her tongue flicking across my skin. "This time, I want a taste."

"My apologies." I kept my voice low and steady as I moved away from Nicolette. Calm. Certainly calmer than I felt. "She's… new to me. You know how it is with wolves, a play for dominance. No one touches her but me."

Grigor halted for a moment, contemplating my words. Then he laughed, and I cringed.

"What a horrible little liar you are. If she was your Source, she'd never speak out like that. Still" — he shrugged again — "it's been a while since we've had a wolf. Your loss is our gain."

I saw it a second before it happened, the tell-tale twitch of muscles before they lunged for us.

My arm snapped out, shoving Summer behind me as Nicolette's shadows hit, banding my arms to my chest. A snarl told me someone was going at Summer, and I growled as I wrenched free of Nicolette's magic, lashing back out with my own. A dark cloud formed as our powers intertwined, but rather than stand my ground, I stepped backwards, forcing Summer towards the doors.

"You're *weak,*" Nicolette spat as she shoved her hands wide, the magical force that held us apart breaking. She slid back into a row of vampires, then flew forward again with a wicked gleam in her eyes. "I should have known that's why you never came back."

She expected me to send out another force of my shadow magic to hold her back, but my entire existence was unexpected.

Shoving my hand into the In-Between, a hole between the angel and earth dimensions, I splayed my fingers wide, pulling on my father's powers as my fingers closed around a long, smooth object.

"That implies I ever *came* to begin with, and I got tired of faking it."

As her eyes widened, mere inches from mine, I sank the stake into her heart.

A wet, choking gasp escaped her lips, her gaze dipping down to the stake, and her face paled. Her wings went first, dissolving into dust, then her body crumpled to the ground, soon turning into a pile of ash.

Grigor let out a roar at the loss of his Second, and before I could move, he rushed to where Summer battled and thrashed with two other vampires. Tossing them off her like they were weightless, he twisted her hair up in his fist again. Trailing a claw down her neck, he broke open her skin in a stream of red.

"Well, I can't let that go unpunished, can I, Dante?" he purred, his veins black as he held Summer in stasis, paralyzed by his vampire powers. I froze, the sight of her blood trailing down her neck sending a bolt of panic up my spine.

"Leave her alone," I growled, my fingers flexing on nothing, but I'd already revealed my party trick — I wouldn't have time to summon another stake from the In-Between before he snapped Summer's neck.

With all my focus on Summer, I failed to notice the vampire sneaking up on me until Grigor's eyes flicked ever so slightly to the right. I whirled, reaching for them, but they were already lunging, stake extended. I twisted enough their stake missed my heart, plunging into my bicep instead.

I clenched my teeth against the pain, and settled for ripping the guy's arm off as I flung his body across the room.

Streaks of fire shot through my bloodstream, the stake poisoning the magic in my veins almost instantly. I hid my grimace, refusing to show weakness while we remained in the den.

Grigor's jaw twitched with annoyance. "That's two vampires you owe me now, Dante. I'd thought of keeping her for a pet, but now, I think I'll drain her dry. Or maybe I should Turn her?"

I lunged forward, pain forgotten as I reached for Summer, her eyes flashing golden. In a heartbeat, she was in her wolf form for the second time tonight, her jaws sinking into Grigor's calf and yanking with a sickening *crack*.

While he yowled in pain, I rushed to her side, then gripped her scruff, took the final step out the door, and called on my darkness, vanishing us away.

Chapter Eleven

SUMMER

My heart thundered in my chest as my rooftop garden reappeared around us, and I quickly shifted out of my wolf form.

I was torn between relief we'd escaped, annoyance and anger that Max had vanished us out of there, fear that we'd nearly died or been kidnapped or whatever Grigor had intended with us, and exhilaration from all the adrenaline.

And possibly the tiniest bit intrigued at seeing Max go all hardcore like that?

No, nope.

Hands on my hips, I settled on annoyance and whirled on Max, who practically choked at the sight of me. Naked.

I ignored the way his blood-spattered cheeks reddened as he struggled not to gape at me. "Seriously? After everything we just witnessed at the den, you're a prude?"

Then he collapsed to one knee, gripping his arm, and my annoyance evaporated as I rushed forward.

"What's wrong?"

Lifting his hand, I saw the stake sticking out of his arm, blood dripping down it, and my hand rose to my mouth.

"Oh, shit. Will that kill you?"

Through gritted teeth, Max panted, "It's fine. I just need to get it out."

"Okay, okay. Crisis mode. Down in the kitchen, I'm sure I have something we can use —"

With an agonized grunt, Max yanked the stake out of his own arm. It clattered to the ground, and he slumped to the floor, rolling onto his back and panting hard.

I gave him a minute to collect himself, pulling a throw blanket off my patio set and wrapping it around my shoulders.

"What the hell was that?"

I lowered onto a patio chair, watching his chest carefully for his breathing and listening for his heartbeat. It was slowing to a more regular beat, and eventually he pushed up off the ground with another groan. Lowering into the chair across from me, he ran a hand through his sweat-slicked hair. Voice hoarser than usual, he said, "*That* was exactly what I was talking about and why I told you we can't do this. It's way too fucking dangerous."

"We barely spent ten minutes there! All you two did was debate whether Quentin and I were property to be claimed, and by whom. And why are we back here?" I gestured to the Rocky Mountains around us, and my blanket slipped, still covering my nipples but just barely. "Half my wardrobe is in Boston!"

Max's gaze snapped down to the table, his hands clasped as he drew in a deep breath. "I can get your stuff later. Right now, we need to let the heat die down in the city. Every vamp in the city is going to be on the alert for us after I staked one of them and you *broke their duke's leg.*"

I couldn't help it. A tiny smile broke out from the corner of my mouth. "That part was kind of badass."

"Unbelievable," Max muttered as he stood and then staggered, his hand shooting out to grip the top of the table. He stiffly paced up and down the rows of vining plants along my rooftop, unaffected by the crisp bite in the spring night air. Rubbing a hand over his face, he spun back towards where I sat. "Not everyone can just be won over with a smile and a joke and a spinach croissant, Summer."

My chest twinged, but I only said, "Okay, but we didn't even *try* the croissant, so how do we know? Riddle me that."

Max glared at me. "Do you have any idea the trouble we were just in? If we hadn't managed to get out of there, and Grigor kept you as a pet like he threatened? Or worse, *Turned* you?"

My smile dimmed, remembering Grigor's words. That part had shaken me up. Hearing the way they talked about their Sources as pets — and referring to *me* that way — had thrown me off, and I'd blind reacted. Just followed my gut and spoken up impulsively. And truthfully, I didn't know enough about vampires to know if I even *could* be Turned. Not exactly a question I wanted to ask West over family dinner, if he'd even know himself.

Maybe my mouth had moved a little faster than my brain.

Still, now I had a better idea of what a den entailed, and I wouldn't make the same mistakes again. For all my flaws, I knew for damn sure my strengths too — I was a fast learner.

"But he didn't," I reminded Max, whose scowl deepened. "And we got out of there, no harm no foul."

Anger seemed to shimmer around Max at my words as he paused his pacing, his shadow powers darkening the night sky behind him. But even with how little time we'd spent together, I could tell they seemed dimmer than before, weakened.

"No harm, no foul, huh?" he seethed, his eyes locking onto the now-dried blood trailing down my neck. His tongue darted out, licking his lips, then he wrenched his gaze away.

I rubbed at it, brushing the blood off my already healed wound. "Just a scratch. A flesh-wound."

He put his hands on the table, leaning down over me with a growl. "*No.* Spilled blood is not acceptable, especially not in a den. Do you understand what the scent of fresh blood does to a vampire? It's like a drug, a tempting high that's almost impossible to ignore. Add in that you're not human, and you're that much more tempting. You're done."

Squinting, I leaned into his space, our faces mere inches apart. "I'll be done when I say I'm done. Like you just said, I'm not some damsel human. I'm a full-blooded wolf shifter, and I heal exceptionally fast. That wound was closed and gone almost as soon as it happened."

He shook his head, stepping back, visibly frustrated which only seemed to egg me on. No way would I let him go back into a den alone — he kept talking about how dangerous it was for me, but what about him? He hadn't exactly received a warm welcome as *Dante*, whatever that was about, and the thought of him walking into danger alone had me clenching my jaw.

"Why can't you understand this is too dangerous? Even now —" He broke off, jaw working.

I threw my hands up, tired of him leaving out information. "Even now, *what?*"

Max met my eye again, his face hard and unreadable as he contemplated answering. His gaze dropped to my lips, then my neck. "Even now, you're in too much danger."

I almost laughed, but stifled it. "From you?"

"Yes," he gritted out, gesturing to his arm. "I was injured back there — fucking *staked* — and it makes it harder to" — a flicker of shadow danced across his skin, lacing up his arms — "control myself. With you."

I frowned, gripping the blanket in one hand as I stood and reached towards his arm. I figured once he got the stake out, he'd be healing quickly, like a shifter would, but the wound still oozed blood. "Are you okay? How fast do you heal?"

"I'll be fine," he snapped, pulling back out of my reach, and I dropped my hand back down to my side.

"Are you always this bad a liar? Because if so, I can't fathom how you ever managed to be undercover." That was a lie — the man literally walked in shadows, only revealing himself when and where he wanted to. And whatever the rumors were in the vampire world about this Dante were enough to have even vampires recoiling from him. Add in the angel powers I'd never seen him use, and I could only imagine how deadly Max really was. A shiver ran through me, and I pulled the blanket tighter around me.

"It might take a little longer for me to recover," he ground out. "Staking affects our magic, even if it isn't through the heart. Add in the vanishing with the stake and…" He sighed.

I took a tentative step forward, but didn't reach for him this time. "Do you need blood?"

His eyes blazed red, then blue again. "*No.*"

"Very convincing." I nodded, puckering my lips in a sarcastic frown. "Look, I had yours, you can have some of mine. It's only fair."

"*Fair?*" he snarled.

I took another step, but stopped when he stepped back. "You're clearly in distress. I can help. It's no big deal."

Max closed his eyes, letting out a heavy breath. "Summer, no. We cannot go down that road."

"Worried you won't be able to get enough?" I tried to lighten the mood, flicking my hair over my shoulder with a smirk. He didn't so much as blink, his gaze intent on mine, then falling to my neck. The air tightened between us, the silence of the night deafening as suddenly I could only hear the pounding of my heart.

In an instant, he disappeared from in front of me, and his fingers wrapped around my jaw, the warmth of his body pressing against my back.

"That's exactly what I'm worried about, *fiore.*" My breathing hitched as he tilted my head, exposing my neck further to him. "Do you know how sweet you smell to me?"

My pulse thundered, but despite everything I'd seen Max

do tonight, everything I'd heard about him, I wasn't afraid of him. He wouldn't hurt me. "I want to help you."

A low, pained growl rumbled against my back, and I couldn't help it. I leaned back, my body melting against his.

His next words came out in a gravelly murmur. "Oh, Sweet Summer." His lips ghosted my neck, a shiver skittering down my spine as my core clenched. "How could a shadow resist your light?"

Fangs sank into my neck, cool and sharp, and I gasped. I sagged back against him even further, and his arms wrapped around me in an unyielding grasp.

My nerves burst like fireworks. With every passing moment, my body caught fire, craving his like I'd never experienced with anyone before. Suddenly, the orgy of the Boston den made a whole lot of sense, since the only thing I could think about was his body filling mine, taking mine, in every way he could. A whimper escaped me as his arm around my torso brushed my nipples, my blanket long since puddled at my feet.

"Max —" I breathed, rocking back against him, reaching for him —

But in a heartbeat, his fangs yanked from my neck with an audible gasp on his end. I whirled around, fully ready to launch myself at him, but he took one look at me, his eyes red and wide, and he vanished.

Alone and aroused on my roof, I blinked hard, pulling fresh air into my lungs in gasps. My shaking fingers traced his bite mark on my neck, already healing, as my heart raced.

What the hell had I gotten myself into?

Chapter Twelve

SUMMER

"I can't get rid of my Willie, not even when I shower," my dad said from where he sat in my café, surrounded by his gardening club that held meetings here every Wednesday morning for the last two years.

Lance, his best friend, nodded along, as if my father hadn't said anything out of the norm. "Have you tried videos? Maybe he needs inspiration to adapt to his new life."

"Tried that." My dad shook his head. "He didn't rise to the occasion."

"Can you *hear* yourselves?" Zara said as she leaned back in her chair, sipping on her coffee that had to be nearly empty by now. The young witch was our local doctor and was about as no-nonsense as they came, which only seemed to spur on my father and his best friend. "We're talking about buffalo, and yet every word out of your mouth sounds like a dirty innuendo, Heath."

"That says more about you than it does me, darling." My dad grinned, then winked at me as I crossed the room to refill Zara's coffee. "I just need Willie to remember he's a wild animal that is supposed to live *outside*, and not in my living room. Not that I mind his company, but there is a whole herd of buffalo waiting just outside my doors, ready to include him in the family."

"How about you start with leaving the door open, and stop feeding him?"

Heath pursed his lips, giving a slight shake of his head. "I *could*, I suppose. But what if he starves?"

"He is a wild animal, not a pet," Zara deadpanned. Lance opened his mouth, but she held up a hand to stop him. "Stop feeding into this insanity."

I chuckled, turning back to the counter to leave them be. It had been a week since I got back from Boston with Max, and my life had returned to normal.

As normal as it could be after experiencing his bite. I still hadn't heard from him since he'd disappeared from my roof, but maybe that was for the best for now, or so I kept telling myself.

The café was empty besides my dad and his club, so I pulled up a barstool and grabbed my notebook, flipping open to the page I'd scribbled my bucket list on. It wasn't as pretty without the visuals I had on the board in my room, but it was enough to let my mind wander.

After our trip to Boston, I was itching for more adventure, and all of these dreams seemed too small now. In the moment, Grigor and his threats had scared me, but in hindsight all I could remember was how *alive* I'd felt.

For once, I hadn't been West's little sister, the baby Larkin, the low-power wolf, or the happy baker girl. I'd crafted my own identity that night, and then lived a life I never could have imagined, even if it was only for a few hours.

Visit a vampire den, I scribbled at the bottom of the list, then crossed it off. "Look at me, doing things."

"Talking to yourself again?" Indi said as she flickered in beside me, appearing out of thin air.

"No, I was summoning you." I drew a pentagram on a page, then wrote her name in the middle.

"Ha ha." Indie grabbed the paper and crumpled it before small flames licked up her fingers and incinerated it. "You know that stuff doesn't work like in the stories. I'm not a demon from hell, sent here to terrorize you."

"Not unless it's a crime of boredom, right?"

"And bad fashion choices." Indi nodded. "I can't allow either of those in good conscience."

"Why I keep you around." I hopped off my barstool and headed to the kitchen. "Want a snack?"

"Sure," Indi said, but there was a beat of hesitancy. I turned around to question her and saw my notebook she held aloft, finger pointed at the line I'd just written and crossed off. "Um?"

My eyes blew wide as I looked from her to my dad and back, then tipped my head to the kitchen doors.

Indi followed me back into the space, and I turned on every appliance I could, grabbing the notebook back from her. "You can't tell anyone. Or, wait," I paused, "Tell every single person on the entire planet."

"Dang." Indi's nose scrunched, and I grinned. Demons had a hard time following direct orders, so if I'd told her to tell no one, she most likely wouldn't keep it secret. But by asking her to tell *everyone*, she now couldn't tell anyone. "Okay, spill it, sister."

So I did. I told her about Max showing up here, about what he needed help with, and how I also seemed to be the perfect candidate for it all.

Indi's eyebrows skyrocketed when I told her about our trip to Boston. "You slept in the same bed as him?"

"I'm not sure he actually *slept*, and that sounds way dirtier than I intended," I added when Indi chuckled. "I don't know where he went, but I think I was alone most of the night."

"That's almost as bad as him sleeping on the floor."

"That's what *I* thought!"

"Okay, so you found the den?"

"Yes, thank you." I resumed the story, happy to have a

friend understand how sidetracked I got with random side-stories that were equally as important but often lost me somewhere in the middle.

"Aren't vampires supposed to be super violent?"

I hummed. "They were not friendly, that's for sure. As far as I can tell, they're interested in feeding, fighting, and fu—"

Indi slapped her hand over my mouth right as my dad walked through the door. She dropped her hand and spun to face Heath, while we both grinned like we'd just been caught red-handed. Subtlety was not our forte.

"Sorry, Heath," Indi said with a sheepish smile. "We were just talking about demon mating habits. My biological clock is ticking, and all."

My dad frowned, looking between us. "Aren't you over a hundred, Indi?"

"Yep." She nodded emphatically. "The perfect time to raise a little hellion, don't you think?"

I smiled as I stared at my dad, doing my best to even out my heartbeat and breathing, reducing any signals his wolf would pick up on that we were lying.

"You okay, sweetheart?" he asked, glancing between us.

I gave him a thumbs up. "Right as rain."

He looked around the kitchen again, then nodded. "You might want to turn off your mixers. You haven't put the ingredients in yet."

I slapped my forehead, then leaned over and turned them off. "I knew I forgot something."

My dad kissed my forehead with a laugh. "Just like your dad, huh? Anyway, we're all done. Dishes are on the counter."

"Okay!" I waved him out of the kitchen, headed back to the neat pile of dessert plates and coffee cups ready to be taken back to the dishwasher.

Indi followed me out, mouthing *talk later*.

I nodded, and she disappeared. Conveniently, we hadn't

gotten to the part of the story where Max bit me and lit my body on fire.

For some reason, I wasn't ready to talk about that yet. Maybe because I kept having to reassure myself it had actually happened and wasn't just a figment of my overactive imagination.

"Bye sweetie!" my dad called as the door bells jingled, waving as he walked down the street towards our family's restaurant.

I grabbed the dishes and headed into the kitchen as the bells jingled again. "Be right there!" I called.

Setting the dishes on the counter, I fixed my ponytail and straightened my apron, then went back towards the café, pausing at the scent I smelled on the other side. Sandalwood and copper.

Max was back.

My heart raced as I opened and closed my hands, trying to think through everything I wanted to say to convince him I needed to go with him on the rest of his den hunting adventures. I'd had a taste, and I needed more. His biting me and subsequently freaking out was just an overreaction and we didn't need to worry about it — or maybe I just shouldn't bring that up at all?

I pushed the doors open, aiming for calm confidence that went up in smoke when the door swung back harder than I'd anticipated, almost nailing me in the forehead.

"Oh, hey Max. Funny seeing you here."

He crooked his head, staring around my café then back at me. "Where you live and work? Yeah, major coincidence."

I laughed way too hard, waving him off. "Good one." Smooth, Summer. Real smooth. "How can I help you?"

Max held up my luggage, the lavender daisy print suitcase looking absurd against his all-black getup. "Bringing this back for you."

Okay, apparently we were pretending the bite never happened. Well, I could play along, especially if it got us past this weirdness and back out on the search for dens.

"Oh, thanks!" I grabbed it from him, wheeling it to the hallway that led up to my apartment above. "So, you went back to Boston?"

Max shoved his hands in his pockets. "I did."

"And?" I leaned my elbows on the counter. "Did you go back to the den?"

"Nope," Max said, his brows drawn down in annoyance. "It was gone. Whatever happened after we left, they decided to move by the time I got back."

"Well, that's unfortunate." I grabbed a dessert plate and a pair of tongs, sliding the glass door open and picking out a rainbow sprinkle sugar cookie, then slid it across the counter to him. "It's almost like you need a partner."

Max looked down at the cookie, then back at me. "No."

I grabbed the plate, then circled the counter to stand in front of him, hand outstretched. The cookie was a guess, but for some reason, I was willing to bet this moody, broody man loved a good sugar cookie. "You need me. Just say it."

Max shook his head. "Are you insane? You remember what happened, right? Or did it get lost in your pretty little head?"

Well, that did it. I slammed the cookie down, plate rattling, and jerked my chin up, but unlike last time we'd been together, I didn't have heels on. I only reached his shoulder in my sneakers, so I hopped on top of a stool to meet his eye. "Excuse me?"

"You heard me." His deep blue eyes blazed as he stared back at me, not giving an inch, but he'd lit my fuse the moment he taunted me. "You've probably already ended up on some vamp watch list after that stunt you pulled, being immune to Grigor's mind hold. Which, speaking of, should have been impossible. The moment he sliced into your skin, you should have been paralyzed by his magic. Even without the blood, his touch alone should have granted him control over your body."

"Really?" I frowned, thinking back to those seconds in his hold. It was all kind of a blur now. "I was stunned for a minute, and definitely creeped out, but certainly not *paralyzed*. Maybe he was just bad at it?"

"Bad at it?" Max huffed. "He's one of the strongest vampires in the U.S., and Grigor is known for keeping his victims in thrall rather than erasing their memories and letting them go like he's supposed to, like he'd kept Quentin. Knowing him, he'll obsess over you now out of spite. And you want to march right back in there, or into some other den, and let any vampire see you and report back to him?"

"Tell me, Massimo dearest" — I poked his chest — "while you were busy posturing and dick measuring with Grigor, did you even notice how the Black vampire to our left watched us? Looked *excited* you were challenging his leader? Or how he locked eyes with the curly-haired female across the room?"

Max's mouth slackened, a frown forming as he tried to remember. But it was obvious he had been too focused on Grigor to notice anything else in the room.

"That's what I thought. Well, *I* noticed. Posturing for power roles is very much a part of pack life, and I'm used to watching for signs my brothers may be under attack. And let me tell you, that den was like a powder keg, ready to blow. Not everyone in that den likes Grigor's leadership style. Dissent is something we can work with, whichever way the dice rolls, and is what you were looking for anyway, right?" I tossed my hair over my shoulder. "See? You." *Poke.* "Need." *Poke.* "Me." *Poke.*

"What *I* noticed" — Max leaned forward almost imperceptibly, his blue eyes darkening as he damn near pushed me off the stool — "was you being unable to take my lead. The safest way for you to enter a den is if you belong to me, silent and obedient like a good Source unless told otherwise. Then you're off limits to anyone else in there. I tried to get us out of there safely, tried to convince Grigor you were mine, and you couldn't do it."

"And yet, you told me none of that first. I'm good at a lot of things, Maraschino, but mind-reading isn't one of them. You didn't even give me the basic rundown so I could pretend to be yours."

"I don't think you can pretend at all. That would take a little impulse control, wouldn't it? After you sprinted down the city streets of Boston in your wolf form, I think we both know that's not exactly in your wheelhouse."

I blinked, but I refused to let him see how that one stung. He wasn't the first person to throw my impulsiveness at me, and he wouldn't be the last. Instead, I flashed him my sweetest smile.

"Oh, honey. You think I can't fake it?" I patted his shoulder, trailing my finger across his collarbone. "I'm a woman. We have to be exceptionally good at *faking it* to keep your fragile male egos intact."

"What?" Max frowned, but I was already scheming.

"Oh, that reminds me!" I tapped the side of my head, like I'd forgotten something. "West mentioned he had something to talk to you about."

"He didn't text me."

I laughed. "Must have slipped his mind. You know Westly, busy busy Alpha. Anyway, I'm heading up to the house after I change, so just tag along. I'll be back down in five minutes, okay? Eat your cookie and relax."

Without waiting for a reply, I hurried across the café and ascended the stairs as I pulled my phone out of my back pocket.

SUMMER

Family barbecue still on for today?

TERRAN

I thought you were busy inventorying the new
merch you got last week?

DAD

Just fired up the grillie with my Willie!

ASPEN

Dad, please. You coming, S?

I swore under my breath, having forgotten she was back in town. I had a lot of lies to sell today, and Aspen always seemed to read right through me.

SUMMER

Change of plans.

JADE

Come on over, Summer! Cooper and Heath are
cooking.

I grinned, knowing that meant everyone would show up. Although Terran and I owned restaurants, our brother Cooper was the best cook in the family.

SUMMER

Sounds good. My boyfriend and I will be there
in an hour.

WEST

BOYFRIEND?

Chuckling, I pulled my apron over my head and slid out of my work clothes, grabbing a sundress instead. "Let's see *your* acting abilities, Massimo."

Chapter Thirteen

MAX

I didn't know Summer well, but I knew enough to be wary of the spring in her step. Her ponytail swished as we strolled up the long winding drive to the pack house, every color of tulip guiding the way up the path.

The full skirt of her yellow sundress flared around her legs. Paired with white sneakers and a denim jacket, she had a decidedly cute style, but I wasn't fooled for a minute. She was a firecracker in a pretty package, and a Roman Candle at that. It would be easy to be distracted by how beautiful she was while she burned your damn house to the ground.

Add in that I now knew how she tasted, how fucking sweet she was, and I was struggling to keep my shit together. Was I an asshole for disappearing without a word for a week after I'd bitten her? Maybe. But I'd barely held myself back from pushing her to the floor and fucking her then and there, right on her roof. The image of her naked and panting was still seared into my retinas, her pupils blown and nipples hard.

Fuck, I couldn't be thinking about this right now, not on the way to meet her family.

There was no universe in which Summer and I should actually get involved. She didn't strike me as the casual fling type, and that was all I was capable of. I had to keep that in mind.

Running away for a few days had been the right decision,

even if my solo hunt for more dens had been fruitless. I only worried a week hadn't been long enough.

Pushing aside those thoughts, I forced myself to remember the other conundrum I'd encountered — not being able to get in touch with Malachi. I'd reached out to share the details of our visit to Boston, but so far, I hadn't heard back from my dad.

Beside me, Summer began to whistle — a bad omen if ever I heard one — and it had me thinking back over everything I'd said up until this point.

She spun around, walking backwards up the hill. "You ready?"

"For lunch?"

The sun backlit the mountains and forests framing the large rough-cut log home, but I couldn't look away from the smile she beamed my way, hiding a level of sinister enjoyment I knew meant I was in for it.

But damn, she was pretty.

Any thoughts of how kissable she looked fled as the front door opened, West's frame imposing against the warm glow of the house behind him. Even from several dozen feet away, a wash of protective aggression radiated from him, and Summer giggled, high and airy. For a second, West hesitated at the sight of me, but his brows quickly furrowed into a glare.

She spun back around, then jogged up the hill as Cooper and Terran took up the spots behind West, blocking the entire front entry.

"Hi boys," she said sweetly, waving her fingers. "Lunch ready?"

"Get inside," West growled, his eyes blazing gold. Under normal circumstances, West had the same brown hair and hazel eyes as Summer and the rest of his siblings, but the gold glare told me his wolf was in charge. As an Alpha wolf, that meant something had truly pissed him off. He was usually as in control as any wolf I'd ever met, except around his mate, but Jade didn't seem to be the issue right now. His biceps bulged under the grey tee he wore, everything about him radiating tension.

I glanced sideways at Summer for any clues as to why we were having a pissing contest as I reached her side, but she still smiled that almost creepy smile.

Terran was slightly shorter than West, but had the same coloring, his shaggy hair hidden beneath a Buffalo Willies snapback. Cooper was taller and looked as feral as the mountain man he truly was, large and imposing just like his mountain lion form. Even though West was Alpha of the Timber Creek pack, it was Cooper I was the most intimidated by.

"Alpha's orders." Summer stood up on her tiptoes and kissed my cheek — eliciting low growls from her brothers — then squeezed sideways between Cooper and Terran into the house beyond.

Hiding my shock at the brief kiss, I moved to follow, but West stopped me on the front step. I looked down at his hand on my black leather jacket, palm splayed as he pushed back. He knew he couldn't take me in a fight, and yet his body language screamed he was ready to try.

Today was not that day, though.

I took a step back, shoving my hands in my pockets, waiting for whatever he wanted to say.

He crossed his arms and stared me down. "*You're* the boyfriend."

I raised a brow, a mixture of sass and pure confusion. Boyfriend? "That a question?"

"Should we kill him?" Terran asked, his voice low.

"Are we waiting on some other male, then?" West asked, dismissing his brother.

Glancing over my shoulder back to town, I shrugged. "Not that I'm aware of, no."

"Were you planning on telling me you were dating my sister? And how long has this been going on behind my back?"

Dating? Who told him we were dating? Still, I didn't appreciate being accosted like this. I held up a finger. "For one, your *sister* is 29. She doesn't need your permission, or anyone else's, to date who she pleases. And two" — I added a second finger — "I wasn't aware I needed to report to you, Larkin."

Terran's nostrils flared, his jaw clenched. "Want to try that again? Permission is one thing, but common fucking courtesy is another."

"We should kill him," Cooper added. While Terran might have been semi-joking, I knew the big cat meant it. Not only was his animal as vicious as they came, he was former military Special Ops — he'd rip me to shreds and hide my body so well, not even another shifter could find me.

West held out a hand to stay Cooper when he stepped forward. "Tell me what the hell is going on then."

Movement inside the house to my left caught my attention and I glanced that way. Summer's face was practically pressed up to the glass as she smiled and waved, then blew me a kiss.

My wandering attention didn't help the brothers' attitudes when I turned back. And then it all clicked.

This was a test. I'd made her mad by expecting her to read my mind in the den, following instructions I never gave her, and now she was doing the same, throwing me to the literal wolves to follow her lead.

I had two options: tell them their sister was making it up and risk looking like Summer and I were fucking around and I didn't want to claim her, or fake it so hard even she believed it.

Two could play her game. Maybe there was no way we could *actually* date, but toying with me like this? She needed to learn I was not to be played with.

"Fine. Yes. I hadn't found the right time to tell you about

us, but apparently Summer was done waiting to share the happy news. What *has* she told you?"

"Nothing," Terran said, a dark smirk on his face. "She hasn't mentioned you even once until tonight. Not a good sign, blackbird. She's chatty. Not many secrets, that one."

"I believe I asked you a question, Max." West's stare was unwavering, and something in me flared at his reaction to all of this, even if it was a lie.

West and I were friends, or at the very least friend-ish, and I didn't have many of those. I could understand he'd be protective of his sister, but still, this reaction from him jarred me. Did he really think so little of me as to hate the idea of Summer and I dating? Was I so far gone, so far beneath her that the idea was as appalling as his reaction made it seem?

Unable to help myself, I gave a hedging shrug. I didn't owe him any explanations, even if I had been Summer's actual boyfriend. "Our relationship is our business. Now, I think we were invited to a barbecue — though, to be honest, I already ate." I smirked at Cooper, flashing the barest hint of my fangs. The cat looking ready to slash my throat, which felt familiar enough to put me at ease. I gestured at the doorway. "May I? Oh, that's right — I don't actually *need* to be invited in, do I?"

I took a pointed step over the threshold, reminding West the whole vampire-invitation thing didn't apply to me. Besides, I'd been in his house before, and was about to have to test whether they'd part and let me through when someone beat me to it.

"Hey Max!" A much smaller figure pushed between the males, vibrant green hair the dead giveaway even before Jade's face became visible. "Two visits in a week, huh? And why didn't you mention you were interested in Summer? I would have put in a good word for you, but I guess you didn't even need it since she says it's pretty serious between you two." She slapped my chest playfully, then pulled me into the house, right past the grumbling males at the door.

I nodded at Jade, following her through the large entryway, open to the floor above, wondering what the fuck Summer had gotten us into. The three brothers walked behind me, their presence like a dark cloud. Fortunately, I thrived in the darkness.

In the kitchen, Summer's dad Heath stood at the island with Terran's daughter River, the young girl stirring a salad that spilled out of the bowl a little more with each stir. At my entrance, Heath's eyes flicked up to mine, but unlike his sons, he only had a moment's hesitation before offering a smile.

"Max, glad you could join us," he said, his voice warm and friendly as he reached out and shook my hand. Just that small gesture had a little of the tension in my shoulders dissipating. Unlike my own father, Heath was the epitome of *Dad*, down to his cargo shorts, white tube socks, and squeaky clean New Balance sneakers. His hair was the same deep brown as most of his children, but shot through with grey. Also, my father would never be caught dead in a red apron with *Daddio of the Patio* written in bold letters. "And just in time. Where's my baby girl?"

"Right here." Summer skipped around the counter, throwing her arms around her dad's neck as she kissed his cheek then looked in the bowl in front of him. "What are we making?"

"The peaches are extra juicy this time of year. I was out tending my Willie last night when an idea struck me. Everyone loves my spicy sausage, but what if I could make it even better?"

"I swear, you do this on purpose," Terran mumbled as he walked into the kitchen, leaning on the far wall with his arms and ankles crossed, laughter lines evident on his face even though he didn't smile.

"I was thinking," Heath continued, completely ignoring his son, the same way West had. "What if I grilled the peaches, and then sliced it, laying it on its side like this" — he arranged a peach half face down, rounded side up on a plate — "then placed the spicy sausage down the center to really soak up the juices better?"

The display was obscenely sexual, and I did my best not to gawk at what should have been innocent food and was decidedly *not.*

"Dad." West scowled, and Terran turned his face away from the room, rubbing at his short beard. Summer's cheeks tinged the darkest pink as she closed her eyes, drawing in a deep breath, then opened them, meeting mine, mouthing *I'm so sorry.*

"Where are your feathers?" River asked, head tilted in confusion at my wingless state and thankfully breaking up the awkward conversation Heath had started. "Daddy says you're the Dark Angel with black feathers my friends talk about."

Summer grinned as she grabbed a grape from a bowl on the island and popped it in her mouth, gesturing for me to join her at the counter.

"Would you like to see them?" I asked. River's blue eyes went wide as she nodded vigorously. I let my wings appear, shrugging my shoulders to settle them close to my body. They were the same deep black as my outfit, but the light caught them, highlighting the dimension in each feather. Although my feelings about my heritage were mixed, at best, I did love how unique my wings were.

River giggled and pointed at them. "Sparkly! You're like *My Little Pony.* I like the alicorns the best, and they have wings just like yours. Twilight Sparkle is prettier than you, though. She's *purple.*"

This time Summer didn't hold her laugh. I frowned, glancing at my own feathers. *Sparkly?* I might have flexed my wings a bit. "Well, not everyone can be Twilight Sparkle. Besides, I think you mean my wings are devastating and intimidating, fit for the Dark Angel such as myself."

River wrinkled her nose and sent a cherry tomato flying across the room from the forgotten spoon-turned-catapult in her hand. "What does that mean?"

"Scary," Summer said, trailing a finger down the edge of my wings that had me shuddering down to my toes. She might not have known what she was doing, but holy shit, were wings sensitive. As quickly as she started, she stopped, patting my shoulder. "*So* intimidating, honey. The *most* devastating."

A chorus of snickers came from behind us from West, Terran, and Cooper.

I vanished my wings away.

Needing a distraction from my body's visceral response to Summer's tantalizing touch, I turned to Heath as Summer shrugged off her denim jacket and pulled on an apron hanging on the wall. "How can I help with lunch?"

Heath opened his mouth to respond but was cut off by Terran.

"What the *fuck*?" He grabbed Summer's elbow, and held her steady, gaping at something on her shoulder. Tiny yellow strings held the sundress up, tied in neat little bows on her shoulders, but her brother wasn't staring at the thin shred of fabric.

"Daddy said a bad word." River giggled with glee, pointing to a large glass jar full of coins on the counter and then to Terran, who fished a coin from his pocket and dropped it in.

"What the he—ck is this, Summer?"

Summer turned slightly, just enough for my jaw to drop at the sight of ink on her shoulder. Black stretched across her skin, slightly blurred as if to appear smudged, but the faint outline of dark wings framed by wildflowers blossomed across the back of her right shoulder blade, stretching down from her nape. Right where I'd bitten her a week ago.

My spine straightened, panic shooting through me.

That wasn't ink. It was a shadowmark, a brand of sorts worn by a vampire's claimed. I wasn't even sure the stories I'd heard about them were true, and I'd never seen a Source with one before, but the dark mark on her skin was hard to ignore.

I swallowed, forcing myself not to let my confusion show. *One* bite had been enough for a shadowmark?

Summer glanced at it, then smirked at Terran, not showing even a hint of her own surprise. Her pulse didn't speed up, her nostrils didn't flare, her eyes didn't glance towards me, even though she had to be as shocked as I was by this turn of events. Surely, she would have mentioned it earlier if she'd seen it before now. I needed to eat my fucking words — Summer deserved an Oscar for this performance. "Like it?"

West circled around close enough to see it, and, unfortunately for me, he was not an idiot. His gaze drifted from the new mark on his sister, to me, and back.

"Who drew this for you?" Terran demanded. "I thought you were waiting for me to draw your art. That's always been the plan."

This time, a flash of hurt crossed Summer's face, gone in an instant that had me glancing between the two siblings. "I know, and I'm still waiting for you to do my pack sleeve. This was just a spontaneous thing. Spur of the moment, like one does."

"You are queen of the spontaneous decisions," Aspen said as she entered the room from the basement down the hall. She was Summer's only sister, and as closed off as Summer was an open book. Gold wire frames sat across her nose, framing hazel eyes that matched her siblings', but held none of the warmth Summer's did as she stared daggers at me. "Massimo."

"Quit it," Summer said to Aspen as she stepped up to my side, sliding her hand through mine. "Be nice."

"I didn't bring a katana, did I? I am nice."

Terran snorted. "Honest? Yes. Nice? That's debatable."

"Good to see you, Aspen," I said, trying to wade my way through this large family dynamic so unlike my own as Summer squeezed my fingers, always so touchy. I'd met all the Larkins at least in passing at one point or another, but facing them all at once — while they all thought I was dating the baby sister — was a whole other thing.

Aspen nodded briefly, her gaze calculating as she watched Summer and I in turns, but didn't say anything else. In a flurry of motion, everyone grabbed plates and trays, carrying them over to the sprawling table. Summer took the seat next to her dad, then tugged me down to the chair next to her.

River sat on my other side, repeatedly moving her chair closer until she was practically in my lap, her eyes flicking back and forth between my shoulder blades and my face. I finally let my wings back out, and her eyes sparkled with delight.

"He's pretty, isn't he?" Summer whispered, leaning across me as she spoke quietly to her niece. River grinned wide, nodding enthusiastically.

"Really pretty."

"The *prettiest*," Cruz agreed as he flickered into the room, dropping into an open chair next to Aspen, then dropped a kiss on her forehead. She recoiled, wiping at her face, and he laughed as he looked around the room. "*Hola, mi familia.* What did I miss? How's Michael?"

Aspen scoffed, waving a hand in my direction. "His name is Max and he's right there. Ask him yourself."

Cruz couldn't contain his grin. "I was referring to your boyfriend, but good to know he's not even on your mind."

"My *fiancé's* name is Matthew. Which you know."

Cruz's hands went up. "Got it. I'll wait." He turned away from Aspen's eye roll to up-nod me. "Hey Max."

I didn't know Cruz well, but the demon was Terran's best friend and basically an honorary Larkin. He wore a backwards baseball hat over his dark hair, tan skin contrasting his bright white smile. His distinctive black irises that marked him as a demon twinkled with amusement, and I got the impression he and Summer would be fiends if they ever teamed up against us.

"Okay, who set the table?" Summer frowned at her place setting, then glared around the table. Innocent eyes met hers all around, and she held up her butter knife.

Looking around the table, I saw the discrepancy — everyone else had a steak knife, except for her place setting and River's.

Her grip changed on the knife, now holding it as a weapon, any hint of her usual smile gone. "Come clean now and I'll consider sparing you."

Heath cleared his throat in discomfort, but Terran broke first.

"Okay, calm down, it was me, but West said —"

West pointed a finger at him. "Hey, you agreed —"

"Unbelievable," Summer muttered, getting up and walking straight to the knife block. Everyone flinched as she yanked out a steak knife for herself and came back over. "I cut myself *one time* —"

"You nearly cut your finger off," Cooper's low grumble cut in.

"I was seven! And we heal!"

"It was pretty bad, honey," Heath said with a sympathetic grimace.

"Not to mention the screaming," Aspen muttered.

Cooper grunted, gesturing to Terran. "Poor T nearly fainted."

"I did *not*—"

"Sweetheart, here, I'll take care of it for you —" Heath made to grab her plate, presumably to cut her steak for her, but she sent him a piercing glare, knife still firmly in her grip, and he yanked his hands back.

"Do I really need to remind you all that I run a *bakery*?"

"Cut a lot of steaks there, do you?" Aspen deadpanned.

With a huff, Summer brought her knife to her plate, slicing through her steak with a vengeance, metal scraping across the porcelain. Heath held up his hands in surrender, and the brothers had the decency to avert their gazes. Aspen just shrugged and continued eating her own food.

I was beginning to see what Summer meant about her family treating her like the baby, not trusting her to know herself. It only served to reinforce how ill-suited we would be for each other, and how much I needed to keep my distance from her going forward. We were polar opposites, and this smalltown girl had no business getting mixed up with the likes of me.

"Summer, you got a tattoo? I thought we were going together?" a new voice entered the room, interrupting the awkward silence as Leif joined us. His black Buffalo Willies tee and shirt said he'd just come from working at the restaurant.

Terran whirled. *"Et tu, Brute?"* He mimed stabbing himself in the chest, his sad eyes settled on Summer. "You had plans with Leif and didn't even tell me?"

Summer scrunched her nose and held her thumb and finger close together. "Only for a very *little* one."

"Wow."

"Her body, her choice," Cooper grumbled from the other end of the table. Maybe I didn't totally hate the cat.

"You'd think she'd want to get pack tats first, though," Aspen added, stabbing at her salad, her gaze resting on me as if she was picturing my face in her bowl. Or maybe my nuts.

"Or at least *my* art —"

West and Jade shared a look, a clear sign of that wolfy mind-speak thing, and then he frowned. "I thought you had a thing about needles?"

Summer laughed, but it lacked some of her earlier breeziness. "Well, I can make my own decisions! And I got over it!"

"Just like that?" West doubled down as Jade rested a hand on his arm. "There wasn't any, I don't know, outside *influence* —"

Heath sighed. "Children —"

Summer gaped at West. "You think Max, what, manipulated me to get a tattoo?" West shrugged, and Summer scoffed. I stared at my plate, trying to temper my agitation that he immediately chose to blame me for decisions his sister made, as if I was a terrible influence. The only problem was, the shadowmark *was* my doing — just not how he thought.

"One, he would *never*, and two, he actually *can't*," Summer went on, and my head snapped back up, afraid she was about to out me. Her hazel eyes expanded as if she'd just realized what she was about to say. "I'm apparently some super-wolf, immune to his powers. So you can take your prejudice and shove it up your asteroid farm." Summer shoved a giant bite of steak in her mouth and chewed decisively as everyone else at the table stared at her.

Ah, shit.

West broke first. "Excuse me? Immune?"

Terran leaned his elbows onto the table. "Super-wolf?"

Cooper's voice was barely above a hiss. "And how *the fudge* did you figure this out?"

Summer froze mid-chew, realizing her mistake, and her wide eyes met mine.

"Did you take my sister den hunting with you?" West growled, rising from his chair, rage rippling off him.

I set my silverware down, ready to push back from the table and leave.

"Den hunting? As in, *vampire* dens?" Aspen asked, her attention snapping to me, staring at my black wings I fought not to hide once more. "Vampires are dangerous, right? Exactly what kind of powers are you immune to, Summer?"

"Okay, this is awkward." Summer chuckled, slipping her hand onto my knee under the table to hold me in place — a move that did not go unnoticed by anyone, least of all my dick. "But if you *must* know" — she looked past me to River, then with two sharp pinches, plucked out my feathers — "here, River, you go play with these for a minute, okay?"

River's face lit up as she took them, immediately running from the table over to the living room, where she put the feathers on some blank paper and started coloring.

I turned a slow, deadly glare to Summer. Did she just *pluck* me? We were going to have a chat about that later.

Cruz and Terran exchanged a glance, clearly stifling laughs at my expense, but West, Cooper, and Aspen looked, if anything, more annoyed than before.

"If you must know," Summer repeated, lowering her voice slightly even though half-wolf River could probably still hear, if she bothered to pay attention. "I was, um, curious about his powers and might have asked Max, *consensually* —"

"Oh, God —" Aspen choked.

"— to experiment a little with me in the, ah" — Summer put her acting skills to the true test as pink tinged her cheeks and spread down her chest — "bedroom."

Four supposedly grown males made sounds of disgust, her brothers and nephew shaking their heads, but also not meeting my eye.

Heath looked like he might be sick.

Aspen seemed torn between anger and horror.

And there I sat, with Summer's hand on my thigh giving

me the boner of all boners, imagining just what Summer said we'd done. Her lying bare under me, totally submissive and willing, golden-brown hair a halo around her as I sent her time and time again over the edge. I squeezed my eyes closed, but that did nothing to dismiss the visual she painted.

Had my heart stopped beating? With a deep breath, I fought to keep the wince off my face, fearing where Summer was about to take Story Time.

"Anyway," Summer soldiered on, confidence returning to her the more she talked. I wasn't sure any of us had enough wits about us left to beg her to stop. "Once we figured out I was immune to his angel powers, we were both curious as to what else I might be immune to. I asked Quentin to try some of his vampire powers on me — um, *not* in the bedroom, that time. Nada. But, let me tell you, suddenly all of those Shadow Daddies I've read about makes a lot more sense —"

"*NOPE.*"

I couldn't tell who said that. Maybe all of them.

Except Cruz, who hung onto every word with delight and even asked, "Which Shadow Daddy? Personally, I'm partial to —"

Terran swatted him, knocking off his backwards baseball cap. "No more."

"Since angels can use mind powers, I had to test it. Could I picture what I wanted him to do without even saying it? Could he control me? I just needed to *know*, you know?"

"I do not," Aspen said with a shudder.

"And, guess what?" Summer shrugged, giving my knee a pat. "Didn't take. Turns out I'm a brat, through and through."

Cooper cleared his throat, his clenched fists on the table holding all of his attention.

West shook his head like a dog shaking off a flea, trying to regain his composure. Something I was struggling with myself, especially as Summer's hand slid higher on my thigh.

"You couldn't see into her mind? Or control her mind?"

I opened my mouth to answer, but Summer beat me to it. "It was more like, I could feel the magic like a sneeze building, and I powered through. Poof."

West narrowed his eyes in thought.

Terran opened his mouth again like he wanted me to make him a target. "Did he bite you?"

Luckily, that earned *him* a slap upside the head this time, from Cooper two seats down.

"What? I'm just asking! Isn't it a thing with angels too?"

"Some things are private, idiot."

"Since when? She shared everything else."

How great it would be to vanish into darkness where I sat. Never had I yearned to use my powers more.

"Can I come back now, or are you still talking about grown-up things?" River had crept back over to the table and now stood right behind us, one eyebrow raised as high as it would go. She'd attached my feathers to a band of paper she'd taped into a ring colored with jewel-like shapes, and now wore on her head like a crown. "Like it? I'm the raven queen!"

Still muttering under his breath about us, Terran hoisted her over the back of her chair and plopped her down until she sat.

"Can we change the subject?" Leif asked with a wince from the other side of the table, and I thanked him internally.

"Absolutely," Heath agreed, clapping his hands together. "Who wants to try my new homemade ice cream flavor? I call it —"

"*No!*"

Chapter Fourteen

SUMMER

"What do you say, Max? Up for a friendly game?" Terran's grin was all teeth as he casually tossed a small axe between his hands. Coop stood beside him, arms crossed but clearly on board with Terran's plan.

I rolled my eyes at my brother and put a hand on Max's arm. We'd all gone outside after cleaning up lunch, enjoying the cool spring afternoon around the fire pit. Up here in the mountains, spring could easily still see snow, but today we had blue skies in every direction. "You do not have to play."

Max frowned. "Play?"

To demonstrate, Terran pivoted and hurled the axe — hitting the bull's-eye of the target nailed to a tree. Much farther away than humans would have been able to throw, but I had a feeling Max could handle it with ease.

"Daddy! Cornhole!" River stomped her foot by the yard game, a handful of beanbags already in her fists.

Terran hesitated for a minute, but Leif hopped out of his chair, headed for her.

"We have a score to settle from last time, River," Leif said, juggling three beanbags with a taunting smugness.

River grinned viciously. "Game *on*!"

Terran turned an expectant look back on Max, and Aspen snorted from nearby. "T, even for you, this is low."

Max gave a resigned sigh and went to stand. "It'd be

quicker to get a tape measure, but if you'd rather lose this way, I'll play along."

I chuckled at Terran's scowl, then froze as Max leaned down over my chair. Time stood still when his fingertips tilted my chin up, his scent overwhelming me as his lips pressed to mine. The rest of the world faded away, until there was only us, until I wanted more, wanted him to push this kiss deeper.

Then Cruz's catcall cut through the air, and Max pulled back.

He gave a wink and a smirk before whispering, knowing full-well every shifter out in the yard could hear him, "Root for me, sunshine."

Of their own volition, my fingers rose to trace my lips where his had been as he turned and strode towards Terran and Cooper. I definitely did *not* notice the way his black jeans clung to his ass, or how his shirt stretched across his broad shoulders when he shrugged out of his leather jacket. My head was spinning with the riot of emotions the smallest kiss elicited from me. Warmth floated through my cheeks as a blush crept over my face, especially when I looked up at my brothers across the yard.

Terran gripped that axe like maybe it wasn't the tree he wanted to hurl it at, and Coop actually growled.

Maybe Max was better at improvising and faking it than I had anticipated. That was all this was, and I had to keep that in mind. If anything, this was just proving *my* point that we could and should keep up this dating ruse to hunt vampires.

Win-win. Right?

"Are there rules to this, or what?" Max called, picking up another axe and flipping it in the air several times to get a feel for it.

Grumbling, Terran and Coop quickly talked him through the rules while Aspen sidled over and took Max's vacated seat beside me, scooting it a little away from the fire pit.

"So," she began, drawing out the word and looking pointedly over at Max while she swirled the ice in her drink. "This is interesting."

"Right?" I chuckled, diverting. "You'd think even Terran would be smarter than this."

"Heard that!"

"I didn't whisper!"

Terran turned away but held a middle finger up behind his back at me.

"Max just doesn't seem like your usual type," Aspen continued. Prodding. Fishing. Interrogating.

Subtlety was not my sister's strong suit.

"What's my usual type again?" I asked, because there wasn't one. I hadn't dated much, and when I did, I rarely told anyone about it. For exactly the reasons Max was facing tonight — my family, all up in my business and treating me like a child.

Aspen pursed her lips. "You do know he's done some… not so above-board things, right? I mean, I know he helped Jade and her sister out and all, but he might be a bit…"

I turned to face her. "A bit what?"

She threw a hand up. "I don't know. Dangerous? Shady? Is he even an angel? Why *are* his wings black?"

"I'm a big girl, Aspen." I took a long sip of my seltzer, ignoring all of her questions. "I can take care of myself and form my own opinions."

Her jaw ticked, gaze swinging back over to the guys. "You say this is serious, so where do you see this going?"

I hummed in thought, not letting it show how much her questioning bothered me. "Maybe Aruba for the honeymoon, then who knows?"

She looked back at me. "I'm serious. He doesn't live here, who even knows where he lives, and you're —"

"I'm stuck here?" My tone came out a little harsher than I

meant, so I laughed. "Have you ever heard of *fun*? Some of us like to have it. You should try sometime."

"Someone's singing my favorite tune," Cruz said, conjuring a camping chair from thin air and sitting with us. "You need a fun times tutor, Aspen? *Estoy aquí.*"

Aspen scoffed. "Pass."

Cruz grinned, then held out his fist to me to bump. "Way to score the bad boy angel. He's hot as hell."

"See? Support." I gestured at Cruz, but looked at Aspen. "How hard is that?"

"Not as hard as your boyfriend was last n—"

"Dude, are you making sex jokes about my sister's boyfriend? *For* him?" Terran called over, then chucked a stick at the back of Cruz's head.

Without blinking, Cruz's demon magic incinerated the stick, the resin crackling as it caught fire and fell harmlessly to the ground. Aspen shifted in her seat and scoffed at the display.

"Who's making sex jokes?" Jade asked as she and West joined us, setting a tray of s'mores supplies on the table by the firepit.

River and Leif appeared immediately, and he helped her spear a handful of marshmallows onto a skewer and find a good spot to roast.

"No corrupting my daughter," Terran shot over.

West tilted his head and rested a hand on my shoulder, speaking into my mind, *"You're really good?"*

I resisted the urge to sigh and instead gave a small smile. For all my family was overbearing, I knew they were just looking out for me. *"Really. He makes me happy, and isn't that what matters?"*

He nodded, then took the stick River handed him and began dutifully roasting a backup batch of marshmallows for her.

"Who's ready to try my blue ball?" Dad came over with a

stack of bowls and what looked like a giant blue exercise ball. "This is my new rolling ice cream maker. Makes ice cream and gives my Willies a fun way to play with themselves out in the field! Turns out, Willies and balls are the perfect match."

"Dad." Terran shuddered, and West made a gagging noise. Cooper just walked away. I held back my laugh at my dad's innuendo, until I saw the shocked look on Max's face.

"Is that why it has what I can only assume is buffalo shit on it?" Aspen pointed to a suspicious smear of brown on the outside of the ball.

Dad turned the ball over to look, then shrugged. "Well, there's none *in* the ice cream."

Aspen's nose wrinkled. "I think I'm good."

Resigned to my fate, I stood and made my way over. "I'm sure it's fine inside. Let's see how it came out."

Dad beamed, unscrewing the ball to reveal ice and a smaller container inside. He scooped out what looked like peach ice cream, handing over the first bowl to me and waiting expectantly for my reaction.

As usual with Dad's creations, the first bite was fine. A little too sweet, maybe, but not bad. But then things took a turn.

I blinked away my watering eyes, trying to stifle a cough. "What's that secondary flavor, Dad?"

"So unexpected, right? I thought, what's something someone would *never* put with peach ice cream? And it just came to me — spicy dill pickle!"

West, Leif, and Jade hid their chuckles behind fake coughs. Unexpected was right.

"Hmm, yes. You are *so* creative with your flavor pairings, Dad." I put the bowl down gently, then grabbed a marsh-mallow and stuffed it in my mouth to chase the taste. It was possibly the worst of his concoctions yet, but the joy spreading across my dad's face each time I volunteered to try his food was worth the momentary pain to my taste buds.

My eyes snagged on Max's dark silhouette as he approached, his head tilted to the side, but his expression unreadable. When our eyes met, one dark brow rose, a small smirk playing on his lips. I swallowed, trying to rid myself of the sensation that he saw me more clearly than anyone here, and turned to my dad. "Maybe a little less pickle next time, though."

Back at my apartment later, Max went up on the roof to make a phone call, leaving me and Aspen — who always stayed in my guest room when she came into town — alone.

Until Indi flickered into my living room, plopping onto the sofa with us.

"You rang?" She smiled, pulling one of my many pillows into a hug.

"Did I?"

"Not you." Indi smacked me with the pillow and nodded to Aspen.

"Yes." Aspen leveled a discerning stare onto my best friend. "Tell me, Indi, were *you* aware Summer has been dating Massimo Russo?"

Indi froze for just a second and glanced over at me. I smiled, unblinking, in a look that hopefully said, *Play along and I'll love you forever.*

Indi raised a brow in a *Do you even have to ask?* sort of way, and turned back to Aspen. "Of course. Good ol' Max."

Aspen's eyes narrowed. "How long have they been dating?"

Indi and I looked to each other and answered in unison, "Since Christmas. Getting serious."

"And you approve?"

Indi patted my knee. "Summer likes him, so I like him. I trust my girl."

My heart swelled knowing, whatever other lies we were spilling right now, that at least was the truth. And damn if it didn't feel good for someone to trust my judgment. To believe me capable of making a good decision for myself, even if all of this was fake and a cover for the actual things we were doing in the vampire underworld. And I refused to think about if *that* was a good decision.

I was also starting to get tired of all these assumptions everyone made about Max. Sure, he might have killed that vampire on our escape from Boston, but they attacked first! It was self-defense. So even if he *had* done some shady deeds in his past, I had no doubt that deep down, Max was a good guy and had good reasons.

"All I'm saying is this seems short-sighted and impulsive, even for you, Summer," Aspen continued. "You *know* there can't be a future with him, so what are you doing? You're just going to get yourself hurt. Life isn't a Disney movie where everything magically works out because love conquers all, you know."

"How do you know?" I shot back, my adrenaline rising at her challenging words, and I could tell by the shocked look on Aspen's face she was just as surprised as I was that I pushed back like this.

"What?"

Indi bit her lip, glancing between us.

"How do you *know* it won't work out? You don't. You can't know I'll get hurt, or anything that will happen in the future. I'm happy now, I'm happy with *him*, so let it be, okay? We're happy, we're having fun, and for now —"

"This is your problem. You only ever think about 'for now' —"

I let out a bitter laugh. "As opposed to you? Because you're so happy with Matthew?"

Indi let out a low whistle. "Yikes."

"How is *only* thinking about the future working for you, Aspen?" I threw my hands up, frustration getting the better of me. "When was the last time you felt *actual* happiness? Felt present and in the moment and content, rather than just safe?"

Aspen's hard glare was familiar enough, but not something I usually experienced targeted at *me*. She stood, shaking her head. "When this crashes and burns, don't come crying to me."

I jerked back, but she was done, already heading to the guest room and shutting the door with a *crack*.

An awkward, heavy silence settled over the living room in her wake. Indi's brows lowered in concern at my chuckle, but what else could I do?

"That was a bit harsh, Summer," Indi said, keeping her voice low.

I waved a hand. "She shouldn't dish it out if she can't take it. Besides, like I'd go crying to *her* anyway. I love my sister more than just about anyone on this whole earth, but no one likes an *I told you so*, which is exactly what I'd get."

Indi grimaced. "Right."

Above us, the rooftop stairwell door opened as Max headed down to us, and I gave Indi an apologetic smile. "Listen, I know we need to catch up, but maybe not tonight?"

I nodded subtly towards the guest room, where Aspen could probably still hear our every word, and Indi got the message.

"Of course," she said. "As long as you don't keep me waiting. Girl, you have some piping hot tea to spill and I am your sponge."

"I think you took the metaphor too far there."

Indi chuckled. "Whatever. You love me. And maybe think about apologizing to your sister."

I mock-gasped. "Traitor."

With a coy finger-wave, Indi flickered away right as Max opened the apartment door.

The minute his tall frame filled my view, his dark wavy hair messy like he'd been running his hands through it, I knew just how to silence any future remarks from Aspen about our relationship.

If there was one thing that could make me double down on an idea, it was someone — especially my effortlessly competent sister — doubting me. Spite was the greatest motivator.

"You. Me. Bedroom." I pointed down the hall as Max blinked rapidly. "*Now.*"

Chapter Fifteen

MAX

Summer grabbed my hand, dragging me down the hall and shoving me through the door of what I assumed was her bedroom.

"Not even going to ask? Consent is a thing, you know. Even for men."

She shot me a glare, then leaned her back on the door, closing it. With a sigh, she wrenched off her denim jacket and threw it towards a chair in the corner, but it fell just short. Everything was pink and white and gold, clothes littered the floor, but the hot pink bra hanging from the curtain rod drew my attention.

Instantly, I was aware of how small this space was. No matter if our relationship was fake, my attraction to her wasn't. I did my best to avoid looking at that pink bra in my peripheral vision again, imagining how it would look on her smooth skin.

I drew my hand over my mouth, trying to think of anything else. Maybe I should have found someone in podunk Kansas to fuck, after all — it had been way too long, but the thought of anyone since I'd tasted Summer was unappealing. As if sensing the direction of my thoughts, Summer dragged a hand across my chest, a sultry grin painting her lips right as she climbed up on the bed.

"Summer —"

She cut me off with a finger over her lips and a twinkle in

her eyes, tossing her head back as she let out a deep moan. *"Max!"*

Fuck. Me.

I glanced at the door where Aspen's room was only a few feet away from ours, biting the insides of my cheeks to keep my fangs from descending.

Fuck, *our* room?

Turning towards the window, I subtly adjusted my pants then looked back, unable to resist. Summer rose to her knees, spread wide on the bed, as if she were riding me. The skirt of her sundress pooled around her, and it was so easy to imagine sliding my hands up her thighs, revealing more of her skin. This was an image I could have painted in my head easily enough, but seeing it in real life had me almost undone.

With that same grin she'd worn looking through the window as her brothers interrogated me on the pack house steps, she rose up, then dropped down, the springs of her bed squeaking with each movement.

I mouthed, "What are you doing?"

She returned, also silent, "Payback." And jabbed a thumb at the door.

I made a cutting motion at my neck, the universal sign for *Stop*.

"Just like that, Max," she groaned, eyes on me as she said it, showing no intention of stopping. "Fuck, that feels so good."

I breathed deep, trying to control my body's reaction, but hearing her talk like this? I had no choice but to give in. Besides, even if this was a show for her sister, Summer was surely aware of the affect it was having on me. And I'd be damned if I let her get away with it without a little torture of my own.

"Such a dirty girl, aren't you?" I growled as I approached the bed, tracing a hand over her jaw. Those hazel eyes locked on mine, blown wide in surprise, and I couldn't hold back my smirk. "Ride me hard, just how you like it, sunshine."

She bit her bottom lip, and I traced my thumb over it while she continued to rise and fall on the bed. "Touch yourself," I ordered, and her eyes shuddered, then reopened, lined with gold. Her hands didn't move from where she had them on the bed, but it took no stretch of the imagination to believe that had this been real, she would follow my orders like such a good girl. Color flushed her chest, telling me she was just as affected by this as I was.

A low moan slid from Summer's mouth, as decadent as any dessert in her store, and I traced my thumb across her lips again, letting my hand fall to lightly grip her throat, tipping her head up to mine as I leaned forward.

"Are you going to come for me?" I said loud enough for Aspen to hear, but in a low enough tone I knew this moment would be imprinted on her mind forever, just like it would mine.

She nodded, her eyes locked on mine, then seemed to remember we were putting on an audio performance. "Yes, Max."

I squeezed my fingers gently, hovering my face just over hers. "Then come, sunshine."

Her eyes dropped closed, and she moaned, long and low, the sound so real I nearly came in my pants like a damn teenager.

I'd never been so hard in my life.

I walked away from the bed towards the chair in the corner, covered in clothes. I cleared a spot to sit, leaning forward to hide my body's reaction to her as Summer opened her eyes, staring right at me with a lust-filled haze.

"How ya doing there, buddy?"

I shot her a look, and she let out a breathy chuckle, defusing some of the heavy sexual tension in the room.

Any worry or thoughts I'd had about being unable to get in touch with Malachi yet again went straight from my mind as the pink bra fell from the curtain rod above me, landing in my lap. I picked it up, running my fingers over the lace, then dropped it on the pile of discarded clothes at my feet. All I could think about was getting Summer to make those noises, for real next time.

Ten seconds later, there was banging on the door. "Would you keep it down?"

Summer grinned and leapt off her bed with a smirk, but didn't respond to her sister, who returned to her own room.

Turning on a speaker, Summer started a playlist and turned it up loud enough it would muffle our words.

"What the hell was that?" my voice came out in a rasp.

"I told you. Payback." Summer shrugged, like she didn't just give me enough material to jack off to for the rest of my life, and she didn't even take off her clothes. "Aspen thinks she wants to judge who I'm dating, so she can suffer through it."

I latched onto her words, trying to read between the lines to focus on her meaning and forget about my painful hard on.

"Your family was a bit protective. For a minute there I wondered if Terran was going to swing that axe at me after I kissed you." I forced a smirk.

"Protective?" Summer let out a deep sigh. "That's one word for it. They all still see me as their baby sister. Like I can't do anything for myself without fucking it up."

I frowned and pointed to the floor. "You run a whole store by yourself."

"Yeah, well. I'm not sure that counts in their eyes."

"Why wouldn't it?"

Summer waved a hand. "Oh, who knows with their logic. The moral of the story here is, they think you're a mistake for me, so I'll show them just how not a mistake this is."

That didn't sound great for some reason. "This?"

"Yep. Buckle up, buddy, we're fake dating for *real* now. You'll be in love with me in no time, and the readers can all squeal in delight that they knew it all along, right up until I break your heart in the third act. Don't try to fight it, it's a canon event."

Somehow, my forehead wrinkled even further, trying to figure that one out before I gave up and shook my head. "No. Summer, if anything, tonight just proved how right *I* was that you need to stay here and this" — I gestured between us — "needs to be done. I'll find another wolf, you'll stay here, hopefully West never finds out about Boston, and I get to stay alive."

Summer gasped. "You'd break up with me *already*? Then West would really kill you, since you broke my heart and all."

I gave her a flat stare, and after a minute, Summer's expression changed. She bit her lip, seeming almost unsure of herself for a change.

"Real talk?" She met my eyes, scooching to the edge of her bed and folding herself up cross-legged. "I need to do this. I *need* to."

"No, really, I'll find —"

"For *me*."

I followed her gaze as it drifted to a corkboard on the wall. Magazine clippings and slips of paper filled it, all tied together like a serial killer murder board. Only in the corner, instead of long-range photos of someone, were the words *Bucket List*.

"What's that?"

She laughed bitterly. "That? Just a whole bunch of stuff no one thinks I'm capable of, either because they think I'd never remember to, or follow through, or make the time, or I'd chicken out, or dozens of other excuses they conjure up as to why I'm still here in town and not marking off those dreams one by one."

What the fuck? For some reason, her words twisted my gut.

I stood, my dick finally calmed down, and went up to the board.

Fly on a plane.
Ride a ~~camel~~ elephant.
Zipline.
Visit the Eiffel Tower.
Eat gelato in Rome.
Road trip.
Get married.

Dozens more scattered the board, but nothing crazy or earth-shattering. Why would her family think she couldn't do these things? I turned back to Summer, and she must have seen the question on my face.

"I tend to have a lot of ideas — too many ideas, maybe — but am not the best at executing them," she admitted, sliding off the mattress and dropping down onto the floor. She pulled two huge rolling containers out from underneath the bed, both filled with assorted craft supplies. "Aspen says my number one hobby is acquiring new hobbies."

"What's wrong with that?"

Summer lifted her head, a slow smile breaking over her face. "Exactly."

Were we speaking in riddles now? "Your relationship with your sister is confusing."

She sighed. "It's complicated." Shoving the containers back under the bed, Summer sat back on the mattress. "You know our mom died?"

I nodded, vaguely aware of their history through West.

"I was a teenager, and Aspen sort of took it on herself to fill that role for me. So, yes, she's my sister, but I also think she feels responsible for me in a way that goes beyond a typical sister relationship. After our mom died, Dad kind of fell apart for a while, so she and West really stepped up for the whole family."

I nodded, having gathered as much over the years from West, but hearing her perspective was different. Not that different from how I felt about working for my father, choosing to hide and protect me for as long as he had.

"I love them so much for that, and we couldn't have gotten through that time without them, but she's also just…" Summer frowned, her shoulders dropping as she stared at her hands in her lap. "I don't know. We're so different. She's always had a direction, known exactly what she wanted, who she wanted to be, and how to get there. Me?" She gestured at the chaos that was her room — a pile of vinyl records in a crate, a bookcase overflowing with books and knick-knacks, clothes spilling from her closet. "I've always been a mess. I've never known what I want — or rather, I want to do everything. How do you make time for everything?"

She stared at me, bewildered, and I realized she expected an answer. "You can't."

Nodding emphatically, she threw her hands up. "I can't! So how am I supposed to choose? What to do, who to be, where to go, what to try?" She flopped onto her back, sprawled over her plush duvet. "Maybe I am stuck here, but I don't want to be."

I looked back over her bucket list items and plucked one off the board. Why I felt the need to help her, I couldn't really explain. Maybe because she helped me out with the den, no questions asked. Or because when her hazel eyes met mine, I suddenly felt like this version of herself, somewhat lost and unsure, was a side she didn't show many people. I wasn't worthy of these vulnerabilities from her, but for some reason, I wanted to be.

I held up the slip of paper. "This one. We can do this, easy."

Summer rolled her head over to see, squinting at the picture in my hand. "Which one is that?"

"Grand Canyon."

She smiled, but it seemed sad. "You're being nice to me. It's not like you."

I scowled, probably proving her point, but the fact it made her smile turn genuine meant it was worth it. "I'm very nice."

"Uh-huh."

"I saved you from bloodthirsty vampires just a few days ago."

"And then *you* turned into the bloodthirsty one. Not sure that counts."

I wanted to banter back, but she had to go and bring that up. Suddenly I was thinking about her blood on my tongue again, that stupid pink bra glaring up from the floor, and words escaped me. My eyes darted to her neck, where my puncture marks had been even though they'd healed now, then to the shoulder where I knew my shadowmark was, and I blinked hard to keep my head.

Summer cleared her throat. "Back to the point. I need to help you with this. For me. I need to prove to myself, if no one else, that I can make my own choices. That I can do something for *myself*. It might not be a bucket list item, technically, but it'll still let me see some of the world beyond the edges of this town. To feel useful and necessary."

Slowly, I nodded. It would still be insanely dangerous, and West would probably kill me for allowing this. But when her earnest hazel eyes met mine? Fuck, I was pretty sure I'd do anything she asked.

My focus drifted back to the cork board, and I decided we might even have time for a few pit stops in our travels.

"You want to see some of that wide world tonight, sunshine?"

Summer scrunched her nose and tilted her head. "What?"

I fluttered the paper in my hand again. "Grand Canyon; I meant it. You and me. Tonight. Who's going to stop us?"

Sitting up slowly, a confused smile rose on her face. "You're serious? Why?"

Why? Great question. I could have told her *because that's not your real smile* or *because I have this inexplicable urge to help you*, but I wasn't sure she'd believe either of those. Or maybe I wasn't ready to say them.

Instead, I played it off, like I usually did, and shot her a smirk. "Consider it my payment for the bite. Are we going or what?"

Summer hesitated only a moment before launching off the floor with a smile — a real one, this time, and my heart fluttered. "All right — show me the world, Aladdin."

I clasped her hand in mine and vanished us into the night.

Chapter Sixteen

SUMMER

The ground dropped out from under me — and didn't return even when the world around us did. I shrieked, realizing we were midair and falling rapidly, and scrambled to wrap my limbs around Max.

"Shit, sorry," he said with what sounded like amusement right in my ear. His wings shot out, catching on the wind, and in the longest seconds of my life, we were soon gliding through the night. "Been a while since I've visited — overshot it a bit."

"Mmhm," I managed intelligently, my heart still racing.

"Open your eyes." Now he was definitely laughing at me.

After a steadying breath, I cracked my eyes open, peering over his shoulder. And my jaw dropped.

As far as the eye could see was desert, bathed in the warm glow of sunset and interrupted only by the giant chasm below us.

"Holy crap," I breathed, doing my best to take in the view without loosening my limbs even a fraction from the vise grip I had on Max like a terrified koala.

"I think this is the least you've ever talked," he whispered into my ear, the words tickling against my skin. "Is this the secret to peace and quiet? Magnificent views and-or terror?"

I pinched his arm, the only violence I could risk at that moment, and his grip tightened on my waist. "As much as I love the birds'-eye view, can we land somewhere?"

"Please return your tray tables to their upright and locked position."

With no other warning, Max tucked in his wings, and we plummeted. I screeched again, eyes squeezing shut involuntarily, every muscle tight as wind rushed past us.

Until, with surprising gentleness, it all stopped.

Max's grip on me loosened, and I pried my eyes open again. Once I confirmed we were on solid ground, I slowly disentangled myself from his body, already missing his warmth.

"That was *not* nice," I said on a shaky breath and shakier legs, staggering away as I fought to steady my heartrate. "But also, let's do it again."

Max chuckled, his hands gripping my shoulders as he turned me around. Now that I wasn't dangling a mile in the air, it was easier to take in the view.

The layers of history carved into the orange and brown colored soils down the walls of the canyon, beams of the fading sun stretching across the chasm. The tiniest sliver of silver glinted down at the bottom, marking the Colorado River snaking its way through time and history. An eagle soared through the canyon so far away, it looked miniscule.

It was everything I thought it would be, and yet — my fingers pressed at the corners of my eyes, coming away wet.

"Hey." Max's voice was as soft as I'd ever heard it as he stepped in front of me, concern drawing his brows down as he tilted up my chin. "What's wrong? I thought this was what you wanted."

I forced a smile. "It is, and thank you for making it happen, it's just" — I gestured at the canyon, the desert, the overwhelming vastness of it all — "It's just all a reminder of how much I haven't seen or done. In Timber Creek, it's easy to forget there really is a world out there, you know? But here..." I trailed off, swallowing heavily before risking a look up at Max.

His blue eyes searched mine, and for a minute, I thought he might give me one of his usual smirks and make a snarky comment. Instead, he gave the smallest nod before stepping back and dropping to the ground, patting the spot next to him. I sat down beside him and, without conscious thought, leaned my shoulder into his.

"I get it, you know."

I almost laughed at that. "Really? You, Mr. I Can Go Wherever I Want, Whenever I Want?"

He didn't respond right away. Belatedly, I realized I might have sounded a little harsh, especially when he hadn't laughed at me. The silence stretched so long, I wasn't sure he would respond at all, until finally he gave my shoulder the tiniest nudge.

"I might be capable of going anywhere, but that doesn't mean I *can*."

I chewed on my lip, casting him a sideways glance. For as much as I'd laid myself bare to Max tonight, it began to dawn on me how little I knew about him. "Why can't you?"

He huffed a laugh. "One, supe. Two, half vamp." He shot me a look. "For most of my life, I had to stay under the radar so no one would raise questions about why the Premier's son has black wings. Why the Dark Angel is so *dark*."

I squinted at him. "You couldn't just go with, emo phase?"

"It's not a phase, Mom."

A laugh burst out of me, and that damn dimple showed up on his cheek. He shook his head, dark hair falling into his eyes. "Then for decades, I've been busy with whatever Malachi assigns me."

"Surely you got to see *some* of the world," I teased, nudging him back.

"Yes and no. Have I traveled a lot? Sure. Have I *seen* the world?" He shrugged. "Most of the shit I do is in darkness, alleys and the shady parts of town. Not exactly the tourist highlights."

I hummed, considering that. "Still, you never took a detour? Watched the sun set over the Grand Canyon? Had a special friend tag along just to see stuff and explore?"

"Special friend?"

"Girlfriend?"

"Not a chance."

I bit my lip, but in the end, curiosity won out. "What about Krista?" Max stiffened, but I went on. "I realize she turned out to be... whatever she was, but weren't you two dating for a while?"

A muscle in Max's jaw twitched, and he shot me an uncertain glance.

"Spit it out, Mascarpone."

"You're going to think less of me."

That brought me up short, and I turned to him. "Well now I have to know." I nudged his shoulder with mine again, and he nudged back. "Hey, I promise not to judge. You didn't judge me when you saw my bucket list."

His lip twitched. "I might have judged you a little. Ride an elephant? Really?"

"Stop deflecting. What was the deal with Krista?"

Letting out a deep sigh, Max tipped his head back, fading sunlight limning his features in gold. "Krista was a means to an end. I needed to get in with the Black Rose Coven to take it down, and she was an easy in. She was cheating on me basically the whole time, and I just pretended I didn't know because I didn't care. She didn't matter."

I blinked at his bluntness.

"And before you think I'm too much of a callous asshole, believe me, she didn't care about me either."

"Did I say I thought that?"

"She wanted someone to give her status in that Coven, and someone to fuck when she was bored."

Ice settled in my stomach at those words. "Guess you were happy to oblige."

He shrugged. "We were using each other. Isn't that what people do?"

Something told me to stay away from *that* with a ten-foot pole, so I tried to redirect our conversation. "Okay, so that's a no on the girlfriend. What about a friend friend, sibling, cousin, whatever?"

"Nope."

I stilled, that single word sinking like a stone. "No, like, you never took them traveling, or…"

"Or."

"Oh." I turned away, ostensibly to take in the view again, but in reality to hide my expression as I took in the knowledge that Max had no one.

Well, he had his father, Malachi, but they didn't exactly sound tight like I was with my dad. But no girlfriends, or friend friends, or anyone?

Was it possible West was his… best friend?

"Stop feeling sorry for me, sunshine."

"I'm not!" I was. A little bit.

"I just don't have time to hang around and make friends or —"

"How old are you, again?"

A low growl sounded from him at my teasing, and I smiled to let him know I was joking.

"So you, what, do Malachi's dirty deeds and go home to your coffin? No friends, no family barbecues, no town peach festivals, no questionable blue balls ice cream, nada?"

"I told you the coffin thing is a myth," he muttered, but didn't comment on the rest.

"What about magical tattoo artistry? No time for that out there, either?"

"What?"

I tapped my shoulder, where the mysterious ink had shown up, and his eyes widened almost imperceptibly.

"Ah, that."

"Yes, that. And I don't think West bought my story about this being a spur of the moment tattoo, so spill it. What is this?"

He scrubbed a hand down his face. "It's called a shadow-mark. It appears sometimes on a Source, especially if there's" — he broke off, licking his lips before finishing — "an emotional connection."

"Like a relationship?"

"Yes."

"Well, that settles it."

"Settles what?"

"You can help me with my bucket list and see the big wide world, and I can show you the joys of small town life. And help hunt vampire dens. Up."

I stood, dusting the red dirt off my yellow sundress, then held my hand out to him, wiggling my fingers.

He stood, and I stepped into his space, grabbing his hand and interlacing our fingers. The gentle touch shocked me as much as an electric current between us, but his bright blue eyes locked on mine as I tilted my chin up towards him. "I'm doing this with you."

He took a deep breath, looking out over the Canyon. "I've already told you—"

"No." I stepped closer, putting my hand on his chest to draw his attention back to me. "I'm telling *you*, I'm going with you. We're going to find these vamps you're looking for and talk to them all nice and friendly, convincing them they need better representation and that the PRICs have their best interest in mind."

"It's too dangerous." His hand rested on top of mine, closing over my fingers as if he meant to pry them off him, but he didn't. "You saw what happened with Grigor."

"I did." I nodded. "But you said if we were married it wouldn't be as much of an issue right? Between a ring and your shadowmark, I'm off limits then."

Max squinted, his heart thundering under my hand. "What are you saying?"

"I'm *saying*, you zip us due north to Las Vegas, and we tie the knot. Screw fake dating. We get married, and then tell my family the happy news while we use a European honeymoon as a cover so West doesn't kill you. Meanwhile, we go hunt some vampire dens."

"Summer."

"Max."

"We can't do this."

"Who's going to stop us?"

His hand tightened over mine, then pulled it down to our sides. "But *why* would you want to do this? Marry me, even temporarily?"

"Because." I jutted my chin up more, making sure he saw every single word I was about to say play across my face and could read the honesty in my words. "You're my friend, and you need help. I want to help you, Max, for no reason other than that."

"Friend."

"You heard me."

"And you get what, in return?"

"An epic adventure with *my* friend."

Max sighed, closing his eyes, and I dropped his hand to reach up and cup his face. "I mean it, Max."

"You're too good for me." His hand framed mine again,

our fingers intertwining once more. "No one would ever believe you willingly chose me."

"So wife me up, buddy, before someone else does. Besides, this is one more thing I can cross off my bucket list."

Max shook his head, then pulled our hands down, turning to face the Grand Canyon in front of us. "Maybe we just tell your family the truth, so your brothers don't to kill me."

"You think telling them we're only fake-married and you're using me for some dangerous scheme is better than telling them we're actually married and happily traveling Europe in love? Trust me, if they believe I'm blissfully happy in love, they won't have any reason to try to kill you."

His blue eyes flashed as they glanced at me, that familiar smirk playing across his lips once more. "Is that a challenge?"

"Happy wife, happy life."

"This is temporary," Max said, his thumb running across the back of my hand where he still held on. "We end it after our work is done, then go our separate ways."

"Sounds fair." I nodded, even though the thought of going back to my routine pre-Max seemed desolate. That was a problem for a later day, though. "Let's say, three months, or whenever the vampire issues wrap up, whichever is first." Three months seemed about the maximum limit I'd be able to lie to my family about this, but I kept that part to myself.

"And what do we do for the next few months?"

I shrugged. "You tell me."

"We—" He swallowed, still not looking at me. "We live together, and act married. Sell it."

"I think I proved my acting abilities if you at least tell me the basic plan."

"And what about dating? You can't have other men around if we want everyone to believe we're madly in love."

I snorted. "Not an issue, trust me. Did you see how my brothers reacted to us dating? Everyone knows how they are, and it's enough to deter anyone who even thought about potentially being interested." When he didn't answer, I squeezed his hand again. "I'm not a cheater, Max. I'm not Krista. I'm yours and only yours until we end this thing."

"You're sure?"

"Positive."

Max held my gaze for a minute longer, like he was giving me one more chance to back out, then he shot me a smirk. "Well? Something you want to ask me, Little Larkin? I'm all ears."

My brows furrowed, unsure what he meant, until his eyes flicked to the ground and back up to me. Rolling my eyes, I started, "Massimo Russo, will you —"

"Uh-uh." He pointed to the ground with a devious glint in his eye.

"Seriously?"

He raised his eyebrows, daring me to back out. Or maybe daring me to do it.

With a huff, I dropped to one knee and adopted my most adoring, beaming smile. He wanted the whole nine yards? I'd give him ten.

"Massimo Russo, love of my week, would you do me the greatest honor of my life and agree to be my temporary wedded husband?"

It was fake. I knew it was fake. And yet, as the words came out, my voice almost trembled. Kneeling before him like that, I felt like I truly was offering him my heart in my hands.

Max's blue eyes glinted. "Why, Summer, I thought you'd never ask."

Chapter Seventeen

MAX

Car horns mixed with the deep bass music from several nearby clubs, and coins clinked on the penny slots to the delight of patrons hovering over them. I held the shadows around us a little longer, savoring Summer's arms wrapped tightly around my waist.

As confident as she was about getting married, I was having a hard time swallowing the idea.

I wasn't sure I'd ever met anyone as selfless as Summer Larkin, and her ready acceptance of this task made me want to hand her the world on a platter.

But that was what this was — a task. A job. She was a tool in my arsenal, like choosing the right ammunition for the hunt, and I needed to remember that.

She wasn't choosing me because she loved me and wanted to spend forever at my side. She wanted adventure, she wanted to feel useful and important, she wanted to shove it in her family's faces.

Now that was something I had experience with.

I leaned down, my arms still inexplicably wrapped around her. "We doing this or what, sunshine?"

"Yep." She breathed deep, then stepped back, looking around the darkened alley, then to the arched LED ceiling dancing with bright colors over a wide atrium just beyond our shadows. "Where are we?"

"Fremont Street. More places to hide in the shadows than on the Strip."

Summer's head tilted up as she stared at the ceiling, stepping just outside my shadow barrier as she approached the crowds around us. Luckily, this was Vegas. No one batted an eye at two people appearing from the shadows here.

The images on the roof changed from psychedelic rainbow patterns to a galaxy of color, and Summer's mouth fell open in surprise. "Look!" she said, reaching back to take my hand as she pointed.

No matter what the ceiling was doing, I couldn't look away from the awe written across Summer's face over such a simple sight. Was it impressive? Sure. But so was the way light danced across her sun-kissed skin, the way her ponytail hung down almost to her waist, curling just at the end. We'd left her jacket back in Timber Creek, so I was left with little to distract me from those tiny yellow bows on her shoulders, not to mention my mark on her skin.

"We need rings." The sound of my own voice seemed to shock both of us, and she looked back at me, her smile growing.

"I happen to love shiny things." She wiggled her fingers to free my hand, but I held tight, navigating us through the crowd towards a jeweler inside one of the casinos.

Her eyes lit up just like they had at the ceiling on Fremont Street, flicking this way and that as she appraised all of the jewels. "Let's trade. Be traditional. I pick yours, and you pick mine."

I frowned, looking around the store full of more options than I knew what to do with, feeling the inevitable analysis paralysis setting in. "No way, you'll make me wear a rainbow ring pop or something ridiculous." That was easier than admitting *I'm scared shitless to pick something you won't like.*

"Oh, damn, you got me." Summer winked, then patted my chest. "Fine, fine. But, just to clarify, is your problem with the rainbow or the ring pop?"

I shot her an unamused glare, and she put up her hands. "Okay, no rainbows *or* candy rings. Plain, boring metal it is." Summer shrugged, then took off towards the display cases of men's jewelry, leaving me standing alone in the store.

"Special occasion?" the saleswoman asked as she approached, and my jaw tensed. She was very much human, and even the single gesture from me was enough to make her scurry back behind the counter, putting space between us. "You let me know how I can help."

With a quick glance behind me to check on Summer, busy pointing excitedly at several things, I approached the cabinets. Light sparkled off the many diamonds below.

Knowing Summer, she'd expect me to pick something simple. A solid gold band, not investing much into this temporary arrangement. But Summer was anything but simple.

The more I got to know her, the more I realized how much she hid from the world, how much she held back to keep from outshining everyone around her.

But Summer was the sun, a living embodiment of her name. Every moment I spent with her pulled me more into her orbit, until I felt like I too couldn't survive without her warmth.

My eyes caught on a large yellow solitaire diamond, different than all of the simpler ones around it. "That one." Like Summer, it stood out in a crowd, and confidence filled me as I looked down the rows of jewelry. Laying on a display further down was a smaller band of diamonds arranged into tiny flowers, like a crown. "And that one."

"Would you like to see them closer?" the saleswoman asked, but whatever expression was on my face, she nodded. "Should I find her ring size for you, sir?"

I nodded, and she scurried off.

Tightness bit at my chest as I leaned back against the display, crossing my arms. Across the store, Summer clapped excitedly and nodded. When the saleswoman approached her, she beamed, holding out her left hand to be measured.

Her eyes sparkled as she looked over at me, her grin spreading further, and damn, I wanted to kiss her. Maybe I wasn't ready for this to be real, but I certainly wasn't mad at the prospect of no one else getting to touch her.

"That was quick," Summer said as she sidled over next to me, as if this moment wasn't monumental for both of us.

"Just the words every man wants to hear on his wedding day."

Summer tipped her head back and laughed, exposing the long column of her neck I desperately wanted to taste again.

"All ready, sir," Summer's salesman said, handing over a small bag with two boxes inside. With quick efficiency, I paid him, waving Summer off when she tried to pay for mine.

Rising on her tiptoes, she laced her hands around my neck then leaned up and kissed my cheek. "Ready for the ol' ball and chain?"

With a brisk nod, I pulled her hands free, then intertwined our fingers, tugging her out of the store.

Vegas made it exceptionally easy to get married. Just down the street from the jeweler was the marriage license department, and right next to it? A tiny but ominous Gothic black chapel, complete with a classic, red-and-black Cadillac parked out front.

"I thought it would be bigger," Summer said, staring up at the building, her shoulders tensing then relaxing when she laughed at herself. "That's what she said."

My fingers tightened on hers. "We don't—"

She spun, putting her hand over my mouth. "Nope. Don't even say it. Mentally, I'm already crossing *Get Married* off my list, and if you make my brain have to erase that strikethrough, I'll riot."

I gave her a brisk nod, and she dropped my hand, walking confidently into the chapel. A whole range of emotions ran through me — indecision, guilt, regret, and maybe even a hint of desire I didn't want to acknowledge — but I followed her inside.

We had a bucket list item to check off.

Tinny organ music sounded from behind the closed doors in front of us, the only indication this was a wedding chapel and not an emo doctor's office. That, and the lingering scent of cigarette smoke. Everything was painted black, and the only lighting apart from the stained glass windows were flickering fake candelabras hanging from the ceiling. A deathly pale woman with dyed jet-black hair and bright red lipstick sat behind a glass window, smacking her gum as she twirled a pen between her fingers. Two other couples sat in red velvet chairs along one wall, both looking equal parts excited and nervous, whispering quietly.

"Lestat's Quickie Weddings, how can we help you have the wedding of your nightmares?" the woman sighed in a monotone as we approached the glass, then slid a clipboard under the partition without so much as glancing at us. "Fill out the forms and bring them back up with your valid Nevada wedding license."

Summer took the clipboard, and we quickly filled out the forms, passing it back and forth. Several of the questions, like my birthday, were fabricated to meet human requirements, but it matched the driver's license I carried and the government's records of me, so we were good to go.

Summer chattered endlessly with the woman next to us

while we waited, her foot bouncing nonstop — a tell she was as nervous as I was. Without conscious thought, my hand went gently to her knee, and the bouncing stilled.

I didn't see a way around this, but the closer our time slot came, the more regret seeped into my bones.

This was a mistake.

I was using Summer, taking this opportunity from her. This was her first wedding, but I wasn't naive enough to believe I'd be the only one lining up to marry her. As much as I needed her help, it felt wrong to take this experience from her.

She shouldn't be doing this just to mark something off her list. It should *mean* something, not just be an item to check off like any other chore.

Images of her family flashed in my mind — of Heath welcoming me so easily, but her brothers and sister too — as I realized with a sickening feeling that this would affect them as well.

Could I survive against a pack of wolves? Or even the one mountain lion?

I swallowed heavily. "Summer."

She turned to me with a bright smile, and our number was called.

"Wait." I grabbed her hand when she went to stand, holding her in place.

"Do you still need my help?" she asked, her brows rising high on her face. "Can you think of a better way for us to do this and come out alive, because I can't."

"I know, it's just —"

"Are you in love with someone else?"

I reared back, meeting her hazel eyes, having a hard time recalling what a single other woman I'd ever met looked like as I stared at her. "What? No."

She shrugged. "Then I'm still okay with this if you are. The last thing I want is to beg someone to marry me though."

"That's not the issue, and you know it."

"Okay, then let that guilty conscience go. Do you trust me to know my own mind? Because" — she dropped her voice so no one would overhear her next words — "fake husband or real, that's nonnegotiable for me."

Fuck, when she put it that way, I felt even worse for questioning her. Slowly, I nodded.

She smiled again, said goodbye to the other couple, and walked towards the doors, stopping just outside. "You coming with me?"

I stood, and my life flashed before my eyes. This marriage may have been purely for convenience, but it was hard to deny her anything.

Music started just beyond the double doors, and we both grabbed a handle, prying them open together. I expected a few rows of pews, some fake flowers, maybe an Elvis impersonator — this was Vegas after all. But that was as far from the scene before me as possible.

Summer chuckled as we walked down the aisle. "Well, this is fitting." A red carpet laid between rows of benches that looked an awful lot like coffins. Everything was painted black or red, with fake bats and hopefully fake cobwebs hanging from the ceiling.

"Reminds me of my childhood bedroom," I said, and Summer elbowed me with a snort. "Did you know this was what we were walking into?"

"When I saw the horror package, I couldn't say no. This is *Lestat's*, after all. Curiosity killed the cat. It also chose our wedding theme. Plus, you know" — she gestured vaguely at me — "seemed fitting."

The generic piano music switched to an organ, slamming out the *Phantom of the Opera* as we walked towards the front of the room. I could hear the heartbeat of a human somewhere in the room with us, but no one was visible yet.

I opened my mouth to ask Summer one more time if she wanted to run, but closed it. I did trust Summer, which was an odd thing for me to acknowledge. Aside from my father, I wasn't sure I trusted anyone, and even he was not a guarantee. Malachi had a reason for everything he did, even if he didn't always share that reasoning, though he never outright lied to me either.

We stopped at the front, the human heartbeat louder now. The room was dark, lit only by flickering sconces on the wall and several battery-operated candles on a table behind a coffin laid in front of us with the lid open. I raised my chin to peek inside when an elderly man popped up, Jack-in-the-Box style, arms crossed over his chest in his best Dracula impression. Complete with plastic fangs and the exaggerated lapels of his cloak sticking straight out. Summer jumped, then burst out laughing, gripping my hand tightly.

"Dearly beloveth, we are gathered here today to thelebrate the union of" — he uncrossed his arms to put on a pair of reading glasses, then squinted at a piece of paper he lifted from his lap inside the coffin, nodded, took the glasses off, then re-crossed his arms — "Thummer Larkin and Max Rutho."

He climbed out of the coffin, coming to stand before us. Whatever I'd expected for my wedding day — which was nothing, if I was honest — it was not the balding white man with a potbelly wearing an old tuxedo and cloak, dressed as the fictional version of a 19th century vampire. "Thorry, these fangth give me a lithp." He spit them out into his hand, and put them in his pocket, wiping the spit on his hand, then extending it out to me. "Hi friends. I'm Jimmy. Ready to get married?"

I stared down at his hand, then back up at his face, until he put his hand back down.

"Right, right. Sorry about that. Should we get started?"

"Yes." Summer nodded vigorously. "Should we face each other?"

"Sounds good to me!" Jimmy said, adjusting his cloak as he put on his reading glasses again, then pulled out a small book and put it on the black podium in front of him.

In a quick succession, we repeated words oddly centered around death to each other, promising things I never thought I'd promise anyone.

"Rings?" Jimmy asked, and I pulled the two small boxes out of my pocket.

Summer opened the one in her hand first, pulling out an all-black tungsten ring with a tiny band of silver running through it, sliding it onto my left hand. "It reminded me of your" — she stopped herself, staring at my shoulder blades where my wings would be, then my eyes — "your eyes."

My chest warmed. And I had to admit, if I'd ever wanted to pick a ring for myself, I couldn't have found something better than this.

"Do you, Summer Larkin, take Max Russo to be your lawfully wedded husband?"

Her smile was bright, a hint of tears lingering along her eyes as she nodded. "I do."

I opened my own box, the yellow glinting absurdly bright in this dark setting, but then again, so did Summer. She was my antithesis in everything, even here.

Her eyes blew wide, mouth falling open as I pulled out the set of rings. With slightly shaking hands, I slid first the yellow solitaire diamond then the ring of daisies onto her finger, closing my hand around hers.

"Do you, Max Russo, take Summer Larkin to be your lawfully wedded wife?"

Lawfully. Wedded. Wife.

I didn't expect those words to do something to me, but they

hit like a gut punch. Something possessive and feral took root in my chest, and I couldn't stop my fangs from descending. I kept my lips curled over them, my eyes intent on Summer, as I made her mine. "I do."

"Excellent!" Jimmy clapped. "Then with the power vested in me by the state of Nevada, I now pronounce you husband and wife. You may bite the bride." My head jerked up at his words, staring directly at Summer. Her heart thundered as her pulse ratcheted up, and the memory of the taste of her blood burst on my tongue as if I'd bitten her yesterday, not days ago.

"Or kiss." Jimmy shrugged when we did nothing. "All part of the package."

Summer stepped closer, her bright hazel eyes locked on mine as she tilted up her chin. I framed her face in my hands, and dropped my lips down on hers.

She shouldn't have tasted this good, this tempting, but the moment her hands closed on the fabric of my shirt, holding me as if I was the only thing keeping her upright, I was feral.

It should have been a chaste kiss, a quick peck to seal the deal, but the knowledge that Summer was *mine* overtook me, and my tongue traced the edge of her lips, seeking entrance.

Immediately, she opened to me, her tongue dancing with mine as the softest moan floated out from her mouth. Her tongue caught on my fang, pricking the tiniest drop of blood and dropping it into my mouth, and I growled low.

She jerked back, pupils wide as she heaved in deep breaths, pressing a shaking finger to her lips.

Jimmy cleared his throat loudly. "I should mention we offer discounted room rates at the motel next door," he chuckled with a flick of his eyebrows, then pulled his plastic fangs back out of his pocket and popped them back in his mouth.

My hands were still cupping Summer's jaw as I tried to regain control over my body, but she nodded, her hands coming up to grab mine. A clock chimed on the back wall, alerting us our time slot was over.

"Thank you for coming to Lethtat's Wedding Chapel here in Lath Vegath," Jimmy said as he climbed back inside the coffin in front of us, then laid back. "May you both live out your scarietht happily ever after."

Chapter Eighteen

SUMMER

"Well, that was exciting," I said as we stepped out of the chapel and back onto the street, the sounds of rushing cars and street performers at odds with the seriousness of what just happened inside. I ignored the fluttery feeling in my chest at the thought I was *married*. "A wedding I certainly will never forget."

"Good thing they gave us the pictures to prove it." Max handed over a black envelope with the chapel's name printed on the front in shiny red ink. "I don't know that anyone would believe we were married by Jimmy, my long lost cousin."

I stared down at the envelope, but more specifically at the *Russo Wedding* scrawled in the corner with the date. "We're married."

"I noticed." Max grabbed my left hand as we crossed the busy street. He fiddled with the two new bands on my finger, sliding them back and forth in a circular motion as if he too couldn't quite believe everything that had happened in the last hour.

"Well, now what?" I looked up and down the Strip towards all the colorful casinos, blinking against the dark night. "Should we go see the Eiffel Tower while we're here?"

Max skidded to a stop, knocking the man behind us off balance as he tried to avoid crashing into him. The guy threw his arms wide and snarled, "Watch it, asshole."

In slow motion, Max turned and glared at the man, who took no further encouragement to hurry in the opposite direction. I grinned up at what I assumed was Max's formidable *run away* look, seeing right past the façade he showed everyone else.

He might scare everyone off with just a look, but this was the same male who picked out the most gorgeous rings I'd ever seen, and I couldn't have picked better myself. The same guy who'd taken one look at my bulletin board full of dreams and immediately made them come true. This wasn't how I'd pictured *Get Married* to play out, but everything about tonight had been oddly and hilariously perfect.

Tugging me out of the crowd of pedestrians on the sidewalk, Max led me towards a side street. "I have a better idea."

My heart raced as he picked up the pace, nearly jogging as we hurried into the shadows away from the streetlamps. He stopped and spun, pushing my back against a brick wall, pressing us into the shadows as magic seeped out of him, black tracing up his arms. I sucked in a breath, not sure whether to watch the shadows grow or the way his face tipped down over mine, so close I could lean up and press my lips to his again.

That kiss at the altar had changed my brain chemistry, disassembling me and putting me back together in a way I hardly recognized. My life was now sorted into *before* and *after*. Once again, Max was never what I expected, and I craved the unpredictability.

His eyes were almost black as he looked down at me, his hands closing over both of mine. "Close your eyes, sunshine."

Between one moment and the next, we were gone.

That same soul-sucking pressure squeezed me as we zipped through space, but the steady pressure of his hands in mine held us together until we dropped into another world.

I sucked in a dizzying breath, trying to find my center, until Max's arms wrapped around my waist and turned me, walking me forward.

"Where are we?" I asked, opening my eyes to look around.

We were in what looked like a residence, soft light drifting in from behind curtained French doors all along one wall.

He stayed behind me, his warm hand pressing gently on my lower back and sending a shiver down my spine, but reached around and opened the doors. *"Bienvenue à Paris, ma femme."*

The Eiffel Tower — the real one, not the little fake Vegas one — was framed perfectly between the doors, all of Paris spread out before us under the soft pre-dawn light. The city was still quiet, only a few pedestrians and bicyclists out on the streets, and the quintessential pale limestone buildings glowed. In the distance, the Seine glistened and flowed peacefully, and I could already scent fresh bread from somewhere close.

My hand rose to my throat as I struggled to breathe, over-whelmed by not only the view but also the gesture. Max stepped out onto the veranda, resting his elbows on the black iron rail, and I joined him, leaning my shoulder into his arm.

"Is it what you imagined?" he asked, and I had to hold in a laugh as I looked out over the City of Love. All that was missing was an accordion player to complete the image, but the day was young.

I smiled, my mind rapidly whirring through all the possibil-ities being in Paris opened up. "Yes, and so much more."

"You sure? We didn't even have the croissants yet."

With a chuckle, I said, "I never once pictured you, *my husband,* here to share this with. I'd imagined a long international flight cramped among so many humans my sense of smell would never recover, and a tiny hotel somewhere wedged into a back corner of Paris with no view. And I always kind of assumed I'd be alone."

Max raised a brow, his lip quirking at the corner. "I can leave. You can have that part of your dream, if that's what you want. Though before you kick me out, I might mention this place is *my* property."

A wave of heat washed through my body as his hand slid down my spine, nothing outrageous about the placement, but enough to have me aware of everywhere our bodies touched, standing like this. When had my entire body become plastered against his? I wasn't sure, but I couldn't pull away now if my life depended on it. "I don't want you to leave."

"What do you want, then?" His eyes closed, head dropping slightly towards my neck as he pulled in a breath, like he was held by the same magnetic force. And damn, if that didn't light a fuse in me.

"For one, I can't wait to see your ferocious fangs biting into a delicate little macaron."

Max hissed out a breath. "Don't say fangs."

I tilted my head, studying him. Was it my imagination, or were his veins flickering with his shadow magic? His eyes opened, glued to my neck again, before he moved to pull back. I gripped his arms, stopping him. "What is it?"

He cleared his throat. "Nothing." Inky shadow flashed across his face like dark lightning as he licked his lips.

"Husband." I tried for stern, but the way his eyes shot to mine, intense and hungry, made me think it might have had the opposite effect. "Is it possible vanishing us halfway across the globe multiple times in one night has drained your magic?"

He heaved a breath, tilting his head back as though asking the heavens for help. "It might be possible. But it's fine. I'll just pop out and find a quick top-up —"

A low growl hit my ears, and it took a moment for me to realize the sound was coming from my throat. "*No.*"

Max blinked, as startled as I was by my response. But the thought of Max biting anyone else, anyone but me, had my wolf snarling in my mind.

Mine, she snapped, and I shook my head at the sensation. It wasn't often I heard my wolf speak like that, so clear and strong. What the heck was that about?

Eyes crinkling with amusement, Max echoed, "No?"

"No," I repeated, trying to come up with a plausible reason he shouldn't go out and find someone else to bite. Something that sounded better than, *My wolf says you're mine.* "We're going to be traveling together a lot, right? So if this is something you need, we should just — get used to it. Right?"

"I'm used to fending for myself. You don't need to do this."

That low growl built in my throat again, but Max's smirk was back as he leaned closer, his lips hovering over my neck. "Careful, sunshine, or I'm going to start thinking you *want* me to bite you."

His teeth grazed my skin, not enough to puncture, but he knew what he was doing. It was right where a mate bite would be for a shifter, and my wolf went feral.

"Just do it," I managed to get out, a husky quality to my voice it didn't usually have, and Max's chuckle said he heard it, too.

He pressed a kiss right behind my ear as one of his hands tangled in my hair, the other steadying my waist. "If you insist, wife."

He pulled me through the doorway back into the apartment, and my heart pounded with each step. Once inside, he tilted my head, and I let out a gasp as his fangs sank into my skin. The steady sucking pull had my knees quaking, and my arms wound tight around him as I held on. Every nerve was alive and firing, making everything feel *more*, his fingers digging into my waist as he pinned me to him, and I was unraveling.

I didn't know if I was supposed to enjoy this as much as I did, but something was so deeply intimate about it, I felt like a livewire. Everything he'd said as I faked it for my sister's benefits earlier came flooding back, wanting every dirty word to come out of his mouth again. For real.

His tongue laved across my skin as he finished, the wound

closing in seconds from the combination of our powers. "Max."

He groaned, all hesitation lost. My back crashed into the wall, and I realized he'd spun us around with his supernatural speed, pinning me in place next to the open balcony doors.

Kissing my neck again, he pressed his hard length into my hip, telling me I wasn't the only one affected by this.

"I'm not a gentleman, Summer. If you're offering, I'm taking."

His words might have been meant as a warning, but they only made my pulse race faster. In response, I hooked my leg around his hip, dragging him even closer.

I could have told myself we needed to do this to prove to any wolves that this was a real relationship, to scent mark and claim each other.

But the truth was I just wanted to.

"I am your wife, *dear*. If there's a reason we should both be celibate for however long this marriage lasts, I can't find it. And I'm already on birth control, so we're good there."

"As long as the marriage lasts," he repeated, mouth against my jaw as the doors flew shut by his magic. "But this is only physical, sunshine. Don't go falling in love with me."

"You think your dick is that magical?"

He ground into me from below, the thick length of him rubbing against me in the most promising ways. "I am an angel, after all."

Before I could respond, his lips caressed the sensitive skin of my neck again, teeth nipping and tongue laving in turns until I could barely breathe, my mind on a never ending loop of *need*.

His hands hooked under my thighs until I was wrapped around him like a spidermonkey, and then he propelled us into a bedroom with that same supernatural speed. He tipped us back on the bed, my hair flowing out behind me as I loosened my legs, scooting farther back onto the mattress, elbows propping me up so I could watch him.

Max put his knee on the bed, his hands dropping down on either side of me. Framing me like this, he was the predator I knew him to be. My breaths came rapidly, my chest heaving as I reached up for him, wanting more.

Unspoken desperation passed between us as he lowered his weight on me and I laid back, feeling the press of his hips against mine. One of his hands tangled in my hair at the nape of my neck, the other pressed into the mattress next to my face as he held himself aloft.

"You're gorgeous like this, Summer."

I grabbed the back of his neck and pulled him the rest of the way down onto me. Again, his face fell away from my mouth and to my shoulder, but I was too lost in the moment, overcome with passion to think on it. Our hips moved, our hands roamed in a dance that spoke of how deeply we both felt this pull, this need.

His palm slid up the side of my thigh, hitching my knee higher up on his hip as he ground down into me, letting me feel everything I was doing to him. "More," I moaned as he kissed along my neck, right over where he'd bitten me. "I need more."

"Can't deny my wife on our wedding day, can I?" Max's hand slid further up my thigh, then traced inside, running along the seam of my underwear. My breath caught as I squirmed, needing him to touch me.

As if he'd heard my silent command, his knuckles traced over me, right where I needed him but with not nearly enough pressure.

"Oh, you're a tease, is that it?" I tried to arch my hips up for more, but Max held me down, not allowing any more pressure than he was giving.

His smirk was all evil delight. "You have *no* idea. But as it's our wedding day, I'll go easy on you."

My jaw dropped open at his implication, and he let out a dark chuckle. His fingers hooked inside my underwear, sliding them down and off. I grabbed the hem of my dress, pulling it over my head as Max watched, eyes hooded with want.

I allowed him a minute to take in the sight of me naked — I knew my body was magnificent — before I reached for his shirt.

He batted my hand away, and before I could blink, he had me on my back, legs bent and hips resting near the edge of the bed as he lowered to his knees on the floor beside it.

I was about to protest, but then his mouth was on me, and my head fell back. He flattened his tongue, running it over every nerve in my body until he kissed at the apex, then gently bit the inside of my thigh. My legs lifted, a full-body shiver convulsing me as he gripped my shins, draping my ankles over his shoulders, and dove back in. Licking, nipping, and sucking everywhere until I squirmed against his face, needing more.

"You like that?" Max said as he kissed along my inner thigh, his tongue tracing over the vein in my leg.

"Goddess, yes."

He held eye contact as his fangs traced over my thigh, long enough it was a silent question, When I didn't stop him, he bit, slow and gentle, into the vein.

Only simultaneously, he sank two fingers inside me, and my back arched at the overwhelming sensations.

"Max —"

"Fuck." He licked over the wound in my leg, pulling back enough to watch my face as he continued to move his fingers. "I love the way you say my name."

A breathy chuckle left me that was quickly replaced by a moan as the heel of his hand pressed into me just right.

My hips moved in tandem with his hand, my heart racing,

and everything was just the right pressure and speed that I was about to —

In a flash, everything stopped, and I whimpered. "Wha—"

But Max was stripping, so despite the glint in his eyes that said he knew exactly what he'd just done, I let him continue.

I ogled him shamelessly, but hot damn, my husband's body was a work of art. That olive-tan skin, all toned muscles that led down to a — my mouth *actually* filled with saliva as he stood, stroking himself and watching me with a smirk.

But something was missing.

I pointed at his shoulders. "Where are your wings?"

His strokes faltered, his brows furrowing slightly. "I don't usually — you *want* the wings out?"

Okay, don't be too eager, Summer.

I swallowed. "I want you. All of you."

Max's eyes narrowed in confusion, then he shook it off. "As you wish, sunshine."

His black wings appeared, flexing as light glinted off the shimmering feathers, and I couldn't hold back my smile.

They were just so beautiful.

Then he climbed on the bed, hovering over me with those wings above us, and I shivered in anticipation. He sank his hips over mine, grinding against me. Reaching up, I ran my fingertip over the arch of his wing, and a groan left him I felt straight down to my core.

Leaning up, I brought my lips close to his ear, giving it a nip with my teeth before whispering, "Fuck me, husband."

Max swore softly, and lined himself up. "You're no sweet summer day, are you?" He was so close to where I wanted him, but not nearly close enough. Then — "You're a hurricane" — he slammed inside me in one thrust — "and you're all *mine*."

Chapter Nineteen

MAX

Summer's back arched off the bed when I moved, her fingernails digging into my skin as she took everything I had to give.

When I agreed to the fake marriage, this was not where I'd seen it going, but not one ounce of me regretted the turn of events. Not only was Summer fucking gorgeous, but the fiery passion she brought to everything extended to the bedroom.

She moved in tandem with me, meeting me stroke for stroke as we came together, words lost to us both. The only sounds were that of skin on skin and our mutual groans of pure pleasure.

I no longer regretted not finding a random stranger to fuck — Summer was worth waiting for.

Leaning down, I pulled one of her pert nipples into my mouth as my fangs grazed her skin. They refused to sink back into my gums when Summer continued to offer herself like a delicious buffet of everything I'd ever wanted.

Her hands tangled in my hair, pulling lightly as she held me in place, urging me on. I bit again, her delicate citrus flavor meeting my tastebuds, as addicting as any drug. Some part of my brain registered how much I'd taken from her already and I should stop, but she was too tempting, too *alive* to deny.

I licked over her breast, closing the wound with my saliva then pulled out of her, flipping her to her stomach before I sank back in and pulled her hips up, giving us a better angle.

"That feels so good," Summer moaned, her head dropped down on the bed but turned to stare at me. Her golden hair was splayed around her, but the shadowmark on her shoulder moved, growing as my magic seeped into her skin, marking her as mine.

Warning bells sounded in my brain at the sight, feeling more permanent than the rings on our fingers, but buried in her like this, I couldn't stop. Couldn't find it in me to regret it. Not when I'd never felt like this before.

I closed my eyes, tipping my head back as my hands dug into her hips, holding her exactly where we both needed it, racing towards the finish line. I might have given her a taste of how I truly wanted to tease her earlier, getting her so close before backing off completely, but I'd meant it when I said I'd take it easy on her today. We'd have plenty of time to play later, if we truly kept this up for the duration of our fake marriage.

A low groan escaped her as her body tightened around me, telling me she was just as close as I was. "Right there. Don't stop."

Even if I wanted to, I was past the point of self control. I dropped my hand beneath her, running my fingers through where we joined. Circling them just right, I pressed down until Summer shattered, a moan ripping from her throat that I'd hear forever.

Her body spasmed, tightening around me until my vision started to black out, the pleasure too intense to deny.

I pushed her down flat on the bed as I pulled out, grabbed my cock, and covered her back in my cum. Seeing her smooth skin dripping with it, marked by me like this — my magic flared with pride, sparks from my angel side skittering up my forearms, chased by the inky shadow of my vampire magic.

Summer made to move, but I held her still with a hand on her shoulder, needing another minute with her beneath me, my knees on either side of her hips, covered in my scent.

A sated chuckle escaped her, her hazel eyes rimmed in the gold of her wolf. "Well, that should do it to convince any shifter we're together."

"We *are* together, Summer. Until this is done, you're mine and I'm yours."

Her smile slipped for a moment, then returned. "At least banging my husband regularly won't be a chore."

The idea of doing *this* again, preferably soon, had me halfway to hard again. But this had been an exceptionally long day for both of us.

I climbed off the bed and walked into the en suite bathroom, grabbed a washcloth, and ran it under warm water before returning to the bed and cleaning her up. Summer's smile was sleepy, but she slid off the bed, kissing me lightly on the way to the bathroom.

Even though it was morning here in Paris, neither of us had slept in 24 hours. I went to the windows, pulling the blackout shades hidden beneath the gauzy curtains closed, casting the room in darkness. The sink turned on as I climbed under the covers, resting a hand behind my head, waiting for my wife to return.

Backlit by the bathroom light, Summer's every curve was highlighted, the perfect body wrapped in a tortuous, troublesome package. I lifted the covers and she climbed in, her hair fanning out behind her on the pillowcase as she turned on her side towards me.

"You said this is your place?" Summer looked around the room, decidedly French in style. We both could see well in the dark, especially as everything in here was white aside from the rich mahogany furniture. Ornate crown moulding framed the ceiling in scrolling floral patterns, here long before my father bought the place decades ago.

"My father's, technically, but I'm the only one who uses it."

"Ah. I should have put this together by now, but you're basically a trust fund kid, aren't you?"

"Don't bite the hand that has the international properties, wife," I growled, and Summer smirked.

"Wouldn't dream of it."

Summer wiggled in the bed, settling into the mattress and fluffing up her pillows a few times to get comfy. When she stilled, her eyes met mine again.

I waited for her to speak, or ask me something, but nothing. "What?"

"Nothing. I'm just taking in that I'm married, and in Paris, and my husband is hot *and* has a great dick." She gave a happy, wistful sigh. "A girl really can have it all."

I rolled my eyes and playfully slapped a pillow on her face. "Get some sleep, sunshine. We have vampires to hunt tonight."

Summer shoved the pillow aside and grinned. "I literally can't *wait.*"

But the way she beamed at me, and those things she said? If I didn't know better, if I didn't know there was no way in hell anyone would ever want me for *me*, I could almost have believed her.

But no, this was a transaction. She'd just laid it out, clear as day — she liked my abilities, my properties, my body. And that was fine with me, because I needed her abilities and liked her body too. Nothing more.

With a huff, I turned away from her, getting comfortable myself and making sure to leave a good two feet of distance between us. If there was one thing I was *not*, it was a snuggler.

Slanted, golden light filtered in through the gap in the curtains when I cracked an eye open several hours later. It must have been late afternoon by now, but a weight across my waist made something undeniably clear.

We were snuggling.

Summer had an arm thrown over my stomach, a leg thrown over both of mine, and my arm, inexplicably, was wrapped around her shoulders. Her head rested on my chest, her hair so close, I couldn't resist tilting my head to breathe in her lemon verbena scent.

I froze, realizing what I'd just done.

Maybe this was a huge mistake.

Chapter Twenty

SUMMER

SUMMER

Okay, two things. One, I slept with my half-angel-half-vampire husband this morning.

INDI

You WHAT? Your WHAT??

SUMMER

And two, I have a husband. Max and I got married in Vegas yesterday!

I snapped a picture of my wedding ring and sent it over. Then I realized what was in the photo's background and added,

SUMMER

Oops. And three, we're in Paris!

INDI

EXCUSE ME!!!!!!

Three dots appeared for a *long* time. While Indi composed herself, I switched over to my family group chat and took a deep breath.

SUMMER

Yoohoo! Hi family. I hate to do this over text, but time is of the essence.

TERRAN

Fuck are you pregnant

DAD

GASP

SUMMER

NO. No.

WEST

Who am I murdering?

SUMMER

No murder!

COOPER

We'll see.

LEIF

Everyone, can we let Summer speak?

SUMMER

Thank you! This is why you're my favorite.

TERRAN

BRB I have a baby gift to return

SUMMER

Okay. Let me get this all out.

One, Max and I got married in Vegas last night.

WEST

Murder is back on the table.

COOPER

It was never off, brother.

SUMMER

STOP

Two: we're taking our honeymoon in Europe!
Um, as we speak!

I sent the same photo I'd sent Indi, which happened to show the Eiffel Tower in the background of my gorgeous ring I couldn't stop staring at. Currently, Max and I were having a very late lunch right in front of it.

TERRAN

Cruz and I could probably get there in ten minutes. West?

West started typing, then stopped, and I held my breath. I didn't really think my brothers would show up, but with three Alpha men whose animals took over, it was anyone's guess.

While I waited, I scrolled back up, trying to see if Aspen had chimed in, but she hadn't said anything yet. It was late morning in Colorado, so maybe she was busy working? Or had she decided it wasn't worth her time to bother commenting?

I hated how much that second thought hurt.

The next text came through in my private thread with West.

WEST

Be honest, are you good?

I couldn't type fast enough, relief whooshing through me. West's protective nature as Alpha of our pack extended beyond just a typical big brother, and his wolf was his own entity — like two souls living under his skin. But I wasn't in danger — yet. Hopefully I could appease both my brother and his wolf.

SUMMER

Pinky promise.

West hearted my response, and I switched back over to the group chat.

I know it's fast, but when you know, you know, right? Maybe this wasn't the wedding I thought I'd have, but Max is great to me and I'm happy and we're having fun. We didn't want to wait to start our adventure together.

There. Not a lie.

I'm happy for you, sweetie. Just promise you'll let your old man celebrate you two when you get back? I can't believe one of my babies is married and I missed it.

I glanced over at Max, frowning at his phone on the other side of the little cast iron table at our sidewalk café. His body language was closed off, but his leg rested against mine under the table, making both my wolf and I elated at the small touch. Without asking, I was sure Max had never experienced the kind of chaos my father's "celebrations" entailed, but I couldn't stop my smile from spreading at the mental image it conjured. We'd cross that bridge when we came to it.

Of course!

Which will be when?

I faltered, since I had no idea when we were returning to Colorado. In fact, I'd asked almost no questions about this whole vampire hunt — were we looking here in Paris? Other cities? Was this just a pit stop because of my bucket list having the Eiffel Tower at the very top, and I'd mentioned it in Vegas? That thought sent little romantic butterflies fluttering in my stomach, but I squashed them, trying to remind myself that this was business, no matter how insane the sex had been last night. Talk about work perks.

SUMMER

I'll let you know!

ASPEN

What's happening with your shop in the meantime?

My heart lurched when her name popped up, and then sank at her words. No congratulations, no support, just pure logic — reminding me of my responsibilities I'd left in the dust.

SUMMER

I have it all squared away with Olive!

That was a total lie, but I was sure she'd be on board to help out longer. And if not, I'd figure it out.

Just then, a giant paragraph came in from Indi, and I quickly flipped over to her chat to avoid seeing my family's response.

INDI

I CAN'T BELIEVE YOU SLEPT WITH HIM.
Nevermind, I totally can, he's super hot. Go you
girl, hot diggity! Also PARIS! Have the absolute
best time! If this marriage is all part of your
track-vamps scheme, tell me EVERYTHING and
if it is real, I swear to God, TELL ME
EVERYTHING. What is vamp sex like? Or
ANGEL sex? By the way, did I know he was a
vamp? I guess I should have with the wings
and all. That makes so much more sense. But
damn, I'm beginning to realize how sheltered I
am, and that's saying something because you
know your girl hasn't been a nun. If vamp/angel
sex wasn't on your bucket list, add it and then
cross it off, because it should have been. Now
I'm kinda curious. Pretty soon you won't have
anything left on that list, but I'm sure after a few
margaritas we can think of some new ideas!

I grinned like a fool as Indi continued to gush with enthusiasm over this turn of events in my life, and I needed it. Indi
was my girl, always there for me. She talked sense into me
when I deserved it, but more often than not, she trusted me to
make my own decisions and hopped right onto whatever my
latest bandwagon was with equal enthusiasm.

SUMMER

I love you, Indi-Go-Go.

INDI

Good because you're stuck with me.

My phone started pinging almost nonstop, so I switched
out of our chat to see private messages coming in from almost
all my family members.

TERRAN

You know I love you, right? If you tell me you're
happy, I'm happy for you.

LEIF

MARRIED?! Wedding pics??

COOPER

Let Russo know if he hurts a hair on your head, he'll never see another day of peace. Nevermind, I'll threaten him myself.

ASPEN

Olive isn't here yet, so I put a sign up on the door. She has a key, right? Heading back to Denver today.

I rolled my eyes.

CRUZ

I've got the keys to your shop sitting right here, and I'll keep an eye on it. Congrats lil sis! Have the best time.

DAD

Ask Max if red velvet is too on the nose for your wedding cake? Or what about death by chocolate?

I bit back a smile.

SUMMER

As long as there's no actual blood, red velvet is great. Thanks, Dad. Miss you!

DAD

Anything for you. And I miss you too, sweetie.

I set my phone down after that, taking a long sip of my *café au lait*, and a bite of my croissant. A kid rushed by on a scooter, his parents following at a leisurely stroll, and for the first time since waking up this afternoon, I let myself take in the fact that I was in Paris.

Chapter Twenty-One

MAX

Summer's phone pinged nonstop with incoming messages as I stared down at my phone, rereading the single text I'd sent this afternoon.

MAX

I have some news, when you have time to talk.

We'd woken up in the late afternoon, starving after our post-sex nap, and I'd texted my father once we'd found a café and ordered sustenance. That was 20 minutes ago.

Summer's shin rubbed against my pant leg, her incessant need to touch me far less annoying today. Switching my phone to my left hand, I dropped my right to her thigh, sliding it under the hem of her skirt just a little. Her breath sucked in, eyes finding mine for a split second before her phone dinged again.

Trailing my thumb across her smooth skin, I scrolled back up through my father's and my brief and utilitarian text exchange over the last several weeks, looking for the last time I'd even heard from him. We'd talked after Boston, and then... nothing.

Clenching my jaw, I bit back my annoyance at his absence, not the first time he'd gone radio silent on me over the years. We weren't as close as the Larkins, but when I was working a job, we checked in every few days. And he usually responded quickly when I reached out.

I wasn't sure how he'd react to Summer's and my spontaneous nuptials, but I also needed him to send over the file on the Parisian news reports about the drained bodies he'd mentioned. Paris wasn't where I'd planned to start this European hunt, but while we were here, we could kill two birds with one stone.

With Summer still busy texting and giggling in turn, I scrolled through the rest of my messages, debating if I had anyone else to tell about our "marriage".

COOPER LARKIN

If you hurt her, you'll never see another day of
peace.

I hid my snort at the mean cat's text, then gave a resigned huff when I realized it was a group chat that also included West and Terran.

MAX

Is this the start of our brotherly bonding?
Should we all FaceTime?

COOPER LARKIN

Not kidding.

MAX

I know, you're threatening me. It's how cats
show their love, right? Next you'll start leaving
dead animals on my doormat. Adorable.

TERRAN LARKIN

Can we maim him just a little, West?

MAX

Listen. I know what you guys think of me, but I
promise —

My thumbs stilled as I realized what I was about to type, but fuck, I meant it. So I continued.

> — I promise, it's not like that. I would never do anything to hurt her.

COOPER LARKIN

> I'll hold you to that.

I set my phone down, glancing over at Summer as she did the same. She let out a little squeak of excitement, kicking her feet under the table and I fought to smother my amusement at how adorable she was.

Adorable was dangerous. A gateway feeling. I squashed the thought right down.

"We're in *Paris!* France!"

"Mmhmm."

"Hurry, we have so much to see!"

I squeezed her thigh. "The first rule in Paris: no rushing. Only enjoying. Relax. We have as much time as we want."

That wasn't exactly true — we needed to find the next vampire den to make contact soon, but there was no harm in a slow day.

Reluctantly, she sat back in her chair and sipped her coffee, giving me a moment to compose my thoughts. First step, get my fucking hands off her.

The loss of contact hummed in my veins when I leaned away, like a dull ache in my chest. How Summer had such an effect on me so quickly, I had no idea, but I ignored the pull to touch her once more.

She gently set the cup down, then took another bite of her croissant, letting out a low moan that reminded me entirely too much of last night.

"This is so freaking good," she mumbled behind her hand, still chewing. A flake drifted down from her lips, falling to the tops of her breasts, exposed by yet another sundress. She wore a red cardigan over a striped dress we'd bought after leaving the apartment, the cut low enough to expose the barest hint of cleavage.

It was classy and cute, not necessarily sexy, but my mind could not separate everything that had happened earlier today from the image of her right now.

I wanted to peel that cardigan off her, remove the thin straps of her dress with my teeth and sink my fangs into her neck again, until I drew out more of those sweet moans.

Fuck adorable. This want, this *need* I was starting to feel for her wasn't just dangerous. It was deadly.

Dropping my gaze to the table, I pricked my own lip with my fangs, the tang of blood not nearly enough to sate me. The thought of her excitedly telling all her friends and family about our fake marriage and fake honeymoon turned my stomach.

For one, when the Larkin males learned the truth about our arrangement and the danger of our mission, I had no doubt they'd come for me.

And two — she truly did seem happy about it, if the grin on her face was anything to go by. That made me feel like the worst asshole in the world.

No matter how much I wanted her, she wasn't mine. She was a temptation I couldn't give in to, a treasure meant for someone other than me. Someone better.

I just wasn't sure I had it in me to let her go.

I shouldn't have been surprised that somewhere between waking up and finishing our coffees, Summer had pulled together a Must-See list of Parisian tourist destinations.

"So, what do you say? Musée D'Orsay first, or do we head to Versailles?" Summer mused, mostly to herself, as she scanned a tourist map of the city she'd picked up on the way over to the café. "That's a little far outside the city though, but you could get us there fast enough. Oh! Notre Dame!"

I shrugged, having seen it all before. "Whichever. We should hit all the main sites."

Summer's eyes brightened, then narrowed in suspicion. "What is this? You're pro-tourism now?"

"The main hotspots are prime vampire hunting grounds, so yes. Let's hit them all."

"What do you mean?"

I waved a hand to encompass the city, resisting the temptation to check my phone for a text that still hadn't come through. "Paris was another one of the cities with drained bodies. Vampires love to prey on tourists, the least likely to have someone notice them missing. We should investigate while we're here."

"Oh." Summer pulled back slightly, her lips tipping down in a small frown for a moment before she plastered a smile on again. "Right, okay. Good idea. To Notre Dame!"

We spent the next few days in a whirlwind of tourism and the best sex of my life. Mornings were spent lazily in bed until Summer was vibrating with excitement for whatever destination she'd picked for us to see. Days were filled with enough tourist stops to put Rick Steves to shame. Nights, vampire hunting, wine tasting, and Summer seeing how far she could push me before I vanished us back to the apartment to devour each other's bodies.

I wasn't complaining.

By day five, there was no part of her I hadn't tasted. Her moans haunted me, her touch set my skin on fire, even the barest hint of gold in her eyes had me nearly feral. I'd never been this gone to lust before, but I couldn't seem to stop myself. And the best part was she met my intensity every single time. I had enough material to fund my spank bank for life.

The only thing we hadn't done was kiss.

Refraining from tasting her lips was supposed to allow me some distance from our relationship, keeping things purely physical. I needed that boundary, no matter how much I hated the rule I'd set for myself. It was too intimate, and I was already falling into what could only be described as an obsession with all things Summer Larkin. My lack of control was frustrating, and so was our fruitless search. We hadn't found anything, not so much as a hint of vampire scent in the air. Half the time, I forgot the whole point of sightseeing was to find vampires, I was so distracted by Summer's enthusiasm for all the history around us. Turned out I was the world's most reluctant tour guide, but I did happen to know the answer to most of her questions.

Once or twice, I thought I felt a prickling at the back of my neck, an uneasiness I couldn't quite pinpoint. But each time, when I looked around, I couldn't see anything out of the ordinary, and Summer didn't mention any odd scents.

Probably just paranoia from decades in my line of work.

Chapter Twenty-Two

SUMMER

"Goddess, why is Paris *so* hot?" I wiped the back of my hand over my forehead and tugged off my linen shirt, wrapping it around my waist. Since we'd come to Paris with quite literally the clothes on our backs, shopping trips had been intermixed with each of our tourist stops, and I now had a small stash of mix-and-match pieces I could layer with ease. Today's outfit was a black form-fitting dress that flared around my legs. I'd paired it with the button-down, white sneakers with red laces, and matching red sunglasses.

Max, on the other hand, wore black. All black. Every day. It shouldn't have been so attractive, and yet the dark fabric clinging to his lean muscles and olive skin had me biting my lip every time I glanced his way.

We'd been wandering the city all morning, my list of top destinations almost complete, and were idling away the afternoon until it was late enough for more vampire hunting.

Max's gaze snapped up, and, to my satisfaction, settled on my now quite exposed cleavage before finally reaching my face. Taunting Max in public places had become one of my cherished Parisian memories. Something about making a badass vampire secret agent blush really warmed my heart.

He cleared his throat. "Heat island effect."

Of course, he knew. I'd come to realize the male was as close as you could get to a walking, talking encyclopedia if you asked the right questions.

Was I a little disappointed Max had brought us to Paris not only to be sweet and romantic, but also for our task? Maybe. But after almost a week here with him, I couldn't find it in me to be mad. It was practical. Logical, even. We'd done far more sightseeing than vampire hunting, and the sex... Goddess, the sex.

I rubbed my legs together at the thought of the orgasms he'd pulled from my body with every tool in his arsenal, leaving me more sated than I'd ever been in my life.

Before Max, I hadn't known sex could be like this, so all consuming. We moved together like we'd been doing this for years, not days, the intensity of every single touch almost alarming. I wasn't sure how I'd ever give this up.

His fingers trailed over my shoulder, the inky mark his magic had left on me expanding to cover more of my back. A shiver ran down my spine, that same *need* kicking in again, but today I was on a mission.

We rounded a corner, and there it was. The Eiffel Tower, the object of countless paintings and photographs and poems, and below it, the equally iconic Champ-de-Mars park.

Subconsciously, I'd been saving this one, this picture-perfect spot.

I took a breath, allowing myself to momentarily forget my job here with Max and appreciate this moment for *me*. I had wanted to see this in person for as long as I could remember, since I needed a stepstool to help my mom in the kitchen. She'd worked in a bakery in Paris for a year before marrying my dad, and she'd always said she wanted to take me one day, that we could visit together. Now, I was finally here, fulfilling at least part of that dream, whatever circumstances had made it happen.

I made it, Mom. And I'm going to do all the other things we planned, too. One by one, I'll do them for us.

Tears gathered in my eyes, a mixture of happy and sad, and I blinked them away.

I scrunched my nose, pushing my sunglasses up on my head as I looked up. The tower rose above me high into the sky, surrounded by the picturesque buildings, ancient trees and colorful awnings over shop stores making everything seem *more*. I could picture my mom here, could feel her arms around me as she hugged me tight for the last time.

Wrapping my own arms around my waist, I breathed in the slightly smoggy air, savoring this moment.

It was everything I'd thought it would be, and so much more. So much grander. I could practically feel the history in the air, in the soils beneath my feet, and I couldn't hold back the awestruck *incroyable* that slipped from my lips.

Max stood just to my right, hands in his pockets, but I could feel his eyes on me, not the magnificent Parisian scene around us. I cleared my throat and dabbed discreetly at my eyes.

"C'mon, I want to sit and wait for sunset." I nodded towards the park.

A red-striped awning caught my attention as I walked towards the park, and I grinned. "*Je voudrais une glace, s'il vous plaît,*" I said in my best French accent, pointing at the ice cream shop. "I can't be in France and not have ice cream."

"Once again, Italy wins."

I rolled my eyes. "Don't remember asking for your opinion. I think I'll test that theory on my own. Let's get some and watch the lights come on."

Knowing he'd follow, I took off, walking through the open double doors into a quaint parlor, the glass cases calling my name. A whole rainbow of colors drew my eyes as I scanned my options. Some of the words I recognized from when I'd studied French, so I ordered a scoop of pistachio for myself and blood orange for Max, for obvious reasons.

He shot me a flat stare, but accepted the bright red cone nonetheless and paid for us, since he was the only one with Euros.

Cones in hand, I led the way to a spot towards the back of the park where we'd have a good view of the tower, unfolded my shirt as a blanket, and plopped down.

"Hold this?" I asked Max as I handed him my ice cream, then pulled a red scrunchie out of my bag and drew my hair back into a high ponytail. "There, that's better."

I smiled at him as I took my cone back, hearing the slight uptick in his heart rate as his eyes bounced between my face, my ponytail, and my cleavage, then back again.

How far could I push him? And what was with the no kissing thing? We'd both had our mouths all over each other, everywhere *except* on our lips since our wedding ceremony.

Did I hate it? No. Far from it.

But I also hadn't been this worked up over a man ever, really. I wanted him to kiss me, or at least feel as out of control as I did.

Leaning back on one hand, I *slightly* arched my back as I licked my sorbet in slow motion, swirling my tongue around for good measure, and let out a low moan.

"*Mon dieu,* I'm not sure Italy can live up to this. I just love the taste of nuts and cream."

Max coughed, turning his head to the side and I smirked, taking another slow lick when he recovered.

"How's yours?"

Max said nothing, so I turned to look at him while I licked my cone again. His dark eyes were glued to my mouth, hardly blinking, as his blood red sorbet began to drip down his hand.

Perfect.

I couldn't hold back my grin as I nodded towards his cone. "Careful there, you're making a mess."

He cleared his throat and took a *bite* of his sorbet, the

barest hint of his fangs protruding before sinking into the side of the cone. I scrunched my nose in horror.

"Have you never had ice cream before, you barbarian? You lick it, like this." I dragged my tongue across the cold cream, circling it as I got to the top, sucking just the tip.

The look he gave me could only be described as hungry, and I. Was. Elated. Pushing his buttons had quickly become my favorite past time.

Despite the cool sorbet, his voice was gravel when he spoke. "Efficiency. This is way too sweet. The only way I'm getting this sugar down is if I swallow it whole."

"How interesting, I also have no gag reflex."

Max missed his next bite, the red scoop dropping off his cone and landing with a *plop* between his legs. He looked down at the mess he'd made, then back at me.

"Shame. You could use a little sweetness." I shot him a sugary smile, then went back to people watching. Couples strolled through the park as streetlights came on, pausing to take selfies, everyone seeming so happy and in love it was almost as sweet as the ice cream in my hand.

I pointed out cute puppies and adorable toddlers, but Max didn't look around much. He was watching *me*, the dark look in his eyes gaining intensity with every swipe of my tongue over my cone, just like I wanted.

Finally, the sun sank below the horizon, and the tower lit up. Twinkling lights shimmered against the dark sky, and I gasped in delight.

"It's so magical!" I breathed, just as the last drop of ice cream landed on my chest. I couldn't have timed it better if I'd tried. The lights sparkled beautifully, casting my boobs with the perfect shadows. I chuckled and swiped my finger through the drop. "Oops," I said, smiling at Max as I put my finger in my mouth and sucked.

His jaw flexed, and in a blink, his fingers gripped my pony-tail as he tossed the rest of our cones away.

Eyes flashing with the inky shadows of his magic, his lips grazed my ear as he purred, "You want to play, little wolf?"

Before I could respond, shadows consumed us and he pinned me to the ground.

My back arched off the cold grass from his hold on my hair, my mouth falling open as his lips trailed down my neck and to my chest.

"Is this what you wanted?" Max asked, the low rumble of his voice sending a wash of heat to my low belly.

I opened my mouth to answer, but the sound that left me was more of a moan than a word. His teeth grazed over my nipple through my dress as a warm palm slid up the inside of my thigh. The light touch was enough to have my body shaking, need consuming me just like it had so many times the last few days.

My hips shifted, making his hand slide further up my thigh until his fingertips grazed across the thin fabric of my thong. Maybe I should have been embarrassed by how wet I already was, but Max's smirk only made me squirm more. "Should I fuck you right here out in the open? Hidden only by the shadows around us? Is that what you want, sunshine?"

That was way hotter than it had any business being, the idea of being so exposed. I tried to nod, but his grip on my ponytail made it impossible. The smallest bite of pain was enough to have my fingers grappling in the fabric of his shirt, desperate to feel his skin.

"Use your words, *wife*." The shadows around us darkened until I couldn't see the Eiffel Tower in front of me, nor the people around us. His fingers trailed across my shadowmark on my neck, and my mouth tipped open, desperation setting in.

My nails dug into his skin, wanting him to feel that same bite of pain I did. To know how bad I needed this. He hissed, his teeth grazing the side of my neck, teasing a bite in my imminent future.

Heat washed across my back, magic humming in my veins as it rippled through my blood, my heart racing at the tiny touch. "I want you so fucking bad."

That deep chuckle made me squirm that much more, his hands drifting down my side and lifting the hem of my skirt. "What should I do about that, then?"

His fingers dipped beneath the elastic of my thong, lifting it to let a cool breeze dance across my skin that had me gasping. I arched, preparing for the feel of him on me when he snapped the fabric back in place. The small sting made me gasp again, my eyes flying open.

My wolf was riding me hard, the desperation for him primal in a way I could hardly explain. I didn't just want Max. I *needed* him. "Kiss me, *husband*."

His head snapped up, eyes rimmed in red as his fangs descended, glistening in the low light. I squeezed his sides, nails digging into his skin as he lowered his face towards mine. My heart could win a freaking marathon with how fast it raced, wanting this more than I'd ever wanted anything.

"Is that what you want?" His eyes focused on my mouth, his tongue licking over his bottom lip as he closed the gap between us. "What made you so wet?"

My breath sawed in and out of me as I gave him the smallest nod. "Yes."

His eyes met mine once more as a slow smile spread over his face, as dangerous a look as any I'd ever seen him wear. He leaned down, his body pinning mine to the grass as I closed my eyes, holding him tight enough to keep him here.

With the barest touch of his lips on mine, he whispered, "I warned you I love to tease."

My eyes snapped open as cold licked across my skin. He

vanished us from the city and back to the apartment, landing us in the middle of his bed.

Backing away, Max stood to his full height as he slowly unbuttoned his shirt, smirking at the way he'd left me flushed and panting. I pushed to my elbows to watch him, not bothering to hide the way my eyes trailed every movement of his hands, every inch of skin he exposed.

"Lie back, wife," he commanded, dropping his shirt completely. "And if you can stay very still, I'll let you come."

I laughed, but lay back as requested. "*Let* me, is it?"

One knee on the bed, Max shifted the skirt of my dress up again, so slowly I wanted to rip it off myself. But we'd been together enough times for me to know that he meant what he said, so I kept still. I sat up when he went to pull it off, and he dropped it beside the bed. His dark eyes roamed me hungrily, then lowered to the space between my legs.

His finger trailed the delicate fabric of the thong, peeling it down my legs.

"So fucking wet for me," he murmured, more to himself than to me. "So fucking perfect."

My core had a pulse of its own, and my hips moved before I could stop myself, pushing up towards him.

He clicked his tongue, shooting me an admonishing look, then his arm dropped over my hips, pinning me down. Lips grazed my inner thigh, then my hip, my stomach. I caught a glint of fang, then my bra ripped and fell away, but his mouth closed over my nipple before I could complain. My nerves lit up as he nipped, sucked, and kissed every sensitive spot on my body. But he still gave me no attention where I wanted it, no friction where I was desperate for it.

"Max —" I panted, and he chuckled, licking over the wound.

"Yes, dear?"

I glared at him, and he licked a drop of blood from his lips.

"You're so gorgeous like this, wife. All spread out and wanton for me."

Finally, *finally*, his thumb grazed my clit, and I gasped at the contact. He circled it lightly, and I whimpered in relief, trying to push up against his arm for more but his grip held me firm.

My eyes squeezed shut as my peak approached. Right before I went over the edge, he pulled back, chuckling at my whimper.

"I thought you wanted me to kiss you. Well, I am." He pressed another soft kiss at the seam of my hips, and I hissed out a breath.

I could have taken matters into my own hands, but Goddess, he was sexy like this. A little dark and sinister and commanding. I loved every second of it, every moment wondering what he would do next.

In my blissed-out state, I must have missed when he stripped off the rest of his clothes. The next moment, he was on top of me again, gloriously naked, wings spread wide.

He lined himself up with me and sank inside in one stroke, both of us groaning at the contact. I was so close already, I was vibrating before he even started to thrust.

"You're doing beautifully, sunshine," he breathed in my ear, and that was enough. The next thrust, I shattered just as his fangs sank into my neck, ratcheting my pleasure even higher. His hips lost their smooth rhythm, moving faster as his breath sawed in and out. Just when I thought I couldn't take any more, Max pulled out, his head tilted back as my blood dripped off his fangs. I couldn't decide whether to focus on his face or the hand moving over his cock as he finished on my stomach, and I swear I could have come again just from the sight of it.

What the hell was happening to me?

Chapter Twenty-Three

MAX

"Okay, if I were a shady vampire duke, where would I make my nest?" Summer tapped her chin in thought as she peered over the map spread across her lap. Her long, tanned legs stretched out in front of her, the city's twinkling lights illuminating her face.

That jaunty ponytail swished as she twisted and turned the map, her bottom lip pinched between her teeth. My hands itched to reach over and free it, or better yet, cover her lips with mine like she'd asked me to an hour ago.

Fuck, I wanted to, but I couldn't bring myself to do it.

Back in the park, Summer's every moan and lick snapped what little control I had, but at least I'd kept myself from giving in to her demands. By the time I had her underneath me on my bed, she'd forgotten all about her request as I brought her to orgasm.

After a short nap and a shower each, we'd moved to the patio for some much needed fresh air and to regroup.

The fact that we hadn't found *anything* on the vampire den in Paris was getting downright annoying. Between the pointed news cast and the size of the city, it was impossible there wasn't a den here. So why couldn't we find it?

Was it this thing between us, this magnetic attraction distracting us at every freaking turn? Because I'd never had this much trouble on a job. Not in a hundred years.

I'd been to Paris dozens of times both alone and with my

father, but experiencing it these past few days with Summer was another thing entirely. She had an opinion and a reaction to everything, and that damn ice cream cone... I'd never forget it.

I leaned over, trying not to notice how my chest brushed her shoulder and her subsequent intake of breath, and pointed to a section of the map.

"Let's try the college quarter," I murmured. "Dumb drunk college kids always make for an easy buffet, and they don't think twice when they wake up the next morning and can't remember what happened."

Summer's eyes were on my lips, then jerked back to the map. "Yep, exactly that." Hastily folding up the map, she headed inside, quickly grabbing her purse and a new pair of high heels to head out again.

Standing, I followed behind her, unable to ignore the sashay in her hips as she strolled ahead of me. Hips I had been gripping only an hour ago from behind, while her ponytail bounced with every thrust.

I adjusted myself in my pants, grabbed my jacket, and followed her out into the night. The temperature had cooled considerably since earlier, so I wrapped my leather jacket around her lightly shivering shoulders.

"Oh — thanks." She glanced up in surprise before sliding her arms into the sleeves. "I meant to grab mine but I forgot."

"I noticed."

Before long, we traded the residential atmosphere where my apartment was for college kids partying out on the town. Dance music drifted out from every corner bar and cigarette smoke hung heavy in the air.

"Let's grab a drink," Summer said, pointing at the closest bar, a small line forming outside highlighting its popularity in the neighborhood.

I grabbed her hand, peering over the crowd for any

lingering shadows or recognizable faces. "Do you already smell something?"

"Not yet, but we should blend in." Summer leaned back, pressing her back to my chest and tilting her head up to look at me. She fit perfectly against me, and I tugged her closer, unable to stop myself. "And I might need a top-up. For the magic." She winked, then ducked inside.

A low growl escaped me at the memory of her sucking the blood off my finger in that club in Boston, and I was right on her heels.

Inside the bar, the scent of beer and sweaty bodies permeated so strongly, I wasn't sure how Summer expected to smell anything else, but she had in Boston, so maybe she could again. We wove our way through the mass of bodies to the wood-paneled bar, pushed closer by the crowd. Summer stood on her tiptoes to lean over the counter and shoved her tits out, smiling coquettishly at the bartender. The guy practically drooled as he rushed over, and I fought back an eye roll.

Stepping forward, I slid one hand under my jacket Summer still wore, settling on her hip. I held up two fingers on my left hand, showcasing my wedding band as I leaned over to order our drinks. "*Soixante-Quinze.*"

"Subtle." Summer smirked as the bartender's smile melted then went to make our drinks.

I squeezed her hip before I let her go. "You started it."

She spun towards me, leaning back against the bar as she fluttered a hand over her chest in mock affront. "I was trying to get service."

"He wanted to *service* you, all right."

The bartender returned with our drinks, and Summer held hers aloft.

"To wedded bliss," Summer said with a twinkle in her eyes as she tapped her glass to mine.

"*Salut.*" I tipped up my drink, taking a long sip but never taking my eyes off her. She stared at my throat working for several beats before taking a sip of her own.

Our gazes locked, neither one willing to back down. The loud music faded to a dull roar, the crowd blurring as my focus zeroed in on her, time slowing around us.

"Quit looking at me before we end up fucking in public again," Summer said decisively, dropping her eyes to our drinks and breaking the moment. "Spike my drink so we can get to work, will you?"

I nearly choked on my drink as I glanced around to make sure no one overheard her, but the lively music and myriad conversations made it too loud for humans to make out our words.

Stepping in close, Summer was forced to tilt her head up and look at me. I leaned in, my cheek brushing against hers as I whispered, "Did you learn nothing, sunshine?"

With a shake of her head, Summer pulled back. "You really are such a prude."

She grabbed my hand, presumably to go find somewhere private, but I froze, something prickling in my awareness again, like it had a few times this week.

My head jerked around the room as I did a quick scan, but couldn't pinpoint what had drawn my attention. Nothing seemed out of the ordinary, just college kids having a night out, but my gut instincts rarely steered me wrong.

Summer whirled on me, then stilled at my expression. "Do *you* sense something?"

"I thought" — I frowned, unsure how to explain it — "I don't know. But I think we might've been followed."

Her gaze snapped up, fully focused now as she surveyed the room like the predator she also was. "By who? A vampire?"

I lifted a shoulder, my senses still on high alert but trying to appear unaffected, just in case we were being watched. "I'm not sure. Just a feeling."

Discreetly, Summer lifted her head, her nostrils flaring ever so slightly as she tried to scent in this busy room. "I don't smell one."

Swallowing, I licked my lips, my eyes unconsciously dropping to Summer's mouth. If someone was watching us, following us, we needed to be subtle. Lure them out of here without their knowledge, get somewhere easier to confront them.

And we might not have long to do so.

Fuck it.

My hand went to the back of her head, and I brought my lips to hers. Swallowing down her soft gasp of surprise, she opened for me, leaning into me like this was where she belonged.

This kiss was intoxicating, just like our first, and I was lost to the heady sensation flowing through my veins. I simultaneously remembered *why* I'd made kissing off limits, and hated myself for denying us both.

Only that same prickling sense of being watched kept me focused, from pushing her into a dark corner where I could vanish us back to my apartment again.

My fangs descended and I let her feel them against her tongue, sending a shiver through her body. Nicking my own tongue with them, I pushed it into her mouth and groaned when she sucked.

She whimpered, clawing at my shirt as my blood hit her system, that same drunken haze taking over like it had in Boston. I pulled back, wiping the corner of my lips with my thumb and drawing my fangs back up.

Summer's pupils were wide, rimmed in her wolf's golden hue. She panted heavily, her face and chest flushed with the rush and arousal. Her eyes kept going to my lips, and it took all my restraint not to wrench her to me again and keep going.

My blood drove her wild, and I fucking loved it.

But we had a job to do here.

"Summer, focus. Scent."

With a deep inhale, she closed her eyes for a moment. Her fingers still gripped my shirt, my hands still held her waist, but neither of us seemed capable of pulling away.

After a few beats, her eyes snapped open, her wolf's gold fully replacing her usual hazel. Looping a hand around my neck, she pulled me down until her lips were at my ear. "We have company."

I skimmed my hands up her waist, tightening my fingers like I had so many times this week. "Vampire?"

She arched her back, her chest pressing into mine deliciously as she nodded against my cheek.

My dick was hardening in my jeans, and I realized at some point I'd slid one thigh between Summer's legs. Fuck.

Exhaling slowly, I forced myself to focus. One of us had to be lucid, and with Summer blood-drunk, that role fell to me. I gave her ponytail a quick tug — part of the ruse, I told myself, but it worked against me more than her as her soft gasp reached my ears — then dropped my hand to hers, leading her back towards the entrance.

Pushing through the crowd at the door, I leaned in close when we were a block or so away. "Still scent them?"

"Yes."

I risked a glance over my shoulder at the crowded road, streetlights shining down except for.... There, to our left — a shadow, moving almost imperceptibly closer.

My blood boiled as I appraised the situation, coming up with a plan. Fucker thought they could sneak up on us? On *me*, another vampire? A growl built in my throat, and I pulled Summer into a dark alley a little harder than I intended.

She yelped, stumbling over the cobblestones in her high heels, but caught her balance quickly. Her eyes glittered as she grinned at me, lust clouding her gaze. "Do that shadow thing again so we don't have to waste —"

Shadow caught the corner of my eye a second before it reached her. I shoved her behind me and called up my own shadow, reinforcing it with lightning. Wrapping it around the stalker, I shoved them against the wall with an audible *oomph*.

"What do you want?" I demanded, my hand firmly around their neck.

"Calm yer tits, Russo," the vampire answered with a Scottish lilt.

I reared back, a wave of shock rolling through me that a vampire had used my real name, not *Dante*. I'd never met a Scottish vampire before, and certainly none that knew my real identity. Slamming him against the brick again, I snarled, "Who are you, and why are you following us?"

Before me, the vampire allowed their shadow to dissolve, revealing a male I'd never met, but who clearly thought he knew me.

He had slightly messy dark blond hair, and was dressed for a night out in Paris — his dark shirt unbuttoned just a little too far, tucked into crisp suit pants. He was big, almost my height but stockier, but I still had no doubt I could take him with my added angel powers.

Amused green eyes flicked between me and Summer, and the fucker tilted his head in some mockery of a bow. "If you'd kindly stop strangling me, we have some things to discuss, Massimo."

I tightened my grip around his neck, my lips peeling back in a snarl, but he only laughed in my face, his fangs shining in the lamplight. "I asked you a question, and I don't repeat myself."

"Rhain Allaway, pleased to meet you. I've been trying to reach you about your car's extended warranty."

Chapter Twenty-Four

MAX

Tension thrummed in the air as shadows swirled around us, blocking the alleyway from views of any passersby.

I had one hand coiled around Rhain's neck, my magic bound tight around us, and kept an eye out for Summer beside me. She blinked rapidly, likely trying to clear the effects of my blood from her senses, but for now all I needed was for her to stay back.

"Why are you following us?" I asked, trying to figure out why his name sounded familiar. He said it with such easy confidence, like I should recognize his name, if not his face. Not for the first time, I was frustrated by how much my father kept me in the dark over vampire affairs and the key players.

Rhain's green eyes slid to Summer and he shot her a wink. I growled and slammed him back against the wall again, *hard*, eliciting a low chuckle out of him. Who the fuck cared if he was someone important? She was my wife, and he would *not* be winking at her.

"Don't look at her. Look at me. And start fucking talking."

Rhain raised his hands in surrender and grinned. He didn't seem bothered in the least about the threat I posed.

"Don't worry, mate. You two have marked each other in ways that cannot be denied — I know she's yours. As for who *I* am" — he waggled his fingers, drawing my attention to a ring on his index finger — "do you not know what this is?"

I looked down at his hand, recognizing the gold band and

the scrolling text along the side, a symbol of vampiric power and status. His had a large emerald, whereas Grigor's was a sapphire. "You're a duke. That excuses nothing."

"The *Scottish* duke," Rhain corrected.

"Max." Summer laid a hand on my shoulder. "I don't think he's a threat."

Rhain's cocky smile faded, and I could have kissed Summer for the underhanded diss she'd just laid out. "I could be a threat."

I clenched my jaw, ignoring him and looked over my shoulder at Summer. "Never underestimate a vampire. It's all an act, just what he wants you to think."

She raised her brows, a silent comment that I wasn't much different, then waved her hand towards Rhain in a silent request to let him go.

I gave Rhain another glare before dropping my hand from around his neck, though I kept the shadows binding him.

He cleared his throat and rolled his head, stretching his neck. "Much better. If we're done with the violence for the evening, we can move on to the conniving."

Summer crossed her arms over her chest, stepping up so she pressed lightly into my side. A silent show of solidarity from a wolf, and one I found myself surprised to relish. "Conniving?"

"Conspiring. Scheming. Colluding."

I scowled. "I don't think her issue was with the definition."

"Right, apologies." Rhain chuckled, then his expression took on a sharp edge. "Haven't you heard? We're planning a coup. The Conclave's days are numbered, and it's time for you to tag in, sonny boy."

A pulse seemed to vibrate through the sultry Parisian air with his words, dots on an invisible map forming I struggled to connect with the little information I had on vampires and their politics.

In a low voice, I asked, "Who's we?"

Rhain smirked, like he knew he'd hooked us. "Want to come see? I'll answer all your little questions and then some."

"You'll answer my questions, now, or we go back to the strangling."

Rhain rolled his eyes before glancing at Summer. "He always like this?"

I fought the skitter of electricity over my skin that itched for an outlet, and Summer pursed her lips. "He has one mode: intense. It's probably better you just explain yourself."

Rhain brushed a hand over his jaw, glancing at the entrance to the alleyway before letting out a deep sigh. "My den is part of Project Oleander, a secret coalition that is working with your father to overthrow the Conclave. I made contact with Malachi a few weeks ago, scheduling a meeting for last week here in Paris. He didn't show up and I haven't been able to reach him. After our first contact, he laid out very specific protocols if such a thing were to happen, which at the time I thought were outrageous. Yet here I am, following that protocol to bring you in. Now, if you don't mind, I'd much rather discuss this over a pint, wouldn't you?"

I kept a neutral expression, but my shoulders tensed even further at Rhain's declaration.

Project Oleander.

I hadn't heard that name in a hundred years, and a flood of memories resurfaced from my youth. My father had never been one to sit on the floor and play with me, but I'd never hurt for his attention either. He set up elaborate schemes and riddles, coded in different languages I'd have to learn to solve them. I learned to read maps, find clues, follow leads, track predators, and use both my shadows and lightning powers to my advantage, all preparing me for a life at his side.

Oleander had always been the ultimate game: a game of life or death. It had always required me to use everything I'd learned, and lives were at stake if I failed. At the time, I'd thought it was all pretend, a chance to let a child be a super-hero like we all wanted. But now the memories were different, the lives I'd saved more realistic. Tangible. Like maybe it hadn't been a game at all.

Even if it seemed far-fetched for my father to be working with a vampire coup, *Oleander* couldn't be a coincidence. This had to be what Malachi had meant when he said he had reason to believe not all vampires supported the Conclave.

Why couldn't he have just *told* me about this?

The riddles and games had been fun as a child, but I was sick of it now. Like everything in my life, he kept me close but in the dark just enough to make me feel adrift, expecting me to figure it out as I went. But now, so far removed from the days when his games had made me feel wanted and special, I felt used. Felt groomed to be the tool he needed. Felt lost, with no sense of my identity outside of the weapon he'd formed me into.

I shoved the familiar ache away, down in the depths of the well of emotions I kept locked up tight.

"When was the last time you heard from him?" I asked, an inkling of worry sinking in, thinking over all my own unan-swered calls and texts from Malachi lately. Not answering me was rare, but it wasn't the first time. Not answering business associates, and ones leading a potential coup at that? Unheard of.

"It's been two weeks now."

Fuck.

Summer moved to step forward, but I shifted my weight, blocking her. Until we knew more, I was staying between the two of them. She was my wife, mine to protect — I would not let Rhain grab her and vanish both of them away in the blink of an eye, destination untraceable.

"What do you mean, working with Malachi?" Summer

asked. "Is the Council involved in this coup? Does West know about this? If he does, he hasn't mentioned it."

Rhain tilted his head back in a pout, whining, "Still, with the alleyway questions?"

"You were watching the apartment." My eyes narrowed as things clicked into place, the puzzle pieces forming in my head just like they always did. "That's how you knew we were here, and have been following us?"

"Technically, it wasn't *me* watching the apartment, but yes, it was being watched."

"By whom, then?"

"Étienne Dubois — well, one of his people."

At our lack of reaction, Rhain scoffed. "Do you know anything about the European vampires? You're in his territory. He's the duke of the Paris den. Luckily for you, Étienne isn't too fond of the Conclave, so he hasn't reported *Dante's* arrival as unannounced. Best introduce yourself quickly and pay your respects before he changes his mind."

Rhain raised his eyebrows pointedly, and it didn't escape my notice that he referred to me by my other identity. Somehow, Rhain knew who I was, but my secret was still intact with the rest of the vampires here.

"And Dubois is one of the other dukes involved in this coup?"

"Yes," Rhain breathed in exasperation. "Dubois, me, and others, who happen to be meeting tonight to discuss said coup, which is why I decided to bring you in. Came to get you myself, mind. Not just anyone gets a duke for an escort." He winked at Summer again, and my hands curled into fists.

"Why should I trust you? That you're not just leading us into a trap to kill us?"

"Other than, I could have killed you without you ever sensing me?" Rhain snorted. "Fine. Malachi said if this situation ever arose, to remind you blood is thicker than water."

I started, trying to mask my surprise.

"*Il sangue non e acqua, my boy*," I'd heard my father say a thousand times when I was a child. I could practically feel his fingers running through my dark hair, calming me when I would get frustrated with my shadow powers, or my mother's absence. "*Blood is thicker than water. You are* my *son, and that's what matters.*"

Between Oleander and now this, I couldn't deny my father's involvement. There was no reason for Rhain to use that exact phrase.

Rhain must have noticed the tension leaving me, because he nodded decisively.

"Now, about that pint."

Twenty minutes later, we'd crossed the Seine and were in a much nicer area farther from the city center, and entered another bar.

This one was less college vibe, more upscale; every man in an expensive, tailored suit and every woman in a silky dress. By contrast, all three of us were woefully underdressed, even Rhain, who'd known he was coming here.

Rhain attempted to put a hand on Summer's shoulder, and I swatted him away. He smirked but leaned in anyway. "Personally, I find Dubois' taste a little stuffy. Someday you should come see my pub near Edinburgh." His eyes glittered with amusement. "We'll have a great time."

I shot him a glare he received with a grin, then strode through the dining room like he owned the place. He shot a salute to the bartender, who nodded back, and moved to a private room in the back. I stuck to Summer like glue, my hand on her lower back, not willing to part from her for a second until we knew what we were walking into, regardless of the meager trust Rhain might have earned.

Summer slipped off my jacket now we were inside, handing it back to me. I couldn't help but stare at her shadowmark, larger than earlier today. Vine tendrils snaked further across and down her back, flowers and stars sprouting outward from where it had begun at her shoulder blade. It covered at least a quarter of her back now, and the sight filled me with dread and fierce possessiveness in equal measure.

"Allaway, what took you so long?" a French-accented voice called.

Rhain spread his arms wide. "A little disagreement, but we're sorted now."

A man in a sharp navy suit stood, grasping Rhain's hand and clapping him on the back. An inch or two shorter than Rhain, who was nearly my height, he had the slightly tan Mediterranean complexion many French did, making Rhain look positively pale. His posture was relaxed, his eyes sharp and calculating in the predatory way typical of vampires, but it was his calm confidence that betrayed his true strength. A self-assurance we weren't a threat to him, whoever we were, that said he was not a vampire to cross.

"This is them?" the man, presumably Étienne Dubois, asked as Rhain moved aside, leaving room for us to step forward.

"*Oui.*" Rhain gestured to us. "Dante, and his wife, Summer Larkin."

Summer's back stiffened under my hand, and I couldn't resist pulling her closer to me. If they'd been following us since we arrived here, no doubt they'd done their homework to find out who we were, but hearing it put so blatantly clearly startled her.

"Étienne Dubois." He held out a hand, and I shook it. "Pleasure to meet you at last, Dante. *Et demoiselle, enchanté.*" He pulled Summer in before she had a second to react, air-kissing her cheeks.

"Oh," Summer gasped, then chuckled, rolling with the custom easily, though my chest warmed as she leaned back into me when they finished. "Nice to meet you, too."

Étienne clapped his hands together. "*Alors*, we have much to discuss. Please, have a seat, *et Vincent!*" He called over to the bartender, already making his way over with a tray of drinks. "*Ah, oui*, okay, have a drink, have a seat. Ah! These are some of the others in my den —" He waved around at the other vampires here with us, rapid-fire introducing them, but it was a blur of French names.

Summer and I found seats and accepted glasses of wine from the bartender. When everyone had a drink, Étienne raised his own glass.

"*Vive la révolution, non?*" His eyes twinkled with humor, but the others joined him, raising their glasses too then clinking with their neighbors before drinking. "What tradition we have in this city."

Long live the revolution, indeed.

Chapter Twenty-Five

SUMMER

I shivered as Max delicately traced his fingers over my shoulder, trying to focus as Étienne described his operation so far.

As we'd followed Rhain through the city, I'd felt the hum of magic tingling along my skin and suspected it meant the shadowmark had grown from our latest blood exchange. Now, as Max's fingers drew swirls and spirals across my skin, lower with each swipe, I was sure of it.

His touch was distracting, feeding off the last of the blood-drunk haze in my system, making me remember just how it felt to have his hands all over me. Suddenly, my mind was right back in his apartment, sprawled beneath him as he bit into my upper thigh, ecstasy bowing my back off the bed. My nostrils flared, my body nearly vibrating with excess energy until Max's hand lifted off my shadowmark.

"Larkin, right lass?" Rhain's whispered voice cut through my thoughts, pulling me back to the present. His lips pursed together to stifle a grin, as if he knew just where my mind had been.

Now that Max's hand wasn't on my shadowmark, the blood high was fading quickly, thankfully. The last thing I needed was to be blood-drunk in the middle of a dozen vampires. Again.

I nodded, reaching behind me to lace my fingers with Max's hand hanging at his side, curious to see if it was touching my shadowmark that left me so unraveled, or just his touch at all. He squeezed my palm, and instantly I was more alert, more centered, more focused. "That's right."

"As in, West Larkin, from Timber Creek."

"As in, *Summer* Larkin, from Timber Creek," I corrected, doing little to hide my annoyance at once again being pegged as West Larkin's little sister. "But yes, those Larkins."

Rhain leaned back in his hair, crossing his arms over his chest. "I met your brother once."

"I have multiple brothers, so that doesn't exactly narrow it down."

Rhain chuckled, but with each passing minute of Max's hand in mine and Rhain's simple conversation, the blood haze faded, and I felt like myself again.

"The scary one," he whispered. "I hate cats."

I chuckled at the idea of Cooper being scary. To most, he was. He towered over almost everyone, and had a deepset frown that screamed *don't fuck with me, I'm former Special Ops.* But to me, Cooper was still the shy, awkward brother I'd grown up with. Always on the outskirts of trouble, but never far enough he couldn't swoop in and save us — mostly Terran, or Terran and me — when we went too far.

I glanced around the room, trying to think like Coop would in this situation. We'd wanted to find vampires tonight — well, mission accomplished.

As the Alpha's daughter, and then, later, the Alpha's sister, I was used to observing from the sidelines, gathering information from body language and posturing even more than from the words spoken. In fact, it was one of the primary jobs of the Alpha's family in the pack — monitoring the other members to watch my brother's back.

Sipping my wine, my gaze drifted across the several dozen vampires here, both seated around the room and leaning against the wall. Most of them were Étienne's, and it was clear they respected him — leaning forward, bodies turned towards him, listening intently, nodding along with his words.

My only other experience with a group this large had been the orgyfest in Boston, but this wasn't the same.

There, lust had ruled the room even more so than Grigor from his lame golden throne. Here, there was a palpable eagerness in the group, a frisson of electricity that skittered through them. These vampires weren't here for sex or bloodlust. They were ready to take action, ready to get to work and overthrow the Conclave.

"Leading those news crews to a dead body in *my territory* was the last straw," Étienne seethed, his fist clenched as he pounded it on the table. Anger rolled off him in waves, so different from the man who'd welcomed me into the room. I sat up straighter, listening as other vampires listed their complaints against the Conclave.

"But certainly not the first," added a female seated near him, her blue eyes flashing to red as she spoke. "They took my sister's husband for a pet, only because he is human. We don't even know if he's still alive."

"My friend, a bear-shifter, went missing a year ago," a male spoke up from where he stood against the wall. "Best we could tell, they took him and sold him to some shady supe fighting ring."

The hairs on the back of my neck pricked up, something about that ringing a bell. "A fight ring? Where?"

The male shrugged. "Who knows? I've heard somewhere out in the American west, but they could have moved by now."

Out west. My stomach turned over at the thought it might be anywhere near Timber Creek.

"I had to flee my home," another, a younger female, added. "After one of the bodies made the national headlines, local news ran wild, theorizing about vampires being real too since 'werewolves' are. Everyone and their neighbor set up cameras all over town, trying to catch a vampire in the act. I didn't feel safe anymore." She set her jaw. "I just want to live my life."

The others nodded along with each story, like they had similar stories themselves or had heard these things from many others before.

"Enough is enough," Étienne said with a nod, bringing the meeting back around. "The Conclave's ironclad rule of our species is done. It's time for a new world for our species, and for equal representation like the others have on the Council."

Rhain, for all his practiced nonchalance, was equally as invested in these plans. He leaned back in his red leather chair next to me, arm thrown wide across the empty chair to his left, but his finger tapping his ring against the wooden frame gave him away. He was just as impatient for change.

"When the Conclave called for an assembly, Rhain tried to reach out to Malachi, to see if he had heard anything about it," Étienne continued, drawing my attention back to him. "Only, he has not heard back."

Max's fingers tensed in mine, a thrum of energy pulsing up my arm at his unease. He hadn't shared much about his relationship with his father, but he also hadn't mentioned speaking to him lately. The hair on my arms stood on end and my foot started tapping impatiently, trying to read the blank expression on Max's face.

He looked relaxed — shoulders down, slightly slumped back in his chair, a small smirk playing on his lips like he knew something the rest of us didn't — but there was a storm brewing in his dark eyes I couldn't look away from. It was gone as quickly as it appeared, his thumb sliding over my hand as if to reassure *me* he was okay.

"And then you two show up at his apartments," Rhain added, gesturing to us. "Dante, the one person Malachi told me to watch for, falling right into our laps. Except you didn't seek us out like I thought you would, instead gallivanting around Paris and having quite a grand time" — he winked — "which leads us to wonder what the hell is going on."

Max's hand stilled. "What do you mean?"

Étienne and Rhain exchanged a glance. "Have *you* heard from Malachi?"

I tilted my head. "You think he's missing?" Another shared glance, confirming my suspicions. "And you think Dante, what, knows something about it?"

"He seems quite unbothered about Malachi's silence," one of the other vampires muttered with a shrug.

Shadow began to creep up Max's hands with the unspoken accusation. I placed my free hand on his forearm, rubbing across the inky darkness as if I could absorb it into myself.

"My husband had nothing to do with it," I shot back, fierceness rising in me for his sake, my fingers tightening on his arm as I fought my claws from punching out. Even if they didn't know Max's true identity and his ties to Malachi, the insinuation that he could be the reason Malachi was suddenly missing pissed me off. "I think I'd notice if he disappeared for some dirty deeds, considering we've been on our *honeymoon*." I glared at the vampire stupid enough to doubt Max's integrity, then turned to Max. "You didn't even know, did you?"

Max shifted, and in doing so, his leg pressed against mine. Whether it was intentional or not was hard to say, but to wolves, it was a show of solidarity.

"I didn't know, but I suspected something might have come up," Max admitted. "I haven't been able to reach him either."

Max had Étienne's full attention. "This is unusual?"

"Yes. To go this long without a check-in is odd," Max hesitated, glanced at me, then continued, "especially when I'm on a job."

"All work and no play, even on your honeymoon." Rhain shook his head. "Not how I would choose to celebrate with such a beautiful lass."

"So, let me get this straight." Max leaned forward and brought our joined hands up onto the table, not sparing a glance in Rhain's direction. I bit back my smile at the silent show of possession it was, claiming me as his for everyone to see. Our honeymoon *had* been a work trip, and yet, he'd spent the last several days lavishing me with more time and focus than I knew what to do with. "You think Malachi is a hostage? Or killed? By whom?"

"Hostage is more likely," Rhain said. "If the Conclave figured out what we have planned, and that he's been orchestrating it, he'd be a prime target."

"Hostage," Max echoed with a huff of a laugh. "He's an *angel*. He could fight off any of you."

"Any one of us, yes." Étienne nodded. "But against more than one? Against a group? Perhaps not."

Max's brows furrowed, the words seeming to permeate his mind, his muscles tightening as he faced the implications.

His father, and Premier of the supernatural world, was possibly a captive of a Conclave of angry, betrayed vampire leaders.

"Fuck," he hissed, pushing to his feet. His hands clenched into fist at his sides, shadow tracing up his veins. "Where is the Conclave? We have to get him out of there."

Étienne shook his head. "It's not so simple. The Conclave maintains utmost secrecy. Assemblies are at different locations every time, and the location will only be revealed to dukes and duchesses right before it's held."

Max cursed under his breath again, and a spark shot from his fingertips. I absorbed the shock through our joined hands, my skin prickling with the electricity, but bit my tongue to hide any signs that it had affected me. No one but Rhain had used Max's real name here, and I knew how important it was to keep his identity hidden, especially now.

Whatever his relationship with his father, Max was a direct

link to Malachi, leverage that could be used to control him. When he'd approached me to help him find these dens, it had been about me helping him while he guarded my back, but now... Now, it was my turn to have Max's back, and it was a position I would gladly take.

"They will likely want to show off their prize, cocky bastards," Rhain added, like that was supposed to be a consolation. "So, he's probably not in immediate danger."

"Great," Max bit out. "Probably not murdered, but held captive. I'm sure they'll give him the finest suite, right? Every creature comfort?"

His implication wasn't lost on anyone. If they had him, and they knew he was involved in this coup, Malachi was in mortal danger. If the situation was reversed, the Council would be trying to get information out of him, by any means necessary. Something told me the Conclave was no different.

Whatever my own thoughts and feelings about Malachi, he was Max's father, and he had done his best for supernatural society during his tenure as Premier. He certainly didn't deserve whatever might be happening to him.

Heaving out a deep breath, Max forced himself to sit back down. "So, now what? We all just sit tight until the assembly location is sent out?"

"*We* sit tight, yes," Rhain said. "But you better believe if *we* were watching you, they are too. You two need to lay low. We can't arouse suspicions."

The thought of more people watching us from the shadows, all because of our connection to a man I'd never even met, turned my stomach.

Max's lip curled in distaste. "Lay low?"

"Wedded bliss, right?" Rhain gestured between us. "My recommendation? Continue your honeymoon, do your sightseeing, and we'll let you know when we have the location."

Étienne nodded. "Then, we go in. Our focus" — he

gestured to his vampires — "will be taking out the Conclave, while you and Rhain focus on finding Malachi and getting him out."

"And if he's not there?"

Étienne turned at my question, sizing me up. "If he's not there, we try to keep one of the Conclave alive for questioning."

"And kill the others."

I didn't say it like a question, but it was one, and I couldn't keep the judgment from my tone.

He raised a brow, ignoring my tone. *"Exactement."*

We took our time winding our way back to the apartment, neither of us all too eager to discuss what we'd learned tonight. Soft music drifted through the night air, streetlights illuminating the Parisian scene like a painting. It had felt perfect, magical even, just a few hours ago when teasing Max with an ice cream cone had been my most important task, but now a dark cloud lingered over us.

Malachi was missing, probably held captive, and had led his son right into the heart of a dangerous coup with little to no information. That had to sting.

Imagining my own father in any such situation made my stomach churn, anxiety creeping up my spine. I'd be in a panic, my siblings and I flying into action to get him back. But Max's relationship with his father wasn't the same as mine, and I was reminded again that I knew next to nothing about my husband.

For all I'd shared in snippets these past couple weeks together, Max was a closed book. Casting a sideways glance at him, I looked for signs of that same panic, that same worry, and came up blank. His dark hair fell in a wave over his forehead, his tanned forearms hanging loosely at his side since he'd given me his jacket back. No tensed jaw. No tight shoulders. No downcast gaze. No clenched hands. And yet...

He was off.

I couldn't see it, but I could *feel* it.

Before I could overthink it, I slipped my hand into Max's and squeezed.

"Never know who might be watching, right?" I whispered, leaning my head on his shoulder as if I was sleepy, headed back home after a late night.

He hummed, but didn't drop my hand.

Now we knew what was truly going on, Paris had lost its luster. There might not be anything Max could do yet, but judging by the energy simmering just under the surface of his skin, he was too restless for more leisurely sightseeing.

My phone buzzed in my bag, and I pulled it out to a text from Terran.

TERRAN

> Hey, I know you're on your honeymoon so I hate to do this, and he'd never say anything himself (you know how he is), but I think Dad is upset about the eloping thing.

> When are you coming home?

> He says he's good but he's been sleeping with his Willies.

> It's bad, S.

"Crap." I sighed, dropping Max's hand to text back. I'd been afraid of something like this.

SUMMER

> I think we'll be back sooner than we thought.

> Does he bring a sleeping bag?

TERRAN

When is sooner?

No sleeping bag. Wolf.

I cursed under my breath. That was bad. A shifter choosing to spend that much time as their animal was a cry for help, an attempt to distance themselves from human thoughts and emotions.

TERRAN

Earlier today I asked if he wanted to run the
dessert special — NO LIMITATIONS — this
weekend at the restaurant and he said NO

SUMMER

Oh my GOD

TERRAN

SEE

I'm telling ya. BAD

SUMMER

I'll give you an ETA when I have one

TERRAN

Shit. He says he just ordered a loom

SUMMER

A loom??

TERRAN

To make buffalo fur sweaters?? I don't know,
and frankly, I'm terrified to ask.

SUMMER

That would be awful. Their fur isn't even soft!

TERRAN

My bad. He is now looking at alpacas.

For fuck's sake, he just showed pictures of baby aplacas to River.

SUMMER

Oh, he's playing dirty dirty.

TERRAN

Using my daughter for his schemes

Help me, Summer Larkin-Russo. You're my only hope.

SUMMER

Shut up. I love you.

TERRAN

I know.

Huffing a laugh at my brother's idiocy, I stuffed my phone back in my bag and took Max's hand again. I sensed his curiosity about my texting, but he didn't need to be weighed down with my family drama. There'd be plenty of that soon enough.

"Well, I guess our work here is done," I said, trying for a lighthearted tone, but it fell flat even to my ears. We had bigger problems now, so it was selfish of me to be disappointed our travels were over so soon.

He raised a brow. "What do you mean?"

"We found the vampires, and your dad was right — they are certainly unhappy with the Conclave. I guess we don't need to keep traveling together since you have Project Oleander at your side now. Case closed." I swallowed heavily, the thought sinking like a stone in the pit of my stomach. "You can take me home now."

Something flickered over Max's face, gone before I could figure out what it meant.

He shrugged. "You heard Rhain, though. We should keep up appearances for now, in case they're watching. Wouldn't want it to seem like anything's amiss."

It shouldn't have given me hope, shouldn't have given me any soft and fluttery feelings, that he wanted to keep up the pretense for a little longer. Because he wasn't doing it for *me* or *us*, but for the job. For the ruse. So the Conclave wouldn't suspect anything had changed.

Still, the tiniest part of me *did* hope. Did flutter. That maybe, *maybe*, he wanted to keep pretending for the same reason I did.

We'd come to Paris newly fake-married and adopted a friends-with-benefits situation, but were leaving with something that felt like a whole lot more. Tonight, feeling his hand in mine, had started to feel just a little bit like it could be real.

I shook the thought from my mind, clearing my throat and giving him a smile I hoped didn't look too forced. "All right. For now."

Chapter Twenty-Six

SUMMER

I slipped silently out of my bedroom, tugging on a hoodie over my tee and leggings as Max laid sprawled face down on the bed. The sun was just beginning to rise over the peaks in the distance, the pink hues emphasizing the fog hovering over the pine trees.

We'd returned to Colorado last night, crashing into bed shortly after our arrival. It was the first night we'd solely *slept* together, nothing more, but yesterday had thrown me for an emotional loop.

We'd started the morning with insanely hot shower sex, then ended the day agreeing to stay together only because the Conclave was watching us.

He didn't stir as I crept out of my bedroom and padded down the hall. Maybe that little bit of physical distance last night was a good thing, giving us both time to sort out our feelings. But this morning, I didn't feel any more settled than I had before.

That was a problem I couldn't solve today, so I tip-toed down the stairs, headed towards a different problem. I needed to talk to my dad first, and alone.

Hopping into my Jeep, I drove the short way from my place on Main Street to the turn-off to Dad's ranch. His driveway was a good two miles long, with several cattle guards to rattle over. Dew lingered on the lush green grass of spring, wildflowers dotting the fields.

A buffalo meandered closer to the driveway, one of a dozen that lived out here on his ranch. I stopped the car, my headlights shining on its beady eyes and the pink bow dangling between its horns.

"Good morning, Willie." I rolled down the window, talking to the buffalo the same way my dad did. Despite having multiple buffalo, he'd decided to name them all Willie, both male and female. It made things both simple and confusing at once, the Heath Larkin specialty. "Seen Dad yet this morning?"

Willie huffed, its breath fogging in the crisp air, then continued to wander past. I rolled forward, craning my neck as I looked out over the land. Mountains rose high on my right, the river cutting through his property to my left. It was beautiful here, a respite from the years he'd spent as pack Alpha, and I loved this peace and solitude for him.

But as much as I knew my dad loved camping out with his buffalo, I hated the idea of him sleeping in the field with them. He could take care of himself, yes, but it was more about his mental state. And knowing he'd been spending more time as his wolf? That was never good.

Losing my mom 15 years ago had wrecked all of us, but none more so than my father, her mate. For weeks after she died, he stayed in his wolf form, something our animals did in a protective state. His wolf mourned his mate, but the range of emotions wasn't the same. Tears gathered in my eyes that I'd driven my dad to that same place.

I parked in front of his little log cabin and got out as the sun just crested over the eastern mountain ridge.

Most of the property was free-range, fenced in only along the property line, but to the right of the little cabin was a smaller pasture for my mother's horse, Tar Baby. Her black mane shimmered in the early morning sun as she chewed on the dewy grass, casting a wayward glance my direction before flicking her head out to the fields beyond. As I climbed up to sit on her fence and scan the field, two grey ears popped out of a thicket of grass a couple hundred yards out.

Waving at him, I couldn't hold back my smile as his tongue peeked out between his teeth, lolling off to the side. He scrambled to his feet, and turned his back to me. Quickly, he shifted, changed into a pair of sweats he must have had in the field with him, then hurried over.

I leapt from the fence and he caught me in a giant hug, squeezing tight. Here in his arms, it felt like home.

"Sweetheart." Dad set me down, pulling back enough to scan my face. His grin spread ear to ear on his tanned, weathered face, his grey hair a mess. Happiness radiated off him, and I leaned into his touch, so glad to have him in my life. "Is everything okay? I thought you were on your honeymoon."

"All honeymoon-ed out," I said with a shrug as we started towards his cabin. I threaded my hand through his elbow, hugging his arm to my side. I'd only been gone a week, but I was surprised at how much I'd missed my family. This was the longest I'd ever been away, as pathetic as that was. "You can only spend so many days in Paris, you know? I thought I was going to puke if I saw another baguette."

He snorted, tapping my hand with his. "Right, that's what they all say. Paris, *Shmaris*. What a drag." Sharp eyes cut at me, his brows drawing together. "Max didn't do something, did he —"

"*No!*" I cut in, harsher than I intended, but my hackles were still up after the meeting in Paris yesterday. For some reason, I still felt protective over Max, whether I should or not. I didn't want to hear anyone speaking against him, least of all my own family. He was my husband, after all. "No. We just wanted to come back." Not totally a lie. "Guess I'm more of a small town girl."

Opening the front door and holding it for me, Dad gave

me the *Look*. The one that said *you might fool other people with that but you're not fooling me*. "You can be whatever you want."

I ducked inside to avoid responding to that, and headed for the kitchen, starting some coffee for us. When it was percolating, I turned around to Dad watching me expectantly, leaning against the kitchen counter beside me.

"You didn't come back for me, right?" His eyes narrowed. "One of your brothers didn't mention something?" His voice trailed off, but I'd never narc like that.

I blinked innocently. "Mention what?"

He grumbled something before shaking it off with a huff and refocusing on me. "*Well?*"

I grinned hesitantly. "Well?"

"*Details*, sweetheart. Tell me everything. I'm not so old fashioned to think he needed to ask my permission, but this was all so sudden. I'm just ready to be happy with you. So, let's hear it. The wedding, hell, the *proposal*, the travel" — he gasped, smacking his forehead — "the *ring*! Tell me he got you a spectacular ring! No daughter of mine —"

I thrust out my hand, and he gasped again, even more dramatically than the first time, as he grabbed my hand to examine the ring.

Over steaming cups of coffee, we sat on his back porch as I told him everything — except that this was all fake — and he gasped and exclaimed appropriately the whole time. He howled, tears streaming down his face as I recounted our ceremony, and I chuckled, surprised at the warmth in my chest as I relived it.

Sharing it with him both healed something in me and twisted my gut. I hated keeping anything from my family, so it was a weight off my shoulders to finally spill some of these details. But it also made me feel even worse that I wasn't sharing *everything*.

When he was all caught up, he sighed contentedly, and it didn't escape my notice that his eyes were a little misty.

"My baby girl, all grown up and married," he murmured, reaching over and squeezing my hand. "Oh, sweetie, I hope it's just the best thing to ever happen to you. A partner for life, for better or worse, to have your back no matter what."

My gut clenched again, but I managed a smile for him. "So far, so good."

"So, you're back. And supposedly all is well with Max —"

"— It *is* —"

"Which can only mean one thing." He clapped his hands together, a familiar glint entering his eyes. "Party time."

I hid my flinch behind a semi-forced smile. I would do anything for my dad, including allowing him to throw me a horrendously extravagant party that I had no doubt would feature every person he'd ever met.

Or so I kept reminding myself. "Um, when did you have in mind —"

"Tonight! Well," he paused, tapping his chin. "Maybe tomorrow. I have to make sure Hattie can come, and who knows where she is at the moment."

Hattie, Dad's only sister, was as much a free spirit as he was, and we hadn't seen her in ages.

"Okay, cool, it'd be great to see Hattie. And yes, I said we could have a party, but maybe nothing *too* big —"

Dad was already waving away my concerns. "Nonsense. My first kid to get married? The bigger, the better. That's what I always say, right, Willie?" He nodded at the nearest buffalo, who grazed just on the other side of the fence not far from the porch, little pink bow tied on its forehead. "Not that you have to worry about a thing, of course" — he patted my hand — "you just relax. Leave it all to your pops here — well, and your brothers. I'll be putting them to work, all right. In fact —" he whipped out his phone, tapping away furiously which I took as my cue.

He had a party to plan, and I had a husband to warn.

I spent the rest of the day mediating disputes between Dad and my brothers, who all suddenly had a thousand opinions on what a post-wedding reception party should entail, while also trying to keep Max distracted and oblivious to what was going on behind his back.

WEST

Dad said you okayed an 8 ft macaron Eiffel Tower? Pls confirm

SUMMER

I cannot

WEST

I knew it.

TERRAN

Thank GOD. That's no better than a cupcake wedding cake.

LEIF

That actually doesn't sound half bad. I like cupcakes.

COOPER

He also said something about a barbeque sauce fountain for the meats? I assume no?

SUMMER

omg ew

TERRAN

Okay, THAT one maybe.

What about ranch dressing? Or is that too suggestive?

On second thought, nothing white spewing out of a fountain for my baby sister's wedding.

Leif has left the chat

WEST

Look what you've done. You proud of yourself, T?

TERRAN

...a little bit, yeah.

SUMMER

Let's just veto towers or fountains of any kind

COOPER

Agreed. On it, sis.

WEST

He just asked me about getting doves.

SUMMER

NO ANIMALS

TERRAN

...

COOPER

...

WEST

...

SUMMER

Shut UP you know what I meant!

Sadly, Max was not an idiot. After my fifteenth exasperated sigh and furious typing session, he dropped down on the couch next to me, moving aside my many pillows to make room. His hair was still damp from a shower, and he'd pulled on a black hoodie and shorts, the most relaxed I'd ever seen him. He should have looked like a black hole against my sunset-colored couch, but instead it was like watching a sunrise, when night turned into day, the promise of a new beginning.

Our thighs touched, and I steeled my face to hide any reaction, relief flooding me at the tiniest physical connection. It was pathetic that such a simple thing would affect me, but after our morning apart, I was shocked by how much I'd missed him.

The sweet smell of my lemon verbena soap drifted off his skin, an intoxicating mix when layered with his natural sandalwood and coppery scent. He reached across me and plucked the phone from my hand.

"Okay, what the hell is going on here?" He wiggled my phone in his hand, but I appreciated that he didn't try to read my screen, despite the ten texts that arrived in just the few seconds he'd been holding it.

I scrunched my nose. "Nothing?"

"Try again."

With another sigh, I held out my hand, and he passed back my phone. "Okay, don't be mad, but my dad is insisting on throwing us a wedding reception party."

Max blinked, his only outward sign of surprise, before covering it with a smirk. "Oh no. Not a party. How dare he. What a monster."

Swiping my phone open, I scrolled to the top of the party negotiations and passed it back over. "One, he wants this party to happen *tomorrow*. Two, he's basically invited the whole town, and then some. And three, he doesn't do things by halves. He's going all out. This is basically a town festival."

Max's eyes widened the further he read through the chat, morphing from surprise to amusement to horror and back again. Finally, he looked up at me, one brow raised. "Doves?"

"I vetoed the doves," I answered quickly, then groaned. "But it's like playing whack-a-mole. I veto one thing, and by the time I turn around, he's got three more crazy ideas for me to veto. I'm trying my best, but I have to warn you. This is going to be a *lot*. And that's me saying that."

Max handed me my phone, lifting a shoulder. "How bad could it be?"

INDI

> Your dad just asked if I had any wedding-y dresses in stock for you to wear to your party.

> Also, did I know you were having a party?

> Also also, are you still in Paris? What is happening right now? Why don't I know every single minute detail of your life?

SUMMER

> You know the Heath Rule. JUST SAY NO

> Also hi, yes. I'm back! And I missed you! I'll text you as soon as I have a minute to chat?

INDI

> K, sounds good! Missed you too!

Eyes widened pointedly, I showed Max the text exchange, Dad's insanity knowing no bounds.

Something akin to trepidation flitted across his face, which, ironically, made me relax a fraction. He was finally getting the idea.

"He won't make us recreate the wedding, right? I can't survive the fake vampire teeth more than once."

I threw both hands up. "We can only hope."

Chapter Twenty-Seven

SUMMER

My thumb tapped the edge of my phone in my pocket, feeling like a lead weight dragging me down. Summer and I had spent yesterday getting her bakery and bookstore organized, the simple tasks taking my mind off the unsolvable puzzle in front of me. Rather than dwell on my father's absence or the impending party, I alphabetized books and restocked ingredients, following her instructions.

The news of my father's absence seemed to have popped the lust-filled haze we'd both been under, but thankfully, jetlag drove us both to an early bedtime. Neither of us had the energy for more than sleep, but our unconscious bodies gravitated together on their own, a tangled mess of arms and legs.

Dawn rose soon enough, and I pried myself out of her sleepy hold to shower early. After making myself a cup of coffee, I took the stairs to her rooftop patio, overlooking the small mountain town. Old pipes squeaked in the apartment below, telling me Summer must also be up and showering.

Today was our wedding reception. Summer had said the party would be "Colorado formal." I wasn't sure how to interpret that, but I'd gone with a simple black shirt and pants, no tie.

We were already married, so it shouldn't have mattered much, but this felt... different. *More.* Intentional, as compared to our spontaneous night in Vegas. But then again, so did the way she'd defended me in Paris.

That hadn't felt staged, or fake.

It had felt all too real, like she cared about me, not just traveling with me to check off her bucket list. It was too good to be true.

No matter how much I was beginning to care about Summer, I couldn't let it distract me from my job. I cleared my throat, pulled my phone from my pocket, and tapped the screen to call my father. Peering over the railing to Main Street below, I listened to the call ring, unsure if I was more nervous that Malachi wouldn't answer, or that he would.

If he didn't answer, then my questions would go unanswered, and Rhain's assumption he was missing might be true.

If he did answer, then I'd have to confront him about Project Oleander, and his decision to keep me in the dark yet again.

The call reached his voicemail, and I frowned as I hit redial.

Five ring-throughs later, and still nothing.

I stared down at my phone, scenarios whirling through my mind. Even if I wanted to leap off this rooftop and hunt him down, I had no clue where to start looking for the Conclave, and that was assuming he was with them. My father was the leader of the supernatural world — it took no stretch of the imagination to pinpoint dozens of people who would love to see him taken down. With nothing else to go off but Rhain's lead, I didn't have much choice but to sit back and wait.

I hated fucking waiting.

Gritting my teeth, I tapped on a different contact, calling Evangeline, another angel who worked closely with my father.

"Massimo, this is a surprise," came Evangeline's smooth voice almost immediately. "Did you get yourself in a spot of trouble and need a bail out? Again?"

There was no hint of concern in her voice, no sign anything was amiss in Headquarters. "Not yet, but it's early," I replied, leaning back on the roof's railing. I kept my tone light, unwilling to reveal my own worry until I knew more. "But I did need to talk to Malachi and haven't been able to reach him. Have you seen him? Old man probably forgot to charge his phone again."

Like Malachi would ever forget anything of the sort, but I kept that part to myself.

Evangeline hummed in thought. "Malachi? Not today, I haven't seen him, no. But that's no surprise — he's out of office this week on a Community Outreach assignment. Something about image control with shifter packs in Canada. Didn't he tell you?"

I ignored her dig, my spine straightening as alarm bells went off in my head. "He told you himself he'd be out for the week?"

"Well, no. But a little over a week ago he sent a memo to a select few of us to let us know he'd be out for the foreseeable future with little to no cell reception." She adopted a mock-pouting tone. "I guess that didn't include you?"

I bit back a few choice retorts. "Goodbye, Evangeline."

"While I've got you, Massimo — that human you brought in a few weeks ago, you remember, the one whose partner you weren't supposed to kill but of course you couldn't follow orders? Again? Well, he's been —"

Rolling my eyes, I hung up before she could have the last word. I didn't have time to deal with whatever complaint that human garbage was trying to make against me. Wouldn't be the first time anyway.

Community Outreach? What a load of bullshit. My father didn't even mingle well with other supes, let alone humans. And besides, why would an angel go lead shifter relations meetings? That was the type of thing he used West for.

That, along with the fact Evangeline and the others only received a *memo*, only confirmed my suspicions.

Malachi was missing.

For all I knew, I was the last one to see him several weeks ago.

Shit.

My skin felt twitchy all over, sparks shooting over my arms with my disquiet. I leaned both hands on the railing, and let my wings burst free, shaking them out to relieve some of my tension.

Soon enough, Rhain and the others would have the location of the assembly, and we could go get him, *if* that was where he was.

But fuck, no one had heard from him in over two weeks. That was a long time when you were being held prisoner, or worse.

My fingers tightened on the railing, shadow magic painting my fingers the same color as the metal as my head tipped forward. Malachi and I might not have had the relationship that Heath Larkin had with his sons, but he was still my father. My only family, the only one who'd known who I really was for most of my life.

I nearly leapt into flight when a soft hand landed on my shoulder, and I whirled around with my shadows coiled around my hands.

"Whoa there," Summer said, holding both palms up. "Who's afraid of little old me?"

Any words, any *thoughts* died immediately at the sight of her, worry over my father ushered quickly to the back of my mind. She was a beautiful distraction, temptation I had no power to resist, a lifeline thrown in the midst of my turmoil.

Her white silk dress was overlaid with a delicate layer embroidered in little white daisies. It hugged her curves in all the right places, and the slit to her thigh nearly had my fangs punching out, desperate to taste her again. She'd painted her lips in a deep red, making them look blood-covered, and they matched the heels peeking out from the hem of the dress.

She smiled self-consciously, swishing the skirt side to side. "I thought it matched the ring." She held up her hand and waved her fingers. "And, of course, I needed to show off my mark."

She twirled and the moment I spotted her back, my fangs punched through.

Perfectly framed by her backless dress was my shadowmark. She'd even swept her golden-blonde hair into a curled ponytail to show it off. Proudly displayed.

My hand reached out of its own accord, tracing the swirls on her spine, and she shivered. I stepped closer, and she leaned back into my touch, tilting her head so naturally.

So trustingly exposing her neck to me.

I couldn't resist her. Skating my lips across her shoulder, to the point where her shoulder met her neck, I inhaled her sweet lemon scent.

She pressed her back to my front, like she wanted more, and I let my teeth graze her skin, but didn't break it.

"Summer," I breathed. My hands wrapped around her waist, tugging her even closer. "Are you trying to kill me, sunshine?"

"Now, why would I do that? I'm not the tease, here." She peered over her shoulder to meet my eyes, long eyelashes fluttering as she blinked innocently. Mischief danced in her expression, the corners of her lips tipping up as she slid her hips to the side, grazing my crotch just right. "That's your job."

I should have loosened my hands around her waist, should have stepped back, should have done anything but lick across her exposed shoulder before placing a gentle kiss there. She sucked in a breath, and my nostrils flared as her arousal blossomed in the air. "Careful what you wish for, wife."

Squeezing her waist, I let her go, already missing the contact. She turned to face me, her chest rising as she breathed heavily. "What are the rules for tonight?" she asked, her eyes darting from my eyes to my mouth, to my chest, lower, and back up.

I smirked, glad she was as affected by me as I was her. "Rules?"

"Yes." She nodded vigorously, blinking several times. "Rules. My family will know something's up if we don't sell this."

I raised a brow. "Do we need to sell this to them?" I didn't relish the idea of coming clean to the Larkins that I'd been using their baby sister to hunt vampires, but it seemed inevitable we'd be found out. "How about I just act like I can't keep my hands off you, and look at you like I know exactly what that dress will look like on the floor later?"

Summer poked my chest. "Quit distracting me. And yes, we need to sell it. They cannot know what's going on, or they'll throw a fit over me coming with you to find your dad."

Her words drew me up short. "You're not coming with me. Once Rhain gets a location for me, I don't need you. And it will be way too dangerous."

She sucked in a breath, and immediately I regretted my words. "Summer, wait —"

"Nope." She shook her head, pulling back from me, but there was fire in her eyes. "You're right. My super nose might not be as useful once you have a direction, but that's not the same as not needing me, and you know it. Besides, who is watching *your* back while you go out looking for trouble?"

I opened my mouth to argue, then closed it again, no retort coming to mind.

No one had ever watched my back, not until Summer.

"This is a terrible plan."

"New plan is *no* plan." She nodded, maybe trying to convince herself. She stuck her left palm out, the golden bands glistening on her ring finger, and I couldn't find it in me to deny her anything. "We stick together until the job is done."

Grabbing her hand, I pulled her into my chest, tipping her chin up with one finger. "How do you suggest we sell this then? Lots of physical contact?"

She swallowed, her fingers twitching against my own. "Yep. Probably that. You know how touchy we wolves are."

I slid my free hand down to her throat, gripping the side lightly as she sucked in a breath. Leaning down over her, I brought my mouth within an inch of hers. "Kissing?"

Her hazel eyes were rimmed in gold, that fiery passion I'd come to adore blazing bright. "Expected. I couldn't stop the glass-clinking tradition even if I tried. You have to kiss me every time."

"Mmm." I tilted my head to the side, skimming my lips over her cheek, feeling her pulse race under my thumb as I brushed it across her neck. The two kisses we'd shared were seared into my memory, and I was dying for another taste. "What about scent?"

A soft whimper left her lips that had my smirk morphing into a full-on grin. "A mate bond sends wolves into a bit of a frenzy, in a permanent state of arousal that is just uncomfortable for all of us."

"Terrible," I said as I dragged my hands down her arms, savoring the feel of her warm skin as a trail of goosebumps broke out over her biceps.

"We're not mated though, so that's not as hard to sell."

"Oh?" My eyes drifted up to hers as I let my hand slip down her back, tracing my shadowmark. "You think you're not mine?"

She gasped at the light contact. "Yours to feed from, you mean?"

My fingers paused at the base of her spine, pressing lightly into her skin. I'd told her previously that a vampire's shadowmark could develop on their Source. It wasn't a total lie, though it wasn't the whole truth either.

But now wasn't the time for that discussion.

Instead, I smirked. "Well, I've certainly done that." Summer clenched her legs together, likely at the memory of the last bite I'd given her on her upper thigh. "And if I have to keep you in a constant state of arousal to sell this, that's what I'll do."

Her eyes widened, and she opened her mouth like she was about to protest that. I pressed a finger to her lips.

"Do you trust me?"

I hadn't meant to say it, but once I did, I realized how desperately I needed to hear her answer. Needed to know she did trust me, before we went out and paraded this farce in front of all her friends and family and then some. I couldn't remember the last time I trusted anyone, but Summer had earned my loyalty time and time again these past couple weeks.

Whatever else we were or weren't, in this we were allies.

Finally, Summer nodded, one side of her mouth tipping up into a smile. "Yeah, I do."

I forced myself to take a step back, to take her hand instead, though I couldn't resist pressing my lips to her knuckles. "Then we've got this, sunshine."

"Turn here," Summer said from the passenger side of her Jeep, pointing out Heath's driveway. "Oh, sheesh."

Cars lined the drive as far as we could see, and Summer muttered under her breath the whole way up the driveway.

The long, *long* driveway. We were on it for a good ten minutes before we even caught sight of the house, a little cabin popping up in the distance.

I raised a brow, glancing at her. "Does he think we'll all fit in there?"

Summer shook her head. "Not in there, no." She pointed in the distance, and I followed her finger to a large barn beyond the house, almost hidden among the trees. Its doors were flung open wide, a space in front of the doors strung with fairy lights. Barrels were spread around as tables in the area, already filled with people mingling with drinks. Off to the side, a dozen kids played lawn games and shrieked happily together.

"Dang it," Summer muttered, taking a steadying breath. "He went for the tower."

I pulled into a spot in front of the cabin — conveniently outfitted with a wood pallet with the words *NEWLYWEDS* spray-painted on it in neon pink to reserve the space.

Switching off the Jeep, I peered out the windshield. "Tower?"

Summer cringed. "Inside the barn."

More fairy lights draped over rafters inside the barn, casting the whole scene in a hazy glow. And there, in the very center, on a table covered in a white tablecloth, rose a giant Eiffel Tower.

"Are those —?"

"Macarons? Yes. Just in case everyone here hasn't heard our entire story yet." Summer sighed, shooting me an apologetic look. "Before we go out there, let me just say one, I'm sorry; two, I tried to warn you; three, I tried to stop them; and four" — she trailed off, pursing her lips like she was trying to think of a fourth — "four, when in doubt, just nod and drink."

I hummed in thought. "You are a paragon of wisdom, wife."

Summer gave her ponytail a flick and winked. "I know."

A series of howls sounded from outside, and a heartbeat later, our doors were wrenched open. My gaze met Summer's as she mouthed *Sorry* before we were pulled bodily from the car.

"Hands off, wolves, I can walk." I shoved their hands off me, straightening my shirt as I found myself face to fang with Cooper, Aspen, and West.

West clapped me on the back — hard — and gave me a nod. "Welcome to the family, Max Larkin."

I frowned. "Not happening."

Cooper hummed, arms crossed over his broad chest, looked me up and down and merely licked his fang. Aspen, in an almost matching pose, narrowed her eyes at me.

Summer came around from her side of the car, followed closely by Leif and Terran.

"Why is West the only one of you idiots who's dressed appropriately?" She laughed, wrapping West, then Cooper, in big hugs.

She turned to Aspen next, and the sisters seemed to have a silent conversation before Summer grinned with a squeal, and squeezed her arms around Aspen.

"Okay, okay — need — oxygen —" Aspen swatted at Summer's back, but they were both smiling as they pulled apart.

I watched the two women, looking for any lingering animosity after their fight the night before we got married. Summer had pointedly avoided talking about Aspen in her ramblings over the last week, but she leaned into her sister, stealing another side hug.

"I was not prepared for how badly I'd miss you fools," Summer said as she returned to my side, grabbing my hand and smiling up at me, and my chest felt buoyed. "Apparently I should have sent Indi to pick all your outfits in my absence."

"What's wrong with this?" Leif tugged at the vest he wore over a plain t-shirt, and which he'd paired with ripped jeans and black Vans.

Summer booped him on the nose. "A for effort, Leify." Then she waggled a finger between Cooper and Terran. "D minus for you two."

"Hey!" Terran exclaimed in outrage at the same time as Cooper gave a disbelieving chuff.

The big cat gestured at his shirt. "This is my good flannel."

"Yeah, and I hosed down these boots for you and everything, sis," Terran added, lifting up one of his hiking boots, then adjusted the hem of his black t-shirt. "And this is brand new last year. Not even a beer logo on it." He lifted up his backwards baseball hat, ruffling his hair, then slammed it back down.

West, dressed in a blazer, dark jeans, and oiled cowboy boots, shook his head at them. "Someday you might want to make yourself presentable to someone, you heathens," he said, giving Terran's hat a sharp tug that nearly had him falling on his ass.

"You —" Terran fixed his hat, righting himself, and raised a pointer finger at West. "This is my favorite hat." For a second, the two were frozen, preternaturally still in that shifter way, then Terran lunged for West, who was already leaping back. Without batting an eye, Aspen and Cooper bodily moved Leif out of the way of their tussling. I slipped a hand around Summer's waist, holding her to me, and felt her soft chuckle beneath my fingertips. Happiness radiated off her, and I felt it to my bones.

"BOYS! Boys," came Heath's booming voice as he joined us. The two brothers broke apart, hands up, letting Heath step between them and shove them apart. West pointed two fingers at his eyes then stuck them towards Terran, the universal sign for *I'm watching you.*

Heath had donned a blazer and dark jeans like West, but paired it with a dark cowboy hat. He beamed around at all of us, then pulled Summer into a hug.

"Sweetheart," he said, stepping back to hold her by the elbows and look her up and down. "You look beautiful."

Summer smiled, blinking. "Thanks, Dad."

He turned to me then, and without realizing it, I braced, unsure how he would react to the male who'd eloped with his youngest daughter. Then, before I knew what was happening, strong arms wrapped around my shoulders, pulling me in tight and thumping my back.

A hug.

"Welcome to the family, son," Heath said, close enough the others wouldn't hear. Just for us. He thumped my upper arms again as he pulled back. "I'm so happy to have you. And may I say you *also* look very handsome, young man."

His hazel eyes glistened a little, and I felt an unfamiliar lump in my throat.

"Thank you," I croaked.

He nodded, holding his arms out wide to the others. "Now, I believe a celebration is in order! Summer? After you two, sweetheart."

With a theatrical bow, he swept his arms towards the barn, and the siblings parted to make way for us.

I met Summer's eye, holding out my arm for her, and she wrapped hers around it.

As we stepped forward, another chorus of howls burst around us. Summer laughed, then joined in with them and broke into a half-skip-half-jog towards the party, tugging me with her.

I hurried to match her step, and we threw ourselves to the wolves.

Chapter Twenty-Eight

SUMMER

There was a distinct difference between being extroverted and enjoying being the center of attention: I was the former, not the latter. A wave of discomfort washed over me as I looked out at the hundreds of people gathered at the ranch, but I put on a smile. After all, I knew how to work a room.

I hugged and waved my way through the crowd in my dad's wake, greeting every person I'd ever met in my entire life, and plenty I was sure I hadn't. Red hair flashed in my peripheral vision, and I turned towards the corner Indi had flickered into, her turquoise dress flaring around her legs.

"Oh, thank the Goddess," I whispered as I hugged her into my side, having lost sight of Max somewhere in the crowd. I was willing to bet he was lingering in the shadows somewhere, if my brothers had let go of him for that long.

"You hanging in there?" Indi squeezed me, then pulled back to look over my outfit. "Damn, I knew that dress would fit you perfectly."

"You never did tell me where you got it." I laced my arm through hers, waving at someone across the room I vaguely recognized as a wolf from Texas. Probably here with my Aunt Hattie.

When Indi didn't answer, I looked back at her, just in time to see her offer a mischievous wink. "Secrets are more fun. I'm just glad it worked like I thought it would." She rose on her tiptoes, scanning the crowd before dropping back down.

"Where's your *husband?* She punctuated the word with a dramatic waggle of her eyebrows that had me chuckling.

"Lurking, probably," I said as I took a glass of champagne off a passing tray Quentin carried. "Thanks Q."

The young vampire blushed, ducking his head before hurrying off.

Taking a small sip, I turned in place, taking it all in.

Small glass orbs hung from the ceiling, clippings of greenery dangling from each one. String lights looped between the rafters over a makeshift dance floor in the center, with tables in a semi-circle around it. A stage off to one side had a microphone and a full band setup. Outside the open doors were rows of hay bales, streamers on maypoles at the end of each aisle. Tears gathered in my eyes as I looked at everything.

"It really is perfect," I whispered, and Indi squeezed my hand. "Exactly how I would have done it."

"It was all Aspen." She nudged my shoulder towards my sister, standing off to the side of the room with Cooper, the two of them all but glaring at everyone. "Quite the drill sergeant, but together we all got it done."

"We?"

Indi nodded. "Your family, me, Lance, Cruz, Atlas and Nova and all the Shields, you know. Everybody."

I wished it was real, that all of them had come together for me for something real, because it filled my heart to the very brim. I knew I was loved — I'd never had to worry there, never had that particular wound — but seeing it like this made my eyes misty. Then the shadow of a thought — of the truth — crossed my mind, of how betrayed these very people who loved me so much would feel when they learned this was all a scam, that I'd lied to them, and I almost wanted to be sick.

"Friends! Family!" my dad said as he leaned into the mic, a broad smile on his face as he held his arms out wide. "Thank you all for gathering here at such short notice to celebrate my beautiful daughter Summer marrying the love of her life, Massimo Russo."

Dad gestured to me as Max slipped an arm around my waist, meeting my eye with something like solidarity. I smiled, but a ripple of muttering erupted in the room, and I faced our guests to see many of them whispering and frowning, their gazes catching on Max.

One guest — someone I didn't recognize — whispered to their neighbor, "Wait, as in *Max Russo*? Wasn't he in prison? Or was it Omega Level?"

I pasted on an even brighter smile and leaned into his side.

"Now, the two lovebirds skipped off to Vegas for their official wedding, but I hope they'll humor an old man and recreate part of the event for us all here tonight."

He beamed at us, awaiting our response, not that it was exactly a question, not when he phrased it like that in front of hundreds of people.

The words "Of course" had barely left my lips before he was directing the crowd outside.

"Now, I know it's a little unconventional, but I trained a Willie to be your ring bearer and he nailed it almost every time last night." He pointed proudly to a buffalo tethered beside the barn, lazily chewing hay.

I clutched my left hand to my chest, cradling the beautiful rings Max had picked for me protectively. "What do you mean, *almost* every time?"

"And, of course, River and Waffles will be your flower girls."

On cue, River and a mini Highland cow appeared. My niece's little pink dress was covered in tulle that billowed out into a giant skirt, and she held the reins to a matching pink bridle on the mini cow. River held a basket of flower petals and didn't seem to notice the cow casually snacking on them.

"Waffles, I presume?" I said, patting the pink bow on the cow's head.

River grinned ferociously. She'd been asking for a mini cow — as well as a pet raccoon, a puppy, or a capybara, depending on the day — for months.

My dad turned, grasping both my hands as he faced me head-on. "Now, I know this isn't a real ceremony, and of course it's your call, but what do you say to me walking you down the aisle?"

His warm hazel eyes were so full of love, I couldn't help my smile meeting his own, but I was spared answering him.

"Uh, Dad?" Terran called from outside, and we rushed over to where he stood in front of the hay bale "aisle," hands on his hips.

The aisle and every row of hay bale seating was now filled with buffalo, munching away on the snack they'd stumbled upon and covering the ground with cow pies. The gathered crowd chuckled and discretely covered their noses.

"Oh, crap," Dad muttered, glancing at them sheepishly. "You know, it's possible I forgot to close that pasture gate."

Just then, a series of crashes sounded from back inside the barn before another buffalo came charging out, a tiny green macaron stuck to one of its horns.

"Tower down, I repeat, tower down!" Leif came running out after the Willie. "I tried to stop her but she wouldn't take no for an answer."

We hurried back into the barn to see the whole macaron Eiffel Tower had collapsed in a shambles. Dad gasped at the sight, whipping his Stetson off and sweeping it over his heart in respect.

"Oh, sweetheart, I'm so sorry!" He clasped my shoulder. "These free-range Willies are being extra spicy today."

I rolled my lips inward to hide my amusement and tried to sound reassuring. "Dad, honestly, it's fine. We didn't need a giant macaron tower or an elaborate re-ceremony or any of that. Just celebrating and having fun with everyone we love is more than enough."

He gave a wistful sigh but nodded, accepting defeat. "All right. But I still get a dance, right?"

Leaning up on my tiptoes, I kissed his cheek. "Of course, Dad."

As he made his way over to the mic to make another announcement, canceling the 'ceremony' and starting the party, I spotted Max again and we met in the middle.

"Crisis averted," I murmured, clasping his hand.

He tilted his head. "In a manner of speaking."

Beyond him, I caught sight of Terran and Cruz — the latter outfitted in a full formal tuxedo, green bow-tie, tails, and all — who shot me thumbs-ups and winks before quickly schooling their expressions when Dad turned their way.

Aspen stepped up beside them, and they both leaned in immediately like a huddle on the field and she was their coach. A minute later, she and Terran stepped back at ease, Cruz gave her a salute — which she ignored — and he flickered away.

I raised an eyebrow at her when she met my gaze, and she only shrugged.

Mind to mind, she murmured, *You'll see.*

Max leaned in and when he spoke, it was low enough even the shifters gathered here wouldn't catch his words. "Did you know that since arriving here tonight, my life and body have been threatened by every single one of your siblings?"

I grinned. "Even Leif?"

He hummed in confirmation. "Your nephew told me if I harmed so much as one hair on your head, he would personally spit in all of my food at Buffalo Willie's." He *tsk*'ed in disbelief. "You shifters can be every bit as violent as vampires, it seems."

"Guess we're a perfect match, then."

His lips tipped up at that, his blue eyes glittering, and my heart stuttered.

I nodded towards the bar. "Time for more champagne, husband."

"Summer, you look so beautiful!"

I smiled at about the twentieth person I didn't recognize who'd come up to greet us and give us their best wishes. The little old witch clasped my hands before reaching up to pinch my cheek.

"Thank you," I said, not allowing my smile to falter, even though my face ached from holding it in place all day.

"Oh, I'm sure you don't remember me, sweetie, but you, your sister, and that little witch Eloise you used to play with came to my camp one year!" She patted my cheek, her own rosy with amusement. "You were a little too young, but your grandmother and I grew up together and she said you wouldn't take no for an answer. Anything Aspen could do, you could do, you insisted. Well, except you opted for interpretive dance instead of fort building. Nearly gave me a heart attack when you fell off the stage at the recital at the end of the week — but it turned out that was just part of your routine about the rise and fall of the Roman Empire. You'd been learning about it in school that year apparently and had taken quite the fixation on the topic."

I tilted my head, still smiling, though I had absolutely no memory of this camp, even if a Roman Empire obsession did sound familiar. I turned slightly, including Max in the conversation. "Do you know my husband Max?"

"Nice to meet you, ah —?" Max held out a hand.

Instantly, the woman's face fell, her eyes narrowing on his extended hand. "Tyra," she introduced herself flatly, offering him only the very tips of her fingers to shake. "That means warrior, young man, and don't you forget it."

Turning back to me, her smile returned as she squeezed my hands again. "So very good to see you again, Summer, dear."

As she moved away, I raised a brow at Max, who only shook his head. His usual smirk didn't budge, but I studied him a little harder, looking for the tells that something was off.

It hadn't been the first time tonight he'd gotten the cold shoulder from our guests. I'd known he didn't have the most stellar reputation to the rest of the supernatural world, but seeing it like this was something else altogether.

And what were any of these people even basing their judgments on? Whispers, rumors of his deeds as 'Dante,' all under his father's direct orders? A prison sentence he'd been excused of, that had only been part of maintaining his cover anyway? None of them actually knew him, knew the truth.

The next time someone gave him the side-eye while warmly greeting me, I was ready to snap.

"What an unusual pairing," said Linney, a wolf shifter from a northern pack and an old family friend, glancing between us before leaning in and lowering her voice. "I hate to spread rumors, hun, but some people are saying your husband" — she gave him a pointed look — "was the one responsible for the Jasper pack tragedy." She gave me a sympathetic grimace, like she wasn't telling me that just to stir the pot and fish for more information. My blood was near to boiling. "Of course, *I'd* never believe such a thing, but some others, you know—"

"Look at my ring," I demanded, sticking out my hand. "Isn't it beautiful? Max picked it just because he knows how much I love daisies. Then he whisked me away to Paris for our honeymoon because he remembered how much it meant to me and my mom." I glared at her. "He's incredibly thoughtful and kind."

Linney blinked, then gave a tittering chuckle to cut the

tension. "Of course, sweetie." She turned to Max, clearing her throat. "How lovely."

Max covered his mouth as Linney moved on, hiding his chuckle. I discreetly stamped on his foot.

"If you go to battle every time someone has a disparaging comment about me, I fear you'll have a very distressing marriage, wife."

Mentally, my knuckles were already wrapped and ready to go. Did it make sense for me to feel protective over him, especially when he could clearly take care of himself? Maybe not, but logic was for another day. "Somebody has to."

He hummed at that, and I felt him watching me from the corner of my eye. He didn't have a chance to respond before Aspen was hustling over to us, the wide legs of her deep green jumpsuit billowing around her.

"Warning," she huffed, eyes wide. "After the tower fiasco, I sent Cruz to hunt down another cake option." She threw up her hands. "He went rogue."

I pressed my lips together to hide my smile. "I'm sure whatever he found is just fine —"

"*Hola, hermanita!*" Cruz skidded up to us, two giant cake boxes in his arms, and said to Aspen, "Whew, you accidentally threw that broom right into me when you took off just now! I nearly tripped and sent both these cakes flying."

"Yes, that would have been a shame," Aspen deadpanned, but Cruz ignored her, turning to beam at me.

"My lady, I have two fabulous options for you this evening," Cruz said, breaking the tape sealing the first box. "At first, I thought, how could I possibly choose between these two? But then I thought, how could I possibly leave one of them behind when they're both spectacular?"

Aspen swiped a hand over her face as Cruz whipped open the cover with flourish.

An extremely detailed dinosaur cake greeted us, complete

with volcano and lava river, and at least 12 candy dinosaurs over the two layers. *Happy 3rd Birthday Tanner,* was scrolled in black icing along one corner. "I can have that off in a jiffy, don't you even worry."

Max snorted, and I nodded appreciatively. "Very nice."

"Right? Okay, that's option one." He shoved the box at Aspen so he could open the second one. "Now, brace yourself, but I really think this one is the winner."

I couldn't stop the laugh that bubbled out of me as the giant penis taking up the entire second box was revealed. Max choked on his sip of champagne until Cruz slammed a hand in the middle of his back.

"Hmm, very veiny." I nodded, inspecting it. "The balls look big enough to feed at least half these people."

"That's what I said to the cashier!"

Aspen sighed, rubbing the bridge of her nose. "This is a disaster. I said to find a *wedding* cake."

Cruz tilted his head back and forth. "Nothing says wedding night like a giant cock and balls, especially since we can all tell these two have already consummated their marriage. T could smell you from a mile out."

"And the dinosaurs?"

He gaped at her, aghast. "Dinosaurs are *always* relevant. C'mon, what's your favorite dinosaur?"

She glared at him, like she was debating not answering him, before muttering a very begrudging, "Pterodactyl."

Cruz grinned. "I knew it. Only a sociopath doesn't have a favorite dinosaur." He gave her an expectant look, which she returned with a stare. "Oh, well, since you asked, *my* favorite dinosaur is a Spike."

"A Spike? That's not a type of dinosaur. He's just a character from *the Land Before Time.*"

A glint entered his eye. "Oh yeah? What kind is he?"

Aspen put her hands on her hips. "I know what you're doing."

"Is it learning about dinosaurs? Because I am all ears."

Her jaw worked. But she bit out, "Stegosaurus."

Cruz bit his lip to keep from laughing, black eyes glittering with delight.

"They're both great, Cruz, thank you for running out to get them," I said, hopefully quelling the fire Aspen looked ready to lash out back at him. "Cake is cake."

Pointing a finger at me, he nodded. "Wise."

The two of them moved off bickering to get the cake set up, Cruz asking her, "What's Mike's favorite dinosaur?"

Aspen groaned and snapped, "Matthew. His name is Matthew."

Max raised a brow at me, a silent question about what was going on with the two of them.

"Safer to stay out of it. C'mon, husband," I grabbed his hand and tugged him forward. "Let's go eat our penis cake."

Chapter Twenty-Nine

SUMMER

"May I have this dance?" Dad dipped into a half bow, extending a hand to me, and I smiled as he swept me into his arms and out into the middle of the barn. He pointed to the band. "Hit it, boys."

The band started up *My Girl*, and tears pricked my eyes. I smiled, memories flooding me of dancing to it with my dad as a little girl, and seeing him dance with my mom to it too. Dad led me through an utterly ridiculous dance as we sang along to every word, belting it out and laughing the whole time.

Wrapping up the dance, Dad pulled me into a giant hug, murmuring, "So proud of you, sweetie. Your mom would be too."

My lip trembled, but my eyes smiled. "Thanks, Dad."

He led me back over to Max as the band picked up the next song, inviting everyone else onto the dance floor. I squeezed his hand again before he meandered off. Turning to Max, I wiped at my eyes.

I gave a breathy chuckle, regaining my composure. "He's such a goof. Mom used to say he could charm the feathers off an angel."

Max wrapped an arm around my waist. "He loves you all so much."

I nodded. "He does." Then I started, something just occurring to me. "Oh my gosh, I'm sorry your dad couldn't be here. Once we get this all figured out, we could have another —"

"It's fine," Max cut in, shaking his head.

"Really, we'd be doing my dad a favor if we said he could have a second party. He'd probably be thrilled for another shot at Maca-Eiffel-ron Tower. It'd be no trouble."

"Don't worry about it. Malachi and I aren't" — Max tipped his head back on a pause, searching for the words — "we're not like your family. Close, I guess."

"He's still your dad."

"Not in that way. Not like yours." I laid a hand on his chest, his heart beating irregularly as a wave of sadness washed over me. "He was always more of a tutor than a father. Training me for my future. Not so much planning my birthday party." Max paused, swallowing heavily. "Anyway, this isn't even real. So." He shrugged.

The tightness at the corner of his eyes. The tension in his neck. I tilted my head, and noted a slight change in his scent too — he wasn't outright lying, but there was definitely more than what he was saying.

Another wave of guests approached to greet us, and I let it drop. For now.

The night wore on, some of the guests beginning to trickle out, saying their goodbyes and wishing us all the best. Those left — mainly the pack, but some other locals as well — proceeded to get increasingly rowdy, cranking the music up and the drinks as well.

My Aunt Hattie made her way over, a sleeping River draped on her shoulder.

"I think we're out," she said, smiling at me and nodding to Max. Her tan cowboy hat had a burgundy ribbon tied around it to match her embroidered dress. Paired with her cowboy boots, she looked every bit the Texan boho queen I remembered.

"Waffles," River muttered in her sleep, her little hand opening and closing. The mini cow trotted up obediently, and I scooped up her pink reins, draping them through River's hand.

"Are you staying around town for a bit?" I asked. We never got to see Hattie enough. She was a Larkin, through and through, but she'd taken off the minute she turned 18, wanting to see more of the world than this little mountain town allowed. Before my mom passed away, I thought that was the life I wanted too. I still did, to some extent, but knowing everyone I loved was right here in this barn was its own sort of dream.

"Few days, you know how it is. Heading up to a rodeo in Wyoming after this, but I need to see your shop first." She nudged me with her shoulder affectionately. "Heath was telling me all about the work you've done there. We'll catch up tomorrow, all right?"

I squeezed her shoulder. "I can't wait."

She headed off to the cabin to get River to a bed for the night, Waffles trotting behind them.

On the dance floor, Cooper, Terran, and West's Shields, Nova, Atlas, and Zion looked like bumper cars trying to do the Macarena, the simple dance nearly devolving into a fist-fight before they yelled at the DJ to change the music. With this many Alpha wolves in one room, I was surprised there hadn't been any tussles yet. Shields were the highest ranked shifters in our pack after Terran as West's Second, and they were usually all business. It was fun to see them let loose like this.

Chuckling at their idiocy, I turned to Max. "I'm going to track down some more of that cake."

He nodded, and the music switched to something low key as I made my way around the edge of the room, eyes peeled for cake. Why was it always so hard to actually eat the cake at a wedding reception?

"Over here!" Indi shout-whispered, waving me over to a corner table where she appeared to be hoarding a small stash of cake plates.

"You're a lifesaver," I told her honestly, swiping up the nearest penis-slice.

"Nearly had to gouge eyes out to save these from your pack," she admitted, tucking into a slice herself. "As it was, I had to threaten to set fire to the steaks."

"Wow," I said around a mouthful. "Well, I thank you for your service—"

"*Ohmygoddess*," Indi gasped, her hand flying to my arm. I almost choked on my cake. "Don't look now but *your sister is dancing with Cruz.*"

I spun immediately, ignoring the smack Indi gave me.

There, in the corner of the room, swaying to the beat, Cruz did indeed have Aspen in his arms. His hands rested on her waist, hers above his shoulders. There was plenty of space between them, but the grin on his face was painted in adoration for all to see. She rolled her eyes at whatever he said, but didn't let go, still swaying to the beat.

My jaw dropped. I swung wide eyes on Indi. We stared at them, then each other, shocked.

"You're seeing what I'm seeing, right?" I whispered.

Indi hummed. "I'm almost afraid to breathe and break whatever crazy spell is happening here."

"I always love an opposites-attract romance. He'd be so good for her. Way better than that human robot, Matthew."

"Not our call to make though," Indi sighed. "Aspen has to make those choices herself."

"You're no fun."

Indi laughed, elbowing me in the side as the music switched to an upbeat dance number, and our shock ratcheted even higher. Because they kept dancing — somehow, Cruz convinced *Aspen* to stay for a happy, fast dance.

"But anyway, this is *your* day." Indi slid us each a second slice of cake. "And correct me if I'm wrong, but you two love-birds look anything *but* fake. Care to share? You know you want to. *Trussst in me.*" She locked her black irises on me, widening her eyes comically like Kaa from *the Jungle Book*, and tapped her fingers on my arm, sending little jolts of her demon magic into me. She'd never really use her magic to coerce me to do anything, to share more than I was comfortable with, but a little teasing, a little toying — always fair game.

"We're really great actors, huh?"

"Summer Rose Larkin-Russo. Or whatever you're doing with your name. You cut the shit and be real right now."

I swirled my fork through the frosting on my plate, trying to sort out my own emotions. "Honestly? It's been a little confusing. We spent a week in Paris, seeing the sights and having — I cannot stress this enough — the *best* sex of my life."

"We're gonna come back to that — I have so many questions — but carry on."

I grinned, but my chest ached with loss at the mention of those feelings. "You already know we said this was just temporary, just for the job, and then we'd go our separate ways. But we found a ton of vamps, and we're still doing this, and it feels like we're" — I shoved another bite in my mouth — "something? Friends? Allies? I don't even know at this point."

"Looks like more than that to me," Indi muttered around a bite of cake, and I chewed on my lip. Tonight had felt real, the small touches, the hand-holding. It was so easy to believe this was my actual wedding reception, and I had a lifetime of happiness at Max's side to look forward to. "Do you want it to be? I mean, it's obvious you like him. He likes you. *Max and Summer, sitting in a tree…*"

"How much wine have you had?"

"Almost none. Or three glasses, but it wasn't demon wine so…"

I snorted. "Practically the same thing."

"You're deflecting."

"That's correct." I licked the rest of the frosting off my fork and set it down. "I don't know. How would we work, if he even wanted it too? I'm here, he's… wherever."

"But you like him."

That part I wasn't confused about.

I peered across the room, where he stood by the wall, sipping slowly at the glass in his hand as he observed the chaos that was my family, my pack. Max was used to being on his own, being able to come and go as he pleased and do whatever he wanted, whenever he wanted. Why would he give that up for me and my overbearing pack who would no doubt insist on sticking their noses in our business every minute of the day?

Even now, after one evening here, he looked overwhelmed and overstimulated. He'd braved it all like a champ, meeting hundreds of people tonight and taking the pack posturing in stride, but he was definitely not a pack animal.

I was sure right now he'd much rather be up on my apartment roof, in solitude, than listening to my dad and his friend Lance, who seemed to be explaining in great detail the finer points of bison husbandry.

Still. I couldn't lie to Indi.

"Yeah. I like him."

Chapter Thirty

MAX

"Next time, we'll have you out to join us!" Lance Morgaine, a witch and Heath's closest friend, said, thumping me on the back. "Nothing like the mating calls of the wild American Bison."

I hid a grimace, fully intending on making myself scarce *long* before that outing. "Great."

"Oh!" Heath snapped his fingers. "Lance, I forgot to show you my loom! Got here last night."

Lance chuckled. "Can't believe you pulled the trigger. Let's see this thing."

The two of them headed off, and I sighed in relief, finally getting a reprieve from socializing for the first time all night. As I scanned the room, I quickly found Summer, my focus magnetized to her lately.

She sat off to the side with Indi, the two smiling and whispering, but something didn't feel right. She *looked* happy, but my gut instinct pulled me across the floor to her, stopping only once I had a hand around her hip, and my mouth at her ear.

"Dance with your husband."

She looked up, surprise written in those hazel eyes. Whatever unease I thought I'd seen across the room disappeared as she put her palm in mine and followed me into the middle of the dance floor.

My hand drifted to her waist, tugging her up against my

chest as we swayed to the beat. Taking our cue, the band switched to *Can't Help Falling in Love.*

I glanced over my shoulder at the crooning voice, trying to place where I knew the dark, curly-haired man who stood at the microphone.

"He's good, isn't he?" Summer said, her chin tipped up to look at me. "I can't believe they flickered Lysander Theroux in for this."

"He's from Deadlights Cove, right?" I slid my hand across her low back, pulling her in closer.

She sucked in a breath, then nodded as she turned her head, breaking the eye contact. "He's also Lance's son. It's complicated."

I squeezed her fingers, leaning forward to rest my chin against her head. She followed suit, her head landing softly on my chest as I led her in small circles across the dance floor.

"Are you happy with the way this turned out?" I asked, suddenly terrified of the answer. I wanted her to be happy, wanted her to enjoy all of this, wanted her to have this many people pour love on her every day. She deserved it more than anyone I'd ever met.

A contented sigh left her, then a soft sniff, but she didn't look up at me again. "It's perfect. Exactly how I would have wanted it."

I kissed the top of her head, holding her tight as images of my own life, my own future, flitted through my mind. It was cold and lonely, just like all my years before now.

Dozens of people stood in a semi-circle watching us dance, adoration on their faces as they smiled at Summer, wanting her to be happy. Those same stares hardened when they looked at me, seeing me as unworthy of her.

And fuck, I knew it.

She was endlessly kind, tenacious, funny, and so full of life, I'd never live up to her. Never deserve her.

My fingers tightened on her, not willing to let go even if everyone here wanted me to. Deep down, I was selfish. She'd given herself to me for three months, and I wasn't done with her yet. I couldn't let go. Not yet.

A glass clinked, then others followed until Summer's steps halted. "Kiss her!" someone yelled.

"You don't have to," Summer whispered, the words only for me. "It's okay."

Dropping her hand, I pressed a finger under her chin, locking onto her hazel eyes, rimmed with unshed tears.

"What if I want to?"

She sucked in a breath, her eyes darting around my face before settling on my lips. "I want that, too."

My fingers slid around the back of her neck, cradling her as I leaned down, my lips touching hers.

What should have been a chaste touch hit me like an electric current, bringing me back to life. This wasn't a kiss with a purpose. Wasn't to seal a bargain between us. Wasn't to pass blood to her discreetly. Wasn't for anyone but us, no matter the clinking glasses that urged us on.

This was for me. Because I couldn't help myself. Because I never wanted to stop.

I licked across her lips to the hoots and hollers of everyone here, not caring that they watched me metaphorically crumble to my knees at the taste of my wife.

My wife.

My wife.

My wife.

The words echoed in my head, a pounding rhythm I was helpless to deny. The rest of the room faded from existence, leaving only the two of us here in the middle of the dance floor. She let out the softest whimper, and my blood heated, need coursing through me like I'd never felt before.

But it wasn't just for her body.

I wanted Summer.

I wanted this to be real.

I wanted to have her back, and know she had mine, every day for the rest of my life.

"All right, we get it!" someone in the crowd yelled good-naturedly, and it brought me back to the present.

Summer pulled back from the kiss, eyes ablaze. A slight blush crept across her face as she looked to her left, noticing the crowd still around us. It took everything in me not to dive in for more, but I skimmed a thumb across that sweet blush and held her to my chest, not ready to let go.

My pocket vibrated and Summer glanced towards it. "Not yet, right? It's too soon for Rhain to have an update?"

I kissed her forehead again, unable to help myself as I took her hand and led her off the dance floor. Pulling my phone from my pocket, I glanced down at the screen.

RHAIN ALLAWAY

The meeting was moved. Tomorrow. Location to be determined, stay tuned.

Like a needle to a balloon, this bubble of happiness popped, and my world crashed back down around me.

Reading the text over my shoulder, Summer nodded. "When do we leave?"

My head jerked up. "Summer, no. I'm not bringing you this time. All the most dangerous vampires *in the world* will be there. My focus will be entirely on locating and extricating Malachi. I won't be able to look out for you."

Summer's eyes flashed with the gold of her wolf, and she cast a quick look around the barn, aware of how much focus we drew even off to the side like this. Grabbing my hand, she pulled me outside, into the dark against the side of the barn, and squared her shoulders to me.

"I don't know how many times I have to say this, but we're

in this together, Max. I'm going, with or without your blessing. If I need Indi to flicker me there on my own and scent them myself, I will. You don't have to look out for me. I am perfectly capable of watching my own back. In fact, I'll be there to watch yours. Now, and this is the last time I'm going to ask you this, when do we leave?"

Cloaked in shadow and limned in moonlight, my wife's inherent fire lit her up from within, her eyes luminous with her wolf. Damn if my pants didn't get tight at the sight of her. Pride swelled in my chest at her fierce determination. How could I say no to her?

"Tomorrow."

She blinked, like she was a little stunned I'd agreed, then nodded.

"They won't meet before dark, so if we leave midday, we should have plenty of time to find them. Assuming we get a location in time." I paused, not wanting to upset her again but needing her to understand the severity of the situation. "Will you tell someone we're going? Terran, or Indi, at least?"

Summer met my eye and held it, comprehension settling in.

Tell someone, so they know where you are.

Tell someone, in case we don't come back.

Finally, she nodded.

Chapter Thirty-One

SUMMER

"This is probably old news, but damn, girl, you should have felt the violent urges zinging around this room when Max kissed you on the dance floor earlier." Indi shook out her shoulders with a laugh, one of her tells her demon magic was lighting up. "I think Cooper nearly cracked a molar."

"I bet he did. Come with me." I grabbed her arm, dragging out of earshot of nosy shifters and into the tack room. Thankfully, the music was loud enough to drown us out as I shut the door. I didn't bother pulling the cord for the single lightbulb overhead, seeing as both wolves and demons could see fine in the dark. Saddles hung along one wall, the scent of leather overwhelming my nose, but not enough to erase the memory of Max's smoky aroma.

"Whoa, there, save the manhandling for your actual man, lady."

I whirled on her, hands on her shoulders. Her skin was supernaturally warm under my hands as a surge of panic rolled through me, but I dismissed it. I had no time for fear. "Indi. I'm telling you this because you're my best friend and you're not one of my siblings."

Her expression turned worried immediately. "What's wrong?"

"Nothing, yet. But" — I took a deep breath — "Max and I are leaving tomorrow. For a head vampires meeting. His father,

Malachi, is missing and we think they're holding him and we're going to try to get him back."

Indi stared, unblinking, then — "*What?!*"

"I know, it's a lot. But I just wanted someone to know, in case…" I grimaced, unable to voice my worries.

"You're meeting with the *head vampires* to steal someone they have *prisoner* who happens to be the *head of our society?*" she whisper-shrieked.

Hearing the intensity of the thing we were headed to do sent a ripple of anxiety through me, but I couldn't let Max do this on his own. Even if I was a little bit terrified, I shook it off, shoving it down with the other useless emotions I didn't dare touch. "I doubt we'll actually meet *with* the head vampires."

"*Summer!*" She shook her head vehemently. "No. Absolutely not. This sounds like a terrible idea, and why do *you* have to go? Vampires are *dangerous*, Summer! I know you're a wolf and can protect yourself, and you'll be with Max, but this isn't just finding dens anymore. This isn't a mostly-harmless-if-not-incredibly-stupid con like a marriage of convenience. I'm not saying you haven't thought this through, but *have you?*"

"We won't be alone," I said calmly, ignoring the last part of her question. After spending the last several weeks with Max, the thought of him walking into this alone was something I couldn't stomach, no matter the danger. I was going, end of discussion. "The vampires we met in Paris are on our side; they'll be coming to help, too."

"But—"

I held up a hand, glancing at the door to make sure we were still alone. "Max is going. He's going to get his father back, and where he goes —"

"—You go," Indi finished for me, but concern laced her furrowed brows. "Please please *please* tell your brothers? Or let me tell them once you've gone at the very least? This is going to eat me alive."

"You know they'll try to stop me if we tell them now." She let out a panicked whine. I launched at her, wrapping her in my arms and squeezing tight. I refused to acknowledge that this could be the last time, if things didn't go well. That wasn't an option. "Twenty-four hours. We leave tomorrow afternoon. If you haven't heard from me twenty-four hours from then, you can tell whoever you want. Okay?"

Indi grumbled, her fingers digging into my sides as she squeezed me back. "If you don't come home in one piece, I will hunt you down myself, young lady."

"I'd expect nothing less."

"Summer?" Terran called as howls broke out in the distance. The door cracked open and he peeked in. Indi straightened, turning towards him with a blush when we separated. "Oh, hey girls. West is calling for a pack run. You gonna join us?"

I nodded, pulling myself back together. "That sounds great, yeah."

He eyed me curiously, but Indi stepped by him, dragging her fingers across his chest as she squeezed through the doorway. His brow furrowed, turning to watch Indi leave. I breathed out a deep sigh, gathering myself. Plastering on my best grin, I said, "After you, brother."

Wolves circled just beyond the aisle my dad had set up for the wedding, some already darting into the woods beyond. Cooper and Atlas stood side by side in their human forms at the edge of the forest, arms crossed as they watched the younger wolves play.

West's storm-grey wolf appeared at my side, his golden eyes glancing up at me for a split second before he brushed by. I let my fingers trail over his fur, emotion clogging my throat as I looked out over my pack.

I couldn't leave Max to this challenge alone, but the thought of losing my family, my pack, my home... "Shit," I muttered as I quickly wiped away tears forming in the corners of my eyes.

"You okay?" Max came up to my side while my dad's grey-and-white wolf and Jade's smaller grey wolf trotted by. Everyone I loved was out in those woods, waiting for me.

"Yep." I turned towards him, doing my best to hide my emotions, capping my connection to the rest of the pack so they couldn't feel my fear and worry. I didn't need West and the rest of the pack figuring out something was wrong. While I couldn't find it in me to regret marrying Max and joining him on this mission, the thought of leaving my family again was killing me.

"Oh, I forgot to ask you," Terran said as he strolled by, now shirtless with his belt undone, getting ready to shift himself. Max cleared his throat, looking away from my brother's nearly naked form and I chuckled at his discomfort. While I certainly had no desire to see my brother's naked ass, nudity was very much a part of being a shifter. "River wanted to ask if she can come over to make cinnamon rolls in the morning."

Feeling Max's attention, I looked up to find his blue eyes focused on me. "We'll be here," Max said, then looked back at my brother. "What River wants, River gets, right?"

Terran and I laughed at the same time, and I squeezed Max's arm, thankful he realized how important my family was to me.

"Good man," Terran said, clapping Max on the back before slipping outside the barn and to the side. Moments later, a russet wolf ran past, his head tipped back as he answered the howls around us.

"Go," Max said, kissing my temple even though no one was around to see us. "I'll meet you back at your apartment."

I nodded, turning my back to him so he could unzip my dress. His warm hands lingered on my skin as the zipper fell, and I sucked in a breath.

Clutching the fabric to my chest, I turned slowly towards him, my wolf's eyes already taking over. Max's gaze turned heady as it raked over me, his hand still on my hip. Every time he looked at me like this, a surge of confidence shot through me, loving the pure *need* I saw there.

I dropped the dress, letting it puddle around my ankles as his eyes widened. With a smirk, I let my wolf take over. Trees rushed by in a blur as I ran through the woods, chasing Aspen's dark brown wolf, Cruz flickering in and out between the pines as his laugh rang out over the night.

This was my home, my family, my everything.

Malachi wasn't just Max's only family, he was the leader of supernatural society. If we didn't save him and the Conclave did everything Project Oleander was worried about, everyone here would be at risk too. The human world hadn't handled shifters coming out peacefully — if the Conclave outed themselves as the bloodthirsty villains hidden in the shadows, it would affect all of us. It would undo all of the work West had done in the past few years to make supernaturals seem a part of peaceful society. We'd be hunted, even more than we already were.

There was nothing I wouldn't do for the people here tonight. That included walking straight into a den of the most fearsome vampires in the world.

Awareness tickled at my brain and I looked up in time to see Max's black wings block out the moon.

Mine. The word rang through my mind, and I could hardly tell whether it was my own thought or my wolf's. On this, we agreed.

Max was mine. I wouldn't leave him, not now.
Not ever.

Chapter Thirty-Two

MAX

Soaring over Summer's pack as they ran, I could feel her joy down to my bones. Whether that was something to do with our connection, my shadowmark on her, or something else, I didn't know. But damn I'd fight like hell to make sure she got to come back here and be a part of this again.

I wasn't sure if flying above them was intrusive, but I couldn't let her out of my sight. The way her wolf tipped up her head, howling at me, made me think maybe she felt the same.

Eventually, the pack slowed near a river so they could all grab a drink. I circled until Summer canted her head and wandered off, a clear signal to follow her.

Out of sight of the others, I shot to the ground right in front of her, silent as a shadow, my lips tipping up as all four of her paws left the earth at once.

In an instant, she was human again and threw herself at me. Cheeks flushed from the brisk air of her run, hair windswept, she crashed her lips against mine with a low, feral moan.

That same electric energy flowed between us when our lips touched, a current I couldn't stop even if I'd wanted to. My hands found her bare waist instantly as I breathed into her mouth, "Summer—"

Her hands found my belt, tugging insistently, and I

groaned. She may have been heedless to the hundred people merely a few trees around the corner, but I wasn't.

"Hold on, sunshine." Grabbing her tight, I vanished us out of the woods, landing in her rooftop garden in case the fresh air was part of this need she'd awoken.

Moaning my name, her fingers dug into my scalp as she swayed slightly from the jolt of vanishing. The decadent sound was too much, and I couldn't stop myself. Without a thought, I bit into her neck, taking the smallest sip. Sweetness washed over my tongue, the taste as addicting as any I'd ever had.

Together we pulled at my clothes, dropping them to the floor piece by piece until I was as naked as her. Our mouths fused back together as if this was the only way we could breathe. With a gentle nudge, I urged her towards the patio chaise across from where we'd landed. Her knees hit the wooden frame, and scooted back on it until she was laid out across the bright yellow cushion, my body draped over hers.

Every kiss I'd denied her came out in a frenzied haze, one after the next, as if we couldn't get enough. Magic hummed between us as I kissed along her jaw and back to the pulse point in her neck, thrumming as hard as my own.

"Touch me," Summer demanded, back arched beneath me. Another time I might have scolded her bossy tone, but I was helpless to resist her breathy voice. Her nails clawed across my back as if she could pull my wings free from their glamour, needing me in all aspects, and I fucking loved it.

My hands drifted down her body to her entrance, pressing everywhere she needed me until her breathing was ragged. Some intrinsic need to make her even more mine than just the rings on our fingers had my fangs out and biting into my own thumb, dragging the drop of blood across her bottom lip.

She sucked in a breath, her eyes flying open as I held myself above her, unable to see anything but this gorgeous woman spread out below me. Her eyes were rimmed in gold as her tongue darted out, licking away the small drop of blood I'd left there.

It was the sexiest thing I'd ever seen, the most *alive* I'd ever felt. In a frenzy, she pulled on my head until I lowered my mouth to hers. She opened beneath me, and I slid my tongue into her mouth, tasting the coppery tang of my blood lingering.

Like gasoline on a fire, I needed her, and I needed her now.

"On your stomach," I growled against her lips. Gripping her hips to help her roll over, I moved to kneel behind her. She did as I said, dropping her head to the cushion as she raised her hips. Gold-rimmed eyes on me, she wiggled her ass in invitation until I smacked it. A gasp had her eyes shifting from gold-rimmed to pure gold, and I lost any ability I had to resist her.

Her shadowmark rippled across her skin, growing in a perfect combination of flowers and the night sky — the two of us, combined into one. I ran a hand across my aching cock, watching the shadowmark grow until it covered the majority of her back.

I ran my free hand down her spine, magic humming beneath my hands until she moaned, the bond strengthening between us while I stroked myself. "You are so fucking gorgeous. My beautiful wife."

She reached a hand between her legs to dull the ache surely building there until I slapped it away. Replacing her fingers with my own, I pushed into her as I worked my thumb in small circles around her apex.

"More, Max." Her eyes fluttered closed as her hips shifted backwards, pushing me deeper. "I need more."

I smirked, high off her little sounds, knowing she was as desperate for me as I was her. "Such a needy girl, aren't you?"

She rocked forward then back, and I hooked my fingers just right until she moaned shamelessly again, squirming against my hand. As she tightened around me, I withdrew my fingers from her warmth and sucked the moisture off them.

"Oh, fuck, Max."

I flipped her onto her back and her knees parted in invitation. Settling between her thighs, I held myself aloft to notch my cock at her entrance.

Before I could tease her more, Summer's foot wrapped around my ass, pulling me into her with a swift motion.

I dropped my head into the crook of her shoulder, inhaling her scent as my mind blanked, lost to anything but the feel of her warmth wrapped around me.

"Move," Summer whined, pushing her hips up into mine. I did as she said, pulling back before pushing in deeper.

"How?" I mumbled against her skin, unable to resist licking across her pulse point again as I continued to move. "How does it just get better every time? Why do you smell like the most irresistible desert? When will I get enough of this?"

She tightened around me, squeezing until I could hardly breathe. "I don't know. I don't know. I don't know." She repeated the phrase over and over, as lost as I was to whatever this pull was between us. I knew there were reasons why we couldn't continue this after my mission was complete, but here, wrapped up with her, none of them came to mind.

My lips found hers as we moved in tandem, her fingers gripping my head. She held me to her until she began to shudder and pulse beneath me.

"That's it, my good girl," I said against her lips. "Come all over your husband's cock."

She tossed her head back, eyes closed as I traced a hand down her chest, feeling her heartbeat slam against her ribcage in a rhythm that matched my own.

"I can't—" she started, licking her lips, then gasping again as I kept thrusting through her orgasm, dragging it out until I couldn't help but follow.

My body folded around hers, a deep groan leaving me I hardly recognized as I came inside her for the first time.

Heart racing, I tipped my body to the side, wrapping my arms around her back as I pulled her with me, not ready to leave the warmth of her body.

Her lips found mine as we lazily kissed, ignoring the world around us including the howls of her pack in the distance.

"Stay out here or find a real bed?"

"Stay," she whispered, and it sounded like so much more. "I want to hear them."

On cue, another round of howls went up, and a contented smile graced her lips.

I grabbed a blanket from a nearby chair, dragging it over us. "They won't wonder where you went and come looking, right?"

"No." Summer's murmur was fading, like she was already half-asleep. "I let them know I'm right where I belong."

I lay awake long after Summer fell asleep, unable to stop tracing the delicate curve of her features and wondering just what I'd done to deserve to lie next to her. To be any part of her world, her life, her family.

Some tiny, long forgotten part of my heart tightened painfully; the dark corner that held the foolish hopes of a lonely boy who, once upon a time, wished for a family like that of his own.

Maybe that was what made me slip off the lounge, careful not to disturb my wife, and pad down to the living room. I found my jacket where I'd hung it on the rack by the door, and took it with me as I sank down on the couch.

From the jacket pocket, I pulled the crumpled envelope my

father had given me weeks ago. The one supposedly from my mother.

My mother, who'd never so much as called me up before. Never spoken to me, never sought me out. Never wanted me.

So why now? Why would she reach out now, and why not just talk to me directly?

More importantly, why was I even contemplating reading it?

But apparently, I was. I peeled open the envelope and pulled out the letter. My mother's cursive handwriting was elegant, old fashioned.

> Massimo Marco,
>
> You must have many questions for me. I wish I could answer them. But I cannot say much, in case this letter falls into the wrong hands.
> When you wonder for whom the bell tolls, follow its ring to the east. Perhaps history will repeat itself where dukes slept and fires lit the water.
> Would that I could cross the bridges between us, but I'm afraid they burned long ago.
> -G.

I read it once, then read it again, anger rising in me.

What the hell was she talking about? The bell? What fucking history? Fire on water?

With a frustrated sigh, I crumpled the letter, tossing it onto the coffee table in front of me. I wasn't sure what I'd hoped to find, but it wasn't this mysterious nonsense that read more like the delusional musings of a vampire with too many years in her mind.

I was so fucking sick of the endless questions with no

answers. My whole life, my father told me just enough to keep me useful, and refused to share anything important. How many times had I asked him about my mother, about my vampire heritage, and he'd just shut me down? I was always feeling my way through my life in the dark, unable to see more than a few feet in front of me, and I was over it. The secrets, the mysteries, the 'need to know' bullshit my father always spouted at me. I'd had it with all these loose threads, never knowing where I was going next or what the next task would be, and now my so-called mother was just adding to the unknown.

The last thing I needed was another unknown. Another fucking mystery to unravel.

My head tipped back on the couch and I stared up at the ceiling, trying to shove my disappointment down. I refused to let her letter have that effect on me. Refused to admit I'd ever expected anything more, anything close to an apology. Anything close to a family.

I knew better than that.

Running a hand through my hair, I stood, shaking my head at the pathetic excuse for a letter and resolving to find my father so I could ask all the questions he'd been avoiding for so long.

He'd raised me to need no one, and job well done.

Consider the bridges long gone, G.

Chapter Thirty-Three

MAX

The smell of lemon roused me, and I leaned in, inhaling deeply. My hands tightened around Summer's waist, pulling her back across the bed into my front until no part of us wasn't touching. Once I'd read the letter and the pack howls had quieted for the night, I'd relocated us to her bedroom.

"You've been hanging out with too many wolves to be sniffing me like this," Summer rasped in her sleepy morning voice.

I smirked, cracking my eyes open. Warm sun rays peeked through the blinds, washing Summer's bedroom in a hazy glow, bringing all the colors to life. "I can see the appeal when you smell like a lemon poppyseed muffin. Makes me want to take a bite."

Propping my head up, I brushed the hair on her neck aside, then grazed my teeth across her shoulder. She reached behind her, running her fingers through my hair as she tipped her head back to give me better access.

Laying gentle kisses across her neck and shoulder, I slid my hand down her naked torso, feeling her body squirm under my touch. She was always so responsive, this wife of mine, and I fucking loved it.

As my fingers dipped between her legs, she let out a soft moan. "Didn't get enough of me last night?" she said with a breathy chuckle, her eyes cracking open as she looked over her shoulder at me.

"I'm starting to think that's impossible, sunshine." I slid my fingers back and forth across her sensitive skin, loving every sound she made.

Somewhere in my mind I knew I didn't have time for these lazy touches. We had things to do before we could leave town and head to Italy, but with my hands on her soft skin, I couldn't think of a single reason any of it had to be right this minute.

Her phone alarm chimed then in insistent opposition.

"Cinnamon roll o'clock?"

With a soft chuckle, she laced her fingers between mine and pulled me upright. "I mean, I'd like to if we have time. You said yourself, River runs the show around here, and I—" She swallowed, and her chin dipped on the words, eyes no longer meeting mine. "I promised I wouldn't leave her like her mother did. I can't help but feel like in the eyes of a six-year-old, that's exactly what I'm doing."

Just like that, the weight of everything ahead of us slammed down on my shoulders. I swallowed around a lump in my throat, my heart racing for an entirely different reason than just a few minutes ago. I hadn't heard from Rhain again since last night, and the meeting wasn't until this evening. If I was working alone, I'd be there already, scoping it out for the best strategy.

But I wasn't alone.

If something happened to me later today, it wouldn't really matter. A few weeks ago, I might have even said no one would even notice my absence. But Summer… Her loss would be profound, not just for me, but for so many people. I was a selfish bastard for thinking my need for her trumped her need for the rest of the people in her life.

I stood, tipping her chin back up. The moment our eyes met, I leaned in to kiss her. "She's important to you, so she's important to me. We have time."

A wide grin spread across her face, and my heart lurched at

the sight. Somewhere in the last few weeks, my priorities had shifted, and Summer's happiness ranked higher than almost everything else. The world could crumble around us, and as long as Summer kept smiling like she was right now, I wasn't sure I cared.

She was more than just beautiful.

She was mine.

I'd thought I'd known what chaos felt like. My life had led me into some pretty unpredictable situations, where danger lurked at every corner, and I'd always met those head-on.

Baking with half a dozen Larkins took 'chaos' to a whole different level.

"Behind!" River screeched at the top of her lungs, and I pushed my front into a cabinet just in time to avoid her clipping me with the giant bowl of dough she did not look big enough to carry by herself.

"Make way!" Summer was on her heels with an armful of ingredients, throwing me a wink before setting everything down on the counter.

She and River were in matching aprons with the Love Bites shop logo on the front, though River's was sized for a child. Shoving a step stool over to the counter, River climbed up and stood at the ready for Summer's instructions.

Leif was slicing oranges and making some fresh-squeezed orange juice. Aspen, Cooper, and their Aunt Hattie stood to the side talking, all of them shooting me sideways glances. West and Jade were preparing a bowl of fresh fruit salad, disgustingly in love as they fed each other blueberries. Terran stood near them in front of the stove, a huge pan of bacon sizzling delectably, and stirred up a bowl of eggs for omelettes.

"Hair, Riv," he called over. His daughter threw her head

back dramatically but pulled a scrunchie off her wrist, holding it out for someone to tie her hair up.

"Um, Max?" She waved the scrunchie in my face, pushing it into my cheek when I hesitated to take it from her.

Summer bit back a smile, not meeting my eyes as she readied ingredients for the cinnamon rolls. Terran was elbow deep in eggs. I glanced around for anyone else to help with this, because what the fuck did I know about kid hair? Cooper leaned against a counter, his stare deadly flat. "We're busy." After a beat, he picked up a few rags, handing one each to Aspen and Hattie too. "Cleaning."

Heath chuckled as he pivoted on his heel and called out, "Getting more coffee beans!" before heading to the storage room.

I narrowed my eyes at him, but accepted this manipulation for what it was. I could do this.

It was just hair. I had hair.

River launched the hair tie, hitting me square in the eye. "Hurry, angel boy! Aunt Summer will do it all without me!"

"You've been around Aspen too much, little Larkin," I told her as I stepped behind the tiny girl, her blonde curls swaying as she faced forward. Her misplaced confidence that I knew how to do this was both startling and endearing.

I slowly gathered River's hair, careful not to tug too hard, and fully ignored the amused glances Summer and Terran shot me.

Once I'd slid the scrunchie on and tightened it, I stepped back. It was a little lopsided, and I'd missed a few strands somehow — River was *not* a still child — but she didn't seem to care.

"Thanks, Uncle Max!"

She immediately dove in to helping Summer form the cinnamon rolls, oblivious to the crack she'd rent in my heart.

Uncle Max?

Fuck. I didn't know how to feel.

No, I did. It *hurt*.

But it was almost… good. A good hurt.

Thoughts I'd never let myself ponder entered my mind, the idea of a future that wasn't so alone, of a family like this one. I blinked, trying to squash the images flitting into my brain as fast as they came on.

Summer must have noticed I was having a moment, because she stepped over and bumped her hip against mine.

"Hey, Uncle Max," she said, a smile playing on her lips. "Grab us a sugar bowl, would you?"

I swallowed heavily, determined to hide the effect a few tiny words had had on me, and nodded. "Sure thing, sunshine."

After breakfast, River insisted we all play Jenga out in the café.

The whole game, I kept mulling over my mother's letter. Faced with the warmth and open arms with which the Larkins embraced me — except maybe Hattie, who never took her predatory gaze off me — her words seemed even colder. Even more impersonal.

For whom the bell tolls. I knew the book. Something about the Spanish civil war.

Was she trying to tell me something about the unrest with the vampires? History repeating itself — maybe a hint about a vampire civil war coming? That didn't seem totally far-fetched — Étienne's group certainly seemed ready for one.

But if my heritage was any indication, didn't vampires have more connections to Italy, not Spain?

"Max! Your turn!" River stomped her foot, impatient with me for holding the game up, lost in my thoughts.

I tugged out a piece, and River shrieked with glee with the top half of the tower toppled.

I paused, piece still in my hand. Tower…

Picturing the letter in my mind again, I went back to the beginning. Where she'd called me *Massimo Marco*, which wasn't even my middle name.

But… maybe that was another clue.

Suddenly, I was sure it was a coded message, the certainty settling over my bones. The pieces were *there*, I just needed to put them together.

"So," came a barked voice beside me. Hattie settled into a chair, tugging it closer to our table and crossing her arms over her chest. "You're the *angel* who eloped with my niece."

I looked up at the Larkin males who all knew my secret, but they all avoided my eye contact. There was something about the way she said the word. Something sarcastic.

I'd be lying if I said Hattie wasn't a little bit terrifying. She was like something out of an old school Western, tough like an Annie Oakley. I half expected to find a set of pistols strapped to her hips under the table, but the energy coming off her told me her wolf was a weapon in its own right. Her long grey hair was braided back, her eyes sharp and assessing, like she'd be ready to attack on a moment's notice.

I sat up straighter before I realized I was doing it. "Yes, ma'am." I'd never called anyone ma'am in my life, but hell if I wasn't going to show this woman all the respect in the world.

Hattie grunted, her nose twitching slightly. In amusement? Or was she scenting me?

"What makes you think you're good enough for our Summer?"

"Hattie," Summer admonished, shooting me an apologetic look.

"What?" Hattie asked, utterly *un*apologetic. "It's a fair question."

Summer opened her mouth to speak again, but I cut her off. "I'm not."

Hattie arched a brow at my response, but didn't say anything, so I went on.

"I'm not good enough for her. I don't think anybody would be." Summer's hand found mine under the table, and I realized the conversations around us had all halted, all eyes on me. I kept my focus on Hattie. "Summer is the most remarkable person I've ever met. She's kind, and thoughtful. She's passionate about everything, smart as a whip. I don't know why she'd want— " I cut myself off, shaking my head. "There isn't one person on this earth good enough for her, but she chose me. So, I'm going to trust her to know her own mind, and spend whatever time she gives me trying to be the man she deserves."

Hattie's eyes bored into mine as silence fell after my impromptu speech. I hadn't meant to say all that, to bare my fucking soul, but the words had just spilled out. My hands turned clammy as I waited for judgment.

Finally, Hattie gave me the barest nod, and conversation erupted again.

"That was fucking beautiful," Terran choked out, pretending to wipe a tear.

"Bad word, Daddy!" River called.

"I think I'm gonna cry," Coop grunted, expressionless. I shot him a glare. The cat was a lot less scary now that I'd seen him scarf down three cinnamon rolls while barely taking a breath.

"Be honest," Aspen said, "have you been reading Summer's books?"

"Aw, leave my son-in-law alone, you barbarians," Heath chuckled. "And you may want to read a few books too, you know. Lots to learn. Your mother loved to act out scenes from my books. How do you think I ended up with so many kids?" He waggled his eyebrows, and every one of his children pretended to gag.

Aspen looked green. "Oh my God, Dad."

"I'm scarred," Terran added, shaking his head.

Cooper merely pressed his eyes shut in horror.

Even Leif pointed a finger at him. "No more book club for you."

Heath's hands went up innocently. "What? It's important to keep your mind active at my age, kids."

Another round of uproar went through the group. But as the Larkins continued to give each other shit, all felt right in the world.

There was so much *love* here. So much goodness, so much heart, so much light.

Did they have room for shadows, too?

Did I want them to?

I was almost afraid to answer that, even to myself.

I closed the dishwasher, pressing to start it, when suddenly, things clicked.

Marco. The bell. Civil war, history repeating itself.

Bridges. Burning.

It wasn't about Spain at all. I whipped my phone out, texting Rhain.

MAX

They're meeting in Venice, Doge Palace.

Saint Mark's Basilica would be the bell tower. The bridges — she was trying to point me to Venice. The civil war, history repeating itself — Doge Palace had been the site of more than one instance of unrest. And once upon a time, there'd been a huge fire there, on the canal side where the apartments were.

Where dukes slept and fires lit the water.

This was it. We had an official location.

Now, we just had to overthrow the oldest, most powerful vampires in the world.

Chapter Thirty-Four

SUMMER

"Anything else from Rhain?" I asked, zipping up my backpack. I packed light, hoping this would be a quick trip.

"He's arrived in Venice, but the others don't seem to be there yet. No sign of Malachi, but that doesn't mean much. My best guess is, he'll arrive with the Conclave, and they'll keep him well-hidden until they want to show him off." Max set his phone down next to his almost untouched eggs. "We'll vanish to somewhere in the outskirts and then meet up with him."

His fingers started tapping on the table, though otherwise he appeared calm. I slid into the seat next to him, laying my hand on his to still the tapping.

"He'll be there. We'll get him out."

He managed a grim smile.

"Not hungry?" I nodded at his plate. After River had carried off the box of cinnamon rolls we'd made, Max and I had come back upstairs and I'd made a more filling late breakfast.

Max lifted a shoulder, but I didn't miss the way his gaze flicked to my neck.

"Oh, I'm dumb," I said on a laugh, and his eyes hardened. "You need more blood, right? Must take a lot of magic to get back and forth from Europe in two days." Sweeping my hair over my shoulder, I tilted my head, baring my neck. "We're in this together, Max. You need to speak up if you need blood."

"One," Max started, his hand on my jaw tilting my head

back upright, "no one is allowed to call my wife dumb, so make sure I never hear those words from your lips again." His hand trailed down my neck, over my shoulder, down my arm, and my entire body shivered at his words. "Two, yes. It does take a lot of magic." His fingers circled my wrist, raising it towards him. "Three, I'll never be able to ask for your blood, Summer. To ask for the life force that keeps your heart beating, to put my needs over your well-being." His lips skated the underside of my wrist, and I had to clench my thighs together under the table. "But when you offer it to me so freely, Goddess forgive me, I can't say no."

His fangs sank into the flesh of my wrist. A gasp left my lips at the sharp pain that quickly morphed into pleasure, nerves all over my body lighting up as he lapped tenderly at my wrist, not spilling a drop. Max's dark hair fell across his forehead as he closed his eyes, dark lashes fanning over his tan skin, and I let out a pathetic whimper.

My thighs squeezed tighter, an aching emptiness taking root inside me as my breathing quickened, my heart rate increasing.

I sat paralyzed by need, overwhelmed by wanting him, his closeness intoxicating. Each time we did this, my need for him grew until it was an all-encompassing thing, blocking out the rest of my logical mind. I wanted to lean over, inhale his sandalwood and coppery scent deep into my lungs, sink my own fangs into his neck, mark *him* as my —

Too soon, his fangs retracted, and he gently laved his tongue over the wounds, sealing them as he retreated.

Turning my hand over, his deep blue eyes met my own as he pressed a kiss to the back of my hand, murmuring, "Thank you, sweet Summer."

I took a shaky breath, licking my lips and clearing my throat. What had just happened? I'd never felt the driving need to 'mark' anyone before.

"A-anytime," I breathed, trying to blink myself back to coherency as Max set my hand back on the table. As I resisted the urge to reach out for him, to pull him in and push him down on my kitchen floor.

"You all right?"

Max had stood, and when I raised my head to look at him, the playful smirk and knowing look in his eye told me he was completely aware of the need coursing through me.

I narrowed my eyes. "Did you do that on purpose?"

"Do what?"

I gave him a look. He flicked up an eyebrow. "What purpose would it possibly serve to distract us both before the most dangerous day of our lives?"

Damn him, he had a point. Some of the tension had left me in the wake of his distraction.

"Touché, Monster Mash." I pushed to stand, my chair scraping over the floor a jarring reawakening to reality. Slinging my backpack over my shoulder, I jabbed a thumb to the ceiling. "Shall we?"

Chapter Thirty-Five

SUMMER

The scent of brackish water washed over me as we rematerialized. In the dark, narrow alley, we were just part of the shadows. I gripped Max's jacket tight, regaining my bearings after the vertigo-inducing trip.

As my spinning mind slowed, the gentle lapping of waves hit my ears, and I opened my eyes.

Venice. Another city on my bucket list that I never really thought I'd see, and here I was, not even a week after Paris. With the time difference, the sun here was already setting, and I almost regretted not arriving earlier.

But I wasn't here to sightsee. And at least this time, I was a fully aware participant in this job.

"You good?"

I blinked up at Max, realizing I was still white-knuckling his jacket. Quickly I let go, retreating a step even if every fiber of my being wanted to hold onto him and never let go.

"Yeah, sorry. I'm good."

He eyed me, his dark eyes unreadable in the shadows, despite the moonlight, and took out his phone. "I'll check in with Rhain. Let him know we're here."

I nodded, stepping a little closer to the end of the alley to sneak a peek at the famous canals. Lights shone from the buildings lining the water, casting a glow over the rippling water.

Laying a hand on the building next to me, the stone was still warm from the earlier sun. I closed my eyes, reaching out with my senses. If there was a den of gathered elite vampires here, would I already be able to sense them? Or would their cloaking be even more advanced than regular dens, rendering them invisible to me?

My nose twitched, a sizzle of magic going through me, and I opened my eyes, ready to tell Max, when —

"If you'll turn your attention to the left-hand side, folks, you'll see the famed Basilica de San Marco." Rhain said in his best tour guide impression and swept his hands towards the end of the alley. Max rolled his eyes.

"Wait, really?" I peered around the corner again, fragments of conversation drifting our way across the water, but too far away to make anything out.

"Well, no," Rhain admitted, sliding his hands into his dark jeans pockets. "'Dante' here isn't dumb enough to land you two downtown. But it's not far from here."

"Focus." Max scowled. "Are they here yet?"

"Right. All business."

"Missing *Premier of the supernatural world*," Max reminded him curtly.

"The Conclave themselves aren't here yet," Rhain continued. "But their lackeys have started arriving. You were right, Max — they're clearing out the Doge Palace as we speak. Dubois and our people are gathering on a boat offshore; we need to keep our larger presence hidden from the Conclave for as long as we can."

My eyes widened. "They're having their meeting *in* the Doge Palace?"

Rhain grimaced. "I know. Bit ostentatious, but the Conclave *loves* a good show of force. Nothing says that like taking over a historical landmark and major tourist attraction for the night to use for their own purposes. Just because they can." He turned to Max, one brow raised. "Have you been before?"

"Inside? No," Max admitted. "But I'm familiar with the city."

"We'll get a floor plan. It shouldn't be too hard to track one down," Rhain said, and I was already searching for one on my phone. "There's a room inside that was traditionally used to question prisoners — and why reinvent the wheel, right? Twenty euro says they'll keep him there tonight."

"Found it." I held my phone out to Max, who quickly scanned the layout, moving the image around and zooming in.

"They'll have the place locked down," Rhain warned. "Not only with guards, but the witches on their payroll are some of the best. It'll be spelled to hell and back. No one in or out."

Max handed me back my phone. "I assume you have a plan for that."

"Well, it's old. There are a lot of entrances, and the Conclave doesn't travel with that many lackeys. It'll be warded, but still, they're not exactly expecting to be ambushed. As far as they're aware, the only people who know about this meeting are on their side, after all. Once they've settled in for their meeting, Dubois' people will work on the wards. As a last resort, they'll take out the guards before going for the Conclave themselves. That's when you can go for Malachi." Rhain's eyes drifted from Max to me, a question lingering there.

Max slid his hand into mine. "She'll be with me."

My wolf lifted her head up, proud, at the words, and the slight widening of Rhain's eyes told me she'd shown herself in my eyes.

A smirk flitted across Rhain's face as he held up his hands. "All right."

"What time?" Max asked.

"Typically, they gather around midnight. Stay close, but inconspicuous. I'll let you know when we've been summoned inside. Once we start, wait nearby until it's time."

"Simple as that?"

Rhain turned his gaze on me, his green eyes glittering in the dark. "As long as everything goes exactly according to plan, yes."

Right. And if not, Rhain and the other dukes might get killed for their treason. If not, possibly none of us would make it out alive.

None of us said it, but we were all thinking it.

"Well," Rhain brightened, clapping his hands together. "Good luck to us all."

He dissolved into shadow, vanishing from our alley.

My lips pressed thin, I glanced at Max. "I guess let's just do everything perfectly, then."

We wandered through the Floating City as it was still several hours until midnight, acting every bit the couple in love, just in case. Hand in hand, we took a water taxi to a restaurant Max knew, huddling close the whole time. Neither of us had much of an appetite, only nibbling on the bread brought to our table but downing the wine with ease.

Max's finger tapping on the table only grew more agitated, and he kept checking the time in between clenching his jaw. I couldn't blame him — my anxiety had sweat beading on the back of my neck, but I refused to give in to the long list of everything that could go wrong.

It couldn't — that was the only option.

I kept one eye on him, though there wasn't much I could do to help his stress, and another on our surroundings. No fewer than three of the Parisian vampires passed by our spot, giving us the barest nod of acknowledgment as they did.

A spark flashed from Max's fingertips, singeing the slice of bread he tore apart aimlessly. Not a great sign.

"Let's walk," I suggested. Movement usually helped my

anxiety, and, at the very least, couldn't be worse than just sitting here.

Looping my arm through his, I led us down the street, no destination in mind other than killing time. Restaurants lined the street, mainly filled with romantic couples, but plenty of groups of friends and family too. Languages from all corners of the globe reached my ears, along with the melodies of street musicians from every corner.

Making our way over a picturesque stone bridge, I tugged Max to a stop on a whim and whipped out my phone.

"Say cheese, husband." I leaned into his chest, smiling into the camera, and his arm wrapped around my waist on instinct. Examining the photo, he hadn't quite smiled, but the look in his eyes as he gazed down at me was heady, his focus intense.

"I'll bring you back sometime," Max said suddenly.

"What?"

He gestured around us. "To Venice. It's on your bucket list, right?" When I nodded, he continued. "This visit hardly counts, I think. But another time, we'll come back. I'll make it up to you for helping me out."

I slipped my phone away, turning to face him. "You know that's not what this is, right? This isn't a transaction, tit for tat. We don't *owe* each other anything."

He studied me, brow furrowing, but didn't speak.

"I *wanted* to help you, so I'm here. That's it."

His eyes held mine for a long moment, like he wasn't sure what to make of that, and I didn't even know if I could blame him. Max, I'd learned, wasn't used to unconditional love or friendship of any kind.

He was spared replying by the loud tolling of the bell, high above the city. It was as ominous a sound as any, each clang a reminder of everything at stake.

I stood on my tiptoes, pulling his face down to mine as I let every drop of emotion I felt for this man show. Hoping he understood how committed I was not just to this task, but to making him see how loved he was.

"Max," I whispered, three little words I'd never said to anyone but my family and friends on the tip of my tongue. "I—"

His phone buzzed, and we both looked down at the incoming message.

"Rhain," he said, reading it. "They're going inside." Nodding back towards the way we came, we turned and walked back towards the Doge Palace.

Showtime.

Chapter Thirty-Six

MAX

Creeping towards the Doge Palace, we found a shadowy corner where we had eyes on a side entrance. I pulled my own shadows around us, cloaking us further, and waited.

After a few minutes, Summer tapped my arm, then her nose, pointing to a man who walked by across the plaza. I saw the vampire too, presumably making the rounds and checking entrances.

"I can't sense any wards. Can you?" Summer whispered from beside me after he'd passed.

I nodded. "They're witch-made, probably layered with the Conclave's own magic though. And you don't need to whisper; my shadow magic has us fully concealed."

"I can't help it," she said, still whispering. "You can't be a secret agent and talk at a normal volume. It doesn't fit the aesthetic."

Even amidst the stress of the moment, she had me fighting back a smile. Another guard went by, their patrols closer together than I would have thought. Had something alerted them?

"What about Malachi? Do you have any connection to him to sense if he's nearby?"

I shook my head. "No, we don't have mental connections like wolves do."

Usually, that seemed like a good thing. The last thing I needed was anyone in my head. But right now? It'd be pretty damn useful if I could sense his presence in the city and use it to track him down.

Time slowed agonizingly as we waited, the only sounds the lapping waves nearby and muted conversations of tourists heading back from their late night out.

I'd meant it when I told Summer I'd bring her back. This was a mission, not a bucket list worthy trip. But I still had trouble reconciling the rest of what she'd said — that this wasn't a transaction. After the wedding reception, everything felt different — felt like we *both* wanted more.

Did I even know how to do that? How to be in a relation-ship without strings? Without scales constantly tipping and rebalancing?

"There." Summer leaned in closer, her voice barely more than a breath, her lips all but brushing my cheek.

Any other time, I'd have her pushed back against the building and take her lips with mine.

Instead, I forced my instincts to behave and followed her line of sight. A man dressed like a tourist — khaki shorts, *Venezia* shirt, white sneakers, camera around his neck — strolled casually by the palace, glancing up at it in interest.

Apparently oblivious, he smacked right into the vampire turning the corner on their rounds. In a split second, shadow surrounded them both.

Silence cut out from the scene, Summer and I both holding our breaths to see what happened. When the shadow retreated, only one figure moved on.

The 'tourist,' arms behind his back again, carried on his stroll.

The guard vampire lay slumped against the side of the palace.

Summer gasped. "Did he kill him?" She tilted her head, listening hard.

"Just knocked out," I reassured her, nudging her attention

to our right as the vampire's body started to disintegrate from the stake in his chest. "Let's get closer."

We crept over to the side of the palace now, crouching near the door itself. From deep inside, a rumble of magic spread, skittering over our skin. I locked eyes on Summer, and we both felt the unmistakable sensation of the wards dissolving.

One quick nod was all I allowed to reassure us both before I wrenched open the side door, ushered Summer in, and closed it behind us.

We'd spent the last few hours memorizing the floor plan, so we took off through the halls, staying quiet but making straight for the room Rhain had mentioned. I kept my shadows wrapped tight around us in case anyone was wandering the halls.

I was about to cross another hall when I froze at the sound of leathery wings rustling behind us. Pushing Summer back into an alcove, I caged her in with my body and covered us with as much of my magic as I could muster.

Her chest moved, but she stayed silent, hands on my sides. My heart raced, the predator within me rising to the surface and all too pleased to have Summer pinned like this. The gold rim around her eyes said she didn't mind it either, but when the rustling faded, I backed away.

Shouts, muffled at first then growing louder, began some-where off in the palace, and my heart rate accelerated. What-ever was going down had kicked off. We needed to find Malachi and get out, now.

I took Summer's hand, hurrying us along until we came to the prisoner's room, the door shut. Indicating the door to Summer, I stepped back, letting her press in close and listen with her shifter hearing.

Heart pounding seconds later, she stepped back, meeting my eyes and shrugging.

Nothing?

I reached for the handle, magic zapping up my arm that made me wrench it back, shaking it out. A ward, but not a strong one. Probably just a trip to let the spell-caster know it had been crossed.

"Shit," I muttered, then forced the door open, the lock breaking with an ear-splitting shriek of metal.

Summer's hands flew over her ears. I entered the room first, the space lit by only one candle. Dim light flickered over the small space, empty except for the figure tied to the chair in the center, iron cuffs around their wrists and ankles.

Their head jerked up, then jerked again at the sight of us.

"Massimo?" My father's voice was hoarse, barely a croak, like he'd been starved or deprived of water, or hadn't spoken to a soul in days.

Dried blood covered his brow, trailed down his neck, though any wounds they might have given him were already healed with his magic. Except for —

"Where are your wings?"

He flinched, even though my words were barely more than a whisper. Summer's eyes widened in horror, looking between us.

Hurrying forward, my shoulders twitched at the thought, my own wings currently hidden. His would grow back, eventually, but it didn't make the archaic practice any less barbaric.

"What about your magic?" I hissed at the spelled hand-cuffs, cursing as I tried to work out how to free him.

He barked a bitter laugh, his head hanging low.

Summer kneeled behind him, trying to free his wrists while I worked on the ones binding his ankles to the iron chair.

"You won't open them," Malachi said, weariness coating his every syllable. "They're coated in endless layers of magic, centuries in the making. You need to get out of here before they see you, before they have any idea you got past their guards —"

A second door on the far side of the room creaked open, and we all froze, staring.

A dark-haired female vampire stared back at us, equally shocked. Her deep blue eyes flashed to her predator's red before switching back as she took in the scene. Silently, she closed the door behind her, her blood red robes sweeping around her.

She made to rush forward. In an instant, I was between her and Summer, shadow and lightning coiling in my palms.

"*Sbrigati*, Massimo. Hurry, hurry!"

My eyes narrowed. Another person knew my real name? Just how many people had my father told about me? If the fancy, brocaded dress was any indication, this female was one of the Conclave herself.

"Max," Malachi's voice broke through my confusion. "She won't hurt us."

I turned slightly back towards him. "What the hell —"

The vampire took my movement as indication to rush forward, quickly going to my father's side and kneeling.

"Hey—"

My protest cut off when I saw the flash of silver, a key sliding out of the long sleeve of her dress.

I met Summer's eyes, both of us too stunned to speak.

"This isn't how I thought we would meet," the vampire said, an Italian accent to her words, as the first cuff clanked open. Malachi let out a breath of relief as he stretched out his leg.

My heart stopped. My gaze jerked to Malachi, seeking confirmation. He gave a tightlipped nod.

"Massimo, meet Giana Lazzari. Your mother."

Chapter Thirty-Seven

MAX

"Gia," the vampire — my *mother* — snapped, correcting my father.

"Gia," he repeated softly, their eyes meeting before she continued unlocking his cuffs.

My mouth opened, blatantly staring at her. All the decades I'd wondered who she was, why she wanted nothing to do with me, and she was one of the *head* vampires in the world?

"You have to get out of here while they're distracted," she said, the last cuff falling away. She reached a hand out to Malachi which he took, letting her help him to his feet.

His hands rested gently on her elbows as she uselessly brushed dirt off his dingy clothes.

"Gia," he said again, lower now, and tipped her chin up with a finger to meet his gaze.

Their eyes locked while my world crumbled around me.

"*Andiamo*," she said, her voice breaking. She cleared her throat. "They didn't anticipate this attack, but we can use it to get you out."

But Malachi shook his head. "They'll know. *He'll* know. Lock me back up."

I gaped at him, incredulous. Lock him back up? Was he insane?

"They cut off your fucking wings!" I barked, my control snapping. "What the fuck do you mean, lock me back up?"

"Max" — Gia *tsk*'ed at my nickname, but Malachi ignored

her — "This isn't the time to explain everything. But the king *will* know Gia was responsible for this, and *I* won't allow her —"

"I know how to handle Osric," Gia snapped.

"You're the only one with the key!"

Gia stepped back, holding her head up tall. "I was attacked. Someone must have taken it from me. Clearly this was an orchestrated attack." She pointed to the door Summer and I had come through. "Now, *go*, all of you."

I caught Summer's eye. "You remember the way out?"

She nodded, already moving forward, like she could read my intentions.

"I'll be right behind you," I assured her, then addressed Malachi. "Go. She'll get you somewhere safe. I'll meet you."

He opened his mouth to argue, but I shoved him forward, and he stumbled towards the door. His obvious weakness rent a fracture through something inside me, but this wasn't the time. He would heal. We just had to get him free.

Casting one lingering look to Gia, Malachi steeled his features, then followed Summer out of the room.

My fists clenched and unclenched at my side. I'd imagined the day I'd finally meet my mother in my head a million times over the years. Planned out all the things I'd say to her, yell at her, blame her for. All the questions I'd ask her.

And now, finally faced with her, my mind was blank. I was tired, and it had been too long.

She wasn't worth the effort. She obviously hadn't thought I was either, for over a hundred years.

Scoffing, I shook my head, turning to go, when her voice cut through the silence.

"That wolf — your mate?"

I stilled. She said the word so casually. Like I hadn't been running from it in my own mind for weeks now.

Since last summer, if I were being honest. When I'd laid a

friendly hand on West Larkin's baby sister, and my magic had thrashed and flared for her, nearly piercing her mind before I knew what it wanted. To search her mind, her memories, and learn everything about her that I could.

It had never done that before or since. I'd had absolute control of my magic since I was a child.

I met my mother's eyes — blue, as deep a blue as mine. My words came out a growl. "What about her?"

"She's mortal."

A snarl built in my throat, sparks shooting up my forearms. Was she threatening my wife?

Gia put up her hands, approaching slowly, but her eyes were calculating. "It's not me you should fear where she's concerned."

"What the fuck are you talking about?"

Cocking her head, Gia looked me over. "You two must be very new to each other. Has it even started yet?"

"Has *what* started?"

Her blue eyes sharpened, magnetizing onto mine in the way only vampires' could. I briefly remembered she was likely extremely old — and therefore, very powerful. But I wouldn't cower before her, no matter the strength of her magic.

"The Fixation."

My brows furrowed, waiting for her to explain further.

She sighed, reaching out like she wanted to place a hand on my shoulder, but I swatted her away. "I realize I did you a disservice by not raising you among our kind, but I didn't think Malachi would be so remiss. The Fixation is unique to our kind. Your father would not have context for it. It's how it sounds, Massimo." She lifted a shoulder, but she almost looked sad. "What we love, we destroy. We obsess and fixate and control until there is nothing left of what we fell in love with."

I had heard some rumors about the phenomenon, but it

had always seemed like a failure of character. Gia made it sound like an eventuality.

Softer, she added, "Why do you think I sent your father away? Sent *you* away?"

I scoffed at that. Maybe that was part of the story — at least the one she told herself — but no way that was all of it.

"So, has it started? Have you felt yourself unable to resist her? Like she's the one temptation you can't say no to? Like you *need* her? Like you're drowning underwater and she's your air?"

I wanted to say she had no idea what she was talking about. That it wasn't like that with Summer.

But fuck. Sometimes I *did* lose control with her. Couldn't resist her.

Hadn't I felt exactly that seeing her in her reception dress?

And last night after her run?

"If you love her," Gia continued, and this time her hand did land on my arm, "you'll let her go. If you don't, you only doom her. She deserves to be more than your Source."

I jerked back, out of her reach, as an explosion and shouts reached us from somewhere else in the palace.

"Massimo, get out of here and never come back," Gia said, urgent and worried now. "Osric can *never* see you."

"Osric? The king? Why the fuck would he care?"

"Because he's my husband. And if he sees you, he'll know I had an affair. He'll kill you. He'll kill you all."

A cry rent the air — familiar, and my blood turned to ice. *Summer.*

Chapter Thirty-Eight

SUMMER

I shrieked as dark shadows wrapped around me from behind and a hand yanked on my hair. Malachi and I had almost made it back to the side entrance — I could see the arched outline in the distance.

My fangs and claws punched out at the threat, my wolf snarling at whoever had snatched me. The hallway was dark, but the scent was sharp, copper and smoke telling me we were surrounded by vampires. I moved my head against the tight hold on my hair, trying to see Malachi beside me, wrapped in the same shadowy magic.

"Well, well. Who do we have here?"

The shadows binding my arms rippled, forcibly turning me around to face —

Grigor's eyes widened in rage. "*You.*"

Without the golden throne, club music, and writhing bodies, the vampire lord from Boston was far more threatening. His blond hair was slicked back from his face, like a Prohibition Era villain in his pinstripe suit. The only thing setting him apart were the long fangs hanging down over his bottom lip, just as dangerous as the guns the bootleggers were known for.

Baring my teeth, I tried to wrestle free from his magic, but even my wolf's strength was no match. Something else was reinforcing his magic, then.

Behind Grigor, two other vampires materialized.

"Get the angel," he ordered with a flick of his fingers, his unblinking eyes focused on me as he pulled on my hair, tipping my head to the side to sniff my neck. "This one is mine."

His magic tightened around my arms, pinning them to my sides. I bit down the edge of panic, focusing on the magic around me, looking for weaknesses to break his hold. They dragged us back through the darkened halls, Grigor and I a few steps behind the others with Malachi.

Leaning in, he tightened his hold on my hair until I winced in pain and hissed in my ear, "I so hope your master is nearby. It will make it so much sweeter to drain you dry if he's here to watch."

I fought the shiver threatening to overtake me at his words. I wouldn't give him the satisfaction of knowing he rattled me.

As we moved through the halls, the noise around us grew louder near a set of large double doors. Grigor spoke in rapid-fire Italian to his men, who hurried to open them ahead of us. Malachi hung limply in their hold as we stumbled into a large atrium behind the doors.

Everything was chaos.

In the center of the room was an immense table, a chandelier crashed down in the middle, glass everywhere. Moonlight shone through the broken windows overhead, casting the room in an eerie glow. The sounds of death were everywhere, snarling vampires filling the large room in a deadly brawl. Some had their leathery wings out, others kept them hidden, all with fangs glinting in the moonlight.

"Where is the king?" Grigor shouted to one of his men, pulling me back towards the doors. Whatever magic held me lessened as one of the vampires holding Malachi took a stake to the chest, launched from somewhere in the distance. My eyes blew wide as he crumpled to the floor, hands clawing at the wood protruding from his chest. In seconds, his body dissolved into a pile of ash.

Bile rose in my throat as I looked back over the room,

looking for any signs of Max or Gia. Even Rhain or Étienne. They had to be here somewhere.

Shouts and cries of agony pierced the air as vampires attacked each other, blood spraying everywhere, roiling shadow magic whipping and coiling as they battled. Two humans lay dead on the floor — either witches under their employ or humans brought in as refreshments, I didn't know. Another three huddled together in a corner under a table, their eyes wide and terrified.

Everywhere I looked lay dead and dying vampires, the entire scene a mixture of gore and ash as their bodies dissolved around stakes protruding from chests. My eyes shifted to my wolf, but even being able to see them clearer, I couldn't tell who was on our side.

"ENOUGH!" a deep voice boomed from the center of the room, followed by a rippling aftershock of shadow magic. Black inky clouds exploded from the man's hands, washing the room in darkness as he levitated above the broken chandelier, floating in midair. The dark rolled over the room like a tidal wave, freezing everyone it touched, paralyzed with his power. The bindings around my arms dissolved and I reached behind me to grab my hair out of Grigor's hold. But as the magic swept over me, my lungs seized.

Eyes wide, I couldn't look away from the huge vampire floating above the mayhem. Grey shot through his thick dark hair, faint lines creasing his Mediterranean olive skin, but nothing was as noticeable as the rage igniting his features while he scanned the room. His eyes were the blood red of his predator, and giant wings stretched from his back, so incongruous with the dark formal brocade suit. At first glance, he appeared mid-fifties in age, but the power rippling off him gave away that he was much, much older.

The room was silent, not a single breath taken without his permission as he floated back to the floor and walked through the crowd, seething with anger. My lungs clawed for air, like being held underwater too long, but nothing I did made a difference to break his hold over me.

When he was satisfied all the fighting had stopped, he lifted the magic just enough to allow us to breathe. Shadows pulled from every corner of the room, soaking back into his skin as black veins ran up his neck and face, then disappeared. I blinked, my heart racing as I considered the amount of power it must have taken to control this whole room, all these people. It was terrifying.

"Pathetic," the vampire said, his laugh a low rumble that held no humor. "This is the best you can do? A coup?" He laughed again, his arms spread wide. "I have ruled the Conclave for a thousand years, keeping us hidden from the humans and supernaturals alike. Biding my time, and yet you dare *turn on me?* On each other?"

Another wash of power exploded out of King Osric, forcing us all to our knees. I crashed to the floor, the tiles biting into my skin as I gasped in pain, not daring to lift my head.

"I will find those responsible for this little attack," the vampire king said, his words echoing off the walls. "I will find you, and your entire line will meet their final death."

The room was immobile, whether by magic or just pure fear, I couldn't decide. He walked through the crowd, black shoes tapping on the tiles, daring anyone to stand against him.

"My king," Grigor spoke up when he neared us, his breaths raspy as if he too had been without air. "A gift."

King Osric stopped, his hands in his pockets as if a coup hadn't been taking place moments before. In slow motion, he turned soulless eyes on us, looking me up and down. Grigor yanked my ponytail until I moved towards him.

"A wolf?" Osric cocked his head to the side, studying me, then dismissed me just as quickly. "That is the least of my concerns, duke. Find me that little French weasel."

He turned away from us, walking on. Grigor tensed, dragging me forward again, needing to prove his loyalty. "Not just a wolf, my king. A *Hunter*."

Osric's head whipped around, nostrils flaring as black inky magic shot through his veins, his eyes flashing red. "Is that so?"

He stalked closer and I couldn't help trying to scoot back, but Grigor held tight.

"She found my den. Found the Conclave tonight."

Panic shot through me as Osric flew forward, shadows erupting around him. Before I could blink, my back smashed into a wall, his hand wrapped around my throat. Osric squeezed as he studied me, his eyes flashing between red and black.

"I thought we killed the last of your kind," he murmured, tilting my head to sniff my neck. My wolf thrashed and snarled in protest, but even my immunity to vampire magic seemed subdued compared to Osric's power.

"Don't touch me," I managed to hiss through his grip on my throat.

Ignoring me, he jerked my jaw until I met his gaze. "Where are you from, little wolf? Who is your pack?"

Steely black eyes bored into mine, swirling with power. I tried to wrench my head back, realizing he was attempting to see into my mind, my memories. Magic tingled at the edges of my awareness, but I clamped my mind shut, just like I did to keep my emotions private from the pack.

Osric growled, his eyes going red again, and his magic turned from a light caress into knives, trying to bore into my mind. This was different than the magic Grigor had used against me in Boston, and the more powerful magic they'd used together in the halls outside. This *burned*, like my skin was being peeled back an inch at a time to see everything inside me.

My breaths sawed in and out as I held firm, sealing my

mind, even as I bared and gritted my teeth, as a tear slipped down my cheek from the effort to keep him out.

There was no universe where I let him see my family, my home.

"Husband."

Gia's voice rang out through the room, and the weight of Osric's magic lifted ever so slightly. As if he couldn't resist her pull, Osric turned to her, loosening his grip on my throat.

Max's mother glided forward, her bearing cold and regal, every bit the queen she apparently was here. Raising an imperious brow, she inspected me like she'd never seen me before, and wrinkled her nose. "What is this stray doing here, *amore mio?*"

My nostrils flared, searching for Max's sandalwood scent, but couldn't find him. He wouldn't have abandoned us, so I followed her lead and kept quiet.

"A remnant of the Hunter line, beloved," Osric told her, stepping away from me but maintaining his shadows that bound me in place.

Gia tilted her head. "The Hunters? They were exterminated."

"Some of them must have survived."

Stepping forward, Gia moved in front of Osric, partially blocking me from his view. "Then we must find their hideout." She lifted a hand to my forehead, but asked Osric, "May I?"

"As you wish, but I believe she's had training. Her mental shield is quite strong."

Gia's fingertips traced my temple as I uselessly tried to yank myself backwards, something flickering in her eyes I couldn't read.

"Shh, be still, wolf," she murmured, and to anyone watching, she was merely trying to calm her prey.

But instead of attempting to force her way into my mind, she let me into hers, a series of images flashing behind my eyes.

Osric, a stake through his chest.

Max, swooping in from the broken window to my left.

Several faces I recognized as other vampires in the room behind her. Presumably, who else to look out for.

Seconds passed before her fingers dropped and she snarled, pretending she hadn't been able to enter my mind.

"Who trained you?" she seethed, raising a hand to slap me.

Osric rushed forward — to stop or help, I couldn't tell — and Gia spun around.

A glint of silver, a choked gasp, and Osric's eyes widened.

As Gia stepped back, a wooden stake with a carved silver hilt protruded from her husband's chest, and he collapsed to his knees.

"You have ruled unchecked for too long, *amore mio*," she said, her hand cupping his jaw as he spluttered for air. "I'll meet you in the next life."

Without hesitating, Gia whipped out a knife, and sliced his throat.

A gasp lodged in my throat as blood spray hit my knees, and his magic dissolved from the room, from the world.

Silence hung in the room for a long moment, and then the frenzy reignited. No longer paralyzed, several vampires launched for Gia while others fought to defend her. I caught sight of Rhain a second before he threw a vampire through the historic stained glass window.

He appeared in front of me with a wink, grabbing my arm to pull me towards the window.

"Contingency plan," he whispered.

Max leapt onto the window ledge, his boots dislodging shards of glass, his dark wings outstretched. His eyes were rimmed in red, his shadow magic dark in his veins, and lightning skittered over his black feathers.

Malachi hurried over to us, but with a snarl, a vampire tackled him to the ground, one of the faces Gia had shown me.

He reared his head back, fangs bared and ready to tear out Malachi's throat, when a heeled leather boot kicked him, hard enough the snap of his neck was an audible crack, even through the chaos.

Straightening her skirt over her boots, Gia reached for Malachi, helping him back to his feet, and ushered him over to us like she hadn't just killed two Conclave members.

The second Max had both me and Malachi in his grasp, Gia shoved all of us out the window, not giving us a second to hesitate. Without a backwards glance, she returned to the fight.

Max's magic wrapped around us as we fell backwards, the sounds of the fighting muffled to silence, and we vanished.

Chapter Thirty-Nine

MAX

The biting cold power of vanishing washed over my skin, blacking out the chaos we'd left behind. My father was a dead weight in my arms, Summer clinging onto his other elbow as we carried him through the In-Between. In an instant, we slammed hard onto a gleaming white marble floor, Malachi falling to his knees from the impact. Summer's face was ashen, but I couldn't look away from her, sick to my stomach over what she'd just endured because of me.

Gathering himself, Malachi put his hands on his knees, lifted his head, and muttered a curse under his breath when he realized where we were.

"Well, where did you want me to bring you?" I said as I held a hand out, helping him back to his feet.

Summer was already on his other side, hand supporting his elbow, as we heard heels clicking across the floor, getting closer. She straightened, alert for danger as she looked around the space, then to me. "Are we where I think we are?"

Gabriella, the angel often in charge of monitoring the Lobby at Headquarters, turned the corner from the atrium into the Lobby, looking down at her tablet as she approached the reception desk. "Massimo, again?" she said, tapping away at her tablet. "You know the rules, same as —"

Her eyes widened when she finally looked up and realized who was with me. "Oh my goodness, Premier! What happened —"

Malachi lifted his hand in a dismissive wave, but winced at the small movement.

"Healers, Gabriella," I said, not bothering to hide the bite in my tone. "Now."

She nodded, hurrying around the reception desk to pick up the desk phone, never taking her worried gaze off Malachi. "Of course."

His breathing was heavy but even, leaning his weight into us far more than he should have been. Angels had supernatural healing abilities — even with the loss of his wings, it wasn't right for him to be so weak. Worry crept into my mind. What else had happened while he was taken for him to be in this state?

"Help is on the way," Summer said, her voice soothing and full of reassurance. I wasn't sure whether it was for my father or if she could see the panic creeping into my thoughts. She reached a hand around my father, squeezing mine.

It wasn't long before a handful of healers arrived in their light grey scrubs, a gurney pushed between them. If they were surprised to see the Premier here and in such a state, their faces didn't betray it as they maintained professional calm.

"Arm around my shoulder, sir," one said, quickly taking Summer's place. I winced at the sight of the dirt and dried blood from Malachi's shirt and hand soiling the healer's white wings, but the angel showed no sign of caring.

Another healer slipped into my place, and they lifted him onto the gurney, pushing him down the hall and to the healing wing.

"I'll be back," I called to him before they rounded a corner.

Too weary to reply, he merely waved a hand and let himself be led away. Gabriella hurried after them, tapping away at her tablet.

I let out a heavy breath, running a hand through my hair before turning to Summer.

Blood spray coated her legs, but I could smell it wasn't her own. Stepping up to her, my hand slipped around the back of her head, inspecting her for further injury.

What we love, we destroy.

My mother's words echoed in my mind, an unending loop, and the picture they painted terrified me.

I tilted her head to the side, revealing the bruise around her neck from where Osric had grabbed her, and a snarl built in my throat.

If you love her, you'll let her go.

I'd hated every moment he'd had his hands on her, and it had nearly killed me to wait for Gia's signal from my perch outside the window.

If you don't, you only doom her.

Summer's small hand came to my wrist on her neck. "It's fine. It's already healing."

"He's lucky he's already dead." The words came out before I realized I'd said them.

Lucky, because otherwise I'd be hunting him down as we speak.

And when I found him, I wouldn't make it slow. I'd draw it out, until he was begging me for death. I'd make him repay tenfold for every hurt he'd inflicted on my mate.

I managed to keep the more murderous thoughts to myself, but I couldn't stop the shadows from coiling up my hands, my forearms. A spark burst from my fingertips, and Summer hissed as it scorched her cheek.

Immediately, I dropped my hand from her.

"Max?" Summer's voice was guarded, her eyes searching my face. I took a step back.

We obsess and fixate and control until there is nothing left of what we fell in love with.

Was this how it started?

With small touches, meant to be tender, that turned into pain?

With comfort and safety, corrupted into control?

I shook out my fingers, taking a deep breath and letting it out slowly, drawing my magic from my hands until the shadows had receded.

Forcing myself to meet Summer's eyes, the concern I met there nearly broke me.

Even covered in someone else's blood, she was stunning. Even in this pristine white room, her brightness, her light, stood out.

Has it started?

Like you're drowning underwater, and she's your air?

A few weeks with me, and already I had her fighting for her life in alleys, dressed in black and covered in blood.

We couldn't fucking do this.

She deserves to be more than your Source.

I clenched my jaw. "Let's get you home."

Tilting her head, Summer furrowed her brow but came forward. "All right."

I grasped her arm, and the Lobby vanished as I transported us from the angel realm to the mortal dimension, reappearing smoothly on Summer's roof.

"Max." Summer's tone was sharper now as I forced my hand off her, distancing myself from her. "What's going on? I can feel you're upset."

My mouth went dry as I struggled to find the words, staring at the lounge chair we'd fallen asleep on yesterday.

"Is it your mother? Let's go back and see what happened, make sure Rhain and —"

"No." My hand cut through the air decisively, and Summer's brows shot up. "You're not going back out there."

Her eyes narrowed. "I will if I say so. I told you, I'm going to watch your back —"

"Not anymore." I straightened up, meeting her eye. "We found the vampires, sunshine. Job done."

"Maybe we found them, but it doesn't really feel like this job is done."

"I don't need you anymore." Summer looked like I'd slapped her, and my gut twisted.

But I couldn't tell her what Gia had told me about the Fixation. She'd only try to say we could find a way around it, all sunshine positivity, and I knew she was wrong.

Summer scoffed. "Well, ouch."

"We did the job, it's done." I choked over a lump in my throat, fisting my hands at my sides. "So, we don't need to pretend anymore. Our arrangement has concluded."

Summer nodded, arms crossed over her chest, but nothing about the move was reassuring, not with her face that stony.

"Just like that."

I lifted a shoulder. "Your little vacay from your real life is over. You knew what this deal was when you signed up for it, remember?"

"Mhm. Yeah, absolutely." If a look could kill, I'd be flayed.

"I'll figure out the paperwork for the divorce." Fuck, had that word always been a weapon? It hit my heart like a stake.

"How magnanimous of you."

Tension coiled between us. I didn't know if I wanted her to hit me or walk away, but fuck, I'd take either. I deserved it.

A bitter laugh escaped her. "Are you kidding me? You're seriously trying to convince yourself this was nothing more than a business arrangement? Even now, after everything?"

"It was," I bit out. "I told you not to fall in love with me."

She gasped, but the shock was gone in an instant. "You're a coward."

I fought my magic down as her wolf glowed in her eyes, begging me to fight with her, and went for a different kind of kill. One I hated myself for, because I knew it would cut deep. But it would be easier, in the long run, if she hated my guts.

Everybody else already thought I was the bad guy. What did I care if one more person did too?

If it would keep her safe, I'd ruin myself. If it kept her from ever agreeing to see me again, I'd reduce myself to the dirt under her shoes.

"Did you honestly expect this to work out, sunshine?" I threw my arms wide, gesturing to the cozy mountain town around us. "I work alone, which is how I like it, not the mess your life is in Timber Creek. Besides, you don't just find danger, you *cause* it. You make cupcakes for a living, and I murder people. You're right, the job isn't totally done, but it'll go smoother without you. Your nose was useful but your impulsivity is just a liability."

Her canines had snapped out. "Well, fuck you, Massimo Russo."

I took another step back. "I have to go."

"Don't let me stop you."

I allowed myself one last look at my wife, gorgeous despite her anger, her hurt, before I wrapped myself in shadow.

Chapter Forty

SUMMER

I was a damn cliché, and I didn't even care. In fact, I was leaning into it.

Ice cream? Check.

Fluffy blanket? Check.

Ignoring the texts from my friends and family? Other than letting Indi know I was alive, check.

Procedural crime drama TV? Law and Order SVU Marathon found. Check and double check.

Stress-knitting? One scarf down.

None of it made me feel any better, but until I was ready to talk to anyone in my family, this was where I'd be. The moment I saw any of them, they'd know something was wrong, and the jig would be up.

I stabbed my needle through the yarn, huffing as I missed the stitch in my impatience. "Stupid yarn," I mumbled, but the only answer was the sound of the TV. Loneliness tugged at my heart, but after I'd gotten myself into this situation, maybe I deserved it.

A single tear gathered on my lower lid, but I brushed it away, refusing to let it fall. His words had been cruel, wielded with the intent to hurt me, and Goddess, they had.

"My life isn't a mess," I huffed, missing yet another stitch. Letting out a growl of frustration, I threw the needles across the couch, slumping back and crossing my arms across my chest.

He told me not to fall in love with him, and I'd laughed in his face, so sure of my abilities to keep my feelings in check. But that was before I knew him, knew how deeply he cared about those around him, knew what it felt like to be the center of his attention.

What a fool I'd been.

I sniffed, trying to focus on the TV through the blurry tears, and debated shifting into my wolf to let her take the brunt of this pain. That was a slippery slope though, and I refused to give Max that power over me.

Whatever Max had said, I knew what we felt for each other was real. I even knew that *he* knew it was real. The way he held me at our wedding, the way he looked at me when he thought I wasn't paying attention, the way he threw himself in front of me when I was in danger. Had I caused some of it? Maybe. But the way he'd flung the accusation at me stung worse than anything else.

We'd never used the words, but I was willing to bet my life that Max was as in love with me as I was him.

What was his deal? Something must have happened in Venice while we were apart for him to make such a 180 from our reception only days ago.

Banging on my apartment door made me jump, gripping my heart. How had I not heard footsteps on the stairs? I glanced at my TV, volume turned way up to drown out my thoughts. Maybe too loud.

"Summer Larkin, open up your door before we break it down."

Aspen. Busted.

Before I could disentangle myself from my blankets and yarn, Indi and Aspen flickered inside. I gave them a flat stare and slumped back down on the couch.

"Why even knock and ask me to get up if you were just going to barge in?"

"Blame me," Aspen said. "I got worried when you didn't answer."

"You gave me literally two seconds."

My sister shrugged unapologetically and joined me on the couch as Indi sat on my other side.

"So? What's going on?" Aspen cast her gaze around my apartment, as though looking for something. Or someone. "You disappear for a few days, we don't see hide nor hair of you, and you feel all… off in the pack bonds. And now this" — she waved a hand at my current setup — "this is a cry for help if ever I've seen one."

I turned to Indi, who raised her hands. "I said nothing."

Aspen leaned forward, her eyebrows rising to her hairline. "Said nothing? About what?"

Resigned to my fate, I took up my knitting again and told them everything. Watching Aspen's face was a show as I detailed how I'd spent the last several weeks: shock at the revelation I found vampires so easily in Boston; amusement at me throwing him to the literal wolves with the fake boyfriend dinner; regret over our fight that lead Max and I to the Grand Canyon; a mixture of judgment and amusement over our Vegas wedding; then terror when I recounted everything that happened in Europe.

"You've been busy," Aspen said, a hint of hurt in her words.

"I couldn't tell you." I squeezed her hand, hating that I'd now caused my sister pain too with this stupid plan. "That he's a vampire was Max's secret to tell, not mine. There's no way West and Cooper would have let me go, and Max needed me. That part, I don't regret."

"What about the rest?" Indi said quietly.

I opened my mouth, then closed it again. Did I regret it?

"I regret thinking I was strong enough not to fall in love with him," I finally said. "I feel exceptionally stupid about that.

I gaslit myself into believing it had changed somewhere in Paris, and it wasn't about needing each other for this task anymore. I just needed *him*, not the adventures he provided. But he's just as stupid if he thinks he doesn't need me too. I know it."

Indi hummed, but didn't say anything.

"And I regret lying," I whispered, looking back and forth between my two best friends. "The thought of telling Dad…" I tipped my head up to the ceiling, blinking rapidly to fight back the emotions flooding me. "He was so excited. You threw me the wedding of my dreams, and it was for nothing."

"Not for nothing." Indi squeezed my hand. "You're worth celebrating, Max or no. If you think Heath wouldn't have thrown you a party on any given Tuesday, you don't know your dad that well."

Aspen's eyes were incandescent with her wolf, ready for murder. "That goth pigeon *bastard*. I'm getting his number from West and luring him here and then I'm going to kill him."

I gripped her wrists before she could reach for her phone, knowing she would do exactly that. "No murder, please. He does still need to save the leader of the supernatural free world."

She growled, but didn't resist my hold. When she sat back, I let go.

"Don't tell the boys," Aspen finally said, and I looked over at her. "I'll deal with it, and let them know where to shove it if they have anything judgmental to say."

I nodded quickly, unable to voice how relieved I was over this. "Thank you."

"This is probably a stupid question, but how are you doing?" Indi asked.

I gestured to the post-breakup nest I'd made for myself. "Right on schedule, I think. Not my first breakup rodeo."

My throat went tight, but I fought back the tears.

"How can we help?" Aspen bumped her shoulder into mine, and a little of my tension eased at the contact.

I sighed. "It is what it is, right?"

"Stupid saying," Indi muttered.

"Well, you're doing the right thing," Aspen said, shooting off a text before reaching for the remote. "When in doubt, look to Olivia Benson."

They pulled my blanket over their legs too, and settled in to stay with me, each resting a head on my shoulders. I tipped my head onto my sister's, savoring the physical connection I had not just with her, but also her wolf.

As much as I wanted a life of adventure, I loved my family, and I loved my pack. Someday when the sting of his words faded, I knew this was a good thing and I would be better off without Max.

For a brief time, the idea of sharing my life with Max had been all I could think about. Family dinners at the pack house, slow nights with my siblings, lazy mornings in bed before I went to work in the bakery, and then letting him whisk me off on an adventure for a few days before returning home to our family.

But that had only been a dream, and the sooner I realized it, the better.

A few minutes later, familiar footsteps pounded up the stairs right as a new episode started. We were mid-intro recitation, the three of us chanting the opening words in unison, as the front door cracked open to reveal Terran, takeout bags in hand. In all-black and his backwards Buffalo Willies hat, he must have come straight from the restaurant.

"Uh—" he froze, like he was unsure if he should interrupt, eyes darting around the messy living room. The episode moved on from the intro, and Aspen waved him in.

"I ordered reinforcements," she explained. "A wolf can't live off ice cream."

My stomach rumbled as the smell of burgers and fries reached me, so maybe she had a point.

"Uh-oh, SVU? Do I need to hurt someone?" Terran asked, bringing the bags to my coffee table and looking between us. He raised a brow at Indi, like she would be the one to spill the beans, but she merely cleared her throat and looked pointedly at the TV. "Dare I ask what's going on?"

"You dare not." Aspen waved him away. "That will be all."

"Where's my tip?"

"Here's a tip — get a haircut."

Rolling his eyes, Terran left, shutting the door behind him.

Indi fell asleep somewhere into the third episode, curling up on the end of the couch. Aspen had assigned herself as yarn-holder and was uncoiling it for me as I knitted.

I was relieved they hadn't pushed me to talk more, instead just being with me. If I was honest, I was sick to death of thinking about myself and my own problems.

Clearing my throat, I shot Aspen a glance. "So. Did my eyes deceive me or did I see you and Cruz getting up close and personal at the party?" I couldn't say *reception*, not after Max had ruined it.

Aspen huffed. "Moment of weakness. It won't happen again."

I tilted my head, squinting at her. "Are you sure? It looked like you two were having fun. Why didn't Matthew come?"

She shook her head, swallowing as she flicked a glance at me. It was quick, so quick you could blink and miss it, that split second of vulnerability. But she was my sister, and I'd recognize it anywhere, even if her next words hadn't been shaky. "Because I didn't invite him. And yeah, I'm sure about Cruz. I can't go there." Then her features hardened, and when she continued, her voice was decisive. "I *won't* go there."

I lowered my yarn into my lap, reaching over to squeeze her hand. My tough-as-nails sister, the one who'd taken care of so much after our mom died, who always seemed to have her shit figured out, was maybe the one of us who'd broken the most.

She wiggled the yarn she held for me. "C'mon. Are you gonna finish this scarf for me or what?"

Knowing I'd never get her to talk before she was ready, I slouched down, getting comfortable, and took up my needles again. A moment later, Aspen joined, slinking down until she was snuggled up next to me.

Disentangling myself from the yarn and blankets, I stood and stretched early the next morning. Aspen had moved to the guest room at some point, and Indi must have gone home because I was alone on the couch.

Yesterday had sucked, but I woke up this morning feeling a renewed sense of purpose. Today was a new day. My heart still hurt, but no matter what life threw at me, I still had my family, the shop of my dreams, and a whole list of things I wanted to do for no one other than myself, made easier when I didn't have to answer to anyone.

There was always a silver lining if you looked hard enough.

"Just a single pringle," I said to myself as my stomach rumbled. "And now I want chips."

With a resolute nod, I started to fold up the scarf I'd been working on, then did a double-take. Somehow, the thing was at least 15 feet long, with some bands of color only a few inches long and others several feet, depending on how much of that yarn I'd had left. I'd just been using up whatever was left over in my yarn pile.

Maybe not the *prettiest* scarf, but at 15 feet, at least it would keep someone very, *very* warm.

Sighing, I tossed it down on the coffee table, then made my way over to the kitchen to start a pot of coffee.

I was sick of being sad over what Max and I could have had. Enough was enough. If he wanted to be an idiot and throw it away, well, I couldn't control his actions.

But I'd be damned if I let his decisions keep me down.

"Oh, my."

Indi covered her mouth with her hand, gaping at me from the door to my bedroom.

Aspen called from down the hall, "What?"

"Found her."

As Aspen joined Indi in the doorway, I gestured to the mess around me. "It's not what it looks like."

From an outside perspective, it probably looked like my arts and crafts corner had exploded, yet again, which wasn't that far off.

I stood, shaking off the paper scraps clinging to my clothes. "First, I decided to update my bucket list, organizing things I was able to check off over the last few years and prioritizing the next ones I want to tackle. Then, I thought, wouldn't it be fun to makeover the bakery?" I gestured to another pile of magazines and a tiny photo printer I'd bought two years ago, then promptly forgot existed. Now, dozens of pictures littered the floor of ideas I'd printed offline. "So, I started planning that. I'm picking up the paint and fabric to redo the upholstery later today, already ordered. But *then* I thought, okay, well if

I'm redoing the whole bakery aesthetic, I probably need new branding." I flipped around my tablet, where I'd been playing around with my logo — a book with flowers blooming from the center, but instead of a few of the blooms, a cupcake, croissant, cookie, cinnamon roll and a whisk grew out from the stems. "Cruz said he had a guy who could put the vinyl up on the front window later today." Then I snapped my fingers. "Oh, before I forget, I booked us that ziplining tour for later this week."

Aspen blinked at me. "You've gone full Heath."

I frowned, ready to protest, then took another look around. She might have been right.

"So what?" I caught a glimpse of myself in the floor-length mirror and noticed my top knot had somehow slid to the right. In quick motions, I pulled the hair tie free, smoothed it out, and pulled my hair back into a ponytail. "I'm going to live my life. My *best* life. I'm going to do all the things I want to do and not feel bad about any of it." I leveled a stare on both of them. "Are you going to stop me, or help?"

They shared a look, then Aspen went for my stack of café clippings and ideas. "You know, if you're renovating anyway, I've been thinking you should add a little outdoor courtyard area. You're on the end of the block, and there's no mayor to protest if you put some tables on the sidewalk when the weather's nice. I can draw up the plans if you want."

I grinned, throwing my arms around her and squeezing tight as she grumbled.

Indi scooped up my tablet and clicked away. "Well, if you have a new logo, then we need new merch. Shirts, aprons, cups, bags. Oh! Maybe some stickers."

My heart swelled, and I blinked the moisture from my eyes. Maybe I wasn't okay yet, but I had my girls at my back, and I could still reach for my goals.

Fake it till you make it.

Well, one thing I knew for damn sure — I was a real tough kid.

I'd handled losing my mom at 15. I could handle this too.

Chapter Forty-One

MAX

"I can walk myself across the room, Massimo." Malachi batted me away, and I raised my hands in surrender.

Despite his words, I trailed close behind him as he made his way to a patio chair and settled into it with a weary sigh. All his clothes here were just as uptight and business-y as he always was, so I'd scrounged up some of my own for him to wear.

I couldn't remember a time I'd seen my father in anything as relaxed as the pair of black joggers and an unbuttoned cotton henley I'd found. The tops of his bandages woven around his chest peeked through the deep v-neck, reminding me of just how gruesome his injury was.

He'd lost his wings.

My back ached at the imagined pain, the brutal invasion, the total devastation and loss of identity he must be feeling. But, of course, my father was as ironclad with his emotions as always.

The healers had kept him overnight at Headquarters, checking his vitals and running tests while they bandaged and spelled his wounds, but then he'd been discharged to recuperate. Nothing other than blood loss and fatigue had shown to explain why he was still so weak, so their best suggestion was to rest and give it time.

At his request, I'd transported us to the Tuscan villa where I'd grown up to recover. It was the closest to the drama happening in Venice, and my father never liked to be far from the action, no matter how injured he was.

I'd called Rhain to find out what had happened in Venice after we left, but other than briefly letting me know Étienne hadn't made it, he hadn't had time to give me a full update yet.

That had hit like a gut punch, even though I reminded myself Étienne had known the dangers going into that battle. I knew vampires had died in the Palace, but Étienne had been one of the good ones. He'd had a good vision for the future of our species, and enough support to get us there. I could only hope whoever replaced him as duke would have his same goals.

Satisfied Malachi wouldn't try to move again, I went inside to fill a glass with water and brought it back out to him. He shot me a look that probably meant *I can get my own water*, but I ignored him.

The patio overlooked the rolling hills of Tuscany, rich green from the spring rains. Everything smelled fresh here, almost enough to wash out the strong medicinal smell wafting off my father. But instead of taking in the view, Malachi closed his eyes, tilting his face up to the sun and finally seeming to relax.

"Is it time to talk about that ring on your finger yet?" he asked, eyes still closed.

I twisted my wedding band, staring down at the dark metal. He'd eyed it in the recovery room at Headquarters, but hadn't asked about it then.

"I called you," I said, my voice coming out shakier than I'd anticipated. Clearing my throat, I looked back over the rows of hazelnut trees just outside our property line.

"Yes, well." He shifted on his lounge chair, his face contorting in pain as he settled again. "I was indisposed."

"Why didn't you tell me about Project Oleander?" I asked, twisting my wedding band again. I knew I should take it off. Summer and I were done. I'd been enough of an ass to her to more than ensure that. Still, the metal felt almost fused to my soul. She was the closest thing I had ever felt to family, to a wholesome and *good* relationship. "About Rhain, about my mother."

He sighed, the sound as weary as I'd ever heard him. "Everything was so uncertain. We'd kept your ruse as Dante for so long, it was a risk to send you looking for dens, let alone get you involved with Oleander. Despite what you may think, I always try to do what's best for you. I want to keep you safe."

A bitter laugh escaped me, the words so close to how I'd felt about letting Summer go, and yet they stung, like a knife plunged through my heart.

"The girl?" My father asked again, and I dropped my hand.

"It doesn't matter. We're over. She was just the wolf who helped me find the dens, and I did what was best to protect her — tying her to me, and then letting her go."

Malachi's eyes shot open, lifting slightly off the lounge. "Wait. You married the wolf who" — he leaned forward, wincing — "the *Hunter*? The one from Venice?"

I nodded grimly.

"Where is she now?" He looked back towards the house, squinting, then swiveled back to me. "Is she here?"

He seemed inordinately upset about this, but I shrugged. "At home. Timber Creek."

His eyes nearly bulged out of his head. "You — *left* her there? Alone?"

"Not alone. She has her pack. Summer is West Larkin's sister, and I trust him."

"Massimo. She's a *Hunter*."

I threw up my hands, frustrated that even now all these secrets stood between us. "Yes, you said that, and the Conclave said that too, but what's the big deal?"

He dropped his feet to the ground closest to me, his shoulders hunched as he leaned forward, pain flashing across his face. "You don't understand. If any of the Conclave survived, they will hunt her down and kill her rather than risk the Hunter line existing. The only reason vampires have been able to stay hidden for so long is because they thought they eradicated the Hunter bloodline, even the ones with latent powers. Hunters are supposed to be gone."

My veins turned to ice, my stomach souring. But she was safe. She had her pack. West wouldn't let anything happen to her. "Why did you tell me to find a wolf then?"

"Because they are the only ones with senses strong enough to even *begin* to detect a vampire den. The magic that cloaks a den from our eyes has a scent, yes, but only if you are right on top of it. Honestly, I figured your presence in a vampire's territory would be enough to draw them to you, curious as to why you were there. You're unregistered with any den, which is rare in itself. Traveling with a wolf only made you that much more noticeable. A regular wolf could track a vampire's victim, the trace of magic enough to follow, and your chances were high of getting lucky. To trace a vampire like a Hunter can is unheard of. I never dreamed you'd find yourself one."

"Once again, don't you think you should have told me you were using me as fucking *bait?*" My voice rose with my anger. "Why do you keep sending me on these missions? Are you hoping I fail? Hoping someone takes me out for you so you can be put out of your responsibility of being my father?"

He jerked back at my words, a different pain washing across his face. "Massimo."

"No." I cut my hand through the air, pacing in front of him. "I don't want to hear your excuses. I don't want your reasoning. You *used* me, once again, and I'm tired of this. You led me into a trap, and put not only me, but *my wife* in danger, all tied up with a cute little name like when I was a child. I'm *not* a child, and I'm through with your shit."

"Max," he said, pushing to sit on the edge of his chair with an audible gasp of pain. "I am so sorry I've hurt you, but I need you to listen to me."

"*What?*" I growled, decades of hurt and anger bubbling to the surface.

"Do you care for her?"

I jerked back, the sudden change of topic jarring and yet so typical of my father, avoiding all the hard conversations. "Summer?"

"Your wife, yes."

If he meant the word to cut, he succeeded. "Of course I do," I bit out. How much of a monster did he think he'd raised?

"Have you gotten a report from Venice?"

I shook my head, not following where he was going. "I haven't heard much from Rhain yet," I said instead, shoving down all the rest as I took a chair near him. "I don't know if any of the Conclave survived."

His hand rested on my shoulder, his brow creased in distress. "Then go back to her. Until we know more, we have to assume she's in danger."

My chest felt like it was caving in, the ache too real to even consider going back to Summer. If I apologized and she didn't forgive me, the pain would be so much worse. But fuck, I didn't even know if I could forgive myself for letting her believe I'd used her just my like father always used me. "She has a whole town to protect her. Believe me, she doesn't want me around her anymore."

Malachi narrowed his eyes. "What did you do?"

How was it four little words could transport me back to my youth? In an instant, I was a child again, caught in the act of some mischief and getting scolded.

And like a child, I scowled. "It was for her own good." The defense sounded weak even to my ears, and Malachi's glare hardened, sensing the lie for what it was. "I'm no good for her. The Fixation — I don't want to —"

"Fucking hell, the *Fixation*," he scoffed, rolling his eyes before bringing his gaze back to mine. "You're not all hers, Massimo. You're also half *mine*. Half *angel*, Max. Never forget that. You can fight the fucking Fixation."

I sat, stunned. He'd never spoken to me like that in over a hundred years.

Still, I heard myself confessing before I could stop the words, "I've already felt it starting. I can't control myself around her. I think about her all the time, want her, *need* her in a way I've never felt with anyone else. It's a compulsion, a need I can't say no to."

Malachi looked to the heavens, heaving a weary sigh. "That's not the Fixation. That's *love*, my boy."

That — *what?*

"Look, I'll level with you." He tipped his head towards me, his grey eyes unwavering in their attention. "Do vampires love more intensely than other species, sometimes leading to an unhealthy obsession they coin 'the Fixation'? In my limited experience with the species, yes. But that doesn't mean the Fixation is inevitable, or that it can't be fought even if it does start to take over. And you, as half-angel, have an even smaller chance of developing it than a full vampire, and a greater chance at fighting it."

I wanted to believe him. Fuck, it was so tempting to agree with his words. "The way Gia spoke of it —"

"Was from the perspective of a full-blooded vampire, and an old one at that," Malachi cut in. "The older vampires are, the stronger everything becomes for them — love, hate, rage, obsession. Her experience has no relevance to yours."

I sat with that for a minute, replaying my interactions with Gia, with other vampires, with Summer. Grigor's obsession with getting Quentin back was beyond that of just vengeance, that much was clear. Even Nicolette had seemed obsessed with me to an unnatural degree given how little time we'd ever spent together.

His words did track with everything I knew of the species, but the fear that I'd hurt her in some irrevocable way was still there. "My shadowmark keeps growing on Summer, almost taking over her whole back. She's wearing me like a brand."

Malachi raised his grey brows. "And you can think of no other reason *a wolf's* magic would intertwine with yours? Tying you together?"

I reeled back, stunned by his words. Shifters had mates, souls their animals identified as the other half of theirs, partners they wanted for life. Up until now, I'd never considered the shadow magic to be anything but my own selfishness claiming what I wanted.

Was her wolf doing the same, spurring on the magic of my shadowmark? My breath caught, the realization that I might be Summer's mate hitting me full-on. A lifetime at her side flitted through my mind: sunny days spent at her side in her café, evenings spent with her wrapped in my arms, taking her on adventures just to see the awe in her face. Fuck, I wanted that more than anything I'd ever wanted in my life. But I knew myself, knew how dark my past was. No matter how much I wanted her, I'd only stain Summer's light with my shadows.

With a heavy swallow, I changed tack, deciding to risk asking some of the other questions I had for my father. "Gia also said — she said she'd sent us away for our safety. From her, and maybe the king. What happened there?"

"That" — Malachi's mouth formed a thin line — "is a long story."

My eyebrows lifted as a bitter laugh escaped me. "Oh, so it's only *my* love life we're interrogating? I've given you a century to explain, and yet I know nothing. Time to fess up."

"It was my fault."

We both started at the voice. From the shadow of an olive tree on the edge of the patio, Gia herself materialized.

Malachi sat up with a wince, his hand going to the bandages wrapped around his chest. "You're alive."

"It would seem so," she agreed. Gia wore a brocaded gown similar to the one she had on the last time I saw her, but then she'd been covered in Osric's blood. I couldn't see any of it left, but the heavy scent of copper and smoke lingered on her, days later.

Now, instead of seeming like the vampire queen, she looked tired, a little tentative. Maybe even guilty, like a mother who'd abandoned her son at birth should. Whatever had softened in me at the thought of a future with Summer hardened instantly, my protective walls slamming up against my parents.

Gia gestured to one of the chairs. "May I?"

My father stared wide-eyed, like a man besotted even after a century, as he nodded. I glanced between them, noticing the pain my father wore like a mask for the first time. Her presence didn't just crack his steely facade, it dissolved it.

His lips were slightly parted, as if he was afraid breathing wrong would make her disappear. His eyes were downturned, lined with a heartbreak I wondered if I'd see in my own face if I looked in the mirror.

Malachi stared at my mother like I did Summer, like she was the only thing he could see. Like she was the best thing that had ever happened to him. Like he was afraid he'd inevitably fuck it up again, and she'd be there and then gone in an instant.

Sweeping her skirts to the side, she lowered herself into a chair across from Malachi, and his shoulders dipped on a deep exhale. "I wasn't sure you'd come."

Her lips curved in the hint of a smile that told me she saw my father's pain as clearly as I did. "You must know I'd always come for you, *cuore mio*. That I would have come for you a century ago, if I could have."

I turned away as my father let out a small gasp, feeling some moment passing between them as I sat there like the worst third wheel.

"How did you find me?" he asked, and I stared at the faded tiles beneath my feet, riveted in place as the man I thought unbreakable shattered in the face of a woman I thought he'd hated.

She sat back in the chair, tipping her head up as she breathed in the Tuscan air. Her posture was relaxed, except for the fingers curled around the armrest, gripping tight. No matter how indifferent my mother seemed, she was just as affected by this reunion as Malachi.

"This was always our place," she said, eyes still closed. "I wasn't sure you'd be here" — her head dropped back down, eyes flicking to me and then back to my father — "but I hoped, after all these years…"

He nodded, looking momentarily to me, then back to her.

This time, that small smile turned into a smirk as she looked at me. "This is the home where you were conceived."

I choked on air, coughing into my hand. "Just what every child wants to hear."

"What I told you in the palace was true, Massimo. I sent both of you away to protect you from the Fixation, afraid of what the curse would do with my love for you both. But it was not my own Fixation I fretted over."

It clicked. "Osric?"

She nodded, a new layer of sadness creeping into her gaze as she looked at my father again. "I won't make excuses for Osric, but the male you met was not the one I fell in love with. The Fixation and the blood madness started to creep in several centuries ago, not only as an obsession with me, but as an unrelenting vengeance against angels, whom he saw as superior to him. It was slow, in the beginning, just a bitter anger." Gia sighed, looking out over the hills. "We fought it together. I helped him rule when he struggled with his thoughts, his coherency. It was my decision for vampires to go into hiding, to remove us from memory, to protect ourselves. I used his Fixation with me against him, knowing he wanted me more than he wanted to destroy the world around him. He was too powerful for his own good, Massimo, you must understand. He was a good man once."

"You loved him." I didn't exactly say it like a question, but it was one. I just wasn't sure if I meant to emphasize the *love* part, or *him*.

How could she *love* someone like him?

Why him, and not us?

A sad smile graced her lips. "Spend a couple hundred years watching one of the loves of your life lose themself, then judge me, Massimo."

I bit the insides of my cheeks until blood welled in my mouth, frustration building with each word of this story. But what could I say to that?

"The problem was, when your father started digging into vampire lore and discovered the truth, I went to kill him before Osric noticed. I had everything planned, ready to keep my people from imploding from a war we couldn't win. But I never planned on *you*, Malachi." Malachi looked grim, but not surprised, to hear this as she turned to address him. "I loved you so much, *cuore mio*. For many years, you breathed life back into me. Your vision for the future of our world invigorated me; I believed in something again. I had forgotten what a pure love felt like, and you reminded me every day." Her voice dropped to a whisper. "I didn't deserve you, and I knew it, but I was selfish, and I *wanted* you more than I'd wanted anything in a very long time."

None of us said anything for several moments, the sound

of the rustling leaves in the trees and birds chirping in the distance our only soundtrack.

"And then *you* happened." Gia almost chuckled. As much as I wanted to pretend I didn't care about what excuses she was sure to give me, I hung onto her every word, a child desperate to understand why I hadn't been enough.

She stood from her chair, moving in front of me. Her sleeves bunched as she lifted her hands to frame my face, cool fingers tracing my jaw and cheekbones. I looked into her eyes, the same deep blue as mine, fighting to breathe evenly.

"I am so sorry, Massimo." She smiled again, but this time there wasn't a hint of happiness to be found on her face. "Sorry to have missed out on knowing you. Sorry to have left you in the dark for so long. Sorry I wasn't there to witness all your firsts."

I pulled back from her touch, feeling electrocuted by the words I'd wanted to hear my whole life.

Her hands fell to her sides, shoulders dropping in defeat. "Vampires are a dying breed, and our birth rates drop every year. The day I found out I was pregnant was the best and worst day of my life. It was a wake-up call, that no matter how much I loved your father, I couldn't have both him and save my people from the power-hungry leader Osric had become. You would be born a half-angel, and it would only be a matter of time until Osric learned the truth, that you weren't his.

"By then, his Fixation with me was too far gone for him to see reason. My affair with your father would have been the ultimate betrayal. He wouldn't have only killed me. He would have killed *all* of us, then gone after the angels too. Everything I'd done to protect my people from a war against the angels we couldn't win would have been in vain."

The weight of her stare was almost unbearable, so I looked at my father. He'd dropped his elbows to his knees, his body hunched over in defeat, and my heart squeezed for the man who had always done his best.

I hadn't understood the drive behind most of his actions, but in this moment, I saw he'd done everything he could to shield me from how deeply his own hurt ran. Here I was, a constant reminder of everything he couldn't have, even looking like her. A reminder of how much he and Gia had given up to protect their kinds.

That he expected me to fall in line with this same level of selflessness made more sense, even if it still stung that he'd never given me all the information I needed to make my own choice.

I didn't want to empathize with him, didn't want to feel bad for the parents who had hurt me, but standing here, it was impossible for me to ignore the fact that they were both *good* to their marrow.

"I sent Malachi away, and as soon as you were born, I left you with him."

"And Osric?" I asked. "Did he never notice you were pregnant?"

"I let him think the baby died," she admitted. "As I said, vampire pregnancy is rare, and miscarriages or still births happen often. It didn't take much convincing for him to buy my story." Her brows furrowed, any hint of a smile long gone. "Even if he hadn't bought it, my mourning was more than convincing. Since I could never see you again, either of you, I didn't have to fake it. You *were* dead to me, in that sense. I had to hope I'd never see either of you again, even if the thought nearly killed me."

Silence settled over the patio as the Tuscan sun set over the hills, its warm orange glow casting long shadows between us.

"You did the right thing." Malachi's words had my brows rising in surprise. "You saved our son."

"I won't ask your forgiveness, nor will I offer an apology,"

Gia added to me. "I stand by my actions. But perhaps, in time, now that things are safer, you would be open to a relationship?"

The tentative hope in her eyes cut me like a knife. But this was a lot. Too much.

I couldn't deal with her question right now. I had the answers I'd wanted for decades, and I needed time to process them. For today, we had bigger issues to return to.

"About Summer." I winced, but pushed through. "They accused her of being a Hunter. I need to know more."

Gia let out a long sigh, walking to the railing. Her deep brown hair fluttered in the wind as she looked out over the land, silent for another moment.

"All of the lore about vampires and wolves as mortal enemies isn't entirely wrong. That you married one" — she looked over her shoulder, a mischievous grin taking over her face as she chuckled — "your ancestors are surely rolling over in their graves."

I bristled at her comment, but she turned to look at me, hands resting behind her on the railing as if she needed an anchor in the weight of this conversation.

"Wolves have always been elite among the shifter breeds. Their pack bonds allow them to hunt with an ease no other animal can claim, and their tracking ability is the stuff of legend."

"Get to the part where my wife might be in danger."

Malachi's eyes met mine, that same disapproving look he often gave for shows of disrespect, but I was at my limit of emotional displays for today.

"One of a vampire's greatest advantages is our ability to mask our scent, leaving us nearly untraceable. It was the only reason our kind could disappear for so long. If we cloaked ourselves in shadows, were untraceable by scent, and kept to ourselves, punishing those who turned humans and erasing the minds of any who thought they'd seen us, we could disappear. The only thing preventing that from happening was a rare breed of wolf shifter."

"Hunters."

She nodded, pushing off the railing to begin pacing. "There weren't very many of them left by the time I decided we needed to go into hiding, so we crafted a plan to lure them to us."

"You killed them all."

She stopped, keeping her back to me. "You have to understand, the deaths of a few to protect my people, to keep Osric's madness in check. He would have killed so many more."

I ground my teeth together, thinking of the lives I'd justified taking for the same reason. But the difference was, I killed those who were a harm to others. She'd killed wolves just because they were *different*.

"I won't harm her. I am surprised any are left, but I won't harm her."

I stood, shadow walking to meet her, wrapping a hand around her throat. She gasped, her eyes tinting red as her fangs dropped at the threat I posed. "But it's not just you, is it? Did anyone survive who might try to track her down because she's a Hunter?"

"It's possible," she hedged, eyes changing back to blue as she stared up at me. "Chaos erupted after you left Venice, a civil war between our kind that has been brewing for centuries."

"After you shoved us out the window, you mean."

The corners of her eyes crinkled, ever so slightly. "Well, you are your father's son. I couldn't risk you staying behind to help with that lionheart of yours." Her palm landed softly on my shoulder, near my heart. "I needed to be sure you'd leave. Safe."

I dropped my hold on her neck, taking a step back.

Her hand dropped, breaking contact, as she continued, "We're still trying to figure out who died, who remains, and what side everyone is on."

That wasn't reassuring, and a bad feeling settled into my chest. "Can't you order them to stand down? Aren't you officially queen now?"

Gia huffed a breath, straightening out her skirts but allowing the topic change. "I believe it's time for some restructuring within our society, so that remains to be seen. I'll need your contact information, but we'll know more soon."

"*My* contact information? Why?"

Her eyes tinged with red once more as the wind fluttered around her, lifting her skirts and hair. Shadows danced across her skin, rising from her fingertips and under her sleeves as she tipped her chin up, a seriousness settling over her features as she stared me down. "Because if I am crowned queen, you are my heir. Welcome to the royal family, Massimo Dante Russo-Lazzari. *Mio figlio.*"

Chapter Forty-Two

SUMMER

"One more," I mumbled as I punched the final staple through the new fabric for my café chairs and flipped it over, smoothing my hand over the new yellow and blue floral. A slow grin took over my face as I stepped back, admiring my work. Everything was bright and cheery, new pink tables contrasting with the floral fabric. Still *me*, but refreshed.

The chairs were the last of the DIY projects I'd tackled in the shop. Thanks to my emotional avoidance, I now had freshly painted tables, crisp new wallpaper on the wall behind the register, springy wildflowers drawn on the front window around my new vinyl logo, and overflowing planter boxes I'd made in my dad's workshop, bursting with color. I was a master at channeling my energy into action. Negativity was a drag no one wanted, least of all me.

My phone's timer went off, alerting me I had 20 minutes to get on the road on time, so I set about cleaning up my upholstery tools and scraps.

In my haste to overhaul everything *right now*, I'd decided to shut the café down for two weeks for renovations, but I was at a standstill until Aspen's plans for the patio were finished. Waking up this morning to one of the first really warm days of almost-summer had inspired me to take a half-day and check another item off my bucket list — white water rafting.

After a quick online search, I'd found one not too far from

here, and texted Indi to invite her. Just like she had a few weeks ago, she rudely declined.

One of the decisions I'd come to in my melancholy over the last few days was that I was tired of waiting for everyone else to be ready for my plans.

Did I hate doing things alone? Yes.

But did that mean I *couldn't?* Nope.

Thankfully, the first adventure I decided to take solo was far from alone — the whole rest of the tour group would be there. I'd have a chance to make some friends, ones unconnected to Timber Creek.

My hands shook as I put my tools back in the basket, placing it on top of the counter and blowing out a long breath. It was a little bit terrifying, but I wanted this — to live my best life here in Timber Creek and still expand my horizons. Indi's words weeks ago about me being stalled weren't as untrue as I hoped they were, but I was determined to make that a thing of the past.

"Today is a good day for a good day," I read the sign leading up to my apartment, hopping up the stairs to grab my things.

Everything was going perfectly to plan.

Twenty-five minutes later, I bundled into my Jeep and took off on the road out of town.

Even just for the mountain drive, this trip was already worth it. Bright green aspen trees dotted the mountain sides, and spring flowers dotted the meadows between patches of dark green pines and spruces in a picture-perfect vision of spring.

In fact —

I spotted a vista point pull-off ahead and eased my Jeep over to the side. It would only take a minute to snap some photos.

Hopping out of the car, I stepped up to the edge where the

dirt-cleared parking space fell away to steep mountainside, hair whipping in the strong winds. The smell of the pines and fresh grass overwhelmed my senses as I trained my camera on the view. In the far distance, jagged mountain peaks still had a healthy snowcap, as they would all summer. But closer, wild larkspur and fireweed and desert paintbrush filled the view with color.

I flipped the camera around and put my back to the scene, posing for a selfie and blowing a kiss to the camera as my hair flew in a cyclone all around me. Switching over to my texts, I sent the pic to Indi.

SUMMER

Adventure awaits!

INDI

Have fun! Let me know when you get back so I can hear all about you drowning multiple times in that death trap of a boat.

I chuckled, then hearted her text.

The crunch of gravel alerted me to another car joining me, and I glanced back to see a blacked-out SUV following my lead at the turn-off to take in the gorgeous view. No one got out to join me, but maybe they'd pulled off for another reason. It was hazardous to drive distracted on these narrow, winding roads, so sometimes people stopped for a break or to make a phone call. I snapped a few more photos before heading back to my car.

I stared at the SUV as I gripped my door handle, but the heavily tinted windows blocked out whoever sat inside. I sniffed the air, my wolf's hackles pricking up, but the wind was blowing right into my face, blocking out any other scents and sounds.

With a shrug, I hopped up into my Jeep, ready to be on my

way. When I pulled back onto the road, the SUV followed shortly after. I stared in my rearview mirror at the imposing vehicle, brow furrowed, but it wasn't like there was anywhere else for them to go.

The hairs on the back of my neck stood up, but I was probably being paranoid. "Quit acting like Cooper," I muttered to myself, looking back at the road.

Winding through the mountains, I glanced behind me every few minutes, that same black SUV tailing me a little too close for comfort.

At the next available passing lane, I pulled to the right to let them go around me.

But they didn't. They moved to the right lane with me, and matched my way-too-slow pace.

Shit.

Fear skittered down my spine, but I tried to shake it off. I was a wolf, after all, and the odds were still in my favor.

Unless they know *you're a wolf.*

The thought hit as they flashed their lights at me. What if they were like the guys who'd kidnapped Jade and Hailey? People *looking* for shifters?

Against my better judgment, I hit the gas as I fumbled for my phone in the passenger seat to call West. This far from town I wouldn't be able to reach him telepathically.

SOS. The symbol in the corner informed me I had no service.

I breathed deep, trying to calm my racing heart.

I knew these mountains. I rarely drove outside of town, but that didn't mean I never had or couldn't. If I could just make it to the next town, I doubted whoever it was would try to cause a scene in public, and I'd be able to find a phone with service.

But every time I upped my speed, the SUV matched me. Every turn I whipped around, they took just as smoothly. Until

I had to admit that whoever was following me must also have supernatural reflexes.

I glanced in my rearview mirror again, but the deeply tinted windows blocked out the sight of whoever drove.

It was only a split-second glance, but when my eyes returned to the road, I yelped.

I grappled with the steering wheel, but it was no use. Too late.

An ungodly shriek of metal scraping metal split the air, the guardrail useless at these speeds, and I braced as my Jeep went airborne.

Chapter Forty-Three

MAX

I stopped dead in my tracks, adrenaline spiking my system as an odd weightlessness hit my gut. Like the crest of a roller-coaster right before the drop.

"Son?"

Rubbing at my chest, I glanced up at my father, already seated at the dinner table, set with a simple meal the house staff had prepared. Gia had left already, having vampire business to attend to, but it hadn't felt right for me to leave Malachi here alone so soon.

"One moment." I backed out of the dining room, heading to the patio as I whipped out my phone. I couldn't be sure what this feeling meant, but my gut said something was wrong.

With my mate.

Before I could overthink it, I hit Summer's name, heaving out a breath of impatience into the Tuscan sunset as the call rang out.

"C'mon, Summer," I whispered. Begged.

Was she not answering because she, rightly, hated me right now? Or because I was right, and something was very, very wrong?

"Dammit." I ended the call, switching over to West's contact and punching his name.

Did he hate me too? He should, if Summer had told him anything.

I exhaled in relief as the call connected. "Couldn't you just pop over if you need something? Marriage has made you lazy."

I cut right to the chase, ignoring his dig. "Where's Summer?"

I couldn't see him through the call, but I could practically feel the way his guard raised immediately, his second of silence tight with tension. "What do you mean, *where's Summer*. She's with you." It wasn't a question. It was a threat. "You two have been holed up in her apartment for days."

Fuck, West Larkin was definitely going to murder me. "No, she's not, and we're not. We haven't been."

More silence that cut like a knife.

"I suggest you start explaining yourself."

That was not a conversation for over the phone. Or ever, preferably. "We don't have time for that right now. Just — track her down for me, and let me know when you find her. I'll be there as soon as I can." My heart was pounding, needing to know she was safe. I swallowed my pride to add, my voice shakier than I wanted to admit, "Please."

Another beat of silence, then, "*Fuck,*" before West hung up the phone.

West would find her. She was pack, and their pack bonds tied them together. There was nowhere she could go he wouldn't be able to track.

Unless someone cloaked her.

That thought got me dialing again, this time to —

"Rhain Allaway, happy to help you today with your car's extend—"

"Not now," I bit out. "Do you have any idea if Grigor made it out of Venice?"

He was the only thing that made sense. The only one who would try to find Summer, who might have any idea where to start looking. The one who had the strongest motive to send her fight-or-flight response spiking enough to punch through our bond to me, halfway across the world.

The only one who had a point to make.

If he was dead, then I was just being paranoid. Maybe experiencing a spot of indigestion.

Please be dead, please be dead.

Rhain hummed. "Grigor… blond lad, Boston duke, little too interested in your girl?"

"That's the one."

"I don't remember seeing him on the casualty list at the palace. Let me check in with some of the others and I'll get back to you."

"Thanks."

I ended the call and stuffed my phone back in my pocket, already moving. If Grigor wasn't confirmed dead, I was going to Timber Creek — there was no way he'd let Summer go if he'd made it out alive. Not after she'd gotten the best of him twice.

Turning, my eyes widened at the sight of my father standing in the open doorway to the patio, concern furrowing his features. But he was standing on his own; he'd been doing better the past few days. His wings had even started to regrow. The doctor we'd called in — a witch who specialized in both human and supernatural medicine — had assured us his magic was just severely depleted, but that he'd recover in time.

Malachi had his staff here, and Headquarters was only a phone call away if he needed anything.

"I have to go."

He nodded. "I heard. I'll be fine." Grey eyes met mine, a knowing resolve in them. "Sometime soon, we do need to talk more, you and me. But for now, just know I'm sorry about all of it, and I love you very much."

My feet moved before I could stop them, and I wrapped

my arms around him, careful of his shoulders where his wing growth would be tender.

Grunting something incoherent, my father gave me an awkward pat on the back. It wasn't quite a Heath Larkin hug, but hell, we were out of practice.

We pulled apart, and he clapped my shoulder.

"Go save your mate."

I allowed myself one moment in the darkness of the In-Between to prepare myself for what would greet me on the other end.

A lot of angry wolves, probably. And I couldn't even blame them.

With a deep breath, I plunged through shadow and materialized just off the Larkin pack house back deck. My wings punched out to slow my fall, and I soared down to land with a thump on the railing. I hopped off onto the deck as the sliding glass door whipped open.

I hardly had a second to register who ran out before three men rushed me, shouting in my face. My hands went up in surrender as green eyes met mine, flashing to amber with slitted pupils in rage, and a snick of metal hit my ears as the tip of a knife pressed to my jugular.

"Where the *fuck* is our sister?"

Cooper and I were almost the same height, but the cat-shifter packed pounds of muscle that a flier like me would never build.

"I'll find her," I tried to get out, but shouts from the doorway interrupted me. I glanced over Cooper's shoulder to see Terran yelling obscenities at me as West held him back.

The knife at my throat pressed deeper, drawing a trickle of warm blood down my neck, and I brought my attention back to Cooper. The more immediate threat.

I tried again. "Let me find her. I can sense her."

"Why the fuck can't *we* sense her?" Terran shouted from the door.

"Coop, stand down," West ordered. "And T, shut up so we can figure out what's going on."

Cooper's eyes narrowed, flitting between amber and green a few times before he eased off. He crossed his arms, but kept the knife firmly in his fist. Noted.

West shoved Terran down into a patio chair, keeping a firm hand on his brother's shoulder to keep him down.

Finally able to take a breath without slicing my throat, I turned to West. "How much do you —"

"Everything," he bit out, his own eyes flashing gold with his wolf. "Aspen told us everything about your little arrangement with our sister. I'm assuming you're also the reason she needed to take off alone today on a solo adventure, avoiding us all."

I winced, but this wasn't the time for apologies.

Then Heath joined us, his own expression pained. Hurt. Betrayed. And fuck if I didn't feel like the most pathetic excuse for a male.

West continued, "What we don't know is why we can't fucking *sense* her. I've never been cut off from any of them like this."

I was vaguely aware of others joining us, emerging from the house, the woods, the driveway. Called here by their pack's distress, their Alpha's emotions.

Jade, who had been through so much. Hailey by her side. West's Shields Atlas, Nova, Zion, Jett. Aspen, who looked angry enough to take that knife from Cooper's hands and gut me herself. I wasn't sure I'd stop her.

"There's a vampire," I began, making myself loud enough for everyone to hear even though I hated my own voice. "We encountered him in Boston, and he fixated on Summer. I think he's taken her. His name is —"

"Grigor."

We all turned at the voice. At the bottom of the steps to the deck, Quentin stood with Leif. Quentin came up the steps, his pallor ghostly pale, his hands trembling.

"He's here. I can feel it."

Terran tried to stand but West shoved him back down, so he settled for throwing out an arm at Quentin. "What does he have to do with this?"

I tilted my head in question at Quentin. It was his story to tell, or not.

"I knew Grigor before coming here." Quentin bit his lip. "He — he's the one who turned me. And then Max found me, saved me."

"So, Grigor is really here because of *you?*" Terran asked.

Leif took a step in front of Quentin, fists clenched at his sides. "That's not what he said."

"*I* brought Quentin here after getting him out of Boston. He needed to be far away from Grigor's den." I'd already dug my grave with this family anyway, so I might as well make sure Quentin didn't go down with me.

Cooper turned to me slowly, glaring. "We keep circling back to this being *your* fault."

"Would you all let him speak?" Leif shouted, and everyone started back, stunned at the usually mild-mannered kid snapping at them.

"I had to get away from him because I'm bonded to him. The closer we are, the easier it is to feel him," Quentin said quickly, like he was afraid he'd be interrupted again. He lifted his head, meeting first my eyes, then West's. "That means I can track him down."

Behind us, the distinctive sound of ammo clicking into a gun sounded. Apparently, while we'd been talking, Atlas had been gearing up.

He checked the barrel of a rifle, then slung it over his shoulder. "Then let's fucking go."

Chapter Forty-Four

MAX

"Is Grigor alone?" West directed the question to Quentin, but the kid shook his head.

"I can't tell that," Quentin answered, sitting on the couch next to Leif. "I can only sense his presence."

We'd relocated inside to the pack house's living room while West dispatched his Shields and Scouts. According to Indi's last text from her, Summer was already outside of pack lands, but had last been in the mountains at a turn-off not far from town. With quick efficiency, the wolves left, headed in all directions from that starting point. Problem was with a vampire who could shadow walk, her last location meant next to nothing. It killed me to sit on my hands, but charging off with nothing to go on wouldn't save her any faster.

"How does that work? Terran asked once everyone else had left, pacing the back wall as he took his hat off and ran his hands through his shaggy hair. "What do you sense through a vampire bond? Location, emotions, anything that can help us."

"Both." Quentin sighed. "Similar to a pack bond maybe, but if you were tied to an Alpha who gave nothing back, only took for himself."

Anger rippled through me, both for the way Grigor had treated Quentin, but also that this fucker now held my wife.

Quentin closed his eyes, likely honing in on his bond. "He's close. In the state, definitely. And he's — upset, but something else? Maybe excited."

Leif leaned his shoulder into Quentin for support. Quentin's eyes shot open, darting towards Leif as he blinked rapidly, flushing at the small touch.

Magic swirled up my arms as I fought the urge to throw a chair through the window. Hearing the duke of the Boston den was upset and excited while holding Summer captive didn't bode well.

West leaned forward, elbows braced on his knees and hands clasped. "What about a location?"

"I can't give you GPS coordinates or anything. It's more like a draw to him, a compulsion to want to be closer. I'll know if we're going closer or away from him."

"That could take ages," Aspen murmured, exchanging a glance with Cooper, whose jaw clenched in frustration.

"I'll go with him," I said. "Together, Quentin and I can track them down much more quickly, and when we have a location, I'll send it to you."

"I'll lead on the ground." Our heads swung around to Hattie, hands on her hips and cowboy hat on her head. Even Heath raised a brow at her. She smirked back at him. "You don't know all my secrets, little brother. But trust me, if he's been around here, I can track him."

I made a mental note to ask her later what that was all about when West's voice cut into my thoughts.

"What makes you so sure he won't just vanish her out of the state the minute you get close?" West's question was a good one, and I hated that I already knew the answer to it.

"Because it's personal." I met Quentin's gaze, remembering the day I'd helped him escape Grigor's control vividly. He was still young now, but the sight of a teenage vampire nearly lost to bloodlust had unlocked a protective instinct in me. Grigor preyed on the young and hopeless, leaving a trail of Turned vampires who had to be put down. Quentin would have been the Conclave's next target in a matter of minutes if I hadn't stopped him from killing that human in the middle of a dancefloor. I'd broken my cover that night, almost risking my life and job in an undercover mission to take down a leader of the Black Rose Coven to free Quentin, but I didn't regret it. "He wants payback for helping Quentin escape his den."

Cooper pushed off the wall and strode towards me, hand outstretched. "Phone."

I raised a brow.

"I'm sharing your location with us, and then you're going to go get my sister."

I handed him my phone.

For some reason, that launched everyone into action. Suddenly, everyone moved in a coordinated motion that made their pack telepathy evident, silently organizing into pairs as Cooper tapped away on my phone.

He passed it back, but didn't let go as I gripped it, instead using the moment to pull me close.

"If he's harmed one hair on her head —"

I shook my head. "As soon as she's safe, do whatever you want to me. I deserve it."

He cocked his head, but gave a terse nod and let go of my phone, following Hattie and the rest of the Larkins out of the house and into the vehicles already running in the driveway.

Left alone with Quentin, I extended a hand so we could vanish together. "Ready?"

"Farther," Quentin panted as we rematerialized for what felt like the twentieth time. Maybe it was.

Who knew this state was so big?

He dropped his hands to his knees, bent at the waist, and I couldn't blame him. Vanishing within one state might not be as taxing as halfway across the globe to Europe, but fuck, doing it this many times in a row? We were flagging, both of us pushing our magic to its limit. But Summer's life was at stake — we had to keep going.

"Back west, then," I said, cross-checking the mental map I had going of all the places we'd tried so far. With each stop, my anxiety rose, the bond between us flaring to life as I felt her panicked emotions.

Quentin held up a finger, breathing deep before straightening up with his hand gripping his side, sweat curling the hair at his brow.

I glanced at the sky, the heavy rain clouds blacking out the setting sun, adding more urgency to my need to get to her. We'd been at it for hours, and everything felt like a ticking time bomb, a desperation I'd never felt in my life. Each time we seemed to get closer, by the next jump, Quentin's connection to Grigor would change, leaving us running around like chickens with our heads cut off.

Unless — shit.

"He's doing this on purpose." I ground my teeth together, heaving an exasperated sigh.

"W-what?"

"He's leading us in circles, to wear us out. Fuck." I was such an idiot. How had I not seen this sooner? By the time he decided he was ready to be found, I'd be so depleted, my chances of fighting back would be severely diminished.

Quentin dropped his hand, his brow creased as he looked up at me. "What do we do, then?"

A sharp pang shot through me, an echo through our bond of what was happening to Summer, and I gasped in pain and shock.

Grigor was upping the ante.

But little did he know he wasn't just taunting me with a pet, with a Source — no, he was messing with *my wife*.

A feral snarl broke out of me as my fangs punched down, lightning crackling over my arms, my wings.

"Quentin," I said, my voice deathly quiet. "I need you to dig deep into your connection to him. I need you to want to go to him more than anything in the whole world."

He winced, but nodded. I raised my arm for him to hold, and closed my own eyes, imagining the same thing.

The one thing I wanted more than anything — to be with Summer.

A cloud of darkness rose around us, lightning skittering through the shadows as our magic combined, weakened from overwork but strong enough for this, tangling and strengthening together. I could *feel* Quentin's intention, palpable in our shared efforts, and I fused mine with his. This wasn't magic anyone had ever taught me, sharing magic *or* tracing bonds — neither vampires nor angels had mates, historically — but we created it together, out of desperation.

In my mind's eye, a grove of pine trees flashed, already dark by a hillside blocking the sunset as rain began to fall. A dilapidated cabin tucked between the trees, windows shattered and shutters hanging askew. But there, in the window, were the red eyes of an angry, hungry vampire.

"Got him?" I gritted my teeth as my lightning lashed out around us.

Quentin's eyes squeezed closed, but his nostrils flared as he nodded.

With all our remaining strength, Quentin and I surged towards that cabin, clawing along our entwined bonds through the In-Between.

As quickly as the world had disappeared, robbing me of all my senses, they came roaring back when a scream pierced the air. I shoved our shadows away, still gripping Quentin's arm as he fell to his knees in exhaustion, panting hard again.

"Max!" Summer gasped as I glanced around the dark space for her. There in the far corner was my wife, sprawled on her stomach across broken and missing floorboards in the far corner of the room. Her hair was a mess, her face covered in bruises and cuts in various stages of healing. She fought to push herself up to a kneeling position but her hands were bound behind her back in iron manacles, locking down her ability to shift or heal, her breath wheezing dangerously as she moved.

I saw red, nothing but thunderous rage in my thoughts. My wings spasmed, and I had to hide my shock as they rippled and changed. My usual black feathers were gone, replaced with the leathery black wings of a pureblood vampire.

Summer's brows shot up, but I clenched my jaw, determined to work this in my favor. Grigor knew me as the vampire, Dante, and this would only help confirm that for him.

I tamped down my angel powers, locking my control over my lightning as a secret weapon.

Summer's eyes darted to the right three times in a row, and I followed her gaze, peering into the shadowed corner where a kitchen once was. Nothing was there now but a broken table and three chairs, but I trusted her silent signal, watching the corner as I stepped forward.

The floorboards creaked loudly under my foot, the sound drowned out by my pounding heart.

"So loud," a voice said as the shadows in the corner dissolved, right where Summer had told me he was. Sitting in the fourth chair was Grigor, one leg crossed over the other as he picked at his nails with a knife, cleaning out blood then licking it off the blade. "You'd think the legendary Dante would be stealthier, hm?"

He looked up at me then, a wide grin taking over his face. His eyes had gone the full red of his predator, and he didn't even try to conceal his fangs. In all-black, he looked every bit the vampire lord cliché, but the sight of the three parallel tears in his sleeve lit a spark in my chest.

No matter how badly injured Summer was, she'd fought back.

"Free her," I said, my fingers tingling with magic as I moved towards him, watching the shadows dance across the blade in his hand.

Grigor chuckled, the sound dark as the storm clouds outside. "But this has been so much fun, right pet?" His gaze slid to Quentin, and his lips quirked into a smirk. "After all these years, it's so good to have you back, boy. You didn't think you'd escape me forever, did you?"

Quentin pushed himself back to his feet, refusing to acknowledge Grigor. By the way his whole body shook, the small defiance was costing him.

"Two against one, Grigor," I called over, trying to stall as I did my best to maneuver myself between Grigor and Summer. I had no real sense on where we currently were, but the steady rain turning to snowfall outside told me we were back high up in the mountains, closer to pack lands again. He'd led us in a circle after drawing us all out to chase him down.

"Hardly." He chuckled, lifting an imperious brow at Quentin as he stood from the chair, circling the broken table to move closer. "Do you have it in you to defy me, pet?"

Behind me, Quentin whimpered like the word was a physical blow, and I wanted to rip Grigor's head from his body twice as much.

"You have no idea what I'm capable of." I raised my arms out, lightning sparking from my fingers as Grigor's gaze flicked from Quentin back to me.

Grigor tilted his head, frowning slightly as he took in the power. "My my, Dante. Aren't you full of secrets. Maybe I need to take you as a pet, too."

My lightning lit the dark cabin, casting spasms of shadows

Grigor observed with interest until his gaze returned to meet mine.

"What are you?" he murmured, but he seemed to be speaking to himself since he didn't wait for an answer. "No matter. Either way, I should replenish myself." His grin was all fang as he appeared at Summer's back and yanked on her hair, wrenching her head back. She gritted her teeth, fighting his hold. His shadows swirled around her, holding her still as he leaned down, meeting my eye as the tip of his fang grazed her neck.

"Wait!" Quentin pushed past me, staggering forward and falling to his knees. Summer's eyes locked on mine, doing her best impersonation of being paralyzed even though I knew Grigor's magic had no effect on her. Clearly, *he* still underestimated the extent of her immunity.

Grigor paused, pulling back ever so slightly.

"*Quentin*," Summer hissed, never looking his way as she held her act.

Quentin trembled so hard, his teeth were all but clacking together, but he tilted his own head, exposing his neck.

"Master." His eyes downcast, his voice was barely audible as he pleaded to save Summer.

Grigor's face lit up with glee, his pet coming home to him. Letting go of Summer's hair, he stepped unceremoniously around her to stand before Quentin. His hand cupped Quentin's jaw, tilting his head up to meet his eyes.

Obediently, Quentin brought his hands behind his back, like this was a routine they'd danced many times over. Grigor's eyes turned feverish as they locked on Quentin, and I was so distracted by their exchange I almost didn't see Quentin's fingers.

Behind his back. Counting down.

Three —

My gaze flicked to Summer, watching as she dissolved the shadow magic binding her in place.

Two —

My ears pricked. A crunch of twigs underfoot behind us.

One.

I dropped a stake from the In-Between into Quentin's hand before he roared, stabbing upward and plunging it into Grigor's chest.

In a flash, I was at Summer's side, wrenching the last of Grigor's magic off her. With a snap of my fingers, I summoned the key from Grigor's pocket to the iron manacles binding her hands and feet.

Grigor's feral growl had me spinning back around as Summer's manacles fell away to see him wrench the stake from his chest, the strike having missed his heart. Quentin's eyes went wide as he scrambled back on his knees. Before I could intervene, Grigor's hands circled Quentin's throat, both of them crashing to the ground.

"Quentin!" Summer cried, moving to rush forward. Her breath was still a wheeze, so I pushed her back.

"*Ungrateful, hateful pet,*" Grigor seethed at Quentin, knees on the kid's chest, holding him down and strangling the life from him. Quentin clawed and scratched and scrambled for the stake that had fallen between the broken floorboards, for a second chance —

I stomped on a floorboard, breaking a piece off as I moved towards Grigor, but a chorus of howls drew all of our attention to the front door as it was ripped from the hinges, a dozen wolves rushing into the tiny cabin, led by Hattie with the glint of murder in her eyes.

Grigor looked over the wolves, then back down to Quentin, his grin wide — he'd vanish them away, somewhere untraceable.

"He's going to —"

I didn't get a chance to finish my shout before a snow leopard leapt from the pack of wolves, jaws closing around Grigor's throat. In Grigor's distraction, I tossed the makeshift stake to Quentin and he went for round two. This time, he stabbed it home, straight through Grigor's heart.

The snow leopard ripped Grigor's head to the side — could never be too careful — and we all watched Grigor's lifeless form collapse to the floorboards.

As quickly as he'd appeared, the snow leopard shifted back, and I drew in a shocked breath.

Leif emerged from the cat form, his naked skin covered in dirt and blood, as he dropped to his knees in front of Quentin and pulled him into a fierce hug, tears streaming down both of their faces.

I raised a brow at Summer. "Since when is he a cat?"

Chapter Forty-Five

SUMMER

I let out a shuddering breath as Grigor's body fell to the ground and Leif wrapped Quentin in a hug. Someone had me in their grasp, holding me upright, keeping me steady, but my brain felt like scrambled mush.

Grigor had been vanishing us all over the place for the better part of a day. Once was enough to set off vertigo; all day? I kept pressing my eyes shut, hoping when I opened them again, my surroundings would stop spinning.

Still, they'd come for me. Max, and even Quentin.

I'd expected the pack, sooner or later. I knew eventually they would figure out how to find me.

But Quentin? I knew he and Leif were friends, or something like it. But enough to put himself between Grigor and me?

I stumbled forward, my legs still shaky, and let my knees give out as soon as I reached Leif and Quentin, shoving myself into their hug with zero shame.

Pressing my forehead to Quentin's, I whispered, "Thank you."

He shuddered a sob, but nodded and wiped his eyes, offering a tentative smile. "Y-you did me a favor, really. I've f-fantasized about doing that for years."

I smiled back, rubbing a hand over his shoulder. "Well then — you did it."

His smile gained a little more strength. "Yeah. Yeah, I

fucking did." He chuckled, glancing sheepishly at Leif, like he was worried what Leif would think of him for that.

Leif positively *gleamed* with pride.

I eased back to my feet, leaving them to it, and turned back to face Max.

Nope, actually, about-face. I pivoted on my heel. I'd deal with my family first.

My brothers and Aspen rushed forward, wrapping me in a giant group hug.

"Did he bite you?"

"Are you okay?"

"Was anyone else with him?"

"Where's the Jeep?"

I gave Coop a half-hearted punch in the shoulder for that last one, but the move jostled my broken ribs and I let out a gasp of pain.

"Almost forgot about those," I wheezed, wrapping an arm around my side.

West shoved the others out of the way, checking me over carefully. "You're not healing?"

I tried to bat his hands away, but gasped again and closed my eyes on a wince. "I am, it's just taking time. Believe me, this is an improvement." I waved a hand to encompass my whole body, which elicited a series of growls from my family.

It seemed safer to return to the questions. "It was just him, I think. I didn't see anyone else. He didn't bite me, thanks to Quentin. And the Jeep, well" — I scrunched my nose — "the Jeep might be a goner. I went off the road; it's probably at the bottom of the ravine by now."

Just the memory of that crash had me hissing in pain. The way I'd held my breath as the car went airborne, then crashed and crumpled through the trees and down the hillside. I wasn't lying — I *was* healing, but my body had had its work cut out for it after the fall. Broken bones, cuts and gashes from the glass, one or two punctured organs.

Grigor whisking me all over the state all day hadn't helped, either.

"You didn't answer my question," Aspen said. "Are you okay?"

I pressed my forehead to hers. "Yes. I'm a bit bruised up but I'll be okay."

Physically, at least. Emotionally — that might take a bit longer. I wasn't sure I wanted to see the inside of a car anytime soon.

On that note — "Where are we?"

"Just southwest of town," Coop answered, jaw tight as his gaze roamed the space. "This is the LeBlanc's old cabin. Practically in our own fucking backyard. Only about a half-hour drive home."

My eyes shot wide. "No — no cars."

Coop, Terran, and West all exchanged a look.

Terran lifted a shoulder. "Run home?"

Coop scoffed. "She's dead on her feet."

"She said no cars!"

"What about a plane?"

"How do you plan to land a plane in this terrain?"

"Okay, Cruz then."

"She's sick from vanishing all day, and you want her to flicker?"

"I'll take her."

Everyone's head swiveled at Max's voice cutting through their bickering.

He'd have been better off keeping quiet. Immediately, my family made a ring around me, teeth bared at Max.

"I think you've done enough." West's tone was lethal, and I winced on Max's behalf.

A muscle in Max's jaw flexed with his frustration, tangible

through our bond. "She said no cars. You can't get a plane in here. I promised you all your pound of flesh, but let me get her home first."

What did he mean by that, their pound of flesh?

Wait.

"Boys. Tell me you're not planning to beat up Max for something Grigor, an *entirely different vampire*, did to me." I shoved my way through their barricade, spinning with my hands on my hips to glare at them. My ribs protested, but I ignored them. "Secret's out now, bat boy. Nice wings, by the way."

None of my brothers met my eye. Terran kicked a splintered floorboard at his feet.

Finally, Coop jabbed a thumb at Max. "Hey, he *offered* —"

"Unbelievable," I bit out, shaking my head at them. "Get yourselves home, and take care of Quentin. I'll make my own way."

West took a step, Alpha energy radiating off him. "Sum—"

"No," I cut him off before he could get out the command laced with the magic that would make me comply. "I mean it."

I held up my chin, meeting his eye, daring him to do it.

His wolf flashed at me, pushing him to take charge and get this — me — handled quickly and safely. But West was able to keep a handle on himself, not breaking eye contact but nodding.

Leaving my pack, I strode over to Max. Was I ready to face him? Absolutely not. But I could get a ride home from him at least. He owed me that much.

His sandalwood and copper scent hit me as I reached him, and it took all my effort not to fold into his embrace. But I had to stay strong. Just because he'd found me here didn't mean he deserved my forgiveness.

Hell, it didn't even mean he wanted it. Maybe he was just here because he felt guilty.

Max's face was unreadable as I met his deep blue eyes, his gaze scanning me carefully.

He held out his hand. "Ready?"

I took a deep breath, preparing for yet another vanishing. With any luck, the last one for a while. Maybe ever.

I set my hand in his, and that same jolt of electricity, of rightness, of *home* hit me, like it did every time we touched. Max's hand closed over mine, gently pulling me into his hold until my free hand wrapped around his waist. He held me there, his breath shuddering as he rested his cheek on my forehead, mirroring our dance at the reception.

"Forgive me." His breath ghosted over the shell of my ear as the world around us faded to black, and I squeezed my eyes shut against the hurtling rush of vanishing. When I reopened them, we stood once again in my rooftop garden, and I pulled back to look up at him.

His blue eyes were streaked with red, earnest and pleading and exhausted as he searched my face.

"Forgive you?" I tried to step out of his grasp, but he wouldn't let me, only tightening his hold around my waist.

"I was wrong. I thought — Gia, my mother, said something to me," he said, and he lifted a hand to cup my face. "Gia came to visit my father and told me everything. How she'd never been able to contact me for fear if Osric found out about me, he'd kill me for her betrayal."

I remembered the manic look in Osric's eye, the ancient vampire terrifying to behold in his power. It took no stretch of imagination to picture him hunting down both Malachi and Max in a fit of rage.

Max's thumb brushed over my cheek, his eyes squeezing shut for a moment, and my heart broke for him. "With vampires, there's this sickness, for lack of a better word. The Fixation. We become obsessed with something, some*one*, and eventually destroy them. It's what's happened to Osric; he

Fixated on Gia and his hatred of angels. And I was afraid" — his voice broke, and he swallowed heavily — "fuck, Summer, I was so afraid I would do that to you. That the Fixation was already taking me, and eventually, I'd hurt you."

I reached up, wrapping my hands around his wrist as I leaned into his touch. He shook his head, then pressed his forehead to mine. "But I'm not just a vampire. Malachi had to remind me I'm an angel, too, and that means I can be stronger than some Fixation. I don't have to succumb to it. I *won't.*" He pulled me even closer, if that was possible. "I refuse. Because whatever obsession I feel with you, Summer, it's not a disease. It can't be. Not when it's the best thing that's ever happened to me, when the best I've ever felt is when I'm with you."

A shuddering breath left me at his words, my heart squeezing with the honesty I heard there. Max's thumb rested under my chin, tipping my face up to his. After a tentative glance to make sure I wasn't going to shove him away, his lips brushed against mine, not quite enough to be a kiss yet, but like he couldn't help himself.

"So, I'm asking you to forgive me for being an idiot," he continued, a self-deprecating laugh escaping him. "All that shit I said before — I hoped if I hurt you enough, you'd hate me, and then maybe you'd move on faster. Forget about me.

"But it was all bullshit. I love you, Summer. I want it all. I want every moment you'll give me for the rest of my life. I know I don't deserve you, or your forgiveness; that this will be hard because our lives are so different, but I don't care. I'm asking anyway. Because I can't go another moment without knowing I laid myself fucking bare to you and did everything I could to win you back."

My heart beat so loud, I knew he could hear it, and my breath caught in my throat. It'd be so easy to dive right in again, but that was how I always got hurt. And what was that saying about doing the same thing over and over and expecting a different result?

"That was a pretty good grovel," I said. "Maybe you've been reading some books after all."

Max chuckled, his lips tipping up in the hint of a smile, and damn if I didn't love to see this man happy. "What else was I supposed to do while trapped in a luxurious Italian villa with a control freak invalid for a father? Now I get the whole Shadow Daddy thing."

I couldn't help but grin. "Told you."

"That you did." His thumb trailed over my cheek again, his eyes soft with adoration.

"I know I should be angry with you, though hate is going a little far," I started, trying to organize my thoughts. I tended to say the first things that came to my mind, but I wanted to get this right. "And maybe I was at first. But it didn't take me long to figure out something else was going on. You might be dark and mysterious to other people, Max, but I can see right through your shadows. You can't hide from me. And it's about damn time you came to your senses and figured that out.

"So yes, I forgive you. Of course I do. I love you too, Max." A true grin broke over his face, his eyes dropping to my mouth before he leaned in, but I put a hand up first, covering his lips. "But I don't want to hear anymore talk about you not deserving me. That's my damn husband you're talking about, and he's the worthiest man I know."

I leaned up on my tiptoes, pressing a kiss to his neck. "You risk your life to help people who can't help themselves." Another kiss to his jaw. "You put me and my safety before your own, time and again. You work in secret, for no accolades, nothing, to make this world a better and safer place for all of us." A kiss to his cheek. "You're like our very own superhero."

He shook his head. "I'm not a superhero."

I met his eyes, waited until he met mine back. "No, you're not. Because you're *real*. And you're mine."

I slammed my lips into his, and he met my kiss with the same desperation I felt. His hand raked through my hair, tilting my head to deepen the angle, plundering my mouth with his tongue.

After what felt like an eon, I pulled back just enough to breathe, "So, does this mean the divorce is off, husband?"

A growl came from his throat. "Never say that word again, wife. I'm not leaving, not now, not ever. Where you go, I go, now and forever. At your back or at your side, however you'll have me."

I smiled. "My very own superhero shadow" — I gasped, my mind flooding with images — "Shadowman!"

"I am not a superhero —"

"I can see it now, the whole storybook! Okay, I need a pen —"

Max's chuckle shook me out my thoughts, and I shoved down the idea of the whole children's book story arc I'd just come up with. I'd deal with that later.

"By my side, husband. That's where I'll have you. By my side, always."

MAX

"That," Summer mumbled, her face pressed into my shirt, "was awful."

I chuckled, wrapping my arms around her as she burrowed further into my chest. Flipping open her lavender notebook, I crossed out the line reading, Ride on a plane like a human.

"Not what you were imagining, sunshine?" I closed the notebook and hugged her tighter. We huddled in a dark corner of Denver International Airport as far as I could get her from the bustling transportation hub. She groaned, and I pressed my lips to the top of her hair, stifling my grin.

"Everything smells. And oh my Goddess, the toilet. I feel bad for the person who couldn't hold it for the 45-minute flight from Eagle Vail to Denver. But not as bad as I feel for myself, having to go through experiencing this with my super super sniffer. And the sounds—" Her body convulsed.

"We still have a longer flight ahead." I rubbed a hand down her spine, her body shivering slightly at the touch.

Instead of giving into another dry heave, Summer breathed deep, her head tilting up to mine. Those hazel eyes I lost myself in were rimmed in her wolf's gold, just like they were every time I touched her shadowmark covering her back. A mixture of love and lust flooded our connection, a combination of her mate bond and my vampire magic. "You're trying to change my mind, aren't you?"

With a gentle kiss to her lips, I trailed a hand down her

back again until she pressed her small, rounded belly into my chest. "Is it working?"

Her gaze flicked to the gate behind us, the next leg of our flight to Paris beginning to board. Dozens of people crowded the area, leaving me feeling far more exposed than I preferred. But after spending two years as Summer's husband, I'd do absolutely anything to make her happy.

Fixation or not, I was obsessed with my wife and the baby girl she was growing.

We'd spent the last two years finding a balance of small town life and traveling the world together. I still took some jobs my father sent my way, particularly if it involved saving innocents in need, but had found a quiet contentment in Timber Creek. No two days were ever the same there, and the chaos was neverending.

Like everything in our relationship, this pregnancy hadn't been in the plans. And yet, the day she told me she was expecting… fuck, the joy emanating from her had been enough to make my heart soar.

The part of me that was absolutely terrified of the unknowns ahead was dulled by the overbearing enthusiasm of the Larkin crew. Besides, River was more than tolerable, so I'd come around to the idea of having a kid.

"Can we rent a car and drive to our babymoon instead?"

"Tempting." I dropped a kiss to her lips, brushing the hair off her face. "But no. Too far."

She scrunched her nose and dropped her hands from my back, turning towards the gate with a sigh. A whole gamut of emotions flitted across her face as she rubbed a palm over her stomach, the bump showing beneath her tie-dye Love Bites tee and leggings.

"Do you trust me?" I whispered over her shoulder, and she leaned against me.

She looked back, our noses inches apart. "You know I do."

"Then if I tell you I checked with Gia, and vanishing is completely safe for the baby, will you let me get us there faster?"

Her brow creased, and she looked down at her hands resting on her stomach. "But how do you know? It's not like there are many wolf-vampire-angel babies running around to see if they've ever vanished before."

I tugged her into my hold, laying my palm over hers as I let my shadow powers expand, cocooning us against the outside world. The baby kicked right where our hands were, and my chest damn near exploded with happiness.

"Actually, there's another wolf-vampire baby in Western Europe. Gia not only spoke to the mother — a wolf — but went there to interrogate her about what to expect. I went with her and even met the little guy."

Summer spun in my arms, her eyes wide. "Are you serious?"

I nodded. "As a herd of stampeding Willies."

"Was he born with wings? Was that an issue? Is she going to kill me trying to get out of the birth canal?"

"What?" I frowned, resting my hands on her hips. "No. You know our wings are just flexible little nubs at birth, like a baby chick's. They don't fully grow in until much later. Where is this coming from?"

"What about blood? Should I be drinking it to sate her vampire needs? Will she die?"

"Summer, no." I fought back a laugh, since the expression on her face was as serious as Summer got. "I promise, you're good. Just like Zara has said at every appointment lately, and Dr Flores on every video call." We'd been relieved to be able to speak with Selene Flores who, on top of being an actual human medical doctor, was also a witch, married to a dragon-shifter, and had had several babies now with no complications.

"Will you have to bite her out of my stomach like a bloody,

disgusting C-section? What about if some wolf shows up and declares he's her mate before she's even born like an absolute creep?" Summer gasped, her hand flying to her heart. "Max. What if she's hideous? What if she looks like bad CGI and her eyes are way too far apart?"

That time I couldn't hold back the laugh that bubbled out of me. "No, to all of that. And if she looks anything like her mother, then she'll be the most beautiful girl I've ever seen. Where is this coming from?"

"I've been reading a lot lately." Summer chewed on her lip, avoiding my gaze. "Maybe romantasy wasn't what Zara meant when she said to read baby books, though. Those women are all very fragile and the logic is almost nonexistent."

"You're telling me someone needed a C-section by vampire bite?"

All traces of anxiety fled Summer's face as her shoulders relaxed and a laugh slipped free. "I know. That one is hard to believe."

"Ready to vanish out of here, then?" I squeezed her hip. "Or should we get in line for our flight?"

With a deep breath, Summer nodded. "Get me the heck out of this airport and feed me, husband."

In an instant, the world faded around us, awash in shadows. Between one heartbeat and the next, we reappeared on the darkened streets of Paris. Hazy light drifted down from the streetlights ahead, a bridge arching over the River Seine. The smell of fresh-baked pastries overshadowed everything, Summer's favorite bakery directly behind us.

Her nose tilted into the air, sniffing out the decadent aroma before her eyes opened, pupils wide, lust-filled, and hungry like that fated day we'd arrived here two years ago. "You brought me back to Paris."

Her gaze drifted to the bakery, and I took the moment to pull a golden padlock out of my pocket. "Thought we could mark this one off your Bucket List next. It's illegal to put locks on the Pont des Arts now. Good thing I happen to be okay with bending the rules."

Hazel eyes shot back to me, then my hand, taking in the padlock I held aloft. She grabbed it out of my hand, holding it up to the moonlight to inspect it.

Max, Summer, and Baby. Famille je t'aime.

"Jasmine," she said, her voice shaky with tears as she gripped the lock on her chest. "I think her name is Jasmine. A little of my sunshine, and a little of your darkness. A flower that blooms at night."

I grinned, brushing a stray hair back from Summer's face as images flashed in my mind. A little girl with black hair and hazel eyes, or golden hair and blue eyes — it didn't matter, as long as she was healthy and happy — skipping through the wildflowers back home. Baking with Summer in the kitchen. Learning how to fly, and shift, and live her life to the absolute fullest. I cleared my throat against the sudden tightness there. "It's perfect."

Taking the lock from her hands, I let my shadows out and encased us in darkness as we walked towards the bridge. The wire panels that had once held over a million locks, a symbol of eternal love, were gone after a part of the bridge had collapsed under the weight of the City of Love. In their stead were glass panels, making it impossible to attach a lock onto the structure.

My wings extended as I pulled Summer close to my chest, holding her tightly. Together, we rose off the ground, hovering beneath the streetlight. Moths fled from my shadows as I took the lock from her hand and attached it to the cast iron lamp, just outside the light. Warmth radiated off the lamp, even in the darkness, and somehow that seemed perfect for us.

A soft snick sounded as the metal clicked in place.

"Forever," Summer said as our feet touched back down on

the bridge. I glamoured my wings and then let the shadows hiding us dissolve. Her fingers tightened on my black cotton shirt, tugging my face down to hers.

"For always."

Thank you so much for reading! If you loved Max and Summer's story, tell your friends by leaving a review on Goodreads, Amazon, or anywhere you brag about books so they can join in on the fun!

Fates Defied

Acknowledgments

This one took a little longer than usual. For that, we'd like to say thank you to all of our readers for sticking with us, whether you've been here since Smoke Show or you're just finding us now. We hope it was worth the wait; we certainly think so.

Every time we get to share more of our quirky, chaotic world with you all, it brings in a little more magic. Hopefully, you fell in love with Summer and Max as much as we did because these two were a blast to write. Their banter flew off our keyboards onto the page, making us chuckle with every troublemaking turn.

To all of our readers, supporters, anyone who's out writing reviews or telling their friends about us: thank you for reading and sharing our names and our books out in the big wide world! Your enthusiastic support for the ever-expanding Vankins universe makes this journey so fun.

To our Wild Willies street team: thank you for always "getting" us, getting our characters, brainstorming ideas, and sharing our posts and your own edits. As most of you know, being an indie author is secretly a dozen jobs in a trench coat, and your help makes all the difference!

To our personal assistant, Britt: holy crap, you made this easier on us. Thank you for diving in and taking the reins so we could finish this book and get it out into the world. We are so glad you joined our team!

To our alpha/beta/proofreaders, Amy, Brit, and Lex: thank you for your eagle eyes and constant encouragement!

You keep us going on the days we doubt ourselves and ensure the final version we put out is as typo-free as we can possibly make it. We would never get to pub day without you.

From B:

To J: thank you for always reading my books, and putting up with me asking "what part??" every single time you chuckle at them.

From Aimee:

To Brit: Consider this my random declaration of how much I freaking love you. You are truly one of a kind and I consider myself the luckiest to be doing all of this with a troll waffle like you at my side. Now that we're both uncomfortable with this level of emotion, my job here is done.

To Lex: Finding you has been one of my favorite parts of this journey. Your constant and unending support, whether it's coming to book signings with me, or taking notes when inspiration hits and I can't stop long enough to write it down... I don't know what I did to deserve you. You are as loyal as they come, and I adore you.

To Dani, Kelli, and Sarah: Never have I wanted to shake it for Kohls Cash like I do with you. Thank you for pushing me when I wanted to give up, plying me with baked goods, Diet Cokes, and an ungodly amount of reels, and just straight showing up. You are the absolute best.

To my girls: Your little squeals every time I say I've met a milestone or show you something new is the best sound in the whole world. I love you both so much, you have no idea.

And to Chris, my very own grumpy hero: Maybe I should just put a heart-eyes emoji here, because that's what I look like everytime I overhear you telling people about my books. No one believes in me like you. Thirteen years ago, neither of us knew this is where we'd be, and man, it's been one hell of a ride together. I love you forever.

XO,
Aimee and B.

About B. Perkins

B. has been making up stories about magic since she learned how to write words on paper. When not immersed in fictional worlds, she enjoys spending time in nature. She has several degrees in various things, and if all they're good for is to provide background in creating fantasy worlds and systems, then maybe they were worth it.

instagram.com/b.p.writes

About Aimee Vance

Aimee Vance writes heartfelt and hilarious romance featuring sassy heroines, grumpy heroes, and small-town happily-ever-afters—preferably with a Diet Coke nearby. Her romcoms blend humor and heart with sharp banter, big feelings, and love stories designed to make readers laugh, swoon, and feel right at home.

A lifelong fantasy and romance reader, Aimee studied public relations at Texas Christian University. She lives in Texas with her husband, two young daughters, and a Labrador Retriever. When she's not writing, she's usually rereading her favorite romances or cheering from the sidelines of her kids' sporting events—occasionally at the same time.

facebook.com/aimeevancebooks

instagram.com/aimeevancebooks

goodreads.com/aimeevancebooks

amazon.com/author/aimeevancebooks

bookbub.com/authors/aimee-vance